Werewolf U
Stories

Brenna Lyons

Fireborn Publishing Copyright Statement

This book is written in US English.

PUBLISHER

Werewolf U

Brenna Lyons

Blurbs

Samara will do anything she can to free herself from her mother's clutches. When she qualifies for a free ride at Lupi Lucania, her life falls apart. All she has left is the father who raised her and an unknown future at Werewolf U.

Samara has been given a full scholarship to Lupi Lucania Universitas Scholarium in Italy. It's a dream come true. The university is one of the best in the world, and she intends to make the most of it. What she doesn't count on is two very distracting brothers who have a different idea of advancing her education than she does.

Usually she-wolves come to the University with full knowledge of Lupine history and traditions. James and Jason will have to teach their little mate everything. Born to a human who refused to take her wolf mate permanently into her life, Samara is nothing like what the duo envisioned...and more than they ever hoped for.

Trademarks Acknowledgement

The author acknowledges the trademarked status and trademark owners of the following wordmarks mentioned in this work of fiction:

Chapter One

"Samara Tyler?"

She turned away from the UMass Dartmouth table at the college fair and eyed the well-dressed, silver-haired man in confusion. "Yes?" But what difference would it make to him? Moreover, how would he know her name?

A smile lit his light brown eyes, and he offered his hand. "Pietro Galvani."

Samara shook it. "I'm afraid I don't recognize your name," she admitted.

Her cheeks flamed at that. Was she supposed to recognize it?

He laughed heartily. "Nor should you." After a moment, he composed himself and gave her a cursory up and down assessment. "I have been talking to your counselor." His hand retreated.

"Mr. Michaelson?" *You mean he actually does something?*

"Quite. I notice you have not come to my table. I had hoped you would." Galvani made an expansive motion toward the far side of the room.

"You did?"

He tipped his head in agreement.

"Which one is yours?" To her knowledge, Samara had already visited all the college tables that were suited to her choice of major. *Well…all the ones I can afford, anyway.*

"Lupi Lucania Universitas Scholarium." A slight bow topped the announcement.

Her mouth went dry and swallowing failed to wet it. Samara worked at clearing her throat. "Uh…there are a few

1

problems with applying there."

"Are there? Please...expound upon them for me?" In the meantime, he waved her toward a few empty seats along the wall.

Once they were settled, Samara took a moment to order her thoughts. "The first problem is that I don't speak Italian, and I don't feel confident I can learn enough Italian in the next year to take college in another language."

"You won't have to. We teach classes in ten languages, including English. You may want to learn Italian to interact in town, and we will assist you in that, but you don't have to do it to learn."

Excitement lit in her chest at that revelation. It died just as quickly.

"Another problem?" He guessed.

Samara nodded. "I can't afford Lupi Lucania. Even if I got a scholarship that covered educational expenses, I can't afford room and board, the flights back and forth... I can't afford much of anything." Admitting that galled her, but it was better that he know her limitations up front. His school was one of the most expensive in the world. Even if her parents could afford it—and they couldn't—her mother would balk at spending the money on her.

And she certainly won't cosign the loans either.

"Ah, but European university education is much different than it is stateside. We have several scholarships designed for foreign students. Those scholarships include everything from tuition and fees to books, room and board, and even transportation and living expenses."

Words stuck in her throat. No matter how hard she tried, Samara couldn't spit them out.

"If you would like to take our entrance exam, we have one—

2

"

"Yes. Whenever. I'll be there."

Galvani smiled widely. Then he offered her a cream-colored envelope with an ornate wax seal. Samara took it with shaking hands, stunned.

"Two weeks from tomorrow, Ms. Tyler. We will see you then." Without waiting for her answer, he was gone.

Samara stared at the envelope, her heart dancing in anticipation. The wax was deep red, the imprint a howling wolf's head with a calligraphy-style LLUS topping it.

"Please," she begged, "I will do anything to get into this school."

It was literally the answer to all her dreams. Not only would she be able to leave home, she would have all the financial support her mother had refused her.

If I pass their exam. If it meant being accepted, she would spend every waking hour between now and the test studying.

* * * *

Sebastian didn't wait for Pietro to clear the doorway at the end of the college fair before demanding a report. "Did you convince her?"

His oldest friend tipped his head in a respectful bow. "Samara will be attending an entrance exam for the university in two weeks. To make a good showing, I invited three other high-ranking students from the county. They will, of course, not place high enough to be awarded the scholarship offered." A wry smile pulled up at Pietro's lips.

"Her mother will protest Samara attending." It wasn't a question. Sebastian didn't doubt the woman would do everything she could to dissuade Samara.

"She is a strong young woman, and…"

The fur at the back of Sebastian's scalp went up in warning. "And?" His eyes narrowed.

"One can smell the need to escape on her. If it means escaping her home life, I cannot imagine Samara will back down."

Sebastian considered his friend's observations. "The scholarship includes university break classes. She need not return home to that…" He stopped himself from specifying his opinion of the mother of his daughter.

"Understood. It will be as you say."

He waved Pietro away, rapt on the vision of his daughter.

In the distance, Samara left the building through another door. She stopped, pulled the envelope Pietro had given her from her bag, and stared at it. After a moment, she placed it carefully back in her bag and smiled. There was a spring in her renewed step.

"Yes. It will be as I wish. At last."

* * * *

Two months later

"I said you're not going." Her mother repeated her protest.

"I am. There's no way you can stop me," Samara shouted. There wasn't. The scholarship came with everything she needed and more.

"You think?" There was a challenge in her tone.

"I know I'll be eighteen long before college starts, and I don't need any money from you to attend Lupi Lucania." What else could she do to stop Samara from going?

Before her mother could retort, her father stepped in. "Back off, Florence. She did well. Samara is going to get a better

4

education than either of us dreamed—"

Her mother turned on him, in a full fury. "Shut up. She's not even yours. You have no say in this."

For a long moment, they stared at each other. Samara's heart raced and her head spun.

She isn't serious. She can't be serious. Of all the insane things her mother had said over the years, this topped the list.

"What did you say? Is that true?" her father demanded. "And you better not be fucking with me, whatever you answer."

Samara backed off a step. She'd never seen him so pissed off before. She wasn't sure what her father would do.

True to form, her mother didn't back down. "I said she's not yours, and yes, that's true."

He stood stock-still for a tense moment. "Samara, go pack your things. Anything important to you. We're leaving."

Her mother reached out to grab Samara's arm, and she ducked away, shocked to silence, her world crumbling around her. Her father stepped between them.

Her mother slapped him across the face. Hard. "You can't take her. She's mine. *Mine.*"

"I have no proof of what you're saying and *my* name is on her birth certificate, too. Even if you prove it, it will take you longer than the four months until Samara turns eighteen to do it, because I can fight you that long, at least. At her age, the courts will let her go with whichever parent she wants, and I *am* her father, whether you prove your claim or not."

Her mother gaped, shaking her head, her eyes wide and wild.

"Samara, go get your things." He hesitated, and his gaze was nothing short of tortured. "If you want to come with me, I'll be packed in fifteen minutes."

"I'm coming. Don't leave without me." *Please, don't. Don't*

5

leave me with her.

"I won't. I promise I won't."

Samara scooped the acceptance package off the table and ran for her room. *He said to take anything important to me.* With the life she'd known falling apart, it was one of the few things she had left that meant something to her.

This, my father, and a few prized possessions.

She slammed her door to the sound of her mother throwing something glass against the wall.

Chapter Two

One year later

James and Jason rushed across campus and up into the administration building. A summons from the Alpha Maestro was a serious matter, and one didn't dawdle when called to his office.

James would worry if he and his brother had been on campus long enough to have pulled a prank on someone, but they'd hardly had time to unpack. What possible trouble could he and Jason have gotten into?

They didn't even have time to introduce themselves to the Alpha's door guard. The old warrior wolf showed them in without a word.

Pietro didn't rise from his place behind the desk to greet them. That could have been bad news, but he offered a strained smile.

"Well, now. I see the troublesome Trudale brothers have arrived."

"As ordered, Alpha." Jason hastened to reply.

James offered a quick tip of his head instead.

Pietro stared at them, seemingly sizing them up. Just as James was preparing to challenge the move, the Alpha Maestro spoke.

"Your mate is coming to campus this semester."

James snarled. As he'd feared, he and Jason were going to be mated to Christiana. *So much for our hopes that there would be a stronger, higher-ranked female a year or two younger than her.*

Come on. I knew this was coming. The two strongest young males, litter-brothers, are expected to mate with the highest-ranking female not related to them. We're fucked.

"She will be moving into the Alpha suite tomorrow morning."

Of course she will. Where else would Christiana expect to stay? By the Night Mother, being mated to that foul beast will be hell on Earth.

Jason shot him a look of disgust that said he was having similar thoughts.

"This will be somewhat…complicated." Pietro continued when they didn't offer comments.

"To say the least," Jason blurted out.

Before James could apologize for his brother's outburst, Pietro was posing a question to them.

"What do you know about Samara Tyler?"

For a potent moment, the brothers stared at each other.

James found his voice first. "Who in the Night Mother's name is Samara Tyler?"

* * * *

"Tyler? Samara Tyler?"

The old woman's accent was a pleasant lightly-British or British colony derivative and her smile warm. Instantly at ease, Samara nodded and offered her hand.

She took it in both of her own. "Ah, bella. I am so happy to meet you."

"So am I…uh…" Samara blushed in the realization that she'd forgotten the name of the woman who would be meeting her at the airport.

"You may call me Marietta."

Samara committed it to memory.

"Well, now… Come along." Marietta turned and looped

Samara's arm with her own. She was shorter than Samara by almost a head and had the slight pouch of a belly almost all older women—even thin ones, like Marietta—had.

"Oh. Wait. Shouldn't I...?" Samara motioned back toward the cart of suitcases and boxes they were leaving behind.

"No. The men will transport your belongings in the van. We will take the car back to your rooms and meet them there."

A glance back confirmed two men in red jackets pulling the cart behind them.

"Sounds good." It did. After spending all day on a jet—thankfully in first class, which was a delight—only to arrive mid-morning in Italy, Samara was exhausted.

She stopped short at the sight of the limo with the school crest on the door.

"Samara? Is there a problem?" Marietta inquired.

"Does everyone get this treatment?" If so, that explained at least part of how expensive the school was.

She chuckled. "No, but you are... What is the American term for it? A VIP?"

"First time I've been called that in my life," Samara admitted.

Marietta frowned, as if the comment confused her.

Samara slid into the luxurious interior. The leather seats cradled her in warmth, and she sighed. Marietta joined her, and the driver closed them in.

They set off, out of the city and into the small villages and farms surrounding it. At first, Marietta pointed out the sights and imparted the history of the area. As Samara's eyes fluttered and dipped, the older woman fell silent.

Sleep dragged her into darkness.

* * * *

"Samara?" Someone shook her shoulder gently. "Samara."

She opened her eyes to the sight of Marietta's smile. "Sorry." Samara yawned widely, stretching her back and arms. She smoothed her blouse while she tried to get her bearings.

"Not at all. Take your time."

That spurred Samara on. It wasn't like her to make people wait. *And I'm not starting now.* She pulled herself out of the limo, ignoring the driver's hand.

He didn't seem offended by it. Once Marietta was out, he shut the door. "If you need anything else, have Marietta call for me."

Samara hadn't quite grasped that statement when Marietta waved him away. He was gone before she could thank him.

The building they'd stopped at was nothing short of a mansion. Samara stared at it, visually tracing it from one long wing to the opposite one. That accomplished, she focused on the cornerstone building, standing a full two stories taller than the three-story tall wings, and that was before one took into account the ornate gilded topper.

"This is the dorm?" she blurted out.

"One of them," Marietta agreed pleasantly. She guided Samara toward the massive front doors. "This one is for VIPs."

They ambled up the circular walk, Marietta speaking the entire way.

"Regina Hall was designed in eighteen-ninety and construction started that year. A large portion of it was destroyed in the fire of nineteen-thirty-nine. The entire hall was demolished, and then rebuilt from the original plans, but with updated building materials.

"The wing to your left is the ladies' dorm on the upper floors. The music room, fencing room, and dining room are on the ground floor of that wing. The wing to your right is the gentlemen's dorm. The ground floor houses the ballroom, gymnasium with swimming pool, and lounge. All ground floor amenities are available to all dorm residents."

Samara nodded, at a loss for words.

A man in the same ornate school livery the men at the airport and the driver wore rushed out to meet them. "Marietta, you may want to take Lady Samara in the back way."

By the way the older woman straightened and looked down her nose at the man, Samara guessed the suggestion was offensive.

"What problem is there?" she snapped, sounding a little too much like a general on the battlefield.

"Christiana."

Samara waited for more, but it seemed the word — or, more likely, name — was enough to make his point.

"Christiana will learn her place soon enough. Come along, Samara."

She didn't hesitate. Something told Samara she was safer at Marietta's side than she was balking her or questioning her, considering Marietta's current mood.

At least until she shows me to my room.

The man sighed, then followed along, seemingly resigned to whatever was coming. He ran ahead to open a door for them.

The complaining from inside was shrill, a tone that set Samara's nerves on edge.

What a whining little bitch.

"I demand to be shown to my rooms immediately."

Samara strained to hear the stomp of a foot that never occurred.

"We are attempting to — "

"Not that way, you witless baboon. *My* rooms are alpha level."

The door swung wide and Samara got her first look at the harpy within. Her hair was as long and as straight as Samara's was, but Christiana's hair was red-brown instead of brown with golden highlights like Samara's. Christiana was dressed in high-heeled boots, suede pants, and a poofy white blouse that looked like something a preschooler would wear. A half dozen sparkling bracelets ringed one wrist, and her nails were long and professionally manicured.

One of the three liveried men facing her took a deep breath. "Lady Christiana, had you read the invitation to campus carefully—"

"I've told you that was in error," she insisted.

"As I have assured you it was not."

"I am alpha level. I have *been* alpha level at every school I have attended."

Marietta stepped forward. "You are not alpha level at this school in this year. Attempt to be an adult, Christiana, and accept your place with grace and fortitude. Or something approximating it."

Christiana spun around in what could only be described as a choreographed move. She scowled at Marietta. "You dare counsel me, servant?"

Who does this bitch think she is? Just because Marietta worked for the college didn't mean she was inferior to anyone else here.

Marietta laughed harshly. "I am no servant of yours," she countered. "Thank the goddess for that."

"You should have been. Your reprieve will be short-lived, I assure you. My father—"

Samara snapped. Her vision went red-tinged around the edges, as it always seemed to when she got angry. "That's it? That's the best you've got? I'll sic my daddy on you?" How pathetic was this girl?

Christiana raked a sneer up Samara's body. "And who is *your* father? Since you've seen fit to mock me, that is."

"None of your business." It wouldn't be, even if Samara knew what answer to give. Sadly, she no longer knew that for certain, and all outward signs said Christiana was the type who quoted which countries her family had manors in.

The idle carts full of personal belongings standing about—presumably waiting for a resolution before they could be transported to Christiana's rooms—held what was easily ten times the amount Samara had brought with her. And that was after a stock-up trip to round out her decimated wardrobe, after Samara's mother 'misplaced' a large number of the outfits she'd left behind the first night.

"On the contrary, I think it is. I don't know you, but I see by the servant attending you that you're the bitch she's taking to—"

Marietta laid a backhanded slap across Christiana's face that rocked her head back on her neck and bloodied her lip. "Be more careful who you call a bitch, dog. No one insults Lady Samara in my presence and walks away unscathed. *That* is my place, as *her* servant."

Students and employees gathered in hallways out to the wings, whispering to each other and watching the unfolding scene. Samara wondered whether they were glad Christiana got bitch-slapped or laying odds on what her response would be to it.

Christiana shot a narrow-eyed gaze at Marietta, then at Samara. "The alpha level is my place. I demand a challenge."

Marietta dropped back to Samara's side. "You are under no obligation to accept this challenge. Christiana is not due what she is demanding."

"She wants to fight *me*?" *Why? I wasn't the one who slapped her, though I agree she deserved it.*

The old woman nodded, her expression guarded. "It is tradition."

"You have a tradition of fighting?" *What kind of school have I come to?*

She'd heard European boarding schools sometimes had hazing and such that had been outlawed in other schools, but Samara had thought all universities had done away with it.

"An ancient one and students only invoke it every few decades. Most are better behaved."

Lucky me to meet the worst behaved student this university has had in two decades.

Enough of that. I need information. "But she has no right to ask for this?" *I'll just refuse her challenge then.*

"No." She sighed, then dropped her voice further. "If you refuse to fight now, Christiana will attempt to back you into a fight later. She hadn't expected to have to fight today. If you win now, she cannot start the same fight again. If you wait and fight her later, she has time to prepare to fight you."

I would have the same time to prepare. "What are the rules?" If they favored Samara, it might be better to fight now, tired though she was.

"Bare hands. One on one. No weapons. No allies. To concession, to incapacitation, or to pin."

Samara nodded. The rules were simple enough.

"Another thing… Christiana has always had men to guard her and servants to protect her."

"She can't fight?" *That's good news.*

"She can, but not as well as your brown belt affords you. Be aware, though. Christiana will try to use her fingernails and those spike heels as weapons. She will play off that anything on her body is fair game in a fight."

She fights dirty. Check. Good to know. Samara shot a sideward glance at her foe, noting everything she could use as a weapon. There wasn't much, thank goodness.

"Do you accept the challenge or not?" Christiana asked archly, clearly believing she'd scared Samara off. She smirked in perceived victory.

Samara's anger simmered its way toward a boil. The release of adrenaline wiped away her fatigue and readied her for battle. "Agreed."

"For alpha level?"

Samara noted Marietta's tip of the head. She trusted Marietta. There was little chance this was a setup.

"Agreed."

Even if she lost, chances were the rooms she would be given were beyond Samara's wildest dreams.

Samara kicked her flats to the far side of the foyer. The liveried men waved everyone back to clear the center of the floor for them.

Christiana glanced toward the shoes Samara had shed, then settled her gaze on Samara herself. "Don't expect the same of me."

"Of course. Then again, I don't need tricks." *Step one: Make your opponent think twice about fighting you. There may not be a fight that way.*

If she backs out after I've accepted the challenge, does she forfeit the right to try again?

Probably so, which means she won't do it. Samara sighed.

Christiana squared her shoulders, which looked more than a little stupid in that poof of a shirt. "Boots are not weapons. They are shoes. Anything on my body—"

"I was told you would say that."

She looked like she would protest.

"Are we fighting or not?" *Step two: Keep your opponent off balance.*

It seemed she'd managed that. Christiana hesitated a full five seconds before she managed a sloppy fighting stance.

Samara flowed into a complementary one and waited for the first attack. She didn't have long to wait.

Christiana tried a front kick. Samara sidestepped it, caught her ankle in one hand, then cleanly snapped off the heel aimed for her chest. She raised an eyebrow and pitched the heel over her shoulder, then pushed Christiana back.

She hobbled for a moment, crimson spreading from her neck to her forehead. "You broke my boot!"

Samara shrugged. "You could take them off, as I did."

"These are four *hundred* Euro boots. You're paying for these."

"You wore them into a fight. If you break a nail, are you going to demand I pay for your manicure?"

Laughter rose around them and Christiana glared at her. Though Samara hadn't set out to do it—*I was just my sarcastic self*—she'd shamed her opponent.

Christiana tried a side-kick with the other foot. Samara managed to snap the heel at the base, but it remained loosely attached to the sole of the boot, stymieing her plan to pitch the second one as she had the first.

I can still make it count. "There. Now you can wear them or remove them and not hobble much either way." That was a stretch of the truth, since the hard soles would keep her feet at that four-inch up angle, which would leave Christiana off balance.

The laughter grew stronger and someone hooted. In the distance, Samara saw someone pump a fist in the air.

Christiana isn't well-liked. Such *a surprise.*

She unzipped the boots, then yanked them off. Christiana threw them aside with a glare that pronounced Samara would be paying for those boots with blood.

Rule number one: Never go into a fight angry. Samara supposed she should be thankful her opponent had given her yet another advantage, but something told her Christiana had just become much more dangerous.

As if confirming that, Christiana launched at her. There were no kicks, probably because Samara had taken her weapons away.

And proven I'm faster than she is.

Samara deflected one blow after another. Though she knew she should simply incapacitate Christiana, something deep and primal demanded she embarrass her first.

Christiana stepped up the attacks, grumbling words that made no sense. Finally, she managed to land a blow; three of her fingernails raked across Samara's right cheek.

Something snapped inside her and Samara started laying blows. The one to Christiana's chin knocked her head back. When she righted herself, Samara broke her nose, sending her reeling several steps backward. Before Christiana could react, Samara kicked her mid-chest and sent her into the wall. She crumpled in a heap, leaving cracked plaster behind.

Samara pointed to the flaw in the once-perfect wall. "*That* I will pay for." *I have no idea how. I may have to get a work study job or something, but I will pay for damage I caused to the school.*

"Nonsense," Marietta announced. "Loser of the challenge pays all damages to school property."

Thank goodness. Christiana can afford it. Samara nodded, then took a shaky step toward the liveried men.

Marietta took her arm gently and stopped her. She whispered in Samara's ear. "You must announce your place before you leave...as a sign of your victory." She took a step back.

Samara considered what Christiana had said during the challenge. She growled out the announcement, annoyed by the pomp and circumstance of their rules. "*I am alpha level.*"

Cheers and clapping echoed around the foyer, returning again from the ends of the hallways.

A redheaded girl rushed to Samara, offering the shoes she'd shed to fight. She tipped her head with a wide smile.

Samara took them with an answering smile. "Thank you…" *I don't know anyone's name. I better start learning them.*

"Eva. My pleasure, Alpha. Anytime." She backed away and motioned the way to a staircase one of the red-clad men had opened the door to.

"Eva." Marietta's tone made it seem she was issuing a summons.

"Yes, ma'am?"

"Why don't you accompany us to Lady Samara's rooms and help the Alpha settle in?"

"If Lady Samara wishes, I would be happy to help." The look Eva shot her was somewhat hopeful.

I could use a friend. Like Marietta, Eva put her instantly at ease. "I would like that. After the long flight and…" Samara motioned toward Christiana. "The help would be great. Oh, and…call me Samara, please."

Thankfully, there were no negative responses to her inviting Eva to call her by her name instead of a title.

Eva smiled widely and stepped in time with Samara as they followed Marietta up the stairs.

Three flights up, Samara slowed, her senses on high alert. She turned, half-expecting an attack at her back. Far from it, she found herself facing two gorgeous guys.

Eyeing me like a hot steak.

They weren't ground round either. They were close in

height, one with hair slightly darker than the other's. Their eyes were a deep brown, not unlike her own. Their skin was deeply tanned…or naturally light olive. The one with the darker hair had a pierced ear that gave him a slightly rugged look, and both of them were beautifully cut.

Heat settled deep in her abdomen and Samara whipped away and hurried up the stairs, her cheeks flaming in embarrassment.

It's just the fight. A good fight had always left her aroused.

She glanced back, but they were gone.

Good thing, because they are so my type. She'd never been more tempted to sate the arousal than she was today.

* * * *

Jason waited in the corridor outside their suite, his nerves humming. The sounds of battle ended abruptly. Clapping and cheers thundered up the stairwell soon after.

He trembled in excitement. *Like a damned pup. What the hell is the matter with me?*

James clapped a hand on his shoulder, grounding him. "Don't worry. There is no way Sebastian's daughter lost to Christiana."

Jason glared at his older twin. "I know that."

"Then what is it?"

The question caused Jason to squirm harder. "What if she doesn't like us?"

James rolled his eyes. "It's tradition—"

"You heard what Alpha Pietro said. She doesn't know our traditions, and Sebastian will consider letting her break with them, if she will not bend."

He stopped speaking abruptly at the sound of footsteps

mounting the stairs. The Alpha's servant came into view first.

Just as she should.

She was a grand old matriarch, and Pietro said she had served two generations of Sebastian's family so far. If anyone crossed Samara, answering to Marietta wouldn't be pleasant.

He wondered if Christiana had already tasted the servant's claws.

As she passed by, Jason got his first look at the Alpha female.

Sebastian's daughter. Our mate. Samara. He stopped himself from saying it by the Night Mother's grace alone.

Samara had more curves than the average she-wolf would.

Most likely due to her human mother.

She dressed casually in stretch jeans and a white button-down shirt.

Not at all like Christiana would dress.

Samara's feet were bare, and she had her shoes hooked onto the fingertips of one hand.

Her golden brown hair reached past her full chest. As Samara turned her head to address the young she-wolf at her side, he spied the wounds on her cheek.

Jason tensed. Their mate was injured. He would rip the one responsible apart.

James closed a hand on his shoulder and squeezed. Hard! The message was clear enough. *Calm down. Don't move. This was a challenge. She took her pound of flesh in return, whatever it might have been.*

Jason forced his muscles to loosen. *This was why Marietta ordered us to stay upstairs. If we gave in to our instincts, we could have cost Samara her place.*

And us ours. Mated to Christiana? Kill me first.

Samara stopped and whipped around, adopting a partial

crouch.

Ready to attack. Ready to pounce.

She took in their scent, her breathing quickening. Her gaze traveled the length of their bodies, bringing his cock fully up in response.

Her cheeks flooded with color. Samara spun away and loped after her servant, leaving her enticing scent behind to torture him.

He shuddered, welcoming the torture. She would be theirs.

James growled. "Oh, yes. She likes us."

* * * *

Samara lounged in the oversized bed, trying to stay awake long enough to reset her sleep to the new time zone.

The paperwork on what to bring had informed her that US-sized sheets would be useless to her but that bed linens would be provided. Samara hadn't been sure what to make of that; she wasn't fond of scratchy sheets, and she'd saved up an extra hundred Euros, in case she had to purchase sheets she would be comfortable with.

Cheap-cut polyester blend wasn't what they were offering, thankfully. The choices had ranged from flannel to Jersey cotton, from 1800 thread count Egyptian cotton to silk, and in a range of deep colors—brick red, hunter green, and navy blue. Though Samara suspected the flannel would be great for winter weather—and said as much—the hunter green or navy blue Egyptian cotton won the toss-up for warm weather. The blue was currently on the bed.

Marietta entered the room again, pausing to check on Samara. She went off to whatever she was doing with a smile on her face.

That's it. I have to sit up or I'll fall asleep.

To her surprise, Marietta didn't protest her resistance to sleep. Samara had never had what other people called a doting mother, but she would bet Marietta fit the profile. The woman hovered, taking care of everything for Samara she possibly could, including unpacking and storing all of Samara's clothing.

The lady in question cleared her throat. She didn't wait for Samara to form words. "There is a second suite of rooms on this floor. It is always Alpha's choice who to offer it to. If you enjoy Eva's company, you can offer it to her. If you prefer to wait until you've met other students—"

"What *precisely* is the Alpha?"

"The highest-ranked student, of course."

What a competitive school. No wonder they are ranked so high in the college standings. "Then why is that challenge travesty allowed to happen? It won't change our SATs or IQs or entrance exam scores."

Marietta smiled widely and went back to putting folded towels in the linen closet inside the bathroom door. "It is an *ancient* tradition. They often don't make sense, when viewed with a modern eye."

"Then why not abolish it?"

She sighed. "We—like most—cling to traditions for the illusion of rich history they provide. Good or bad, we are loath to let them die a natural death. We *have* done away with many of them. This one is slower than most to die out."

"Why not that one?" Were there really worse traditions that went first, because they were more glaring?

"I trust one of the future presidents of the university board will see things your way. So far, none of them have been as evolved as you are." Her tone said she was joking.

Samara wasn't sure how to answer, so she remained silent.

22

"If you prefer to wait—"

"No. Offer the room to Eva." The afternoon with her had been very enjoyable. They'd been laughing and joking in no time. It was rare for Samara to find someone she clicked with so quickly.

Marietta turned smartly. "As you wish, Samara. Can I bring you anything else?"

"No. I'm fine." She leaned back against the plush pillows, listening to the patter of Marietta's feet disappearing down the hall.

I'm top dog here. For the first time in my life, I am.

That thought warmed her, and long before Marietta returned, Samara was fast asleep.

* * * *

Marietta entered the Alpha Maestro's conference room, where they had reportedly been meeting with all manner of servants and guards for Samara all afternoon. Not that Samara would be informed of their presence. They would simply shadow her when she left campus, protecting her from the humans who might harm her.

She didn't bow to Pietro. Since Sebastian was in the room, Marietta showed proper respect to the highest-ranked member of their pack.

I changed his diapers when I worked for his mother, but he is still my Alpha.

Sebastian waved her closer, and she complied, taking a seat halfway down the table.

Not close enough to be deemed presumptuous, but not far enough away to be seen as fishing for a compliment when he decides whether or not to invite me closer.

23

Sebastian seemed content with her choice. He got straight down to business. "Has my daughter settled in well?" he inquired.

"Very well. She is...leery of the challenge. Samara wonders why we still permit it."

"She will understand in time." He dismissed her concerns.

It is never smart to disagree with an Alpha, even one who is somewhat fond of you. "As you say. Regardless, her first sight of her mates was promising, and she has chosen a den sister."

The muscle at the back of Sebastian's jaw twitched. "And her choice?"

Marietta tried not to take that personally. Did he really believe she would fail to discourage a bad choice? She cleared her throat. "A sound one. A lower noble daughter but loyal and pleasant. They get along well together."

"Do I know the family?"

"I believe you do." She knew he did, but it never hurt to act as if she didn't, in case he'd forgotten the couple. "Eva's mother is Trisha, and her mate is Dane Howell. Eva is their youngest daughter."

"Adored but not pampered and spoiled." He tapped a fingertip against his lower lip, deep in thought. "She has an elder brother and two elder sisters, as memory serves. And this will mean a social jump for the entire family." He nodded. "Good. Tell the girl what she needs to know, and keep me informed."

"As you wish, Sebastian." With that, she was off to her work.

Chapter Three

A week later

"Welcome, class of two thousand and nineteen."

Samara clapped politely and hoped it was the end of the Matriculation ceremony.

"Finally," Eva huffed. "I cannot wait to get out of this gown."

"That makes two of us," Samara agreed.

The day was sweltering, and the scarlet, velvet-trimmed graduation gowns were overkill, considering the weather.

When the board members left the stage, they were both out of their seats, stripping off the gowns with sighs of relief. Marietta and Suzanne, Eva's servant, appeared to take them with silent nods that said they would be in the dorms if there was need of their services.

Around them, other servants did the same, male servants for male students and female for female.

Ladies' maids and gentlemen's gentlemen. But Marietta isn't just a lady's maid. She was also a bodyguard of sorts, a teacher, and—for all that it galled Samara—something of a nanny. Were all the servants the same, or was Marietta simply responding to the fact that—unlike the other students—Samara didn't know the rules and traditions already?

In the distance, Christiana pushed her gown at her servant as if she loathed the sight of her...or of the gown. Samara couldn't be sure which, but she suspected it was the servant that irritated her.

"Is there a problem, Samara?" Eva asked, her golden-green eyes narrowing.

Samara looked away from Christiana before the other

woman could catch her staring. Deciding what to say or ask was difficult. She never knew who was listening in. Beyond not wanting to start a war with Christiana with a misplaced word, Samara didn't want to appear naïve or stupid.

She'd never realized how much there could be to learn about the university. The first full day she'd been on campus alone had consisted of Eva and Marietta teaching Samara rules and traditions. None of the remaining ones involved fighting, as far as she could tell, and her two tutors had promised to head her off at the pass if it seemed she was about to commit a faux pas of some sort. So far, she hadn't.

Eva and Marietta answered her questions patiently, even when Eva's expression announced she found them odd. Samara trusted them, but she didn't doubt her standing with the rest of the student body was precarious. She couldn't undermine it with a poor choice of question or comment in public.

A hand closed on Samara's shoulder. She met Eva's gaze and managed a weak smile.

"I'm fine." She offered before Eva could ask.

"Well, that is good, I suppose. Marietta would lock you in your room and call in doctors from the clinic, if you weren't."

Both laughed heartily, mostly because they knew she wasn't exaggerating. Arm in arm, they made their way out of the amphitheater. Once they were in the clear, Eva tried again.

"What is bothering you?"

"More...confused than bothered."

"Okay. What is confusing you?"

"Each section of the seating was a dorm building. I could pick that out by the heraldry and the order of seating."

"You've got that right. It doesn't sound like you're confused."

Samara considered how best to broach the subject.

"Depending on the dorm building, there were varying numbers of servants. In our dorm, more than three-quarters of the students have a servant. Then half, less than half, a few...one."

Eva nodded sagely. "The Alpha and her chosen friend—and the alpha level males below—get a servant supplied by the school."

The Trudale brothers. I saw them the first day.

"If it's possible, the school employs a servant who has worked for the students' families before. For instance, Suzanne was my mother's servant when she attended."

"That's why Christiana thought Marietta..." Oh, that's a bad way to phrase it.

"You can say it. Christiana acted like she owned Marietta. Though they would likely have reassigned Marietta and hired one of Christiana's family's servants, had you lost the challenge, she would have been stuck in the position for the first few days until a replacement arrived."

And Christiana would have made life hell for Marietta. I am so glad I won that match.

"She's quite the little bitch, as you might have noticed. You need to understand this. Christiana and Lorilea feel you've stolen something from them. Not just the alpha level rooms—because you *know* Christina would have given my room to Lorilea, had she been Alpha, but the school servants they felt they were due."

Samara winced. "And the rest of the servants?"

Eva questioned her silently.

"Who employs them? Why doesn't everyone have one?"

"Families who can afford them—those who want to show off that wealth or who want to pamper their children—provide a servant for them out of their own pockets."

"And the servant you would have had?" Had the woman

lost her job, or had the school simply taken the expense of Suzanna off of her family's hands?

Eva's smile faded a bit. "I wouldn't have had one. My family isn't as well-off as Christiana's."

She isn't embarrassed by that, is she? I don't care how much money she has. "I guess I wouldn't have had one either," she admitted.

"But...you're an Alpha." Her expression said Samara had said the wrong thing again.

"Sure. So I rocked the test. Another day, I have a head cold, my score drops ten points... I'm not Alpha." Academically highest was a fleeting thing.

Eva stopped and stared at her. Samara held herself stock-still, certain she'd just made a major faux pas. Hiding her attack of nerves was nearly impossible, but she thought she managed it.

"Samara... Being Alpha has nothing to do with tests and scores." She said it carefully as if she was afraid Samara might be angry with the answer.

"Marietta said the Alpha was highest-ranked." Had she lied?

"Of the highest-ranked ancestry, the most powerful line. That's why there are so few challenges. The lines of ancestry are rarely contested, and when they are, it is usually someone's parents disagreeing, not students."

After a moment of silence, during which Samara found herself unable to form words, Eva continued.

"The traditions we're teaching you... They aren't just traditions of the university. They are traditions of our people, a proud and ancient race.

"Whatever your family line is, it's much higher than mine. Higher than Christina's. I admit I don't know your line. Tyler isn't a recognized lineage. What is your mother's maiden name?"

"O'Connor."

"Neither is that." Her brow furrowed and she seemed genuinely perplexed. "I don't understand this. You *are* of our kind, or you wouldn't have been invited to the school."

Samara considered how to phrase the truth. "Liam Tyler is…was my mother's husband. He raised me as his own."

"He's not your biological father then." The usual animation returned to her face in a flash.

"No. He's not biologically my father."

"So, who *is* your father?"

Before Samara could decide whether or not to admit the truth, a snide voice interrupted them.

"I see the poor cousins shop at S-Mart together."

Samara didn't bother to look at Christiana. "S-Mart is where Ash works in the *Evil Dead* movies. I think Kmart or Wal-Mart would be the insult you are so *desperately* seeking." She didn't bother to point out that the dress had been purchased at a formal shop for her prom. It wasn't a designer dress, and Christiana's likely was.

"I notice you are familiar with the stores."

A twitter of unkind laughter let her know they had an audience of Christiana's cronies.

Samara turned to face her and forced her mouth into a vicious smile. Christiana wanted to embarrass her? Two could play that game.

"I notice your daddy didn't manage to make you Alpha. Face it… No matter how well you dress up, you will be masking the fact that you are *second* best." *I may not know who my father is, but I know hers isn't up to par.*

For a potent moment, Christiana's cronies gaped at Samara. Christiana stood, shell-shocked, much as she would if Samara would have slapped her across the face.

Just when Samara would have stalked away in disgust, Christiana launched toward her. Samara moved to block the swing toward her throat and something sliced deep into her arm.

She has a knife. She's trying to kill me! Though Samara knew it would drive the blade deeper, she forced her arm forward to throw Christiana off-balance.

The bitch went sprawling. Her cronies stopped laughing and went ashen. They stepped back, waving Samara off.

"We had nothing to do with this," Lorilea assured her. "She said it was a joke."

Samara didn't doubt it was true. All the same, the drive to rip them to pieces rose up. A tinge of red clouded her vision.

Two male bodies bracketed her. Samara's move to attack Christiana and all three of her so-called friends ended with her wrists trapped by one man each. She pulled at their hold, growling out a warning to release her.

"Move." The one to her left ordered. "Take that bitch with you."

Christiana paused in the act of dusting off her ruined dress. "How dare you call—"

Samara lunged for her and Christina squealed and ran the opposite direction. The other three took off after her, one of them passing Christiana in a matter of a few footsteps.

The man on Samara's right released her for a split second. There was a flurry of white from his direction. The sound of fabric ripping jangled her nerves.

Samara fought for a decent breath, her head spinning. Her entire body ached and twitched.

He yanked the knife from her arm and Samara screamed. Her knees weakened. In a dizzying series of movements, he wrapped something around her injured arm and pulled it tight.

"You're going to be fine, Samara."

She focused on the shirtless man addressing her. Had he sacrificed his shirt to make a bandage for her? That seemed likely.

He was one of the two men who lived on the floor below her. *The Trudale brothers.*

The wind whipped around them and their scents surrounded her. Samara looked from one to the other, arousal beating at her nerves.

The one who'd stripped off his shirt leaned toward her. "Oh, yes." It came out little more than a breath of air, teasing at her lips.

Her arm went numb, giving her relief from the pain.

"Jason! Wrong time!"

He pulled away, going red-faced. "Right. Wrong time."

No. No. No. Right time. Very right *time.*

There was no time to voice her complaint. The one behind her scooped Samara into his arms and they rushed toward a building.

The clinic. I need a doctor. As if in agreement, her heart started racing.

"Eva, take that to the Alpha Maestro," Jason yelled back. "Be careful not to cut yourself."

Samara looked up at the man carrying her. "What is your name?" She knew his brother's name. She supposed she should know them both, since she owed them for helping her.

He seemed stunned by the question. At last, he found his voice. "James."

"James and Jason." Samara closed her eyes, suddenly exhausted. Unconsciousness closed over her like a thick blanket.

* * * *

James stamped down the need to howl out in fury. If Samara was seriously injured, he would hunt down Christiana and tear her throat out himself.

If Sebastian doesn't get to her first. That was unlikely, at best, so he focused on Samara fully.

Jason raced ahead and pulled the clinic door open for them. James vaulted through it with Samara held tight to his chest, and Jason rounded them.

"Alpha with an emergency," his brother shouted. "Move ass. Now!"

Two doctors came from the far reaches of the clinic.

Probably playing cards or inventorying their stock. It's not like wolves need them often.

The first one to reach them tugged at the knot on the make-shift bandage.

"No." Jason cautioned him. "It was a Hunter's Fang."

Both pulled back. One swallowed hard. In the next moment, they were checking everything from her pulse and breathing to her pupil reactions. One raced for the back again.

James tried to reconcile it. *A Hunter's Fang?* "Are you sure?"

"That's why I sent it off to Alpha Pietro with Eva. However Christiana got it, this has to be addressed. Now."

"In here," the remaining doctor ordered.

James followed him, his senses reeling. *Christiana swung for her throat. A throat shot with a Hunter's Fang would have killed Samara.*

"Here, James."

The snap of the doctor's commands brought him to his senses and James lowered Samara to the king-sized bed in the Alpha room. *When an Alpha needs care, he or she has an Alpha's comforts.*

She was alarmingly pale and seemed to be having problems taking in a lungful of air.

The other doctor rushed in with a dusty, ornate glass jar. "I never thought we would need this," he grumbled. "Steven!"

"Working on it." He unwrapped Jason's shirt from her arm.

James cursed fluently.

Her entire lower arm and hand were crimson and swollen. The knife wound had blackened edges and was weeping a mixture of blood and yellowed pus.

A Hunter's Fang. There was no question about it. Nothing else would cause that reaction in a wolf. *Damn the wolf hunters of the seventeenth and eighteenth centuries.*

The doctors didn't waste time. They used the ointment to scrub out the wound, leaving it red and raw. Then they put more ointment in the laceration and wrapped it loosely.

"Will she recover?" Jason asked.

Steven looked up and smiled at them. "I take it you are her mates?"

James glared at him. "I believe my brother asked you a question."

The other doctor straightened and offered his hand. "My name is Benjamin. My partner is Steven."

"Did we ask your names?" James inquired coolly. *Benjamin. Yes. That's how he knew my name. He treated me when that prank went wrong first year.*

Benjamin sighed. "All signs point to a full recovery, but it will not be an easy one. The poison moves quickly."

"Perhaps a scar." Steven added his observations to the discussion. "With a Hunter's Fang, that is possible."

"Yes. Perhaps. Samara will have to stay here for the next day or two. After that, she will need a week of recovery time in her rooms."

"Then we stay here, too," Jason decreed before James could.

"Of course," the doctors replied in unison.

* * * *

Sebastian smiled at Pietro over his glass of wine. "She *is* beautiful." The photos his men brought him over the years didn't do justice to the woman Samara had become.

"I hear she also has the temperament of an Alpha female."

"I knew she would. Human though her mother was, the woman had spirit." He still loved that about her, though he loathed the woman in general. *She was fine stock to create my daughter, though lacking in other ways, not the least of which is the fact that she's not a wolf.*

Pietro leaned forward. "If it wouldn't be impertinent to ask—"

"It would." The memories put a damper on his happiness, just as they always had.

Wisely, Pietro didn't respond. They sat in a pleasant silence, sipping their wine.

The shout of a warning to halt brought Sebastian's head up in shock, and they both vaulted to their feet, their glasses abandoned on the conference table.

What in the red hell is this? Human hunters hadn't breached the campus for well over a hundred years, and how would one make it to the administration building without a general alarm being sounded?

He couldn't. It's impossible.

"N-need the Alpha M-Maestro," a young woman stammered out.

Pietro made it to the door two steps before Sebastian did. He wrenched the door open, and the young lady rushed toward them. Pietro dodged left, and Sebastian took his cue, dodging right. If this was some kind of attack, they would have her flanked.

She came to a halt an arm's length away from both, which left Sebastian staring at a frightened she-wolf. Worse, the youngster was holding a bloodied blade, and her hands and dress were stained with the same.

"What happened, Eva?" Pietro asked.

Eva? Samara's den sister. He could see the likeness to her father in her.

"Christiana attacked Samara with this. I think..." She sobbed. "I think it's a..." It seemed she couldn't force the words out.

Sebastian focused on the blade, his blood running cold. "A Hunter's Fang." But they were outlawed within the wolf community. He had passed that law personally, his first decree as Alpha.

Eva threw the blade onto the table with a whimper of distress. She backed away from it, trembling and sobbing.

Sebastian made it to her first; he wrapped an arm around her, supporting Eva to the far end of the table. "Where is Samara? Is she well?" *With a Hunter's Fang stained with blood? The more appropriate question would be "Is she alive?"* Sebastian couldn't face asking it.

"James and Jason took her to the clinic. Her arm. Christiana sliced into her arm."

Even that could kill, but not if they got her there quickly enough. He released her and turned toward the doorway, but Eva's whisper stopped him short.

"She aimed for Samara's throat. Night Mother, what was she thinking?"

Sebastian didn't turn back, trying to hide his shifting

features as best he could. "I want Marcus here. Now! And I want that bitch gone within a day."

"It will be done."

He loped away toward the clinic, his vision red in bloodlust. Wolves gave him a wide berth as he passed.

Damned right, it will be done and no one will dare try again. I made those abominations illegal. Now I'm going to make that law hurt.

Chapter Four

Sebastian sat brooding in one of the wing chairs set before the fire in his residence den. He'd been to see Samara twice and nothing had changed so far. His daughter lay unconscious and lightly fevering, her breathing shallow but stable.

She could be dead. If Samara was slower or less skilled, she would be dead.

He raked a hand through his hair. *A Hunter's Fang. How lost have I been in my misery that a wolf dared balk me and keep one of those abominations? Are there more of them?* A show of force was warranted.

The polite knock at the door put his nerves on edge. "Yes?"

"Marcus is here, Sebastian."

"Thank you, Roberto. Show him in."

Sebastian knew Roberto would have left Marcus waiting in the sitting room. That meant he had plenty of time to get to his desk before Roberto opened the door and waved Marcus through it.

He strode through as if he had not a care in the world. Then he bowed sharply.

Not cordially.

"You called for me, Alpha?"

At least he didn't presume to use my given name. In his current state of mind, Sebastian might leave scars if Marcus displayed such presumption. "Yes. I did. I need to speak to you about several issues."

Marcus moved toward one of the guest chairs.

"Did I say you should sit?"

He jerked to a halt. "No, Alpha. Of course not."

"This is not a business meeting. Neither is it a friendly chat. Make no mistake. This day may mark the end of your den, Marcus. Tread lightly but honestly with me."

If I learn your daughter knew what the weapon was, she dies today. Though it pained Sebastian to take a wolf's only child away, some crimes required that punishment. *Moreover, if I learn you knew of the existence of the weapon, you will die.*

Marcus went pale. "Alpha? What have we done?"

"Your daughter tried to take the life of her Class Alpha today."

He ground his teeth. "The Alpha. I should have known. I have heard nothing *but* complaints about the Alpha from my daughter in the last week."

Sebastian tensed at the implied criticism of Samara.

Marcus waved him off. "Not that I am excusing my daughter's behavior. If you and Pietro say this...Samara Tyler is Alpha female, I trust your judgment." He hesitated. "But... Why have we never heard of this Alpha before? Where was she schooled? Whose line does she come from?"

His frustration set Sebastian off. Before he could talk himself down, his ears, eyes, paws, and muzzle had shifted.

Marcus shuffled back a step, then dropped to his hands and knees in a sign of submission.

My reaction told Marcus what Samara is to me. He knows now. He knows only my own blood would make me lose control this way.

"You need not know the details of my daughter's life," Sebastian informed him. What his pack would assume was shameful enough. They didn't need to know the whole sordid truth. *Only Samara needs the awful truth. When she is ready to ask for it.*

He forced himself to shift back, but it cost him in effort. "This is not to be shared, Marcus. Not even with your daughter."

If you live that long.

"Yes, Alpha. My daughter will be dealt with. I assure you, she will."

"She will indeed. At the least, Christiana is no longer welcome at this university or at any of the ones I sit on the board of."

Marcus was silent, probably working his way to the fact that Sebastian sat on the board of three of the five wolf universities worldwide. Since it was a safe bet Christiana didn't speak Japanese, he'd just proclaimed she would have to attend university in northern Norway, above the Arctic Circle.

Hope you like snow, Christiana.

He nodded. "I understand. It is most fair of you."

"She will be leaving campus with you tonight, Marcus. Pietro has already ordered her packed out to leave. That is assuming, of course, that she survives my judgment."

Marcus snapped his head up, his eyes wild at the bluntly-stated threat to his daughter. "Alpha, surely nothing Christiana could have done would really en—"

"Stand. I want you to look me in the eyes when you answer my questions, and may the Night Mother have mercy on you if you lie to me."

Marcus made his way shakily to his feet. He nodded, his expression strained.

Sebastian pulled the blood-stained blade from the towel on his desk. He held it between them.

"That's—"

"A Hunter's Fang. I am well aware of *what* it is."

"Christiana used—"

"Yes, she did. So, I am sure you can understand the severity of this crime."

"Is she well? Your daughter? Samara?" He tripped over his

words, nearly in a panic.

Sebastian shot him a quelling look.

"I-I mean…" He swallowed hard, going red in the face.

"Samara is alive. Thank the Night Mother for that favor. Had your daughter's blow bit skin at her intended target, my daughter would be dead now." Marcus would know what that meant.

"Artery, lung, or heart?" Sebastian barely heard him.

"Throat."

Marcus winced.

Sebastian dropped the dagger, letting it clatter to the desktop. He savored Marcus's cringe. *I have him where I want him. He won't dare lie to me now.*

"I am sure you are aware of the laws governing a Hunter's Fang."

Marcus nodded. "I swear I knew nothing about it."

"Then where did your daughter get it? Since she is an inept fighter, I assume she didn't take one off a hunter personally."

"I can ask, but I suspect—"

"You suspect what? Who? Where did she get a Hunter's Fang?"

Marcus sighed, then rubbed a hand over his mouth. "My father didn't want to give up his collection. When the new law was announced…he resisted turning them over. I turned in five of his blades for destruction."

Sebastian's stomach churned. "Five?" He hadn't realized anyone had an arsenal of that size.

"It was all I could find. My father swore I'd found them all. He cursed me out of his house. We never spoke again." He shifted from foot to foot, as if he felt the need to pace.

Sebastian wasn't in a giving mood. "You believe your father gave Christiana the blade before he died?"

"Perhaps not intentionally. You see, my father left me nothing. Everything was left to Christiana and to my sister, Aubree. I checked everything that came into my home, but my father was fond of false-bottomed drawers and trunks, hidden compartments... Anywhere he could hide his prized possessions. I believe the blades came to my daughter hidden in some larger piece of furniture. He was addled near the end. He may not have remembered where the blades were stored or that he'd hidden some from me at all."

"In other words, you're guessing."

"Yes, damn it! I'm also guessing Christiana didn't know what the weapon was. To her, it would have been nothing more than an impressive piece of workmanship."

That was likely true. Since Marcus didn't own one, and the law was passed before their daughters were born, Christiana may never have learned about them.

Sebastian took a calming breath. "Get the answers from your daughter, Marcus."

"I will, Alpha."

"Have her off this campus and away from Samara before sunrise, but do not leave without giving me the answers I'm seeking."

"You have my vow on that." He was gone without a backward glance.

Roberto appeared in the doorway. "Samara has awakened, Sebastian. Steven reports that she is still fevering and is quite befuddled, but the wound is healing well."

His muscles relaxed in a rush of released breath. "Good. Thank you, Roberto."

He left silently, as he had done for years.

Since he was my servant here at university.

Sebastian laid his head back, exhausted. All these years, he'd pined away at the loss of his daughter, at the stolen chance to be a father to her. A week with Samara at the periphery of his life, and he wasn't certain how parents survived decades in the role.

* * * *

"Can we do anything for her?" a deep male voice asked.

Samara licked her lips, trying to place it. For that matter, she tried to make sense of where she was and why.

No dice. I can't think of anything, roasting as I am. She pushed the sheets and blanket away, trying to cool off.

"Tepid water. Bathe her face, arms, legs… Let's bring this fever back down."

"Right."

One soft cloth started at her forehead, worked down her face to her chin, then caressed her throat. Another slid down the inside of one thigh.

Male musk surrounded her and Samara arched up to their touch. There was a moment of stillness, and their scent intensified.

"Get out," one of them ordered.

Footsteps moved away, and a door closed with a click of metal on metal. Water rippled and splashed.

The cloth on her face returned and traced the path down the opposite side. She spread her legs, and the other worked its way from the opposite knee to nearly her core.

All manner of erotic visions paraded through her head.

* * * *

Jason shivered. *Damn, this is hard.* For that matter, *he* was hard and had been for the better part of the week since he'd first scented Samara. *I am getting a ferocious case of blue balls.*

Stop thinking about it! This is for her health and safety. Bathe her. Bring down the fever.

That in mind, Jason refreshed his rag and started bathing her head and neck again. Droplets of water fell on her clinic gown, turning the lightweight material translucent.

Samara shifted every time a droplet fell. She gasped at the first time one landed on a nipple.

Jason stared at the erect tip, his breathing ragged.

"Do it." James rasped.

Jason snapped his head around, issuing a silent question. James couldn't be telling him to suck it into his mouth. *Not while Samara is semiconscious.*

"Bathe her. Through the shirt. Don't undress her, but help her shed the heat…everywhere."

Which will mean she'll be as good as nude. He nodded. Samara needed wetting down to reduce the fever. *There's a reason we're doing this instead of the doctors.*

Jason left the rag sopping and started working it down her chest. The gown stuck to her body, outlining every curve.

Pass after pass with the rag prompted moans from Samara. She arched her back, offering herself to him.

To us. She's as affected by what James is doing as she is by what I'm doing. He didn't doubt that.

His cock pressed tight to his jeans, weeping fluids that would ease him inside her body.

Samara cried out and Jason looked toward James's position. His brother had done the same job of wetting Samara down on her lower half. That meant they could see every inch of her, from a front view.

They say Alpha females are created in the Night Mother's image. I know Samara must be.

James leaned over her and Jason prepared to warn him off. No matter how enticing she was, they couldn't take advantage of her blind lust.

His brother didn't put his mouth on her. Instead, he blew air over her core, bringing Samara off the bed with a whimper.

"It's an old trick for keeping cool," James explained. "Wrap yourself in wet linen or cotton, then blow air over the fabric to draw off heat."

Jason swallowed hard. He leaned down and breathed on her throat. Samara shivered, and her scent took on a potent edge. Jason moved on to her shoulders and then her nipples.

She grabbed him by the head and dragged Jason's lips to hers. Samara parted her lips and invited him in.

I can't deny her this.

James didn't protest it. His twin moved up Samara's body, trailing his lips over her abdomen, blowing puffs of air over her sensitive skin.

Jason eased out of the kiss and made way for James to share in the taste of her passion. At the first breath James released against her cheek, Samara turned to him and pulled him into a similar embrace.

Goddess, that's sexy. Visions of her touching them had his cock screaming for more. Jason reached down and adjusted himself. He seriously considered stroking himself off.

James pushed to his knees. "Help me get her up."

"You're not—"

"No! I want you to bathe her back. Besides..." He smiled. "I want her to feel us on either side of her.

Jason hurried to help him. In moments, Samara was astride James's thighs, Jason sliding his knees between his twin's.

When Jason set to work bathing her back, Samara started shifting back and forth over James's cock. He hurried through the rest of the bathing, watching the curve of her ass appear through the dripping hospital gown. He stared, rapt, at the interplay of muscles as she rode his brother.

At the edges of self-control, Jason pressed to Samara's back. She went still for a moment and he held his breath. Had they pushed her too far too fast?

Samara moaned and pressed back against him, swiveling her hips. James moved closer, and she stroked up and down their erections.

"That's right," James whispered. "Get used to the feeling of us."

"Yes." She breathed her reply into James's chin. She moved faster, grinding into them. "Yes." Samara tensed, and her scent went straight to Jason's head. She shouted incoherently.

She came. It was all Jason could do not to come in his jeans in response.

"Next time will be inside you," Jason promised.

Samara nodded weakly, her head sinking toward James's chest.

"Do you want us to sleep with you?" Jason offered. *Please, say yes.*

Another nod.

Jason lowered her to the bed, then brushed a kiss across her lips. He lay down to her right, facing her on the wide bed.

James did the same, then settled to her left.

Samara cupped a hand over Jason's cock. By the way James tensed, Jason guessed she did the same to his brother.

Oh, yes. She wants us.

Not to mention, she feels cooler.

* * * *

45

The knock on the door was undoubtedly Roberto again. *It's unlikely to be news about Samara.* Updates had already informed him that her fever had spiked dangerously high but James and Jason had brought it down again. The latest reports were that she was past the danger of complications—her breathing, heart rate, and the swelling in her arm all greatly improved—and sleeping soundly with her mates.

That means it's Marcus's answer. I need to hear it, whatever it is. But he admitted to himself that the idea of killing one or more of his pack members exhausted him.

"Yes?"

"Marcus has returned, Sebastian."

"Show him up."

Sebastian went through the formality of moving to his desk.

Roberto showed Marcus in and closed the door behind him.

One look at the younger wolf gave testament to the fact that Marcus's evening had been no less stressful than his own.

Marcus took a step toward the desk and held out a small wooden chest to him. "My sincerest apologies, Alpha."

He took it carefully, set it on his desk, then opened it. Inside were another three Hunter's Fangs, along with what appeared to be a similar weapon, shaped as a set of brass knuckles with a smaller blade at the far end.

"Dear Goddess." Sebastian choked the words out, past the lump in his throat and the stomach acid rising.

Marcus went to his knees. "My daughter assures me that is all of them, but I will have everything of my father's searched again to make sure there are not more hiding places we have missed. I have also alerted my sister to do the same."

He raised his face to look at Sebastian. "She didn't know what they were. By the Night Mother, she could have killed

46

herself with a nick of the blade." He took in a deep but halting breath. "Christiana gave me everything and let me determine what was a hunter's weapon and what was not. I fear other young wolves may not know any more than Christiana did. Who knows how many are in danger and don't know it."

Sebastian nodded wearily. "I have already told Pietro and the other Alpha Maestros to have a required class about it this week, and I will be making another proclamation on the matter."

"We await your judgment, Alpha."

I don't have the heart to kill them. Admitting it made him feel weak.

"Take your daughter home. Search for more weapons. Spread the word that anyone caught with Hunter's Fangs, from this day forth, will face death for it. My daughter will live. So will yours. This time." He let the threat hang between them.

"There will never be another incident," Marcus vowed. "Thank you, Alpha. Your consideration is more than I dared hope for."

"Go on. It has been a long night for all of us."

He scrambled to his feet, bowed, then made his way to the door. The nod he sent before he walked out let Sebastian know he'd won the loyalty of Marcus's line, as long as they remembered this day.

Chapter Five

Samara shifted in bed, stretching her arms and back. She went still at the feeling of bare skin under her hand. Not her own skin but rather that of someone else in bed with her. The crisp hairs and ridges of muscle attested that it was a man.

This is new. A twitter of laughter stuck in her throat and she swallowed it down.

Okay. Before I panic, retrace my movements. How did I get here?

Christiana attacked me with a dagger. Those gorgeous brothers who live downstairs showed up. Jason wrapped his shirt around my arm.

Everything after that was a fevered blur. A not unpleasant one though. Someone was bathing her.

With my clothes still on? No, not my *clothes, but clothes.*

Touching led to kissing. The delicious feeling of two men pressing on either side of her, their cocks hard and long against her skin.

Through clothing. Samara corrected herself.

Movement on both sides of Samara prompted a gasp from her. Dual groans answered her.

Lips pressed to the back of her shoulder and Samara trembled in arousal. A second set of lips nestled to her throat.

"W-wait," she pleaded.

They both pulled back slightly, and Samara focused on the one in front of her.

"James?" She vaguely remembered learning their names before she passed out. Were they the ones who bathed her? Why wasn't she in a hospital?

"And Jason." The one behind her grumbled his response, his

voice husky in what she didn't doubt was arousal.

The bed was nearly as wide as the one in her rooms, but this room wasn't hers. Instead of dark, masculine colors, it was decorated in shades of pale peach, blue, green, and butter yellow with almond accents for the trim. There were blinds on the windows instead of curtains.

"Samara?" James prompted her.

"Where am I?"

"The school clinic."

Okay. Not their room, but still... The clinic allowed this?

James cupped her cheek in one large, rough hand. "It looks like your fever has broken."

"So...um...you won't have to bathe me again." She only just stopped herself from making it a question. *It shouldn't be a question.*

He smiled. "You remember that?"

Her cheeks flushed in heat. Oh, yes. She remembered it.

James raised one hand in a Scout promise motion. "I promise we won't bathe you again, unless you want us to."

Jason chuckled darkly, and Samara's nipples came to hard points. Memories of one of them stroking them made them harder.

Jason purred in her ear. "Oh, she wants."

Samara straightened, certain she should be offended at their familiar address. "I don't know precisely what happened when you bathed me, but I know I wasn't myself."

James raised one eyebrow and scanned a blatant look down her body between them. "Are you now?"

"Am I what?"

"Are you yourself?"

His teasing tone irritated her. "What kind of question is that? Of course I am."

49

"Really? Because your scent, those perky little nipples, your eyes and lips... All of them say you would like to see where a night with us would go."

The protest stuck in her throat. *Damn him! I do want to know. I don't have to tell him that.*

A knock at the door saved her from figuring out how to answer him.

"Come in." James shouted out the invitation as if he had not a care in the world.

Samara stared at him, shocked to wide-mouthed silence. They thought they were just going to stay in bed with her?

Two men in white, medical coats bustled in, carrying an armload of supplies each.

"Ah, excellent. You're awake." The dark-haired one punctuated the statement with a glance up and down her body.

"And her fever has broken," Jason added.

"Wonderful." The doctor placed the jars and bottles he was carrying on a rolling tray. "My name is Benjamin. That is Steven." He motioned toward the other doctor.

"Thank you both." Samara searched for how to phrase her question. "But...ah..." *Sure. How do I say it? Why aren't you reacting to these two men sharing a bed with me?*

Benjamin stopped to stare at her. "But?"

"Nothing."

"You really should thank James and Jason." Steven's comment sounded like a correction. "Their early care and their speed in getting you here made our job much easier."

Samara noted James's smirk out of the corner of her eye. She cleared her throat. "Thank you." It wasn't quite as cool as she wanted to make it, but Samara guessed cool would be seen as rude. They did, after all, save her life.

Benjamin reached out and lifted her injured arm.

James and Jason tensed so abruptly, the hair on the back of her scalp stood on end.

Steven sighed and shook his head."Stand down, men."

They did so, but only minutely. Samara took a long, slow breath in response. Why did nothing they did make sense to her?

Benjamin ignored them. He snipped the bandage carefully, then unwrapped it. Samara strained to get a look at the damage, but Benjamin turned her arm away.

Maybe to get better light?

Steven went to work, wiping her arm with cloths that smelled of isopropyl alcohol. He folded them carefully before dropping them into a kidney bowl. On the third drop, Samara noticed the yellow-brown stains.

Brown could be dried blood, but yellow is bad news. "What is that? The yellow stains?"

Steven didn't hesitate. "The blade introduced an infection into your system, but it's well on its way to being healed now."

"Infection? How long was I out?"

"A little over a day," Benjamin responded.

A day? "Isn't that fast to get an infection from a wound?"

Steven shook his head. "We didn't wait for the infection to reach your bloodstream and go systemic, as some doctors might. As soon as your body reacted with heat, swelling, and pus formed, we started treatment. That happened very quickly."

"Oh." Something told her there was more, but she couldn't figure out what to ask. *I should find out how severe it is.* "I don't feel stitches." There was no way she hadn't needed them.

Benjamin took that question. "We had to leave it open to drain, but it looks like we can put butterfly tapes on it today."

She winced. "I guess I'll have a scar then."

"A small one."

James grumbled a curse. Jason settled a hand on her

shoulder. There was something comforting in both of their reactions. She found herself paying more attention to them than she did to the doctors working on her.

At last, Benjamin wrapped a fresh bandage around her arm and secured it. "The bandage will need to be changed twice a day. You will have oral and topical medications. You will be on bed rest for a week or so. We will send you back to your rooms with instructions for Marietta."

Steven took over. "Would you like James and Jason to take you back to your rooms, or should I call Marietta to come collect you?"

"James and Jason." She studiously avoided looking at them. *I just don't want Marietta hovering.* It was as good an excuse as any other and Samara vowed to stick to it.

"Very well." Steven piled used supplies onto a metal tray. "Marietta will have a meal waiting for you when you arrive."

Benjamin passed him on his way to the door. "I will order the car to the side door for you."

"Car?" Samara protested. "It's only the other side of campus." She could walk there in a matter of ten or fifteen minutes.

"Bed rest." Jason forced the words out through the end of a yawn.

James snuggled closer. "I could carry you instead."

That sounds waaaay too appealing. "The car will be fine, thanks."

His expression was nothing short of mock disappointment.
Any more cheese on that and he would be pouting.

The doctors left the room with what looked suspiciously like imperfectly masked grins on their faces.

James didn't waste any time. He vaulted from the bed, then strode across the room in nothing but a pair of jeans.

Over deliciously tight buns. I bet he's commando.

He collected a plush blue robe and headed back with it, giving her an enticing view of his sculpted abs and the outline of his cock.

"Maybe I do want to know." Samara considered the idea carefully. *College is supposed to be the time you experiment, right? And it's not like I can get pregnant from it. Why shouldn't I find out for myself if they are as good as their promises — and my vague memories of last night — attest they are?*

James stopped short, shooting her a questioning look.

Time to go for broke. "Maybe I do want to know where a night with the two of you would go."

His cock lengthened and thickened behind his jeans, fighting containment therein.

Jason laid a kiss on her neck that made her shiver in delight. "That can be arranged."

She sighed. "If Marietta ever lets me out of her sight again."

James grinned widely. "Marietta likes us."

Samara doubted she liked anyone that much.

* * * *

Jason rearranged his cock, cursing the tight jeans for the third time since awakening in bed with Samara. She didn't look in his direction, but her sudden intake of breath said she was well aware of what he was doing.

"One of the servants mentioned a back way into the dorms?" she hinted.

James shot a look of confusion her way. "There is, but why would you want to use it?"

She fidgeted for a moment, then stiffened. "It's just... You carrying me in. Everyone watching." Samara shrugged.

"I could see how that might be embarrassing," Jason admitted.

The time would come when Samara would know there was nothing shameful or weak about being carried by her mates, but that day had not arrived.

James tipped his head and ordered the driver to pull around to the back. "We can take the servants' elevator up."

"There's an elevator?" She was probably wondering why she had to walk the stairs all the time.

"You can use it anytime you wish." James waved toward the approaching door.

If she's going to, she might as well know the facts about it. "It's a freight elevator and not all that comfortable."

"Or fast." James crinkled his nose in distaste. "You could walk the stairs faster than the beast moves, but if you have an injury or are very tired, it is available to you."

"Sounds good." Samara sounded tired.

Jason wondered if she might beg off the night with them, out of sheer exhaustion and the need to heal.

The car pulled to a halt and James moved to pick her up again. Jason shot him a look of frustration, and his brother relented, probably realizing that he was monopolizing carrying their mate and leaving Jason to be the fifth wheel.

Samara fit in his arms like she was born to be there, and Jason memorized every sensation as he made his way through the door James opened for them and then into the elevator.

James hadn't been exaggerating about the speed of this ancient piece of junk. Though it was meticulously maintained and smooth-running, it could lose to the mythical tortoise.

Jason didn't mind that, since it meant all the more time with Samara in his arms. She didn't question why he was carrying her...or why James had earlier, though it seemed the hierarchy of wolves within the pack was still alien to her.

Yet another thing we have to teach her. He didn't begrudge her not knowing. Every piece of information she was lacking granted himself and James the time to teach it to her.

The elevator opened, and James led the way out, then to the hall doorway. It wouldn't be appropriate to cut through Marietta's rooms, so they went the long way, down the hall and into the front door to Samara's room.

Marietta was there, waving them in and giving useless commands.

Does she think we won't show Samara the care of putting her in bed and tucking her in?

The servant chattered on and on.

"I will have your meal brought up immediately."

"Let me fluff the pillows for you."

"You're so cold! I'll bring another quilt."

"No, don't you dare get up! I will help you to the toilet, if you must go."

That was where Samara drew the line, her Alpha personality coming out to play. And it was glorious.

"I am more than capable of walking to the bathroom."

"Benjamin said—"

"He is as overprotective as you are."

"If I relent and let you go by yourself, *will* you get into bed and rest for a while?"

Jason swallowed a snort of laughter. He never would have guessed Marietta could be so flummoxed. *And by an injured Alpha who doesn't know her own power and is unsteady on her feet.*

Samara seemed to consider that. "Yes, but you should know I invited James and Jason to come back after dinner for a movie tonight."

Marietta moved her lips as if to talk, then clamped them

shut into a thin line. She nodded, then waved Samara toward the bathroom.

Once she disappeared inside, James let loose a laugh, muffled into his hand.

Marietta turned on them, a fierce warning glare on her face.

Jason cracked a smile sure to infuriate her.

"She needs her rest," she whispered.

"We know more than a few ways to help her sleep." James's falsely innocent answer wouldn't fool a complete stranger, let alone Samara's servant.

"She enjoyed sleeping between us." Jason hurried to offer an explanation before the old she-wolf decided to gut his brother.

Whatever she might have said next short-circuited at the sound of Samara flushing the toilet.

Samara left the bathroom wearing a long, silken sleeping gown, having shed the medical gown and robe in the other room. Their mate made her way to the bed, then slipped under the covers, revealing an enticing peek at her legs in the process.

Jason salivated at the thought of touching her again.

"Well, now," Marietta said. "If you two don't mind… Samara should eat and rest. That way she won't fall asleep during your movie."

The need to protest rose up strong. He swallowed it at Samara's wave and smile.

"Eight?" Her suggested time confirmed that Samara ate an early dinner, in the American style.

Jason's heart lightened at the invitation. "Not a minute later. You have my vow."

James executed a formal bow. "Until tonight."

* * * *

Samara watched them leave, the slow simmer warming her belly. *And below.*

Marietta disappeared for a moment, then returned with a tray of soup and crackers and a plate of fruit. She set it on the table beside the bed and laid a large napkin across Samara's lap.

She'd hoped for something more substantial and her stomach growled in complaint.

As if she'd spoken the thought aloud, Marietta answered it. "Benjamin says you can have a full dinner, if you keep this down."

Don't rock the boat. She's not complaining about James and Jason spending time in my room. "Makes sense. Take things slowly. Right?"

Marietta seemed surprised at the capitulation. She sat on the edge of the bed and smoothed Samara's hair. "This has been a strain on you, I know. Why don't we do this? You eat. After that, I will help you get a nice hot bath, we'll change your dressing, and you can rest until dinner."

Samara leaned closer to her and gave Marietta a hug. If questioned, she couldn't have recounted why she chose to do it, but it felt right.

Marietta rocked her for a moment, then settled Samara back into the pillows with what appeared to be a heartfelt smile. "Now, let's get some food in you."

* * * *

Samara watched the line of servants carrying flowers, stuffed animals, and boxes, her eyes wide. "What is all of this?"

One of them turned and offered a stiff bow. "Well wishes for the injured Alpha."

"But... But I don't even know this many people." That

wasn't an exaggeration.

Marietta laughed. "They know you. It is our way to offer comfort when someone is injured or ill."

Our way. That reminds me, I have questions for her about that subject.

Samara realized the servants were standing there, seemingly waiting for her to say or ask something else. "Thank you."

The one who'd addressed her smiled and nodded. In moments, the dressers and tables in the room were covered in gifts. The male servants left the room and closed the door behind them.

Samara sighed. "I suppose I should write thank-you notes to everyone." It was one of the many courtesies her mother had drilled into her.

"When you feel up to it." Marietta dismissed her concern with a flitting of one hand. "If you wish, I can make a list of the gifts and who sent them to make it easier."

"That would be nice. Thank you."

Marietta pulled a pen and tablet out of the desk drawer and started recording the information. "Is there anything you would like closer to the bed?"

"The lavender…and maybe a few of the stuffed animals?"

Marietta smiled. "The lavender is from James and Jason."

"How did they know…?"

"That it's your favorite?"

Samara nodded.

"My two best guesses are that they either realized you favor soaps and perfumes that include the scent or they saw you in the gardens. You tend to sit by the lavender."

"I suppose that makes sense." *And it means they've been paying attention to what I like.* Samara couldn't decide if that bothered her or impressed her. *Think about it later.* She scanned her gaze along the gifts, wondering what the boxes held.

"Oh, here is something from Christiana and her family."

"Has anyone checked it for poison?" The question was out before Samara considered how rude it might sound. *Who cares! She stabbed me.*

Marietta stiffened. "She wouldn't dare!"

"Oh, she dares a lot."

"True, but I doubt that will continue."

"Was she at least punished?"

Marietta shot her a look of disbelief. "Of course. Though all evidence points to her making a mistake—"

"Please tell me you're not defending her." *Are you kidding me? Seriously?*

"No. Nothing like that. And I fully endorse her being expelled, as she was." She hurried over to the bed, the tablet in one hand and a box in the other. "You see... Christiana had two types of daggers. The one she used was lethal, but she'd *thought* she grabbed the nonlethal one...a trick blade, I believe they call them. She meant to scare you, not kill you."

"And you actually believe that?"

Her expression hardened. "Even Christiana wouldn't lie to the Alpha."

"Mr. Galvani?"

"No. He's the Alpha Maestro...the head teacher. The Alpha is..."

"The head of our people?" Samara guessed.

That seemed to shock her. "Yes. You know about our people now?"

"Eva was telling me about them when Christiana attacked me. I haven't learned much yet. I guess I should."

"Yes. Absolutely."

"Do you know who my father is?"

Marietta went stock-still. "It is not my place to impart such information to you."

She didn't say she didn't know. She only said it wasn't her place to tell me. "So, you know, but—"

"Oh, look. They gave you McKinnon's candies. Those are the best."

She's afraid. She can't tell me, and she's afraid to let me know why she can't tell me. Samara decided to drop it. *For now.*

The scent from the box taunted her. "I can't eat chocolate. I'm—"

"Allergic. I know. I let anyone who asked know as well. McKinnon's makes the best carob candies. Nearly indistinguishable from chocolate in taste, but won't set off allergies."

"Christiana actually *asked* that question?" It didn't sound like her.

"Her father, Marcus. He's a lovely man. He would like to offer his apologies personally, when you're feeling better."

She'd expected as much. "Maybe."

"Would you like to try a carob?"

Samara smiled. "I'm sure Benjamin wouldn't approve."

Marietta leaned closer and offered a conspiratorial smile. "I am sure I'm not going to tell him. Are you?"

"No." Still, she hesitated.

"I'm sure Marcus bought them. I can guarantee they are safe."

I may not trust Christiana, but I can probably trust Marcus. It made no sense to come to that conclusion, but she felt it was correct. *It's most likely because Marietta trusts him.*

"I'll give it a try."

* * * *

"Do you need anything else?" Marietta asked.

"No thank you." Samara tried not to sound as nervous as she felt. *I probably failed.*

If that was true, Marietta showed no sign of it, and Samara breathed a sigh of relief.

"Thank you for the popcorn, Marietta." Jason popped another piece in his mouth.

She shot him a smile. "Let me know if you need anything." With that, she turned on her heel and strode away.

Samara forced herself to take several calming breaths.

"Not yet." James smoothed a hand across her cheek. "Give Marietta time to settle into her own rooms."

"And what do we do?" she whispered.

"Watch a movie."

Laughter bubbled up from inside her.

Jason put the DVD in, then returned to the bed. The two of them curled up on either side of her. It was comfortable and exhilarating at the same time.

The movie was in Italian with English subtitles, so she focused on it, trying to follow the plot instead of obsessing over what she'd decided to do.

And with two men, no less. What am I thinking? The answer to that was simple enough. She was thinking how hot they were. She'd wanted a piece of them for a week. *And now I'm going to get the taste I want.*

Twenty minutes into the film, Samara guessed why they'd chosen it. The couple on screen had decided to go skinny-dipping. *Vincent* dropped his trousers. Unlike most American movies, there wasn't a cut-away. She had a full-view of his tight ass, then of his half-erect cock surrounded by a thick nest of black curls.

Samara glanced at her partners' cocks, hard behind the sleep pants they'd worn to her room for the *movie*. She looked back at the screen, torn between hoping they didn't notice and hoping they did.

It seemed James never missed anything.

He leaned close to whisper to her. "Do you want to see ours?"

"Yes," she admitted.

They stripped off their sleep pants and tossed them aside before she could catch her breath. The movie abandoned, she scanned their bodies, hungrily.

As she'd guessed earlier, they were muscular, without excess fat anywhere she could see. Their cocks were long and hard. Both much bigger than the actor they'd been watching. Droplets of clear liquid dotted the slits in the heads.

"If you're comparing..." Jason teased. He trailed one finger down her arm, raising goose bumps in his wake. "I'm longer, but James is thicker."

Damn. They know just what to say to turn me on.

James reached down and levered his cock up. Jason followed suit.

Samara compared their dimensions. *He didn't lie about that.*

In a daze, she reached for James's cock. He groaned at the feeling of her fingertips sliding down the thick veins on the underside of his length. The fluids slipped lazily down the foreskin, and she rubbed at the slit, testing its feel.

"You're making James feel really good." Jason laid a kiss on her shoulder.

And ignoring Jason. As little knowledge as she had about a threesome, Samara was fairly certain giving unequal attention to one or the other was bad news.

She did the same for Jason, shivering at his moans and pleas for more.

Jason reached a hand between her thighs, stroking at the gathering wetness moistening the silky fabric. "You are so hot."

"Maybe you need to bathe me again." It was out before she thought about what she was saying.

"Not tonight," James replied.

"At least...not yet." Jason's tone said he'd like bathing her.

Good. Because that's not what I want.

Jason sat up, threaded his fingers in her hair, and parted Samara's lips in a slow, deep kiss. James trailed his hands up and down her chest and abdomen. Her arousal stepped up, notch after notch, and the kiss heated in response.

"My turn," James grumbled.

Jason released her mouth, and James turned her toward him. There was no slow start with him; James's engine was running, and he was clearly in high gear.

Jason leaned back and eased Samara to his chest. James leaned with her. While James plundered her mouth, Jason slipped a hand under her pajama top and cupped a breast.

Oh, yes! Her entire body burned and begged for more of them.

As if he could hear it, Jason swore a blue streak. He pulled his hand from beneath her top and started unbuttoning it. She arched up, driving her now-bare breasts against James's chest.

Jason stripped the top off and tossed it off the bed. He cupped both breasts in his hands, teasing at the nipples. The calluses on his thumbs pulled and massaged with each pass.

"You have got to feel these beautiful breasts, brother."

The kiss was over that quickly. Samara lounged against Jason, her senses reeling, while both brothers fondled a breast apiece.

"I say we share her." It wasn't a question; James fully

intended to, and his tone said he didn't intend to open it to discussion.

"Oh, yes." That was what she'd wanted since she first saw them.

Jason slipped from behind her, and they lowered her to the mattress together. Before her senses righted themselves, each of them had a breast in his mouth—sucking, licking, and nipping at the tender tips and the surrounding flesh. Samara wrapped a hand around each of their necks, encouraging them.

One of them worked a hand down the front of her pajama pants, then beneath the panties.

James. She spread her legs as far as she could between their bodies.

He took the hint and made designs in her pubic curls, moving lower and lower, until he circled her clit. Samara cried out harshly, then tensed in anticipation of Marietta rushing in to find them in flagrante delicto.

"Marietta likes us," Jason reminded her.

Samara wasn't sure how she felt about Marietta knowing her sexual exploits. *Especially this one.*

Who am I kidding? She's not going to miss anything that happens in this room. That much was a given.

James stroked her clit again, a silent reminder of where they'd left off. It wasn't silent for long. Samara moaned.

He started working her pajama bottoms and panties down together.

Jason urged him on. "We really don't need those."

Samara tried to convince herself that she should be offended by the way they handled her. *Why should I do that? This is what I wanted. Nearly, anyway.*

James pitched her clothing away, leaving her as nude as they were. He spread her legs, seemingly rapt on the view.

"Even better than I imagined."

That was reassuring to hear.

"I think we should share her again, Jason."

Samara gasped at Jason's abrupt movement. Before she could decide what to ask, they'd levered her legs up and out.

Two tongues played between, searching out every crease and plane. One backed away slightly to allow the other to suck, then they switched places.

Her heart hammered, and the tension inside reached a painfully sweet razor edge. Realization that was she was about to come made her balk. "No. Stop. I'm going to—" Samara wondered if they would push her over, just to prove they could.

It seemed that wasn't in her game plan. Both backed off in a hurry. Jason moved toward her head, and James positioned himself between her thighs.

"Not without us," he grumbled.

Then he was inside her, filling Samara as she'd fantasized he would. There were so many overlapping sensations—*Pleasure. Pressure. Pain. The drumbeat of need*—Samara couldn't make sense of them. The sudden need to push him off assaulted her.

Jason grasped her wrists and laid a kiss on her forehead. "You don't need to fear us, Samara."

She relaxed, and James started thrusting. In moments, her arousal had rocketed toward climax again. *And this is only one of them.*

* * * *

James breathed deeply, savoring her scent. *Blood. We're her first. Her only!*

Her lunge toward him came so fast, he might have taken on scars, had Jason not captured and soothed her so quickly.

It wasn't completely unexpected, he supposed. A she-wolf's first sexual experience was confusing for her and often resulted in her first partial shift.

It wasn't her first. Memories of Christiana's attack brought his fang tips out. *By the Night Mother, we're lucky Samara never took a human lover...and was never attacked by an armed combatant. She might have gutted him in the rush of the shift.*

The need to make her come was instinctual, and she'd forced his wolf to the surface. James started moving, rapt on the proof of her wolf heritage so apparent in her features.

He'd seen her golden eyes, the mouthful of deadly teeth, and her thickened fingernail-claws when she'd been stabbed with the Hunter's Fang. The blade was designed to prove wolfhood as it killed their kind.

But her ears hadn't shifted last time. The sight of the tufted tips, peeking through her hair, confirmed that she was fully engaged in the sex.

One thrust led to another and another. Her inner muscles fluttered, then clamped rhythmically. Her moans turned to screams of delight. She came around him, prompting James to follow her over. He howled in triumph, emptying his sac into her in spasms.

"Jason," she pleaded.

He met his brother's eyes and smiled. There had been the slight chance she would refuse the younger brother this time. It was good that she hadn't. The last thing they needed was jealousy in the pairing.

James eased out of her, shushing Samara's protest with a kiss brushed against her lips. He switched places with Jason, his mouth going dry at the sight of his younger twin sliding home inside their mate.

His cock twitched, coming erect for more she might or

might not grant him tonight. He hadn't realized how exciting watching her take Jason's length would be, and James wondered if Jason felt the same when their places were reversed.

"I want to feel both of you," she pleaded. "Like when you were bathing me."

Jason snapped his head up. "Lift her." His brother usually deferred to James, but the scent and feel of their mate had brought out the full Alpha tendencies in Jason.

James didn't hesitate. They'd discussed this already. They didn't want to rush Samara to double penetration, but it was natural for an Alpha female to want to feel both mates touching her. *Especially since we've already introduced her to the sensation.*

He snuggled to Samara's back, savoring every movement as Jason thrust into her. James pressed kisses to her neck and shoulders, shivering at the idea of laying his fangs instead.

Jason pushed her tighter between them, and the scent of his brother's blood assaulted him.

James forced his eyes open in shock and disbelief. *She hasn't started the blood exchange already.*

Samara hadn't. She was raking Jason's back with her claws.

Lucky bastard.

Jason stepped up his pace. "You have such a lovely little pussy."

Samara didn't miss a beat. "All the better to take two big cocks."

James's cock responded to the compliment, releasing more cum onto her lower back in a spate of aftershocks.

That spelled the end for her. Samara climaxed again with a shout and Jason indulged in response.

They came down to earth slowly, hands trailing over bodies. Her ear tips retreated, and his fangs did the same.

The time will come. Eventually, her instincts will demand Samara taste our blood. The question was, would she learn about their world another way first? If she didn't, the event could traumatize her. *Damn Sebastian's rules.*

Samara took a deep breath and they lowered her to the mattress. Jason's attempt to join her short-circuited at her statement.

"We shouldn't. We might fall asleep."

James bit back his frustration. *Marietta is a servant, damn it. And she's a wolf. She knows what traditionally happens when Alpha males join the Alpha female in her bed.*

Jason nodded. "As you wish, Samara. We will bring your class work for you after breakfast, if that is acceptable to you."

She smiled. "I'd like that."

They left the bed and tucked her in. James scooped up Samara's clothing and tossed it in the hamper. He grabbed Jason's sleep pants and prepared to lob them in his brother's direction. Jason had already tossed James's pants over his shoulder.

He doesn't want Samara to see his back. Smart move, brother. James did the same with the pants he held. He forced a smile to his face. "See you tomorrow."

"Absolutely." The invitation underlying that single word was impossible to miss.

"Good night to you, Samara." While she'd been focused on James, his brother had moved halfway toward the door.

Jason waited until James was between him and Samara before he turned his back to her. James stared at the scratches weeping blood as they walked away. They would be healed by morning, but James didn't question that Jason would relish every moment he could feel them.

I would if it was me.

They closed the door behind them and came face-to-face

with Marietta.

James straightened, well aware of how they looked—sweat-misted, their cocks half-erect and coated in sex fluids and Samara's blood.

She has no right to judge. She knows what is expected.

"Why are you leaving her?" she whispered harshly.

James reminded himself not to snap at her. "She doesn't know our laws and traditions. Samara is nervous about falling asleep together. She's afraid of what you will think or say."

Marietta shook her head in frustration. He didn't question what she was thinking. If it wasn't for Sebastian, they could simply tell Samara.

Tell her. Show her. Reassure her. Seduce her to her destiny.

"What next?"

Thankfully, she deferred to them. James was in no mood to take orders.

Jason shrugged. "We study with her tomorrow. We work toward putting her at ease. We wait for an opportunity to tell her who and what she is." He turned away and started down the stairs.

Marietta gaped at his retreating back, then hid a giggle behind her hand.

James smirked at her. "You can tell Sebastian her shifted form is lovely." He loped down the stairs, smiling at the servant's wide-eyed look.

She wouldn't pass the message along, but she didn't need to. Saying it to the straight-laced servant was enough.

Chapter Six

"Samara, James and Jason are here with your class work. Do you feel up to seeing them?"

"Yes. Thank you, Marietta." At the very least, she didn't hover when the brothers were around. She would offer them something to eat and drink and then disappear to whatever other chores awaited her until lunch time.

Marietta waved them in. "Anything I can bring you? Coffee? Juice? A light snack?"

"Juice and some fruit and cheese, please," Samara requested, knowing Marietta would keep suggesting something until she agreed.

Jason tipped his fingers. "The same."

James's request followed close on his brother's heels. "Coffee. Thank you, Marietta."

"Right away." She left through a back door Samara had never investigated before.

I'm not sure why. I guess I always assumed it led to her rooms, and it wouldn't be acceptable for me to intrude.

"In addition to her rooms, there is a small kitchen back there." James wrapped an arm around her shoulder, pointing the way back and then to the right. "At meal times you take in your rooms, the main kitchen sends a chef to help her prepare the meal for you."

"Oh. That's why it never seems to take her long to bring back food." Samara supposed it made a certain amount of sense, though it was an incredible waste of resources to pamper one person. *Well, two, since Eva usually eats with me when I eat in my room.*

"Samara?" Jason prompted her.

"I suppose I should see what work is waiting for me." She sighed. *Two days of missed classes already, and another three to come. What a lousy first impression I'm making.*

Jason started pulling books from his knapsack. "It doesn't look like much, and all your professors know you're ill, so if you need more time to complete the work, they will be lenient."

That was good to hear. She started to rise to go to the table.

James placed his hands on her shoulders to stop her. "Bed rest. Remember?"

"How am I supposed to—"

He raised a finger for a moment of silence, then reached into the large shoulder bag he'd carried in and pulled out a lap desk.

"You two think of everything. Don't you?" Samara wasn't sure whether to be annoyed or amused by their solicitous care. *Amused. Enchanted. Damn it, how can I not enjoy two hot men seeing to my every need this way?*

"Yes, and the sooner you learn that, the sooner we can get down to business." His smile said James was joking, but there was an underlying tension in him she couldn't make sense of.

Samara didn't try to. She took the books and papers from Jason's hands, then sent James to her desk for her notebooks. Well before Marietta returned with the tray, all three of them were lined up on the bed, studying hard.

* * * *

"Enough. My brain is turning to mush." Samara moaned and rubbed at her temples.

James smiled at her exaggeration. *She is so playful at times.* "You've been at it for three hours straight." *And she really doesn't have much left to do. Samara is a dedicated student.* "We should probably ask Marietta for some lunch." If he concentrated on it, James could hear her padding past the door, probably weighing the length of time she should wait before demanding Samara stop to eat.

Her stomach rumbled. "Probably a good idea."

"Roast chicken or grilled salmon?" Jason recited the lunch menu from memory.

She considered it, seemingly torn.

James didn't question that she wanted both. "We could get one choice and you the other and share."

"That sounds good."

Feeding you off my fork sounds more than good. There was little a wolf enjoyed more than providing for his mate.

Jason rose and went to the servant's door. He knocked politely and relayed their order to Marietta. Then he returned to the bed.

The question that had been plaguing him all morning gnawed at James. It would take Marietta time to bring the food, and Samara needed a break from studying. It was time to broach the subject.

"Are we invited back for another movie tonight?"

She blushed a bit. Since she was still pale from the trauma of the attack, it looked good on her. "Of course."

Jason grinned widely, and James followed suit. His brother leaned down and laid a kiss on her throat, probably daydreaming—as James often did himself—about laying his mark in claim on her.

"Was it everything you'd hoped for?" Jason purred.

Samara hesitated, and James's blood ran cold.

It wasn't. We failed her.

Jason beat him to the question. "What didn't we do for you? What would make being with us perfect?"

72

Her cheeks went scarlet.

She was a virgin until last night. She doesn't have the confidence to ask for whatever it is. James reached out and cupped her face up to his for a sweet kiss. "Now. Be honest with us. Believe me when I tell you we would do anything to fulfill your fondest wishes, and I doubt there is anything you could ask that would be uncomfortable for us." *Well...one thing, but how likely is she to ask for that?*

"It's just..." She seemed to struggle for the words to explain it.

"Tell us," Jason pleaded.

"When you are with two guys..." She peeked up at them.

James nodded. "You wanted to experience double penetration." He didn't question it.

She squirmed. "Well, I...expected it, I guess."

"Dearest, if you want that, you will have it."

Jason nodded. "We didn't want to rush you."

James considered it. "Would you permit us to suggest something that may make it easier for you?"

Samara nodded and waved them on.

"Jason, you know what to get."

His brother didn't question it. They'd been planning for this day for a week. He rose from the bed and loped away toward the stairs to their rooms.

"What is he getting?" she asked.

"After lunch, we'll show you," he promised.

James pressed another kiss to her lips, his blood heating. Concentrating on his studies this afternoon was going to be difficult.

* * * *

Samara didn't look up from the lap desk when James and Jason came into the room. She squirmed, feeling the butt plug they'd put in earlier more acutely when she moved.

Her cheeks flamed at the memories of the day.

Putting it in had been a sensual delight, and the brothers had taken turns showing their appreciation by introducing her to new sexual positions. More than once, they'd captured her groans and screams of delight to avoid Marietta coming into the room to check on her.

As if the thought of her had summoned her forth, the servant appeared at her side and placed a hand on her cheek.

"Hmmm... I should call Benjamin."

"I'm sure I don't have a fever." Samara snapped. "It's just a little warm under the blankets."

Marietta's raised brow said she wasn't convinced.

"Could you drop the temperature another five degrees or so, please?"

"As you wish, but if you are still warm in the morning—"

"I know. You'll call the doctors again." She sighed.

Marietta offered James and Jason a nod. "I've left your food and drinks on the table. I'll clear the tray in the morning."

"Thank you, Marietta."

Samara managed to stifle the pleasant shiver by the skin of her teeth. There was something about the brothers speaking in unison that aroused her.

"Have a good evening." In the next moment, she was gone.

The temperature started to shift within a minute, and the brothers were stripped and on the bed with her a heartbeat later.

Jason took the pen from her hand, and James removed the lap desk. She let them, shocked by the speed of events.

Jason reached out to untie the lace robe she'd donned over a short negligee.

She covered the top tie with her hand. "Shouldn't we give Marietta time to settle?" They had the night before.

James grasped the next tie down and pulled the lace out slowly, watching it unfurl. "We *can,* but last night proves we won't be seeing her again tonight. She said so on the way out."

Samara let her hand drop to her lap, spellbound by the sight of him licking his lips.

Jason took advantage of the situation to open the tie she'd been covering. "Of course, if you're still not sure of that, we could put a movie in and pull the blankets up." He stroked one callused fingertip over her ready nipple. "But I don't promise not to touch."

"Yes. Let's—"

She made it no further. They were already under the quilt and sheet with her.

"What about the movie?"

James grabbed the remote from the bedside table and started pushing buttons. It was a different movie than the night before...and more blatant. It started off with a couple fully engaged in heavy petting, over clothes and under.

Jason raked a hungry gaze down her chest. "You seemed to enjoy the scenes last night."

"When did you...?" She swallowed hard at the sight of the man on the screen sucking an engorged nipple.

James leaned down and pressed a kiss to hers, through the negligee. "When you were in the toilet after lunch."

"I always knew you were the one with the wickedly sexual ideas."

Not to be undone, Jason pulled the bodice on the gown back to uncover one breast and suckled on the other nipple.

"And I bet you are responsible for the lavender." She bit at her lower lip.

He licked the hard nub. "I am."

James nuzzled at the other breast. "I bought you sex toys and movies we can share together."

"Watch, Samara," Jason whispered.

The couple on the screen was wearing less clothing, and engrossed with each other. Her body responded to what she was seeing.

Just as the man on the screen slid his fingers into the woman's body, James did the same to her. Samara gasped, her inner muscles gripping him tightly.

James hummed low in his throat. "She likes it. She likes watching and being touched."

"Good. Keep watching." Jason slipped the other side of the bodice down and went to work on the opposite nipple.

James pumped his fingers in and out, and his tongue played at her clit, making her head spin pleasantly.

I'm going to come. Oh, God, I am going to come so hard.

She glanced at the screen, trying to make sense of what she was seeing. The actor was applying some sort of oil to his cock and rubbing it in, his head thrown back and his arm muscles tightened.

It took a moment for her to realize Jason was no longer sucking at her. Samara glanced in his direction, her mouth going dry at the sight of him doing the same.

"Watch, Samara." James reminded her.

"This view is better." It was. She expected to hear them laugh at her observation, but they didn't.

Instead, Jason edged closer to her on the bed. "Move her."

James lifted her to her knees and positioned Samara at the edge of the mattress. Before she could make sense of their actions, he was back between her thighs, kneeling on the floor, using his lips and tongue to increase her pleasure.

Jason grasped the base of the butt plug and worked it in and out slowly, stretching the ring of tissue. He added lubrication to soften the muscle.

Out of the corner of her eye, Samara saw the actor easing his fingers out of his partner. He worked the head of his cock into her.

"You want to feel my cock inside you, don't you?" Jason breathed.

"Oh, yes."

The butt plug was abruptly gone, and the soft tip of his cock replaced it. Samara gasped.

On the screen, the actor was buried to the hilt in the woman. She pushed her ass back into the cradle of his hips.

Samara did the same and the head popped past the restraining muscle.

Jason groaned. "That's right. Keep pushing back. I want you to feel all of me."

She wanted the same. The gentle rolling of his hips picked up speed and force. Samara gasped and moaned, her body coming to life.

At last, he went still, deep inside her. Samara wiggled against him, aching for more.

"I think she's ready, brother."

James came to his feet before her, working his cock into the conspicuously empty fore-hole. In moments, she was stuffed full of Trudale cock, her breathing coming in ragged gasps.

They stayed there for a moment, letting her adjust to the pressure of them overlapping inside her body.

Jason moved first, drawing back. As he returned, James withdrew. It was a potent dance that made her dizzy.

"I'm not going to last," Jason admitted. "You're so tight and so hot."

Samara had no words to answer him. Climax was already clawing at her. She wouldn't need much to finish her off.

As if James knew it—*and he might*—he started handling her nipples roughly, adding a layer of pleasure-pain to the rest. The patchwork of sensations shot her over the edge.

Her scream of delight was muted in James's mouth. Still, the climax went on and on, driven by their quickening motions.

Jason came next, his entire body going tense inside her, his fluids heating her.

That left James, cycling his cock in and out, while Jason's was still and deep. The change sent aftershocks through her system, and their kiss deepened.

As if that was what James had been waiting for, he lodged himself deep inside her and let loose his own wave of cum.

After a few moments of shared panting, Jason started to withdraw.

"Don't you dare," Samara warned him.

He went still, half-buried inside her.

James smiled a wicked little smile that made her heart flutter in excitement. "What do you want, Samara?"

She pushed up further on her knees, then slid down the length of their cocks again, drawing twin moans from the brothers. "I want more of you. More of this...for now."

"And later?" Jason asked, his hands stroking her still-hard nipples.

"I want the two of you to find a movie with double penetration."

Aftershocks wracked them...and then her, in response.

James laid a solemn kiss on her lips. "That is a wickedly sexy idea."

"I think you may be rubbing off on me." *That's not right.* "Both of you." *Better.*

Jason nipped at her ear. "Maybe you'll let me bathe you in lavender, then."

"After." Right now, she had two very talented males in bed with her, and Samara didn't intend to waste a minute of it.

* * * *

"Marietta has arrived, Sebastian."

He waved her in, anxious for news about Samara. "Bring some tea, Roberto. You know Marietta's favorites."

"Just a few minutes." Roberto closed them in together.

Marietta tipped her head in a bow, then settled in the wing chair across from his. "Thank you, Sebastian."

He didn't waste time. "How is Samara healing?"

She smiled wearily. "Very well. Her arm will scar. Weak as she is, keeping her on bed rest is nearly impossible. She is a wolf, and—no offense intended to you—your daughter has all the energy you had at her age."

Sebastian cracked a smile at her tactful handling. "And the rest?"

"If she is not sleeping, or spending time with Eva, she is probably in the company of James and Jason. Samara has been...intimate with her mates for the last two days, but she resists letting them spend the night in her bed."

"What? Why?"

"Apparently..." She shot him a measuring look out of the corner of her eyes.

"Yes?" Sebastian drew the question out, demanding an answer.

"Apparently, she is worried about my reaction to such a move. We have only just established a lasting peace between us...and she doesn't know our traditions. If I could only tell her —"

"No!"

The lines around the old woman's eyes tightened in tension, and she nodded.

He considered the problem. "Give them room."

"Sebastian? I don't understand."

"You have other duties."

"My *only* duty is to Samara." Her resistance to the idea wasn't difficult to understand. Hers was a sacred post.

He narrowed his eyes, letting them shift in frustration. His shoulders tensed. It was a clear warning, and her eyes widened in response to the threat.

"You. Have. *Other*. Duties."

"Of course." Marietta tripped over her words, and her eyes shifted left and right, as if searching for something. "Things I would have to do when Samara was in class. She will have James and Jason with her as protection, so I need not worry about that."

An impressive idea. Then again, I've always known Marietta was intelligent. "You get a few days and nights off once a month. That is coming due, I believe."

They both knew she didn't, but Marietta had followed the game this far.

Her brow crinkled, though she didn't voice her opposition to the plan.

"Yes?" he prompted her.

"Yes, of course. Coming soon." But something remained unsaid.

"Is there a problem?"

"Your rules about Samara's protection."

He smiled. *Well done. You even seek to protect my daughter from my own short-sightedness.* "All *Samara* has to know is that you are absent. She doesn't need to know about the guards stationed out of her sight. When her mates are not in the room with her or are sleeping with her and not actively on watch, the guards will protect her back for you."

Marietta nodded. "Done. My first night away will be tomorrow."

Sebastian bit back a laugh at the wondrous subterfuge they were planning. It was like a chess game with another master. "Is there any other news?"

Her cheeks darkened, and she cleared her throat.

He raised an eyebrow in surprise. The old woman had seen everything, from what he'd heard. Family stories had it that his parents had shown no decorum at all in mating. What could possibly embarrass such a woman? Sebastian cleared his throat, a gentle reminder that he'd asked a question.

"It was a rather…rude message from James. It would hardly be appropriate to repeat it." She didn't meet his gaze.

James. According to Pietro, he was the more outgoing – and outrageous – of Samara's mates. "And the message is?"

Marietta winced, then sighed. "Your daughter's shifted form is lovely."

Sebastian laughed long and hard. So hard that tears pooled in his eyes and rolled down his cheeks. It wasn't until after Roberto delivered the tea that he composed himself again.

"Such a bold challenge," he marveled. "Of course it is simply his frustration speaking out of turn." Sebastian considered the message. "Still… It is good to know Samara can shift. I wasn't sure she would."

Marietta took a dainty sip of the hot tea. "It is also good to know her mates excite her so."

"Yes. It is." To his surprise, Sebastian found it also bothered him. *More than a little.*

He would like to deny he had secretly hoped Samara would refuse the brothers and stay close to him for a while. *I can't.*

Samara is an adult. If she wants James and Jason, she'll have them. They will protect her well.

That settled, somewhat, he picked up the second cup of tea and started planning Samara's protection with Marietta.

Chapter Seven

Samara considered putting on the robe, then tossed it across the mattress. The short nightie Eva had given her was scandalous, but it was just the impression she wanted to make on the brothers.

Besides, with Eva attending a late study group and Marietta gone for the night, who is going to see me?

That thought in mind, Samara opened the door and peeked down the hall. *No one. Just as I thought.* She padded barefoot over the hardwood floors.

At the staircase, she took a moment to right her senses. It seemed the vertigo was still with her.

I could take the elevator...or call them to come to me. Or even wait another hour, and they will come up on their own.

Samara dismissed those ideas nearly as quickly as she thought them. Any of them would undermine the independence she was proclaiming by going to them, whether James and Jason knew about it or not.

Besides that, I want them. Now. Right now.

Hold the rail. Take it slow. She repeated the mantra silently as she inched down the stairs.

At one point, Samara was sure she heard someone behind her. She turned to look, cautiously, wary of slipping on the marble stairs. There was no one there. A shadow moved, retreating further down the hallway of Samara's floor.

Suzanne? Getting something for Eva?

It wasn't important. *Getting to James and Jason before anyone sees me is.* Not only was she half-naked, Samara was supposed to be on bed rest, and it was a safe bet Marietta left instructions with someone about that.

She rushed down the last six steps and made it to the door to their suite. Samara stood there for a moment, trembling lightly.

Calm down. You know what you want. Tell them. With that, Samara knocked on the door.

James answered it, gloriously naked. He looked up and down her body, then reached for her, wide-eyed.

She shoved back against his chest, rocking James onto his heels. "If you *dare* pick me up and treat me like an invalid, I will go straight back to my room and leave you with that erection all night."

It took him a moment to recover from shock. James laughed darkly, then guided Samara inside. "We can't have that." He pushed the door shut, leaning close to her to accomplish the job. "Why don't you tell me why you're here...and dressed so deliciously." It wasn't a question.

Samara walked her fingertips up his chest, smiling as his eyes narrowed and his abdominal muscles tensed. "There's something I want, something you haven't done for me. You're going to. Now."

* * * *

That piqued his interest. This was a side of Samara James hadn't seen yet. "Tell me."

He breathed in her scent, confirming what he suspected was true. His instincts went wild. Samara was an Alpha female in her fertile window, her pheromones heated, and she was demanding sex from him.

Anything she asks for.

"Where is Jason?"

Even better. His brother wouldn't handle it well if she chose James without him. *Neither would I, if it was reversed.* "In the shower."

Samara pressed to his chest, humming in pleasure. "Good. We can get started, and Jason can join us when he's done."

"Tell me."

She drew his hand to the back of her thigh, then pulled it upward to the crease of her ass.

The breath caught in his throat at the feeling of the butt plug embedded in her. *Night Mother!* His cock strained toward her.

Samara didn't hesitate. She nudged him backward into the main room. "It occurred to me that Jason has my ass every time we do double penetration."

He didn't argue it, though that wasn't *entirely* accurate. James had had her mouth while Jason had her pussy only that afternoon. Still, James knew what she meant.

"I'm going to have you exactly as I want you."

"Oh, yes. You certainly will." *If she wants Jason to walk in on us, we don't have much time.* James led her to his bed. Though they would likely have Samara in every room of the suite, he was determined it would be his bed first.

James lifted her onto the mattress, facing the center, then pushed down on her shoulders to position her for what she wanted. He worked the plug in and out, gritting his teeth as she moaned and met his inward thrusts.

The shower turned off, and James pitched the plug aside. Before Samara could finish her protest, he was working his cockhead back and forth through the pliant, tight ring of muscle.

It didn't take long for him to move from teasing preparation to balls-deep thrusting. James cursed himself for monopolizing her pussy for himself—unconsciously hoping to sire their first pup, he was sure. He had missed out; James hadn't realized how good it would feel to have Samara's ass clenching against his cock, the sensation of a great hand job, mixed with the fine control of sex.

Their noises rose in unison, so markedly James was afraid they were going to come before Jason could join them. With her fertile cycle riding her, it was a safe bet she would want them as often as she could get them, and it wasn't as if they hadn't indulged with her singly over the last few days. Still, she wanted something specific from him, and James didn't intend to fail.

That wasn't going to happen. Jason rushed into the room, a towel wrapped around his shoulders.

After a moment, his brother's indecision hit James solidly between the eyes.

He thinks she's offering a reversal of earlier today. Jason is afraid of her lack of control. Letting her fellate him is the last thing Jason wants to do.

James eased down on his knees on the edge of the mattress, pulling Samara upright between them, still impaled on his cock. "Plant one foot on the bed and spread your legs. I want to invite Jason in properly."

Samara followed his instructions, and Jason gasped in surprise. James spread her nether lips, thrusting slowly into her to demonstrate that he wasn't in her pussy. She tipped her head back, moaning.

James smiled at his brother's quickening breathing, at the narrowing of his eyes. "Samara requested this in specific, Jason. You're not going to keep a lady waiting, are you?"

The towel went flying across the room. Jason stalked across the floor, every muscle notched down tight. His cock went from half-mast to fully erect from one step to the next.

"Watch him, Samara."

She levered her head up and swiveled her neck to watch

Jason come for her. Her breathing went ragged, and her fingernails sharpened against his thigh.

Jason captured her lips in a heated kiss. When he pulled back, he thrust inside her in one smooth movement, his cock crowding James's inside her. "Is this what you wanted, Samara?"

It was a taunt, and she shivered in response to it. Her claws raked lightly at James's thigh, an instinctual show that she could fight them off.

But she isn't. She's submitting to us, as a pair.

"Yes." It came out a rough release of breath, no doubt spoken through sharpened canines.

James and Jason matched their movements, retreating and thrusting in near unison. There was no play at taking turns filling her; Samara was their mate, and she would know what being full of them both felt like.

Their sounds moved from pants to growls and grumbles. Samara closed a hand in James's hair, tugging lightly. She cupped the other around the back of Jason's neck and dragged him closer. She dragged her lips up and down Jason's chest and throat, her mouth opened a bit.

His brother's fangs peeked past his lips. James watched them, spellbound. Had her fertile cycle prompted her to demand their blood?

Samara jerked her head back, and James swallowed a curse. As if Jason agreed, they sped up at the same time.

She stiffened, her inner muscles pulsing in sweet release. Her howl echoed off the walls.

James bit back a laugh at that. Chase, their servant, was certain to have broken sleep tonight.

He scowled at a further thought. *If I learn he beat off to the sounds of Samara with us, I will gut him.*

James and Jason joined her in climax, their own little den

staking territory as a unit. They clung to each other, sharing breath, supporting each other.

Samara started laying kisses down Jason's chest, her need to mate driving her to more, no doubt.

James eased out of her. "That's right, Samara," he whispered, well aware that her hearing would be heightened. "Jason will give you what you want while I wash up."

Before James climbed off the mattress, the two were engaged in a passionate kiss.

* * * *

Jason restrained himself. If he didn't do that, he would take her down and fuck her hard and fast. James had promised anything *she* wanted, and her pheromones said Samara likely had distinct ideas about the subject.

I just wish they included marking each other. The sight of her preparing to choose a site to plant her teeth had nearly stopped his heart in excitement.

Soon. She'll need to taste our blood soon. If she didn't do so within the next week or so, a burgeoning pregnancy would force her to sate the need.

Will that alienate her? If she finds herself carrying our pups before she knows what she is? What we all are?

Samara dragged her face away, forcing his mind back to the present.

Her shifted eyes were hard in warning, her ear tips twitching. "I will have you as I want you."

What a glorious Alpha female she is. "Whatever you want." A male would be a fool to deny a female satiation of her choice, when she offers such boundless delights in her heat.

She pushed him backward, forcing Jason flat on his back on

the mattress. The part of him urging Jason to dominate her was silenced at the first lick over his nipples, a long swipe from right to left, her roughened tongue raising more than his interest.

Jason settled his hands on the back of her head, encouraging her. The licks alternated with nips. Her tasting moved lower. By the time she reached his abdomen, he was praying Samara intended to suck him as she had James.

Fuck the teeth. She could maim me, and I'll heal. And if Samara draws blood, she may need to taste more. We could be mated before James reaches the bed. Blood-drunk, she would bind herself to James as well.

It seemed Samara had no intention of maiming him. Her lips and tongue played at his cock, bathing him, enticing him. She slipped lower and sucked on his sac, causing it to fill again.

Jason arched up with a strangled groan, burying his claws in the palms of his hands. *James isn't crazy for allowing this. Not at all. I would allow Samara to grant me this every day, were she willing.*

She circled her tongue around his sac lazily, and she murmured against his skin.

Probably reacting to my arousal. To the increase in my scent.

In the next heartbeat, Samara was sucking the length of his cock down, engulfing him in bliss. He was on the verge of exploding when she moved.

* * * *

Inside. Damn it, this isn't enough!

Samara rushed to straddle his hips, then slipped down over Jason's cock.

He feels so good. So right. They both do.

She started rocking back and forth, then up and down, driving him deeper inside her. Samara stripped off her nightgown and dropped it to the floor. She drew Jason's hands up to her breasts, offering them to him.

He wasn't gentle.

Not that I want him to be.

Jason rubbed and tweaked at her nipples, sending bolts of pleasure through her body. He licked his lips, a sure sign that he would be leaving love bites if the position were move favorable.

Yes, bite. The idea of him leaving tender marks on her drove her on. Samara rode him harder, needing to feel him climax inside her again.

He started meeting her movements, taking her deeper. Suddenly, he surged up, suckling hard at her breast. Jason pushed down on her hips, embedding himself tightly inside her.

Her senses scattered at the change. "Yes. Oh, yes. Jason, please." It ended on a keening wail. Her body tightened, seeking his heat. Craving it.

His climax set off hers, and Samara pitched backward...into James's chest. She came hard, screaming in release. Still, it wasn't enough.

I can't get enough of them. I can't even define enough.

"That's right." James smoothed his hand down her back to her hip. He nipped at her earlobe. He shifted his hips, letting her feel how hard he was. "Say you want me now."

"Yes." Her body held tight to Jason's cock, but she wanted James's between her thighs, moving, enflaming her lust further. "You, James. Now."

In a whirlwind of motion, he lifted her off Jason's still-hard cock, laid her back on the mattress next to his brother, then thrust deep inside her. Samara screamed, the conflicting sensations making her head spin.

James crooned to her. "We're going to make love to you all night long, Samara. In Jason's bed. In the shower. In the living area. On the furniture, on the rugs, and against the walls." He stroked slowly inside her, setting off aftershocks. "Tomorrow, we're going to share you all day long in your rooms."

"But—"

"Tomorrow is Friday. We will have all weekend to do class work. Well, aside from the football game."

Soccer. James and Jason were at practice this afternoon. Samara nodded. *Tomorrow will be the last full day Marietta will be gone. She's due back an hour before the game.*

James didn't pause. "You're ours, Samara. Can we share you?"

"I always knew you were the one with the wickedly sexy ideas."

He smiled slyly. "So you've said before. Can we share you?"

Another climax rocked her. Catching her breath seemed to take far too long. "Yes. Definitely."

Jason reached between their bodies and stroked at her sensitive clit, making her gasp. "The shower next."

She arched up off the mattress, her senses in overdrive. *Oh, yes.*

Chapter Eight

Two days later

Jason snuggled up behind her and Samara smiled. She still wasn't sure if what she was doing was depraved or not, but it felt right.

All those stories about Dad growing up in a commune rubbed off on me? She supposed it was possible.

Eva breezed into the room without knocking. She started bustling around, then turned toward the bed with a grin.

Samara gaped, waiting for a reaction. Eva crossed her arms under her chest and started tapping one foot on the thick carpet. Before Samara could form words, Eva was issuing orders.

"You two are supposed to be at the field already. Report time was ten, as I recall. Instead, you're here, putting Samara behind schedule. She has to bathe and eat before we take her to the stadium, you realize. Get up. Go on. Move, before the coach benches you for the game." She waved her arms in wide arcs toward the hall door.

Samara's cheeks flamed. "Could you—"

James sighed dramatically. "Very well." He turned and laid a lingering kiss on Samara's lips. "We'll continue later?"

She nodded, breathless, her body throbbing in want of immediate consummation.

Jason appeared over her as James retreated. There was nothing soft and slow about his kiss. It seemed he was intent on defying Eva and seducing Samara right in front of her, just to prove he could.

When he pulled away, she moaned in protest.

"Until then." It sounded like a promise.

"Up." Eva pointed to the door imperiously.

They're naked.

That didn't seem to bother James and Jason. They eased out from beneath the quilt, collected their clothes, then made their way out of the room, delightfully nude and erect. James offered an irreverent little wave for Eva on the way.

Eva turned her head to watch them go, and Samara cringed, anticipating the explosion of anger or disgust that was likely coming.

"Mmm-mmm." Eva purred when the door closed behind them. "Those two have gorgeous asses."

"And cocks. And everything else." It was out before Samara could rein herself in.

Eva started laughing, doubling over, her face going scarlet.

"I don't know what's wrong with me," Samara grumbled.

"Wrong with you?" Eva's eyebrows bunched in a look of confusion. "Don't you enjoy your time with James and Jason?"

Samara's cheeks burned in embarrassment. *That would be the understatement of the century.*

Eva laughed heartily, collapsing at the foot of the bed. "Oh, Samara. You are just a hot-blooded Alpha."

"Not the term my mother would use."

Why should I care what she thinks? I shouldn't. She's a prude. Worse, she's a hypocrite masquerading as a prude. It felt good to acknowledge that.

Eva sighed. "Your mother isn't our kind. No offense, but she can't understand running barefoot in the meadow under the bright lovers' moon."

"She doesn't even like walking barefoot in the park in full daylight." *She* loathes *nature. We couldn't be more different.*

"You see. Our people are free and wild. We are true to ourselves, our innate natures, and to our communities and the natural world we are brothers and sisters to."

"Are we some sort of upscale Romani gypsies? Or maybe Native Americ…well, native tribesmen from wherever?"

Eva smiled. "Close. More than two and a half millennia ago, we started as two separate groups. One was from Eastern Europe—close friends and sometimes kin to the Romani, actually. The other was from mainland Greece."

Samara settled in to hear the rest. This was the most information she'd ever gotten about their people.

"The early ones… They were stupid and shortsighted. Rather than working together, they went to war. It took more than four centuries to resolve their differences. In the end, the leaders of both sides sat down and formed a pact and a line of succession."

"Succession? How does that work?" If she was an Alpha, did that mean she was in the line of succession somewhere?

"Well, the first two fought for the position. We've rarely fought since then, unless someone went rogue or individuals argued the line of succession. The rules put in place made sure it was a one-on-one fight. There would be no more wars over leadership."

As there were rules when I had to fight Christiana to confirm my place as Alpha. She nodded. "Much better than wars."

"It is." Eva paused for a moment. "Since then, the rules handle peaceful succession…usually. If the current leader has a son or sons, the eldest takes leadership. The younger brother takes leadership, if the eldest dies without heirs or without adult heirs."

"Sounds pretty misogynistic to me. What about his daughters? Or if he only *has* daughters?"

"A daughter can only take leadership if her brothers have died or if she has no brothers. She shares the leadership with her mate or mates, as a male would with his mate. However, the ruling family switches to the family of the mates."

"Because...she becomes part of that family when she marries into it." Samara was guessing, but it seemed a logical assumption.

Eva nodded. "It's really quite brilliant. The leader's family changes with some regularity...at least once a century or so. I admit that the original rules called for arranged marriages between the sides to force intermarriage of the Alpha class, to facilitate the two factions passing leadership back and forth. They have so intermarried now, no one has to trace back lineage to make sure it happens. We truly see ourselves as one people now.

"It's still...*traditional* for Alphas to mate with Alphas, but I suppose that makes sense, all things considered. Strong-willed individuals will tend to choose mates who match them in temperament, it seems."

Samara dissected what she'd heard so far, certain she was missing something basic. *She said mate or mates, didn't she?* "And our...people are good with the idea of polyamory or polygamy?"

"To be honest, it has always been encouraged for Alpha females. I'm sure James and Jason would be crushed if you ultimately chose only one of them and rejected the other. Their bond as brothers might not survive the loss."

She realized she was gaping and forced her mouth shut. It took a moment to finagle her way to speech. "Really?"

Eva nodded sagely. "Absolutely."

"Why?"

"Have you seen yourself?" Eva quipped in return.

Samara nudged Eva's arm with her toes. "Not that."

Eva turned to her side, staring up at Samara with a teasing smile. "Then what?"

"Why was a threesome encouraged?"

"Some say it was to strengthen the bloodlines, but that's obviously bullshit. One brother would be as effective as both.

"Others say it was to protect the female better. That one has a ring of truth to it. It also ensured she had a chance to reproduce, in case one of the brothers died."

The thought of one of *her* two brothers dying sent a shaft of fear through Samara. She pushed the thought away and tried to focus elsewhere. Eva continued on before Samara could question why the female couldn't simply marry again.

"I prefer the other reason people speculate on."

"And that is?" Something told her she had to know.

"An Alpha female is so strong and sexual, it takes *two* males to sate her and match her strength."

Samara swallowed hard.

"And I do wish you would get on with it."

"With what?" Her voice sounded strange to her ears, her head spinning as it was. *Everyone* expects *me to be sexual. They expect me to take two men to bed.*

Eva raised an eyebrow and waited for Samara to catch up with the flow of conversation.

"I think it's safe to say we've gotten on with quite a bit." Samara smiled at the memories, then chuckled.

"Yes, but when are you going to get *serious*?"

"Serious like what? Going steady?" Just the thought of James or Jason sexing up another woman made Samara see red. She would kick whichever of them did it so hard in the balls, he would need surgery to right it.

"More serious than that."

"What? Marriage? Now?" *Now I know she's joking. We've known each other all of a week.*

"Ask James and Jason. They'll answer any questions you

ask. For now, I think I heard Marietta moving around in her rooms. She'll be in here to draw your bath any time."

"I guess I don't need a robe."

Eva laughed. "In this group? Hardly. Though James and Jason would be more than a little jealous if you paraded around naked in front of other men."

"Should I be jealous that they did in front of you?"

"Of course not. I have no interest in them. Neither would Marietta. But any male would have an interest in you. Few would be brave enough to chance James's and Jason's reactions to it, but they would have an interest."

Samara pushed to her feet, scowling at the bandage on her arm. "Can't I ditch this yet? The cut is nearly healed."

"When we take the bandage off, the ointment is still yellow-brown."

Samara waved her on, unsure what that meant.

"That means the medicine is still leeching toxins out of the wound. When it comes off the same color it went on, we can stop wrapping it. Doctors' orders."

She sighed. "Doctors' orders." Samara was starting to loathe doctors.

* * * *

Jason had half his attention on the coach and the other half on Samara. She entered the Alpha's box, Marietta on one side and Eva on the other. They settled her in what appeared to be a comfortable, overstuffed chair, and Marietta spread a light quilt over her lap.

"Trudale," the coach snapped.

He winced and focused on him. "Sir?"

"Nice of you to finally join us. Have you got your mind on

the game, or should I bench you now?"

Though it was unlikely to happen—James and Jason were the cornerstones of the playbook—it was tempting to push the old wolf to benching him. Jason would love to be in the Alpha box, tending to Samara. A glare from James set him straight.

"I'm in." *Maybe I can impress Samara with my prowess on the field.*

"Good. If that changes, get your ass off my fucking field."

"Understood." It was. One thing wolves didn't fuck around with was any sort of contest or challenge. *Even an intramural football match.*

Jason threw himself into the game, working as a team with James as they had since they were pups. Within the first ten minutes, they were five points ahead. Wolf sports were fast-moving.

By fifteen minutes in, Jason was so immersed in the game he nearly missed the disaster unfolding around him.

One of the strikers on the opposing team was a first-year wolf, still hot-blooded and easy to anger. The stopper on their team had stymied every move toward the goal, pissing the young player off completely.

So much so that the youngster shifted mid-stride. He got tangled in his uniform, which pushed him further over the edge. In moments, he was snapping and snarling.

Jason shot a horrified look at James, and they turned toward the stands together, just as the ref threw a flag on the play.

Samara was on her feet, trembling hard, wide-eyed and focused on the rampaging wolf. In a heartbeat, that changed. She crumpled, and Eva and Marietta eased her down into the chair.

James pivoted as if he couldn't decide whether to gut the oaf or to go to their mate.

Jason didn't hesitate. He took off at a run, vaulted the fence into the stands, and headed for Samara. Behind him, he heard James following his lead.

Good. I won't have to smack him around for ignoring our mate's need.

He pushed Marietta away, then cupped Samara's pale cheek in one hand. "Samara? Samara, answer me."

She recovered slowly. Marietta produced a cool glass of water and Samara drank some.

"Trudale, in or out?" Brand shouted up to them, probably relaying the question for the coach.

Brand was a mountain of a wolf, and his rumbling voice would have made a lesser wolf cower. Jason and his twin were *not* lesser wolves.

James answered before he could, and in roughly the words Jason would have chosen himself. "Out. Tell coach we are removing ourselves from his fucking field for the day."

"Got it." There was a note of amusement in that.

Jason laid a kiss on Samara's forehead. "Let's get you back to your room."

"We're not..." She motioned vaguely toward mid-field. "We're not going to pretend *that* never happened, are we?"

"No I assure you we are not."

"When we get back to the room, ask your questions." James sighed. "We will answer them if we can."

"Okay."

Jason scooped her up in the quilt and started walking. Usually, James got to Samara first. This time, the honor was his.

* * * *

"He shifted? *On. The. Field!*" Sebastian rubbed at the tense muscles in his neck, which heralded a vicious headache gaining steam.

"He's a late bloomer." Pietro tried desperately to explain the latest fiasco. "Thomas didn't shift for the first time until two years ago. He lacks the control most first-year students possess. He hasn't had time to develop it."

Sebastian buried his head in his hands.

"This...*could* be a good thing," Pietro offered carefully.

Sebastian stared at his oldest friend in disbelief. "Good? What is wrong with you? How could this possibly be good?"

Pietro crossed the room and squatted next to him. "We never decided how to introduce Samara to her true heritage. We've coasted along, chancing her conceiving to James and Jason or coming to her senses with a mouthful of their blood before she finds out who and what she is. This may not be the way we would have preferred to broach the subject, but it's done now. Now she knows. We move forward."

"Or she runs screaming in the other direction." *I'm stating the obvious, but it needs to be said.*

"To where? Our information says she's estranged from her mother."

"Samara maintains a relationship with her stepfather. She speaks to him on the phone, sends him letters, and receives them in return. You know as well as I do that Samara lived her last year of high school with the man, after she left Florence's home."

Pietro nodded. "Even if Samara returns to him, she cannot discuss this with him. Eventually, the need for information will bring her home to us."

"Maybe." *Probably. Damn Pietro for always being right.*

"Of course, you could be the father she runs to."

It was tempting, but... "No. That goes according to plan." *Does anything?* The odds seemed to be against it, at this point.

* * * *

Samara was no more certain what to ask them when Jason tucked her into bed than she'd been at the stadium. Or on the trip back to the dorm, for that matter. Her mind had been in a flat spin since the moment she'd seen a player turn into a wolf on the field.

James and Jason stood at the foot of the bed, waiting patiently for her to find her voice. At a loss for something better to do or say, she motioned for a moment of peace.

"When you're ready," Jason replied.

"Take your time." James's answer overlapped with Jason's.

What should I ask? Hundreds of questions circled in her mind.

Keep it simple. Ask the most basic questions and let the answers to those lead you into more complex subjects. "I saw him turn into a wolf," she blurted out. *Okay. Not a question.*

James nodded. "Yes. You did."

Samara stamped down the urge to laugh. She realized she'd secretly hoped they would say she hadn't seen anything of the sort, that she'd been hallucinating.

Ask a question. "And precisely *how* did he do that?"

James and Jason shot each other a look she couldn't interpret.

"If you lie to me—"

"Never," Jason promised.

James scrubbed a hand across his mouth. "That's what our kind are, Samara. Wolves."

Words stuck in her suddenly-dry throat. "*Our* kind?" He might mean himself and Jason. *And that other student.*

As if! No one else in the stadium seemed shocked.

Jason shifted closer to her, but he didn't reach for her. "Our kind, Samara. The two of us. You. Eva. Everyone at this university. And more, of course."

She tried to ignore the part about her being a wolf. "Werewolves are real?"

James snorted, his lip curled up in disgust.

"We aren't called werewolves," Jason instructed her. "Most of the fiction you read about our kind is bullshit. But wolves... Wolves that can shift forms and live among humans do exist."

"And you're...?" *They don't look like wolves. Then again, neither did the other one, until he changed.*

The brothers shared another potent look. They started stripping off their clothes.

Her arousal peaked.

Stop it. This isn't about sex.

"What are you doing?" *Focus on talking. Focus on anything else.*

James shrugged. "I don't intend to get tangled in my clothes like Thomas did."

"Oh." She watched them strip, numb, her mouth going dry.

In a flash, the pair were replaced with two dark wolves. They raced around the room, playing a game of what looked like tag. At last they bounded up on the bed and dropped down on either side of her.

They want me to be sure they're real. Samara reached out with a shaking hand and buried it in the wealth of fur to her left.

"James." How she knew which twin was which in wolf form was beyond her, but there was no doubt in her mind about it.

As if in confirmation, he reached up and licked her cheek.

Samara smiled, then turned to scratch Jason under the chin. He stared at her with soulful eyes, and she knew what he wanted.

"Jason."

He yipped happily.

"Okay... You're wolves."

They changed back, stretched out on either side of her, much as they had been for the last week.

Samara felt compelled to add the inescapable truth. "You're wolves, but I'm not."

"Of course you are." Jason stated it with certainty. "Everything about you screams it, from your temperament and your affinity with animals to your scent."

James took over before she could protest. "Your mother was human, but she carried a wolf's child, and you *are* a wolf."

"Do you know who my father is?"

"Yes, but he wants you to decide when to meet him. Be sure before you ask to."

His tone raised the hair at the back of her neck. Was he insinuating she wouldn't want to meet her father for some reason? If so, why?

A question for another time. "But I'm not a wolf. I can't..." — she circled her hand, searching for the term — "shift." *That was the word they used, wasn't it?*

Jason chuckled.

James smiled. "Females don't. Well, not fully, as the males do. Perhaps it's because shifting would be bad while carrying young. I'm not really sure why males shift fully and females don't."

"I don't at all." The sense of loss was heart-wrenching. *Why? What have I lost?* It wasn't like Samara had hoped and dreamed to be a wolf. She'd learned what she was only a few minutes ago.

Jason groaned, his cock going hard and twitching in excitement.

James trailed a fingertip down Samara's neck, making her shiver in delight. "Oh, you do. It's sexy as hell when you do."

"Except when Christiana stabbed you with the Hunter's Fang." Jason growled. "It scared the hell out of me when I saw you shifting."

"How can I shift and not feel it?" Samara demanded. She tried to push away a dozen new questions that popped into her mind.

"You're usually otherwise occupied." Jason trailed his fingertips up her thigh.

She gasped at the implication. "Show me."

James smiled, showing the tips of his fangs. "It would be our pleasure."

* * * *

"What are you doing?" Samara could have smacked herself for asking such a stupid question. *Obviously Jason is filling the tub.*

James stepped up behind her, his breath heating the back of her head. "See the mirror?"

She looked at it, her breathing going shallow. She'd seen the mirror, of course. Who could miss it? It reached thigh to ceiling and half the length of the wall across from the tub. *The same half the tub itself dominates.* The reason for the positioning was impossible to miss.

"You're going to get me sexually excited and then—"

"Let you see your wolf come out." He finished the thought for her.

James pulled her flush to his body so Samara could feel the length of his cock pressing to her lower back. "Of course, if you want to use it to watch us have sex later…"

Samara swallowed hard, the mental image making her dizzy in need.

"Thought so."

Jason turned off the water, then returned to them. The brothers bracketed her with their larger bodies. There was no rush. They trailed their hands down her body, unbuttoning clothing, pushing it away, caressing her skin beneath as each piece of clothing fell to the floor.

Each of them closed his hands around her waist. They lifted her together and set her in the tub, then they joined her, standing knee-deep in the water. Jason helped her to sit on the far side of the tub, and James spread her legs wide.

"Look at the mirror." Jason tilted his head in that direction.

Samara had barely had time to comply when Jason buried his face between her thighs and started feasting on her. James paid attention to her breasts instead.

It didn't take long for them to push her toward climax. That had been true since the first time James had suggested they share her. Samara had believed there were limits to sexual exploits, that a woman would suffer from rubbing or bruising or Honeymooner's Distress.

Maybe wolves don't have those problems. They say I'm a wolf.

As if in answer, Samara saw the change happening. Her eyes went from brown to golden, her irises spreading until they covered most of the visible whites of her eyes. Her vision sharpened. The tufted tips of pointed, furry ears rose at the sides of her head, one catching on a lock of hair.

Her teeth felt...wrong. Samara ran her tongue along them, groaning at the sharpened tips.

It took her a moment to realize they'd both stopped trying to arouse her.

"So beautiful," Jason murmured.

Samara looked at her hands. Dark gray claws stood out in the place of her fingernails, and brown fur surrounded the bases of them.

She wasn't sure she agreed with the assessment of "beautiful". It was…different, but she wasn't sure she would call it beautiful.

James plucked the hair off of her ear and let it fall. "You're always beautiful. Sexy. Fierce. Gorgeous."

Her tongue caught on the tip of a fang. Hot, salty blood made her mouth water, and she swallowed. Her senses rioted.

I've wanted to bite nearly every time we've had sex. "Wolves mate for life." *Eva said Alpha females usually had two males, but were they both mates? Or was one a mate and the other a concubine or something similar?*

They stared at her for a long moment.

James found his voice first. "Is that what you want, Samara? Do you want to become our mate?"

They would both be my mates.

Jason took over. "If you do—"

"Is that why I want to bite you?" Her cheeks flamed at the admission.

The male musk mixed into the steam increased, and her body responded to it, sex fluids running lazily down her perineum.

"Trust me, we want to as well." Jason's upper lip undulated, as his fangs descended.

Her heart skipped in excitement. She sobered just as quickly.

"What is it?"

Jason. Always the more sensitive of the two. Spitting it out was hard. Would they still want her when they knew?

"Samara?"

James. The leader. He takes control when something is wrong. Usually. Jason did at the stadium.

She forced her mind back to the present. "What if I can't…?"

He nodded, urging her on.

Be clinical. Maybe it will hurt less. "Reproduce."

The brothers shot each other a sidelong look. Jason broached the subject first.

"Because you're half-human?"

"Because I don't cycle like—"

"Like a human does." James nodded his agreement. "We know."

Jason smiled widely. "You're all wolf, in that respect."

"I...I am?"

James raked a look down her body that said he wanted to lick her from head to toe. "You thought you couldn't." He stated it as a fact.

He's not wrong. "The doctors—*human* doctors said it was highly unlikely. Not without major medical intervention, most likely." *In my defense, I thought I was human.*

He didn't let it drop. "And if the odds had worked out that way? If you *would* have gotten pregnant?"

"Well..." Samara cleared her throat. Why had she dismissed the possibility so quickly and completely? "The timing wouldn't have been ideal, but I would have figured it out."

Jason trailed his fingers between her thighs, playing the tips inside her. "You mean *we* would have. Together."

"You're not saying you want to. A-are you?" She held her breath, waiting for a reply. It wasn't smart to hope for a positive response.

The fact that they never asked if I was on any sort of birth control and never used condoms says something. Doesn't it?

Jason stroked his fingers deeper inside her, and she let out her breath in a rush.

"Give us a chance. You have no idea the devotion of a wolf male to his mate and his offspring."

James trailed a hand up the opposite thigh and joined Jason in finger fucking her. "Let us." He said it softly, an invitation.

"What are you offering?"

Jason leaned down and pressed a kiss to her mound, heating her blood. "Everything you're willing to give us. Just ask, and we are yours."

"What do I have to do?"

James flicked his tongue around one turgid nipple. "Do what your instincts have been telling you to do…if you want to."

Sink the fangs I grow into them. "Then I want you inside me. If my instincts are calling me to bite, I want to bite and allow you to bite."

James growled low in his throat. "We mate for life. You with the two of us."

Thank goodness. Her heart hammered in her chest. "Now."

"The bed. This is best done in a bed." Jason swept her up in his arms and started walking.

Samara pulled him down into a kiss, her body in the same fever it had been for the last two days.

In moments, the three of them were kneeling on the bed together, trading kisses, hands stroking bodies. Samara encircled one cock in her hand, bringing it up. It didn't matter which one it was; she needed one inside her.

Now. Now. "Now."

James settled her astride his lap and thrust inside her. Samara levered herself up and down his shaft and he met her. It was animalistic, nearly violent, but it was exactly what she needed.

The fangs sprouted. Her mouth watered, and the salty scent of blood enticed her.

"That's right." Jason urged her on.

He ran a fingertip over her lips, then stroked one fang. With a yank, he sliced his fingertip open and pulled it away, letting a drop of blood land on her tongue.

Her senses went wild.

"Taste." Jason sealed his lips over hers and parted them.

The blood on his lips ramped up the thirst for more. Samara kissed him, sucked at his lips and tongue, wrapped her oddly-shaped hands around his head.

Jason pulled away. "Finish with James. Now. I can't wait much longer for you."

Samara focused on James's neck, the pulse of blood under his skin visible to her sharpened vision. The temptation was too much and she bit down. Her jaw felt unnaturally large, but she ignored that and riveted her attention on the hot flow of James's essence coursing down her throat.

Climax exploded, sending warmth and pleasure from the center of her body out. She arched back, releasing him, rivulets of blood dripping down her chest as she gasped for air.

James guided her face back to his shoulder and sank his fangs into her neck in return. She screamed, half in pleasure and half in pain, raking her claws down his back, while his cum filled her with heat. Her climax waned, and her resistance with it. Samara sank into his arms, moaning as he licked at the bite.

"My turn." Jason's voice was all it took to bring her body to life again.

They switched her from lap to lap, and James's subsiding cock was replaced with Jason's rock-hard length. Her fangs itched to bite immediately. As if he could read the need in her body language, Jason drew her mouth to his neck, baring the unmarked side of her own for him.

She didn't question his intent. The lure was maddening. Samara bit down, savoring his flavor, not as wild as James's but rich and creamy as the finest carob replacements she was gifted after Christiana stabbed her.

Climax raced through her again, and she gasped in surprise. Jason bit down, groaning as he emptied into her in a series of spurts that massaged her inner muscles.

Consciousness was abruptly a rare commodity. Mouths meshed and parted in steamy kisses. One of the brothers covered her body with his own, thrusting hard inside her. Samara pulled at the tight muscles of his ass, dragging him deeper inside.

A slightly-roughened tongue bathed her chest and throat.

Cleaning off the blood that was spilled during the mating bites. She sought out the same on the chest before her and moaned at the flavor. *Jason.* Her inner muscles fluttered at the knowledge of which brother was inside her. Until that moment, she hadn't realized how exciting it was not to know.

They came hard and fast, and Jason moved aside. James didn't take his place. Instead, he spread her thighs and laid a long lick up her sex, bringing Samara up in an arch.

One fang nipping at her nether lips dragged a scream of pleasure from her. James suckled and licked, his breathing going ragged.

Cum splashed against her core, then his cock was inside, delivering the rest of the load.

"Give me room," Jason demanded.

Samara wrapped her legs around James's hips. Both brothers stopped and stared at her.

"Both of you. Now."

Dual growls of pleasure answered her.

Chapter Nine

Two days later

Samara descended the stairs between her two mates. A shiver of delight worked up her spine at the truth. After they graduated, she would be sharing a home with them. In the meantime, they were already working on the first of their babies.

Pups, though they are born babies and not as pups.

Moreover, none of them were capable of cheating on the others. *I know more than a few human women who wouldn't mind this life.*

If she lived to be a hundred and five, Samara was sure she would never understand how her mother could turn down a devoted wolf mate.

I've said it before and I will say it again. We are polar opposites.

"What is going on in your mind?" Jason teased.

"This is a big day." It was, and not just because it was the first day she'd been allowed to leave her bed.

"You don't need to worry about our parents." James repeated it, the third time he'd done so since they announced the couple were coming to meet her the night before. "They are going to adore you."

"Yes, but they are going to ask the sixty-four thousand dollar question. Aren't they?"

"The what?" Their voices overlapped.

She sighed and raked a hand through her hair. "The sixty-four thousand dollar question is the jackpot question in a quiz show. It's the tough one, the one that always trips people up."

They stared at her in seeming confusion.

Jason's face brightened in understanding. "You mean the

question of who your father is."

"Bingo."

That reference didn't throw them.

James stopped and took her hands. "Would it put you more at ease to meet your father before meeting our parents?"

Samara staged an inner debate on that. "It wouldn't be right to call off your parents now. They've been waiting more than a day for this."

"You won't have to. I'm sure you could meet your father today, before we meet our parents for dinner. If you want to."

The niggling of unease returned. "You've said that before. Is there some reason I shouldn't want to meet him?"

"No! Of course not."

Jason wrapped an arm around her waist, then planted a kiss on top of her head. "If your heart has room for him, he is there for you. His greatest fear is that your love for the father who raised you will preclude you loving the father who gave you life."

James raised one of her hands and kissed the knuckles. "The question is…are you ready to hear him out calmly and attempt to accept him into your life?"

"What would I have to hear him out about? My mother already admitted she cheated on my dad with him."

James looked over her shoulder, probably at Jason. He shrugged, then released her hand. "Okay. Let's go in to breakfast."

While they walked, James pulled out a cell phone. He texted someone. The answer came a few moments later. He read it, sent another text, then put it back in his pocket. "We're meeting him for lunch."

Samara's stomach squirmed in apprehension. *Maybe he should have waited until after I ate to tell me that.*

Jason sighed. "Yogurt and a muffin?"

She laughed heartily. "How did you know?"

Each brother wrapped an arm around her waist.

"We know you so well." James teased.

"In other words, Jason notices everything, and you make sure I'm never left wanting."

Jason barked in laughter. "It is an equitable division of labor."

"I suppose it is."

Halfway to the table, Samara startled at the sound of a high-pitched squeal.

Eva sprinted for them, enfolding Samara in a hug and dragging her away from her mates. She tugged at both sides of Samara's collar, uncovering the mostly-healed mating marks on her neck. "You did it. You *finally* did it."

"Finally, she says. We've only known each other for a little over a week, Eva."

She turned on her heel with a flip of her hair. "I'll show you how it's done."

"How...? What?"

Eva didn't answer. She marched across the room to a group of male students, then tapped one on the arm. "Excuse me." The sing-song voice and the bounce in her step made Eva appear even younger than usual.

He turned toward her, and Eva went up on her toes, grasped his head in both hands, and laid a full-out carnal kiss on him. He pulled her toward him with a growl.

At last, he straightened and left the kiss. Eva let her hands slide to his shoulders.

"Are you inviting my attentions, little wolf?" The question sounded like a challenge.

Samara bristled. "He doesn't even know her name."

Jason gathered her to his chest, stopping her march over there to leave scars. "I assure you, he does."

Eva trailed a fingertip down along one broad shoulder. "Mmmm. Yes, I am."

The male's teeth and eyes shifted. "I warn you, I am fond of the ancient rites."

Eva nodded, but Samara noticed her knees shook just a bit.

Don't rush in. Think. "What does that mean?" she demanded of her mates.

James whispered the answer to her. "It means he is intent on making Eva his mate. Brand is going to take her to a bed and seduce her until she agrees to let him lay his mark. Dissuading him, now that she has invited him, will be very difficult."

Samara swallowed the lump growing in her throat. Eva wasn't a high Alpha. Could she fight off a male as large as Brand, if it came to that?

"Eva will be fine," Jason promised.

She looked up in time to see the male lifting Eva off her feet in a show of strength.

"Brand!" There was a cut of order in James's voice.

He looked their way, as did Eva. She went wide-eyed, pleading for something Samara couldn't name.

"Take care with our little sister, Brand."

Jason tensed a notch. "Our mate would be very displeased if her den sister were injured, and what upsets our mate upsets us."

Eva blushed, but she smiled widely.

Brand tipped his head their way. "Rest assured, Alpha Samara. There is no wolf Eva is safer with than me."

"Thank you," she replied.

Brand didn't wait for more discussion. He carried Eva from the dining hall and turned toward the far staircase.

114

His rooms. He's taking her there instead of to our shared floor.

James and Jason will kill him if he hurts her. That simply, her stomach settled.

* * * *

Samara had seen the residence at the edge of campus before, but she'd assumed it was Pietro Galvani's home. Since they'd passed by the Alpha Maestro in the commons, it was a fair bet they weren't going to meet him.

James rang the bell and a silver-haired man answered it.

"Lord James. Lord Jason." He tipped his head. "You are expected, and—" He looked in Samara's direction, and his olive skin went a waxy, gray-beige. "I did not know..." He straightened and backed away quickly. "My apologies for keeping you waiting. Please, come inside."

"Thank you, Roberto," James replied, ignoring the servant's fumbling and shock.

Her mates guided Samara inside.

With another unreadable look at Samara, Roberto turned away.

"Am I not welcome here?" Her stomach churned and tears stung at her eyes.

Roberto whirled around, seemingly horrified. "Anytime you wish, Alpha Samara. I am honored to serve you. I simply did not realize you would be accompanying your mates today. I would have liked to have been able to prepare for your arrival. I fear you will find my attention to detail lax."

His response stunned her. "I'm sure I won't, Roberto."

The servant smiled widely at her trust in him. He led them up one level, then down a long hallway. At the last door on the left, he waved them inside.

"Can I provide you with any refreshments while the meal is prepared for you?"

"No, thank you," Samara replied. Her stomach was still complaining, and she wasn't sure how she was going to eat lunch, let alone anything else.

"A coffee tray," James requested.

Roberto smiled widely and tipped his head. He was gone in the blink of an eye.

As if she'd questioned them, Jason offered an explanation. "Roberto has dreamed of the day you would come here. If there was nothing he could do for you, he would be disappointed."

"I see." She didn't understand it fully, but it was a small thing to ask to make an old man happy.

He was back in what seemed like moments, while Samara was still wandering around the library, admiring the leather-bound books, the paintings, and statuary. Roberto appeared at her side a moment later, offering a small cup of the coffee. Samara stared at him for a moment, confused.

He lost his composure a bit, and his face darkened. "Kona with two creams, no sugar? This is your preferred, is it not?"

"Yes. Thank you." Samara took it from his hands, trying to make sense of it. "Marietta told you?"

He smiled. "She...confirmed it, but we knew long before that."

"How?" Her senses went on high alert at that. Was someone spying on her?

James stepped in. "Your father will explain."

Samara nodded her agreement. It wasn't fair to put pressure on a servant, since they were bound to the orders they were given. She'd decided that about Marietta when she learned the servant couldn't tell her who her father was.

Roberto hovered. It took a few heartbeats for Samara to put

together the reason for his hesitation. She sipped the coffee, then smiled.

"Perfect. Thank you, Roberto."

He tipped his head and hurried away.

I think I just made his day.

Jason watched him go. "That was nicely handled."

"I'm learning," she admitted.

Still, her father's lack of an appearance bothered her. Didn't he want to meet her?

* * * *

"She is enjoying coffee with her mates in the library, Sebastian."

He couldn't help it. Sebastian winced. He'd thought he was ready to face his failures, but apparently he was being outted as a coward.

"Is there a problem?" Roberto pressed him.

"I'm...nervous." Admitting that galled him. He was Alpha, and Alphas rarely showed such weakness.

"So is she. This is not a situation a wolf often finds himself in."

Sebastian snorted, baring his teeth in frustration. "One should hope not."

Roberto placed a hand on his shoulder, something he rarely did. "I was there for you then. I am here for you now. You did all you could. Your daughter will understand that."

"I did too much. I only *hope* she will understand."

Roberto straightened, glaring at him. It was all Sebastian could do not to squirm in place.

It's because he was my bodyguard when I was a child. Early lessons die hard.

Sebastian scowled at him, and Roberto smiled, showing fangs.

"You're good, old man. I'll give you that. But don't push me too far."

"Never, sir. I wouldn't dream of it."

Right. Sebastian smoothed his shirt, then took a calming breath. "It's time." *Far past time.*

Roberto didn't presume to follow him. On some level, that was better. If he made a fool of himself, it was probably better for his servant not to witness it.

He's witnessed more than a few of my mistakes.

Sebastian made his way down the corridor and slipped into the library. His breath caught in his lungs at the sight of her. *My daughter. In my home. At last.*

She didn't notice his entrance. Samara was busy examining the portrait on the far wall.

"That was your grandmother. My mother. You look quite a bit like her."

Samara whirled around. For a moment, she performed a slow visual assessment of him. Then her shoulders eased. "Was. I guess that means she's…passed away. I would have liked to have met her."

"She would have loved to have met you, too." It wasn't a stretch of the truth. His mother would have doted on Samara.

"Why didn't she?" It was a blunt question.

Oh, but you are a perceptive one. "If I had told my parents about you, they would never have let me live to the agreement I made with your mother."

Her color drained away. "I see."

You don't. You really *don't.* "Please, allow me to explain."

For a moment, he was sure she was going to refuse, storm out, walk away from him right there.

At last, Samara nodded. "I promised to hear you out calmly. I can't guarantee the *calm* part, but I'll hear you out."

More than I'd hoped for. Sebastian proffered his hand. "Over lunch. Roberto will be setting it out now."

Samara hesitated and her mates came to her side. They led her toward the door.

Sebastian stared at his hand for a moment, his heart aching. *Give her time. She doesn't even know the truth yet.*

That could be good or bad for me.

* * * *

Samara settled into the chair Roberto offered at the foot of the table. She considered pushing the plate away. It was filled with her favorites, but she wasn't sure she could stomach it.

Her father sat at the opposite end. He waved off the plate Roberto offered.

Is he as nervous as I am? Maybe so, but what did it matter?

Roberto took his leave and disappeared into the kitchen. Silence fell around the table.

"I suppose you should know who I am, to start with."

"That makes sense," Samara conceded.

"My name is Sebastian Travalian."

It had a nice ring to it. *I won't be using it. I'm a Trudale now.*

"I met your mother when I was visiting America. Our kind maintains a close kinship with many human groups, including several Native American nations. I was there to revisit and revitalize our pacts with them.

"I knew Florence was my mate. There was really no question that she was. I also knew she reeked of another male...a male I soon learned was her husband."

Samara's temper simmered, and she did her best to hold it

in check. "You knew she was married and decided to break up her marriage?"

His jaw tightened. "I don't mean to speak ill of your mother, but—"

"Oh, don't stand on ceremony. I know what she's like."

That drew a wry smile from him. "Yes. So do I." A look of misery replaced it. "Your mother was more than willing to carry on an affair with me. She's quite convincing, and I truly believed she intended to allow me to mark her as my mate."

"You *knew* my mother was married and *intended* to break up her marriage?" Samara was quickly losing her patience.

"Yes, damn it, I did." Sebastian motioned for a moment of peace. He took several deep breaths. "I was young, newly advanced to my position. I believed she would choose me over a...mere human. Yes, I admit I was more than a little bigoted back then. And...I was afraid of losing her and never being able to mate." He motioned again, before she could protest. "I've since learned the very hard truth that no mate is better than one you cannot trust."

Samara considered that. Jason covered her hand with his, and she grasped it, needing their connection. James did the same on the other side.

She couldn't imagine life alone after being part of their mating. "I see."

"When she caught pregnant with you, I pushed the issue. It was time to end the dalliance we were carrying on and for her to commit to what we...were to each other."

"And she refused you." Samara didn't question it.

He swallowed what looked—from his expression—like a sour wave of disgust. "In a word...yes. I wasn't content with her decision, of course, but Florence threatened to expose what she knew of our kind.

"Sure, most people would think she was a crackpot, but there are societies of people, enemies of our kind. They are always listening for news of us, for disgruntled humans who will point the way. Mind you, it wasn't just a duty to our people that convinced me to back down. If Florence shared the wrong stories about me... They would kill you, Samara. And I wouldn't be with you to protect you."

James squeezed her hand, then loosened his grip. "Leaving her unprotected had to be a torture."

Sebastian laughed harshly. "That was one thing I refused to do."

"I don't understand," Samara admitted.

He sighed. "I made a deal with your mother — a deal that ensured your protection. I would walk away and let her and her...husband raise my child."

"He's a good man," Samara argued. "I know you have your reasons for disliking the situation she created, but if it had to happen that way... I couldn't have had a better father raise me."

Sebastian waved her down. "I know. Had he ever been a danger to you... Had he not been the perfect father, I would have killed him myself, agreements be damned."

She shivered at the threat, but his admission put a temporary damper on her fury. "So, what *was* this deal?"

"They would raise you, happily. I warned her up front that I wouldn't stand for any abuse or neglect of you.

"She would provide me with updates and pictures of you, as you grew. Florence tried to claim she 'forgot' some of the time, but my men filled in the blanks and — "

"Men?" Samara questioned. "*What* men? What were they supposed to do?"

His face darkened and Sebastian cleared his throat. "I told her a few of my trusted men would stay close, making sure you were safe. Thankfully, they rarely had to intervene in your life, fleeting moments where they...dissuaded someone in the shadows. They also helped train you."

"Pardon me?" What was he saying?

"Do you recall two males from your self-defense classes, named Trent and Dale?"

She nodded. "Two older guys. They were in their late twenties when I was a pre-teen." They were also often paired with her in sparring practice. *I learned a lot from them.*

"I'm sure they would like to see you again."

"I guess I should thank them."

Sebastian tipped his head. "Not necessary, but they would certainly be touched if you did."

"Were there any other parts to this agreement?"

"Three more. The first was that she wouldn't tell anyone about your wolf heritage or about meeting a wolf." He paused for a moment. "The second was that I wouldn't try to reveal myself directly to you or contact you, unless you sought me out."

"But...coming here. Pietro Galvani approaching me—"

"I only promised *I* wouldn't contact you. That didn't mean I could allow you to remain dangerously ignorant of your inner wolf."

Samara couldn't argue that. "What was the last part of the agreement?"

"Your name. If she balked me on that one thing, all bets were off. You were born a wolf, Samara, and I was determined you would have a name from my family. It was the least she owed me, if she wasn't going to give you my last name."

"Who am I named for?"

"My mother."

"The one in the portrait?"

He smiled. "Yes. I'm glad you favor her; it makes your name

all the more fitting."

"Where do we go from here?"

Sebastian leaned across the table. "Where do you want to? We could get to know each other, at your comfort level. You're all welcome to stay here with me...Eva and her mate as well. Or you could stay in the dormitory. I would like to get to know you, Samara. The choice of how is your own."

"I need time to think."

"Of course."

* * * *

Samara twirled in front of the mirror, trying to check from every angle the red dress James had bought her. She still wasn't sure she should wear it tonight.

As if she'd spoken the thought aloud, the brothers appeared in the bathroom doorway, dressed in matching tailored suits. Their heated gazes gave assurances she hadn't asked for.

"Yes, I'm obsessing," she admitted.

"You don't need to," Jason said.

For the fifth time today. "Now that I have a name for my father, I guess not," Samara quipped in return.

"Not before that," James corrected her. "But certainly not now."

"Should I feel judged by his name?" *I'm being peevish, but it feels that way.*

"No one would *dare*," Jason cut in again. "You're not the kind of person who would name drop just to get special treatment—"

"Like Christiana would," she guessed.

"Precisely. But if you were to name drop your father, you would find wolves falling all over themselves to ingratiate themselves to you."

James nodded in agreement. "A fair number of humans as well. Your father isn't a poor man, and he's well known in industrial circles."

Jason motioned to the room around them. "Everything in these rooms was provided by Sebastian."

"I see." She hadn't known that. A sneaking suspicion that he had also provided the scholarship plagued her. *I won't ask. Not yet. If I found out — right now — that he has, I might walk away. I have to get to know him and find out why he does things.*

Samara made her way back through the bedroom and into the sitting room, lost in thought, her mates trailing in her wake. She glanced at the clock, noting that their parents were expected soon.

Before she could settle on the couch, there was a knock at the door.

Early. "Yes?"

"Your guests, Alpha Samara," one of the household servants replied.

"Send them in."

James and Jason stood just behind her and to the sides. It was comforting to feel their heat, to know they were watching her back.

The door opened and the couple stepped inside. The brothers got their height from their father, but their dark hair and eyes came from their mother.

Their father tipped his head, but their mother crossed the room and took Samara's hands in her own. She leaned across and kissed Samara on one cheek, then the other.

"My dear, you are so welcome." Her voice was smooth and lightly accented.

Spanish, Samara was sure.

"Thank you."

James spoke up. "Samara, this is my mother, Aurora, and my father, Jacob Trudale."

Jacob moved to Aurora's back, offering another tip of his head at the introduction.

"It's nice to meet you." How Samara managed spit out words, stunned as she was by their mother's beauty, was an uncertain thing.

Up close, she was still having trouble noting signs of age. If she hadn't known the woman had adult sons, she would have guessed Aurora was in her early thirties.

Aurora smoothed a hand over the bandage on Samara's arm. A long spate of Spanish followed.

Jason sighed. "Samara will be fine, Mother. Every day, the wound gets better. The doctors say it will only be another day or two of wrapping. No, she doesn't need to see our family doctors, and yes, we are watching closely. Please, for the love of the Night Mother, speak English for Samara."

Deep points of color rose in Aurora's cheeks. "My apologies, Alpha Samara. I was not aware you did not speak my language."

"I'm working on it," Samara admitted. "I have required language lessons, and I'm taking Spanish right now. I'm afraid I took French in high school, and I never cared for it much."

Aurora and her mate shot each other the sort of questioning look Samara was starting to loathe.

I said the wrong thing again.

Jacob broached the subject first. "You weren't required to learn multiple languages in your youth? You didn't travel extensively to learn them as you did?"

"No. I lived in the same city my whole life." *The same house, until I was seventeen. Thus starts the inquisition.*

"Who are your parents?" Aurora asked, seemingly confused by the conversation.

James leaned forward to faux whisper to her. "Time to name drop."

"Are you sure?"

"Certain." Jason nodded emphatically.

Samara prepared for whatever fallout there might be. "My father is Sebastian Travalian."

They stared at her, unmoving.

Not reacting. This is bad. "My mother is…was supposed to be his mate, but she—"

Aurora enveloped her in a hug. "No wonder you were strong enough to survive the Hunter's Fang! Oh, my poor dear."

"That was because of James and Jason." Didn't they know their sons had saved her life?

Jacob placed a hand on the side of her head. "You will never be endangered with us, Samara. Never again. You have my vow. I will step up your security immediately."

"I don't understand," she admitted.

James groaned. "I *knew* there was something missing in Sebastian's meeting."

Aurora released her.

"What are you talking about?" she demanded.

Jason guided Samara to the couch. "Sit down. This may be a bit of a shock to you."

She sank to the cushioned surface, ill at ease. What hadn't she been told? What other secrets were there?

James squatted to one side of her and Jason to the other. The elder twin seemed to struggle with where to start.

"I'll explain." Jason took the lead in an atypical move.

"Thank you." James sounded relieved, which intensified her unease.

Jason looked up at his parents. "Samara was raised by her mother all these years. She only met Sebastian today."

Aurora went a vivid shade of burgundy, and Jacob put his hand on her shoulder, probably in soothing.

"You've seen how wolves call you Alpha."

Samara nodded. "Of course. We're all alpha level."

"No, Samara. You aren't *an* alpha. You are *the* Alpha, the only child of the current reigning Alpha."

Her head spun at the truth of it, and Eva's lessons on line of succession raced through her memories. That meant she — along with James and Jason — would rule after Sebastian. The Trudale family had just become royalty.

James cleared his throat. "For all intents and purposes, you are a princess, the heiress apparent to the throne of our people."

A wild laugh bubbled up, and Samara swallowed it with no small amount of effort. "Heiress apparent and I don't even speak Spanish." *Or Greek. Or Italian.* "How many languages do our people speak?"

Aurora straightened. "Never fear. We will teach you all you need to know. If you wish it." There was a hopeful note in that.

"I do."

Chapter Ten

Three months later

"The car is coming in, Samara," Marietta reported.

She smiled, then started pacing. At the far turn, she collided with James's chest. Jason stepped in behind her and rubbed her lower back, easing muscles under far too much stress. She moaned in response.

"Have you decided how to tell him yet?" James teased.

"Oh, stop," she pleaded.

Jason laughed long and hard. "You really *are* more afraid to tell your human father you're a wolf than you are to tell him you're married to two men or that you're pregnant, aren't you?"

"He grew up in a commune with his mother, for pity's sake! He's one-quarter Cree, and the Nations tend to be progressive about alternative lifestyles. Pregnancy and sexual...tastes aren't likely to throw him."

"This way, Mr. Tyler," Marietta intoned.

Samara sighed and turned toward the door, just in time for her father to turn the corner. His smile went brittle and he stared at her well-rounded midsection.

"Dad?" She prompted him, hoping for a positive response.

"Was *this* why you said you couldn't come home this year?" His voice held a note of awe.

"My doctors aren't happy with the idea of me traveling by air, and I'm not sure a ship would be much better. If we ran into rough seas..." She shrugged, though the thought of sea sickness made her more than a little queasy.

He walked across the room to her, then reached out to touch her distended abdomen. He hesitated and met her gaze, probably seeking permission.

"Go ahead."

He stroked from side to side. "After all those doctors saying you couldn't... I'm so happy for you. But, you're so big."

"Twins will do that." James offered his hand. "James Trudale."

Liam shook it.

Jason extended his as well. "Jason Trudale."

He was slower about shaking that time. Liam looked from the rings on Samara's hand to the matching rings on both of her mates'. "Would it be rude to ask what the situation is?"

"Of course not." Samara hastened to assure him. "Yes, I'm married to both James and Jason."

"Brothers?"

"Twins." Jason tipped his head to punctuate it.

"Aha. So her carrying twins is—"

"Possibly our doing," James finished for him. "There hasn't been a set of twins in Samara's line for at least four generations."

Samara reached back to rub at a sore spot, and both her mates moved at once, leading her to a gliding rocker. Once they had her settled, she searched out Liam.

He'd seated himself on the couch, and was watching them, a speculative look on his face. "This makes you happy?"

"Completely." Every day was a new delight with her mates in her life, and Marietta's descriptions of Alpha wolf life with babies was more than she'd hoped for.

He smiled. One eyebrow went up. "Which one is responsible for..." Liam motioned up and down her body.

"Both of them."

"Both of us." Their voices overlapped with hers.

That seemed to satisfy him. "This is quite the house." He moved smoothly to another topic.

"Sebastian's house." But he knew that. She'd told him as much as she dared in letters and phone calls. He knew she'd met her biological father. He knew that she was temporarily staying with him, while they got to know each other. Most importantly, he knew she still considered Liam her father. *One of my fathers.*

Marietta wheeled in a cart loaded with food and drinks. "Roberto will be in with coffee and tea in a moment," she told them. "In the meantime, can I get anyone food or juices?" Her focus on Samara let her know the intent was to feed her.

Again. "I would *love* some meat, cheese, and crackers. And an orange juice. Thank you, Marietta."

She set to work, making the plate for Samara.

"Servants. Antiques. It's not the life I can give you." Liam sighed.

"And you know that doesn't matter to me. Next year, it's Christmas back home. I promise. If you don't mind us crowding you in, that is."

He laughed. "Crowd away. I'll build new rooms on."

"The Trudale family would probably join us for the holiday, but they can stay at a hotel or a house in town. They'll be here for dinner, so you can meet them then. Oh...and Eva and Brand stayed to meet you, as well."

"And Sebastian?"

Samara smoothed the turtleneck she was wearing to cover her mating marks. "He's around somewhere."

His eyes narrowed. "There's something you're not telling me."

Both her mates tensed a bit. Marietta cast a look his way that told Samara she was ready to defend her charge.

"It's...nothing. Really." But it was. *And I still don't know how to tell him.*

His expression said he wasn't convinced.

Before he could push her further, Sebastian strode into the room. He went directly to Liam and offered his hand. "Welcome to my home, Liam. It's been a long time."

Liam hesitated, then shook it, calculation in his eyes. "I know you. You visited my grandmother more than once."

"Rain Cloud was a wonderful woman. One of the finest diplomats our people have ever dealt with. My deepest condolences on your loss."

"You?" He looked from Sebastian to Samara and back again. "*You're* the one Florence cheated on me with?"

"I have no right to expect your forgiveness, but there were extenuating circumstances I would like to explain, if I might. Not that I'm excusing my actions. I wronged you, and Florence wronged us both."

Liam snorted. "Rain Cloud always did call you a wolf."

The room seemed to hold a collective breath.

"Do you remember the old stories Rain Cloud told?"

"My grandmother had stories for every occasion."

"Do you remember the story of the Wolf-Brother?" Sebastian pressed him.

"Talking wolves who befriended our ancestors. There were several variations, but the wolves were always supposed to be loyal, wise, and vicious." He sighed. "Look. I don't know where you're going with—"

Sebastian performed a partial shift, allowing his head and hands to take on wolf form. Liam stared at him, his breathing going ragged.

When he'd returned to normal, Sebastian stood and offered his hand. "Come with me. There is a lot we need to discuss."

Liam looked toward Samara, seemingly too shocked to form words.

"It's okay, Dad. Consider yourself Wolf-Brother. You're not

the one he'll be vicious to."

"If he was, he would have to answer to us," James added.

Jason finished with the usual threat. "What upsets our mate upsets us."

"Okay." He pushed to his feet, still a little pale and unsteady. "See you at dinner?"

Samara smiled. "Or earlier, if you two are done talking that soon." It was unlikely, but it was possible.

They disappeared up the stairs together.

She watched them go, nervous but oddly relieved. *I don't have to tell him.* "Sebastian did this so I would stop stressing. Didn't he?"

James and Jason started laughing, and Marietta joined in.

"You could have told me," she groused.

* * * *

Sebastian laughed heartily and refilled Liam's drink. "She was a piece of work."

"Still is." Liam swallowed a mouthful of the whiskey. "She's *still* trying to argue the divorce settlement."

"What would it take to settle it?"

His smile disappeared. "No. I can't take your money."

"The way I see it, I am at least partially responsible for what you're facing now. It's only right that I make amends for it." Sebastian had been considering how to do that for weeks, and there were few options a proud male like Liam Tyler would accept from him.

Liam seemed to weigh that argument. Before he could form an answer, someone knocked on the office door.

"Yes?" Sebastian called out.

"There is *someone* here to see you, Sebastian."

"Someone I won't want to see," he whispered under his breath. "I am busy right now, Roberto."

"I know, sir, but... Oh, hell." He opened the door and shot Sebastian a look of misery. "For Samara's sake, this visitor is best dealt with and dismissed quickly," he imparted.

"Marcus?" Surely, he hadn't brought Christiana with him.

"No. Mrs. Florence O'Connor-Tyler."

Sebastian's stomach churned, and he fought not to bring the whiskey back up. "I see." He looked at Liam, noting the tightening of his jaw. "Show her in."

Liam started to stand. "Maybe I should —"

"If you don't mind, I would rather have a witness when I send her packing."

He settled back in the chair and drained his glass. "It would be a pleasure." There was a bitter edge to his tone.

While they waited, Sebastian refreshed both their drinks. He wasn't sure about Liam, but Sebastian was honest enough to admit he needed the fortification.

Florence didn't wait for Roberto to announce her. She pushed the servant away and breezed through the door. If she was surprised to see Liam, she gave no outward sign of it.

"I should probably warn you that my attorney has been trying to reach you, Liam." She smiled sweetly.

"I don't exist to fulfill your attorney's whims...or yours," he replied. Liam took a sip of the whiskey, and the first volley was over.

"This would move so much faster if you just —"

"You came for a reason, Florence?" Sebastian interrupted her.

Liam was, first and foremost, a guest in his house. He wouldn't allow this badgering to continue.

She searched out Roberto, standing where she'd left him.

Most probably waiting for my word to throw her out.

"What about some refreshments?" She didn't so much as suggest it as she deigned to order Sebastian's servant to do her bidding.

Roberto raised an eyebrow at that.

Sebastian swirled his drink. "No, thank you," he answered. "We're going to have dinner soon. Roberto, would you see to that, please?"

Florence shot a look of disbelief his way, and Roberto closed the door with a smile and a bobbing throat that said he would be laughing before he reached the kitchen.

If she's hoping for me to extend her a guest's welcome, she's in for a rude awakening. "You came here for something?" He reminded her of the question, hoping to spur her on to what he suspected was her aim.

She sauntered across the room. "I thought we might discuss the past. I made mistakes, Sebastian. I know that. I want to make up for lost time and past hurts. I really do." Her expression might be mistaken for earnest concern by someone who didn't know her.

I know her better.

Liam snorted and took another sip of the whiskey.

Sebastian joined him. *I'll need it, for what I'm going to do next.* "Mistakes? I think it all worked out for the best."

That seemed to confuse her. "If you're concerned about the…unpleasantness about my divorce from Liam, I'll drop that. I swear. I won't take a dime, and we'll be divorced in no time."

"Not a dime. Except what the local laws claim you're due, of course," Sebastian guessed.

That was quite a bit, considering the pair had been married for two decades.

"Well…*that*, but I can't help that. It's the law."

Sebastian met Liam's eyes, noting the other man's red-faced, tight-lipped fury.

I can make this right. "Liam and I were just talking about this, as a matter of fact." He waved off the other man's attempt to protest. "I was just telling Liam about my stateside attorney. I'm sure he could iron out some of these difficulties."

Liam hid his smile behind the whiskey glass, his eyes twinkling in seeming amusement.

Florence's look of horror was short-lived. She pasted on a sickening smile. "Well, that's *good*. I'm so glad it will be over...and amicably."

"If that was all—"

"Of course not. I told you, I want to discuss our past. I should have done what was right, Sebastian. I've hurt you, and—"

"I hold no grudges. You can leave with a clean conscience." *Not nearly, but if it gets her out of the house, I'll tell her all is forgiven.*

"But... You said we're mates." Florence affected a look of supreme hurt that shredded him.

It has to be done. I've known for the last decade and a half this was necessary. "We are, but, amazingly enough, I have learned very well how to live without a mate during the long years we have been apart. I take lovers on occasion. I have no one to answer to. I find myself in no need of you, Florence."

Liam raised his glass to Sebastian. "Sounds like a good life, my friend."

Tears pooled in Florence's eyes.

Crocodile tears. Don't let her fool you. Words stuck in his throat.

"How *could* you!" She sobbed. "You said..."

"A lot of things. As did you. It turns out neither of us could be trusted, in the end." *You could have trusted me. Had you not turned on me, you would never have had to question my sincerity.*

"Always a wolf." Liam laughed.

Sebastian nodded, struck by the sad truth of it.

Her eyes narrowed. "And what if I leave here and tell everyone about you? About this place?"

Not to be trusted. I knew she couldn't be. Sebastian drained his glass and set it on the table between them. "Let's be honest with each other, Florence. You don't want me or a place in my life."

She opened her mouth to protest.

"You want money."

She didn't deny it.

"Fine. I'll tell you what... Roberto!" He knew the servant hadn't gone far. *Probably just far enough to warn James and Jason to keep Samara away from anywhere Florence might be. He would have sent word to the kitchen about any dinner preparations.*

The door opened and the servant popped his head in.

"Bring me my check book, would you please?"

He dipped his head and disappeared. Roberto was back a moment later with the leather-bound book and Sebastian's father's fountain pen.

The sight of it choked Sebastian up a bit. This was the pen they used when issuing an order that might result in deaths. *Yet again, Roberto proves he knows my mind well.*

He whipped the book open on his lap and started writing. "I'm going to give you money. Quite a bit of money, Florence. In exchange, you are going to accept the bare minimum the law allows you in your divorce proceedings, you are going to leave here and never return, you are never going to attempt to contact me or Samara again, and... Not that I believe anyone would pay attention to your mad ramblings about wolves, but you will *never* mention it to anyone. Am I understood?"

"We'll see."

Sebastian wrote the check for two million dollars and signed it with a flourish. *It's probably a good thing that she doesn't know I have ten times that amount in cash in the bank, plus securities, business holdings, and personal holdings.* He held the check out to her, the back to Liam, so he couldn't see what the payoff amount was.

Florence's eyes widened and she took the check from his hands. "I think we understand each other, Sebastian." She folded it and started to place it in her purse.

"I think you need to understand one thing more."

"Which is?" She challenged him, taunting him with her belief that there was nothing Sebastian would or could do to her.

"With a word, I could have you killed before you left this campus. I can do so later, if you cross me. I am a wolf, Florence, and you have twice threatened me and mine. I do not suggest you try that a third time."

Her face paled, but she pasted on a slightly wobbly smile. "We understand each other, Sebastian." She turned to leave.

"My plane will take you home today." The last thing he wanted was for Samara to run into her mother in town.

"Trying to get rid of me?"

"Yes."

Florence didn't respond to that. She left, and Roberto hurried to see her on her way.

When they were alone, Liam took another sip. "How much did you—"

"She's a cheap bitch. Can we leave it at that?"

The human howled in laughter. He refilled Sebastian's glass and raised his own. "I'll drink to that."

A laugh bubbled up from Sebastian's chest and burst free. "To freedom."

"Amen!"

They drank together until Roberto announced dinner was ready.

Our daughter is waiting for us...my den brother and I.

The Ancient Rites

Eva and Brand

Note from Brenna: *Eva and Brand really wanted to get their two cents in, but the scene just didn't fit into the book. Still, not one to deny them their chance to tell a story, I decided to let the readers see their mating.*

Eva held to Brand's shoulders, her heart hammering when he turned away from her rooms and toward his. As if she'd spoken aloud, he replied to her unease.

"Tell me, Eva. Are you intact?" The rising musk said he suspected the answer and was enflamed by it.

"Yes. I am." *But I won't be for long. Brand favors the ancient rites. I'll be full of his cock in short order.*

"Then you will shed your blood on my bed, as the ancient rites decree." He slowed a bit. "That doesn't frighten you. Does it?"

"No. You don't frighten me." She'd done nothing but fantasize and dream about him since she'd sighted him at Samara's challenge match.

"If you wish to return to your alpha level room, with me, after I breach you, I will happily seduce you wherever you wish to lay your head."

In your lap. The thought of it had her weeping sex fluids down her thighs.

He took a deep breath and his eyes shifted. "Such a sexy little thing you are. And all mine."

His voice alone raised her nipples against her blouse. He noticed and a rumble of satisfaction escaped his lips.

"Yes. All yours." She wondered how large his cock was. Eva had heard rumors that Brand was long and thick, and she hoped they were true.

Brand opened a door and stepped through.

A soft "oh" of surprise came from the far reaches of the room, and Eva stiffened.

Most likely his servant.

"Leave us." Brand barked the order out in a tone few wolves would ignore.

The sound of skittering feet was punctuated by a door slamming.

Brand kicked the door behind them shut and settled Eva on her feet. His eyes were hard in challenge, his muscles strung tight.

Some foreign corner of her mind urged her to run, but Eva stiffened her spine and raised her chin instead. He didn't smile in reply, though her response probably pleased him.

Instead, Brand dragged the shirt off over his head and let it drop to the floor. While she was busy taking in every millimeter of flesh he presented, he went to work on his pants. Brand went from half-dressed to nude in what seemed like the blink of an eye.

Then his mouth was covering hers, his tongue parting her lips in a kiss that made her heart falter a beat or three. Eva wrapped her arms around his shoulders, her fingers tangling in his hair.

Night Mother, this is good.

He unhooked and unzipped her long skirt and pushed it over her hips, leaving her nude, save her blouse and shoes. One large hand closed over a globe of her ass, and he tested her readiness for him with a thick fingertip.

Eva gasped and arched toward him, her knees trembling at

the feeling of his cock teasing at her ribs.

He's so big, so strong.

"No panties?" he questioned.

Eva fought to order her thoughts. "I heard males following the ancient rites often destroyed clothing in their haste to have a female beneath them."

Brand hesitated a moment. "You planned for that?"

She nodded, picking up his personal flavor on her lips.

His hands closed on the front of her blouse, and he pulled it apart. Pearl buttons went flying around the room, and the sound of shredding cotton shot her arousal into overdrive.

Brand yanked the blouse off her arms and threw it over his shoulder. "You are mine, little wolf."

Trying to force speech was impossible, Eva conceded. She nodded instead.

He backed her across the room.

Toward his bed. She didn't look to see if she was right. Brand had promised she would shed her blood on his sheets. There was nowhere else he would want to take her.

The mattress pressed to her thighs and Eva took a calming breath.

Brand captured her lips again, leading her from one kiss to another and a third. He stroked his hands down her body, his lips leaving hers so he could catalog her attributes to himself.

Eva panted in need, his descriptions of her body making her blood heat for more.

"And all mine." He claimed her, his voice rough.

"Yes." *Make me yours.*

He turned her and folded Eva over the edge of the mattress in a series of smooth motions. Brand forced her legs wider.

"You liked my descriptions," he murmured.

"Yes." It seemed that was all she could manage to say.

"You will like them better when I revisit each one."

Her inner muscles clenched and she moaned.

"But, for now, I will claim what you offer, little wolf."

Eva fisted her hands in the rumpled quilt, prepared for him to thrust hard and deep.

He didn't. Brand spread her nether lips and went to his knees. His tongue traced the seam, inside and out, and he recounted his senses of her: the tang of her musk, the silk of her body, the quivering of her excited body.

Her moans gained volume and Eva's palms started to itch. *I'm shifting.* She wracked her brains to remember hearing of a female shifting her first time during sex *before* he'd even made it inside her.

I don't think I've ever heard of this.

Her instincts took over and she tried to turn to attack him.

Brand came to his feet, capturing her with ease. He pressed her wrists to the quilt and thrust inside her, his howl of pleasure overlapping with hers.

The fur teasing her inner thighs attested he'd partially shifted as well. Growls escaped his mouth and Eva shivered. She was being fucked by the half-beast, and it was just what she'd always wanted.

His hips retreated and slammed home, over and over, his cock stretching her intimately, in every direction. Her nipples brushed the quilt with every forward thrust.

The tightening in her womb broke free, and she cried out in ecstasy. Brand lodged himself deep, and his heat flowed into her, a hot stream that made her breathing go ragged again.

He released her arms and trailed his fingers up them, claiming her again in action.

I'm his to touch. His to seduce. His to protect.

Aftershocks coursed through her at the thought of it and he

growled again.

Brand left her body and lifted Eva to the edge of the mattress. He spread her legs, smiling at the sight of blood and cum spilling onto his bed linens.

"Do you wish to return to your rooms now? With me?" He offered the invitation, though surely he knew he didn't need to offer her anything but safety, care, and pleasure. The ancient rites meant he expected to be in charge completely.

"I guess we should share our scent there as well."

Brand walked across the room and picked up his shirt.

He's giving me his shirt to replace the blouse he ripped off me. She warmed to the idea. It was so...male. "Would you grab my skirt as well?"

One eyebrow went up in challenge. Before she could make sense of it, he turned and picked up her skirt. In the next heartbeat, he shredded it and tossed it to the floor. His meaning was more than clear.

I'm his, and I will be wearing nothing but his shirt back to the room.

Her body heated in arousal, and her eyes shifted in the force of it. Brand stopped and watched, no doubt trying to decide if she was aroused or angered by the move.

Eva spread her legs and invited him in. "We can go back to *our* rooms later."

The shirt hit the floor a second time and Brand made his way to the bed, his fangs showing.

Dear Night Mother, how am I going to last three days? Any less would make it seem she was an easy catch.

He thrust inside her again, holding to Eva's hips, positioning her to his best advantage.

Not easy. He's just that good.

Brenna
Lyons

Younger Daughter

WEREWOLF U II

Blurb

Aurora is a wolf princess who has never fit the Alpha female mold. Unlike her older sister Talia, Aurora likes getting her hands, feet, and any other part of her body dirty. She would rather wear Daisy Dukes than designer gowns. She keeps her hair cut short instead of long, the way most alphas do. Moreover, she doesn't like alpha men...alphas who aren't related to her in general. When she meets Nolan, Aurora finds focus...and maybe more, but will her family approve of her taking a mate who isn't an alpha?

Younger Daughter

WEREWOLF U II

"I apologize profusely, Lady Aurora."

She smiled, though his apology confused her. "Whatever for?"

"That the Alpha level rooms are not available to you."

"I'm sure my rooms will be sufficient." They would. No school would want to be found lacking when it came to caring for an alpha, especially when she was the daughter of the current ruling mates. "It is hardly your fault my sister and I were born less than three years apart." Talia would graduate that year, and the Alpha level rooms would be Aurora's the following year.

If only her sister would commit to her mates, they wouldn't be having this issue. They would surely produce young and decide to move to more spacious quarters at the Alpha house across campus. *Grandfather Sebastian's home, though he isn't in residence right now.*

Talia was not so obliging. She'd met her mates. She liked them. Talia had even slept with them and made it clear she would commit to them...in her own due time. Since the pair were four years older than Talia was, her older sister wasn't subjected to their constant presence as many Alphas were, so she felt little pressure to complicate her life with a mate and young while she was in school.

"Still, I humbly apologize that you were given a lesser

room."

She didn't bother to assure him it was acceptable again. As the head porter, he would see this as a personal failure, no matter what she said.

The room he showed her to was far out in the female wing, a lovely suite of rooms that overlooked the gardens on one side and the forest on the other. It took a moment for Aurora to realize he was waiting in the doorway, red-faced and discomfited.

Aurora offered him a broad smile. "It's wonderful. Perfect. Right above the sunflowers. They are my favorite, you know."

His smile was slow coming. "I didn't, but I am glad it is to your liking." He waved the porters in with her belongings. "Marietta said she will arrive from the main house with her belongings in an hour. Is there anything I can do for you until then?"

"No thank you. I believe I'll take a walk in the gardens until then."

"As you wish, Lady Aurora. Call if you need anything." With that, he was gone.

Aurora took a calming breath and made her way downstairs. At the edge of the gardens, she stripped off her shoes to walk barefoot between the rows of flowering plants and bushes.

She turned her face up to the sunlight, closing her eyes. This was what she enjoyed best. Like her older sister, Aurora had been raised with designer dresses and tours of the world. Unlike her sister, Aurora preferred running barefoot on her parents' wildlife preserve in North America.

I'm going for a walk in the gardens tonight. She smiled. *In my cutoff jean shorts. The ones Marietta hates. The Daisy Dukes.*

* * * *

Nolan wandered from plant to plant, making a survey of the gardens behind Regina Hall. It was a rare privilege to be the one named to maintain these gardens. Only the highest scoring student, with the best teacher recommendations, was given duty here.

If he did well, this post would make his career. If he did poorly, he would be replaced faster than he could cry out in despair.

He was so engrossed in the topic, Nolan nearly tripped over someone laying between the bed of sunflowers and the one of hollyhocks. He jumped back, as she vaulted to her feet with a gasp.

"I'm sorry."

"Sorry." Her apology overlapped with his.

Nolan took a moment to appreciate the view. Whoever she was, she was exceptional. From her tight v-neck sweater to the cutoff denim shorts that barely covered the essentials, from her long bare legs to that enticing scent, the young woman was enough to make any male wolf hard.

Her dark blonde hair was clipped in short waves around her face, and her eyes were a stunning golden-green.

As if she was discomfited by his examination, she crossed her arms over her chest.

Not quickly enough to disguise that her nipples are hard. And she's not wearing a bra.

"I'm sorry," he repeated. "I'll finish my survey and leave you alone."

"I...I should go anyway." She started to back away.

"I won't tell on you." For some reason, it was important that she know that. She could get in a lot of trouble for using the Regina gardens, if she wasn't a resident of the dorm.

Her clothing says she's not.

She stopped and stared at him, seemingly shocked.

"You like the gardens. Don't you?" Even as he asked it, Nolan questioned what difference that could possibly make.

"Love them." A stiff smile pulled up at the edges of her lips.

There was something endearing about her wistful look at the sunflowers. "I will be maintaining these gardens. If you would like to...tag along in the evenings and learn about them, I would be glad to teach you." He didn't question why he would make such an offer. She was enchanting, and anything was worth more time in her presence.

Anything but screwing up my internship. "But you cannot work with the plants without my permission. You see, it's my responsibility to—"

"I'd like that. Thank you." She smiled widely, offered a

wave of her fingers, then loped away. "Tomorrow evening," she shouted back.

"Seven o'clock."

Nolan wasn't certain she heard him, until her reply of "See you then." reached him from the far reaches of the gardens.

He stood there, a sappy smile pasted on his face. She'd agreed to meet with him again.

Nolan sighed. "Time to finish this survey." Still, he took a moment to look the way she'd disappeared one last time.

* * * *

A date. I have a date.

Sort of.

He was interested. There was no denying that. If his cock was any indication—*it usually is with guys*—he was more than simply interested in her. He was intent.

But he thinks I'm lower ranked than I am. Aurora slowed, biting her lip, considering that problem.

It's not that much of a problem. Maybe it's better that he doesn't know who I am. After all, she'd never met an alpha outside her own family that she got along well with. Maybe accepting a lower-ranked mate was a good thing.

My family won't approve of this. That was admittedly a problem, but what could she do about it?

Who says I have to do anything? Aurora smiled. Which male or males to accept was ultimately the female's choice, though her family might voice opposition. It wasn't like she

151

was in Talia's shoes. She wasn't expected to take the highest ranked twin males around.

I have a choice, and damned if I'm going to let anyone take it from me.

Especially not when that choice involved a delicious male like this one. His hair was as dark as her fathers', though his eyes were more dark gray than brown.

In fact, he looked more like her siblings than she did herself. Aurora looked like her paternal grandfather and — reportedly — like her maternal grandmother. Since Aurora had never met the latter and had no urge to do so, she'd long ago decided to take that on advisement from her family members who *had* met Florence.

Good riddance! It was much more pleasant to think about the male she'd met that night.

He wasn't as tall as her fathers were, little more than half a head taller than she was herself. Though all wolves were muscular, his physique said he worked hard at his trade, which was more than passably appealing to her.

Aurora had never cared for lazy wolves and tended to do a lot for herself, something that drove Marietta mad on a daily basis.

She breezed back into her suite of rooms, on top of the world, making plans for seeing him again.

Him. I don't even know his name yet. And he doesn't know mine. Maybe I should use my nickname. It was a good idea.

"Oh, Koukla." Marietta sighed. "You're filthy."

"I'm sure you walked barefoot in the dirt when you were my age. I'm sure you watched the stars, flat on your back on the cool earth." She smiled sweetly and headed for the bath. "Besides, it washes off."

"Dinner?" her servant offered.

"Steak? I'll eat when I get out of the tub." Though it was unlikely Marietta would scent the male on her, Aurora wasn't taking any chances.

"Very well."

That easily, she escaped scrutiny. *It won't be as easy once we scent each other.*

* * * *

Nolan maneuvered the John Deere Gator down the paved garden path and toward the area he would be working on tonight. Though one part of his mind was focused on the pruning and planting he'd planned for this first evening, another was wandering.

To her. Haunting memories of her scent had him searching out the same on the breeze.

Not yet.

Even so, his cock was half-erect in anticipation of seeing her again.

He stopped the Gator at the Rhododendron bushes, cast one last look around for her, then dismounted with a sigh. *She isn't here.*

Of course, that didn't mean she didn't want to see him. She might have been caught entering the Regina gardens...or leaving them the night before. She might have been roped into first-year duties she hadn't anticipated. *She doesn't have my name, so there's no way for her to let me know if she can't make it.*

Whatever the case may be, I can't do anything about it now. I have work to do.

In moments, Nolan was lost in his work, pruning the bushes, humming to himself as he worked.

"That doesn't look wilted."

He tipped his head back and met her gaze, offering a smile. "It's not. It's too densely packed here. It will choke itself off if I don't prune a little."

"Ah. I see." She folded herself onto the path, where she would have a good view of what he was doing but wouldn't be in the way. "Sorry I'm late. My mother called, and I got caught up in the conversation."

Nolan went back to his work with a nod. He'd be late for his evening work if his mother called. She didn't, but only because she knew his schedule.

"How do you know which branches to prune and which to leave?"

"That comes with experience. It's not so much a number but how they crowd and push each other, whether or not the individual leaves will get enough sunlight... It's something of an art."

"I think I understand." She was silent for a long moment. "At the risk of being rude, I realized I don't know your name."

Nolan peeked at her over his shoulder, noting her nervousness. "I don't find that rude at all. I was wondering the same thing about you. My name is Nolan."

She didn't hesitate. "Koukla."

"Really? That sounds Greek." He wouldn't have guessed she was of Greek stock.

"It is. I was born in Greece. Prematurely, no less. It's a nickname, but anyone who knows me uses it, so I use it."

"Interesting. The name stands out. Nolan is... Well, there are enough of them around that it doesn't, I suppose." He shrugged, then moved along to the next bush. "Would you mind putting the clippings in the cart behind the Gator?"

Koukla hurried to do so. "It seems counterintuitive, doesn't it?"

"What does?"

"Cutting off healthy limbs to make the plant healthier. I understand why it's necessary, but it would be like cutting off a healthy toe to make a wolf healthier."

He bit back a chuckle. The last thing he wanted to do was offend her. "Wolves don't grow back toes, but plants do grow back branches, if they are allowed to."

She laughed. "I suppose that's true enough."

Nolan scanned his gaze up and down her body, marveling at her willingness to do manual labor. Most beautiful females like her avoided it. "What is your major?" Females were underrepresented in his field of study. Encouraging one wouldn't be a bad idea.

"I'm undeclared, at the moment. I haven't decided what to major in yet."

"But you enjoy working in the gardens?"

Koukla sighed. "I think this would be my dream job."

"Then you should sign up for some of the basic classes while you can, just so you don't fall behind. If you don't like it, you can always decide on another major later."

She hesitated. "That's a good idea." She met his gaze. "Can I continue to meet you? To learn from you as well?"

Answering that was easy enough. "Of course." Was there any doubt?

* * * *

Two days later

"So the soil you plant roses in is usually sandy."

"Precisely. A little more right there, please." Nolan pointed out the area she'd missed.

Aurora added more sand to the mix and patted it down loosely around the immature plants. He smiled and nodded, and her heart skipped a beat at the unspoken praise.

So far, she was enjoying her botany classes. It seemed she'd found her calling, and it was all because of Nolan.

Why did I never consider working with plants before? Because my family and servants have always considered that a servant's job? How ridiculous!

Moreover, working in botany gave her an excuse to wear her comfortable, old jeans and t-shirts, as a matter of course.

"You said you have an idea of where you might want to work with a degree in botany?" It was a reminder of where their conversation earlier had been left.

How much should I say? "Some wolves run animal sanctuaries and similar businesses. I imagine a botanist on staff would be exceedingly helpful." *It wasn't a lie. I just didn't mention it was my family's business.*

He placed another young plant in the ground. "I imagine it would. I hadn't considered that."

"What are you going to do with your degree?" He was a fourth-year student. Surely he had plans by now.

"I want to be a groundskeeper...eventually head groundskeeper for the Alphas' homes."

Aurora pretended to consider that. In reality, she was biting back more than a few things she could say to him. *You're a shoe-in, if I suggest you. Becoming my mate would secure your position. There isn't only one; each estate has its own staff for that.*

All bad choices. Instead, she formulated an answer that wouldn't tip her hand. "That sounds like a lot of work. Interesting work, but difficult. The homes are all over the world, so each one would have different types of plants."

"That's what makes the job so appealing to me. It's a challenge."

His excitement was infectious, and she smiled in return.

"Oh. There you are."

Aurora stiffened. She knew that voice. *Darian, Tyler's den brother.*

Please don't let him say my name. I don't want Nolan to find out this way. She turned to him, pasting on a brittle smile, though she'd never really liked Tyler's choice in friends.

"Your brother wants to see you."

Thankfully, he didn't mention Tyler's name. It wasn't a common wolf name, and Nolan was sure to know it.

Aurora checked her watch, then sighed. "I should go."

"Don't forget, Koukla," Nolan instructed her. "Roses —"

"Sandy soil," she finished, as she made her way to her feet. "Thank you, Nolan. See you next time." She hurried down the path, making Darian lope after her. The sooner Aurora got him away from Nolan, the less chance there was of the jerk ruining this for her. She turned the corner, leaving him behind.

Darian caught up and pulled her to a halt with a grip on her upper arm. Aurora shook his hand off, adding a glare for good measure.

He had the good grace to look embarrassed, then took a step back and stiffened his spine. "Who is he, Aurora?"

She bit back the protest that it was none of Darian's business. That would likely convince him to dig deeper. "He's my botany tutor," she answered in half-truth.

"He calls you Koukla. That's awfully familiar, don't you think?" One brow went up in challenge.

"Everyone who knows me calls me Koukla," she dismissed him.

"Not everyone."

"Everyone I like." *There. The snub was clearly stated. Darian doesn't call me Koukla, because I don't like him, and I've never invited him to do so.*

His eyes narrowed, and they shifted to wolf eyes for a

few heartbeats. He visibly calmed himself.

"Well, I suppose I should see what Tyler wants," she announced. Aurora turned on her heel and headed for the nearest door into the dorm building.

"Oh, Tyler didn't ask to see you."

The admission stopped her short, and Aurora swiveled her head to question him. His smirk made her blood burn and her fingertips itch.

I'm mad enough to shift my first time. That realization forced her to calm a bit. "You lied? To *me?*"

He didn't seem the least bit sorry for it. If anything, his smile widened. "Digging in the dirt with that...lowborn wolf? That beta? Someone had to save you from yourself."

"You are overstepping your boundaries, Darian. Moreover, you interrupted my studies. I don't appreciate either and I *will* see you punished for it, if you try it again." Though she really didn't want her family looking into her relationship with Nolan yet, Darian didn't know that.

His smiled faded, and his jaw notched down in apparent frustration.

"I am pursuing a degree in botany, which means I will be digging in the dirt. Nolan is my tutor, which means I will be digging with him routinely. Beta wolf or not, he is the best at what he does, and an Alpha wolf gets the best. Always. Now *none* of this is your business, and this is the only warning I will give you not to attempt to *save* me from my schooling again."

He didn't offer comment, though she would lay wagers he was within millimeters of a temper fit.

"Good night, Darian. I trust I won't see you again."

* * * *

"And the work so far?" Maestro Ty asked.

Nolan walked at his side, dressed for the office, trying to appear as professional as possible as he gave his report to the head of his department. "Going very well. I decided to focus on maintenance and fit in a bit of planting each evening. After all, problems left unchecked will only create more work in the long run."

"Very true. A sound decision."

He bit back a smile and offered the written report. When the Maestro took it, Nolan continued.

"The rose beds are complete, and I'm moving on to weeding in the..." He paused, staring at the crowd milling around the rose beds. Nolan hoped they hadn't trampled the immature plants he and Koukla had planted the night before.

Their conversations were too low for him to pick out, but the sounds of confusion and upset were impossible to miss. Nolan sprinted for the site, wondering what might be wrong.

He slipped between two onlookers and stopped dead in his tracks. The blood drained from his face. The rose beds were destroyed, plants ripped up and torn apart, the new plants dug up and strewn about, wilting in the heat of the morning.

The destruction reached further, into other planting

beds. His heart sank at the sight of hollyhocks shredded, alstroemeria trampled and uprooted, and sunflowers ripped to shreds and scattered through the gardens.

Sunflowers are Koukla's favorites. She's going to be crushed by this.

The person to his right shifted away, and the Maestro joined him. His mentor's litany of curses made Nolan wince. He'd never seen the old wolf lose his composure before.

"The onlookers have destroyed any scent we might use to identify the bastard who did this."

Nolan nodded, his stomach in knots. "I'll get to work on this right away," he promised. *All our hard work.* It hurt to see it destroyed this way. "It's going to ruin my budget, but—"

"In a real-world situation, damage of this kind would be considered an extenuating circumstance, meriting an expansion of budget. It might even be covered by insurance. I will approve anything you require to fix this." His hand closed on Nolan's shoulder. "Order what you need. Let me know how many assistants you require. In the meantime, I will consult with security and the Alpha Maestro. This cannot be allowed to happen again."

"Right away." Nolan stared at the destruction, his heart aching. *Who would do such a thing?*

* * * *

"I'm telling you it was Darian." Aurora waited for her

sister's reply, her nerves on edge. "He was angry at me, so he destroyed the garden."

"Can you prove that?" Talia asked, seemingly more interested in her manicure than their discussion.

"What? I'm telling you Darian is dangerous, and you're questioning me?"

Her sister sighed dramatically. "The security team couldn't confirm the scent of the vandal. You didn't witness the crime. How do you intend to prove it was Darian?"

"What if I'm right and he decides to attack me?" *Or Nolan.* The urge to gut Darian was growing stronger.

"Look, Koukla. I know you don't like Darian, but you can't toss around unfounded accusations."

"Stop calling me Koukla. I'm not a baby anymore." Though she loved the way the nickname sounded on Nolan's lips, she found Talia's use of it grating.

"Then stop acting like one. You have security. If you don't feel safe, let Marietta know, and she can order guards for you on campus."

And I will lose my chance with Nolan before it's more than a glimmer in our minds.

"Right. I get locked up, because our brother chooses an unstable prick as a den brother." *If I went to Tyler with this, he would be even less sympathetic.*

"Part and parcel of being the Alpha mates' child." That simply Aurora was dismissed. There was no question that Talia considered the matter closed.

Bitch.

Aurora made her way out of Talia's suite of rooms and

down the staircase. At the Alpha male floor, Darian was leaning against the wall, that same smirk painted on his too-pretty visage. She ignored him, silently willing him to start something.

He didn't, and she made her way to the dining room. Though she wasn't overly hungry, Aurora decided she should try to eat heartily.

It will be a long night of work.

* * * *

Three days later

Nolan paused, looking toward the amphitheater at the sound of applause. It took a moment for the explanation to resonate with him.

Matriculation. Koukla is a first-year student; she'll be there.

He changed direction and headed that way. If he was lucky, he might spot her and have a chance to talk to her for a few minutes on her way to change clothing.

He couldn't deny he wanted to see Koukla. The hours between their evenings in the garden were long and empty. Nolan found his mind wandering to the woman when he should be working.

If she invited me, I would be in her bed in an instant. Though it would slow down his progress toward his career goals, he would even mate with her and take a job with the university until she graduated.

Maybe we could work together. He'd heard mates who worked together had the best lives.

Even the current Alpha mates did so. Samara Trudale worked with wild animals and had a preserve in the northwestern United States. Her mates, James and Jason, were an architect and a businessman, respectively. Between the three of them, they had the skills necessary to plan, build, run, and oversee such a complex operation.

Koukla suggested working for a similar operation. What if she worked for the Alphas? Would we be able to work together? Perhaps me working at the houses while she worked for their business ventures? It was an enticing idea.

Not as enticing an idea as finding her at the ceremony, but nearly so.

Nolan came to a halt at the foot of the large staircase to the left of the stage and started scanning the first-year students for her. He went back and rechecked the first three sections in confusion. She wasn't there. He was sure of it, but what would make a first-year student miss Matriculation?

Polite clapping and movement indicated the end of the ceremony. Nolan didn't pay attention to it. He was still mired in the mystery of the missing student.

A sea of crimson velvet interrupted his train of thought. In the closest group, he spied a familiar-looking flounce of dark gold hair and focused on it.

Koukla peeled off her robes and handed them to a waiting servant, a rather grim-faced crone of a female. The woman beneath the trappings was nothing like he'd seen from Koukla before and more than he'd dreamed to see of her in some time.

She wore a knee-length white gown, her shoulders and arms bare, save the single line of silk attached at the bodice, trailing over one shoulder and down past the curve of her ass. That wasn't the dress of a lowborn wolf, and lowborn wolves didn't have servants like the dowager serving Koukla.

Neither was she seated in one of the lower sections. The section Koukla had risen from was the one reserved for Regina Hall students.

She's an Alpha. She lied to me.

Some rational corner of his mind opined that she hadn't lied to him. She'd simply never corrected his assumption that she didn't belong in the Regina gardens.

She should *have corrected me.*

Why?

He couldn't answer that. Nolan suspected his reason was as flimsy as the belief that she'd stolen something precious from him, the belief that they might have a future together.

She's interested in me.

Was she? He couldn't say for sure. All the signs of attraction he'd thought were so clear suddenly weren't.

Koukla turned, coming face-to-face with him. Her eyes went wide.

"Good day," he offered crisply. "My name is Nolan Gibbs."

Her cheeks went a vivid red. "Aurora," she answered his unasked question of what her real name was.

"Aurora." Something resonated with him, and the

pieces started falling into place. Her brother was on campus. She was familiar with the Alpha mates' business. She came and went from the Regina gardens with no questions asked. "Aurora Trudale, I presume."

She nodded.

Other students stopped to stare. Neither of them turned to look. The servant approached, and Nolan ignored her as well.

He wanted to wish her a good day, but he couldn't find the words. Or couldn't force them out. Nolan wasn't sure which, at the moment.

Instead, he tipped his head, turned on his heel, and marched away. Whatever game this was, he wasn't sure he wanted to play. *Alphas ruin a man on a whim.*

They could also make a man, but the last thing Nolan wanted was to find his success that way. He worked for his advancement.

"Always have. Always will."

* * * *

"Koukla?"

Marietta's soothing tone made Aurora want to cry. Instead, she swallowed down the lump in her throat.

"I am not a baby anymore."

She left the hated pumps Marietta had insisted on behind and took off after Nolan barefoot. Aurora wasn't sure what he thought, but no matter what it was, it was likely wrong.

"Nolan!"

He ignored her and kept walking.

Aurora laid on speed, ducking around other students. They started moving aside for her. Of course, they were also giving Nolan a wide berth as he stormed toward the Regina gardens.

She didn't call out to him again, somehow certain that it would only make him move faster.

As she expected, Nolan went directly to the area where his classmates were still working on repairing the damage Darian had done. He bustled about, checking their work, giving instructions.

Aurora slowed down, walking the last ten meters or so instead of running them. Nolan didn't react to her approach. She wondered if he was actively ignoring her. Following him from person to person, she became more sure of it.

"Can I have a moment of your time, Nolan?" Aurora asked.

"A little busy." His voice was cool and dismissive.

One of the other males peeked up at her; his gaze lingered. That was all it took to cause Nolan to wheel around and face her. He grasped her arm and led her away from the other students.

"What is it, Aurora?"

"This is not what you think." She motioned for calm.

"You lied to me," he accused. His eyes flashed, a momentary shift that revealed how upset he was.

How furious. "I didn't. I told you Koukla was a

167

nickname. I told you everyone uses it for me, so I tend to use it." She winced. "Though I admit I'm getting sick of it. I'm not a baby anymore, and I'm tired of being called one."

"I thought... You *made* me think you weren't..." Nolan motioned to Regina Hall, seemingly furious with her.

"I didn't. Yes, I knew you assumed it, and I didn't correct you. Maybe that was wrong. I didn't think it mattered. Honestly."

"You didn't think it mattered?" He went red in the face, then pushed a hand through his hair, gritting his teeth in what she could only assume was aggravation.

Explaining it was more difficult than she'd hoped it would be. "You didn't know who I was. You treated me like any other wolf. Meeting me in that context... I liked it."

"I would have treated you like any other wolf, even if I knew who you were," he countered.

"Would you? If I was my sister, would you have treated me like you did?"

"Do I look like I want to die?"

Her head spun at the topic skipping that seemed to be going on. "What?"

"I'm sure her mates would kill me on sight." There was a snide undertone to that remark.

"Well, I'm *not* Talia, am I? I don't have preordained mates waiting to kill you." Against her better judgment, she let her frustration show.

"That doesn't mean you're someone I can—" Nolan clamped his mouth shut, as if he'd admitted something vital.

If he stopped himself from saying what I think he did, I want him to admit it. Aurora calmed herself, thinking through his comment. *Continue as if he said it. Let him correct me if I'm wrong.*

"Who says? Who I choose is no one's concern. I'm the *younger* daughter, remember? I have an older brother and sister and a younger brother. The odds of me ever taking the throne are so remote as to be impossible." *Even if I did — on some far-away day — my mate will be my mate.*

"So you're making a choice?" The question was more subdued than he'd been moments before.

"Today? Not a permanent choice. Am I interested in you?"

He looked at her, his expressions shifting.

"Yes. I am," she admitted. Aurora swallowed the lump rising in her throat. She was putting herself on the line and hoping Nolan would be kind to her, despite his anger.

He was still for a long moment. "I have plans, Aurora."

"Then follow your plans. Did I ever ask you not to?" *I've never demanded anything of him.*

"I've worked for everything I have. Worked hard. You know what my plans are."

She nodded. "I do."

"I don't want anyone saying I was handed those dreams. Can you — ?"

"I understand. Then go on with your plans. I'll even find someone else to teach me, if you want me to. Maybe someday, when you have your dreams, we can be more." *I can do that. Talia has made it clear she won't be mating until after she graduates. That would give Nolan five or more years toward his goals.*

He seemed shocked by her answer. "You'd be content with that?"

Aurora straightened. "I'll live with it."

His eyes narrowed. "Live with it?"

"If you're asking if it's what I *want*, no. It's not, but you have to follow your dreams, right?"

There was a tense moment of silence between them. "What do you want?"

Her heart hammering in a mixture of fear and anticipation, Aurora stepped toward him and went up on her toes, sealing her mouth to his.

For a heartbeat, Nolan didn't respond. Then he wrapped his arms around her and pulled her flush to his body.

The kiss took on a potent edge that made her dizzy in need.

"Nolan!"

The shout from one of the other students broke them apart...just in time for claws to cut deep into Aurora's cheek.

She fell back into a patch of Stella de Oros, stunned and in pain.

* * * *

Nolan spun around to face their attacker, noting the flow of blood down Koukla's face in rising fury.

He'd seen the male before. He was a Regina Hall snot of some sort, usually seen in the company of the young Alphas.

Aurora's siblings.

"Your brother wants to see you."

Damn it, I didn't remember who he was back then. Aurora's dress and demeanor had put him at ease. He hadn't searched for the wolf's identity, because he felt safe with Aurora...thus, safe with anyone she associated with, by extension.

The wolf facing him was anything but safe. He was half-shifted, showing his teeth and claws. The latter were stained in blood.

Aurora's blood. How dare he!

That simply, Nolan's vision went red-tinged. He pulled at his shirt with shifting paws, tearing the fabric and throwing it aside. Growls rose from his chest.

"No." Aurora's protest was a strangled whisper of sound.

Nolan didn't turn toward her. He wasn't about to give this beast his back.

The other male's voice was guttural and stank of malice unleashed. "You were supposed to be mine."

Aurora gasped at that. "I never invited your attentions. I made it clear I couldn't stand you long ago."

"An alpha stakes his claim."

"Only if the female accepts him. I don't. I will never accept you, Darian."

"He moved and left you open to attack. You want a

male like that?"

Before Nolan could call him out as a liar, Aurora did. "You attacked his back from downwind, like a jackal. Neither of us knew who was attacking or from where. You are a coward, Darian."

As if that pushed the alpha male past his limits, Darian shifted, and Nolan did the same. Darian, focused on Nolan, then turned his attention on Aurora.

Nolan's fury rose like a tsunami. Darian intended to attack Aurora. It was beyond contempt. Everything he was doing was nothing short of treason and foul play.

"Me and me alone," Nolan barked at him in wolf language.

Darian offered a tip of his head and attacked.

What Nolan lacked in practice, he made up for in speed and agility. He worked for a living, and it showed in how they fought.

When Darian tried to attack his feet and come up at his belly from below, Nolan pushed off his back, driving the larger wolf into the dirt as he leapt away, leading his enemy further from Aurora. Darian tried to attack from above, and Nolan jumped, powering his shoulder into Darian's rib cage to send him sprawling.

I have to end this quickly. Aurora is bleeding from her wounds.

Nolan came down over Darian before the other wolf could right himself. He used his claws to dig furrows in his enemy's chest and belly. When Darian tried to push him off with his paws, Nolan clamped down hard on a forepaw, snapping bones.

Darian yelped like a frightened pup, then started pleading for mercy in whines and cries. Though it galled him to let the bastard go, Nolan backed off and shifted back to human form.

He ranged his gaze along the horrified students watching them, savoring the blood in his mouth. "You all heard him. He conceded to me."

Several nodded, and Darian whipped away. He lifted Aurora gently from the ground and cradled her to his chest.

Then he took off at a run.

"Where are we going?" she asked. "Nolan, you're not dressed."

"You're injured. I don't give a damn about my clothes."

She smiled. "I think I may love you."

You better. Even with witnesses, the Alphas might ruin him over this.

* * * *

Aurora pressed harder at the gouges in her cheek, trying not to panic. She'd never had a wound that bled for more than a few minutes; she'd never had one that bled this much.

"It will be all right," Nolan soothed her. He kicked the clinic door open before them. "Injured Alpha," he shouted at the top of his lungs.

Doctors came running. They showed him to the Alpha

treatment room and started to work on Aurora.

As she'd feared, the claw marks were deep, requiring not one but rather two layers of stitching to close them appropriately. The doctors assured her more than once that they were unlikely to scar...or scar deeply, at any rate.

"Alpha injured," someone shouted from the hall.

Darian's whining was impossible to miss, and Aurora winced as it grated at her nerves.

Two of the doctors started to move toward him.

Nolan stared at them, his features flexing and tightening between forms. "If any of you see to that traitor before Aurora is taken care of, I will deliver your hide to her parents myself."

They looked at each other as if they weren't sure what to make of the threat.

"Darian attacked us and did this." She pointed to her cheek. "Then he challenged Nolan...and lost."

The eldest of the doctors sighed. "Put him in a room. We'll get to him next." His order shook the walls and sent tremors through Aurora's body.

The other two returned to their places, handing supplies off to the elder doctor and cleaning the spilled blood from Aurora as best they could without changing her clothing.

Nolan didn't thank them, though he seemed content with the response.

Putting in the stitches seemed to take an inordinately long time, and the initial shot of painkillers wore off. The doctors spoke between themselves and gave her a shot of pain relief mixed with a mild sedative to finish the job.

She relaxed on the wide bed, the doctors' voices buzzing in the background, as they discussed her condition with Nolan.

At last, the door closed behind them. Nolan came to the bed and sat on the edge. He trailed his fingertips over the thick bandage on her cheek.

Aurora opened her eyes and smiled up at him.

He managed a strained smile in return. "I know you're not ready to make a permanent decision, but when you are, I want you to know I feel the same way about you."

That was enough to clear some of the fog in her head. Aurora wrapped a hand around Nolan's neck and urged him closer. He didn't fight the move, and in moments, they were engaged in another heated kiss.

His cock rose between them, taunting her with what she wanted.

She didn't ask. She didn't formally invite him. Aurora pulled up at her gown, trying to free her legs so she could straddle him or spread her legs further. *Or something. Anything to make what I want clear.*

Nolan rose and turned, keeping his mouth meshed with hers. In the next coherent moment, he was lodged deep inside her.

The itch of shifting tissues stole Aurora's breath.

Nolan didn't bother to immobilize her, as she was told males did. He stared at her, his eyes golden, his expression starkly serious. "Do you want to hurt me, Aurora?"

She shook her head, a solemn promise that she wanted

nothing of the sort. Instead, she raked her claws lightly down his body, leaving trails that would heal in minutes.

The move inflamed him, as she'd heard it would. One thrust became two...then three... His muscles tightened and released with each shift forward and backward, his cock blazing a trail within her.

Claiming me as his.

Her breathing went ragged, and she bowed up from the mattress, seeking more of him. Nolan grasped at her hips, positioning her for deeper thrusts.

The tightening inside her unraveled with a snap of sensation. Aurora screamed in the release of climax, and Nolan growled, his teeth sharpening.

He let loose a wave of heat into her that stole her breath and set off aftershocks. Nolan's howl of triumph echoed off the walls.

He didn't move again until his cock subsided, and she moaned a protest when Nolan slid free of her body.

"Shhh," he soothed her. "You need some rest."

* * * *

It was all Nolan could do to rein in the need to laugh aloud. He was nestled under the quilts with Aurora, both of them nude and her dress thrown haphazardly over the bedside chair, surely ruined by blood and dirt stains. The lady in question slept peacefully in his arms, full of his seed. It was everything he wanted.

Nearly. Nolan hadn't lied when he'd told Aurora he

had plans, but he was no longer certain those plans had to exclude her until he attained a position with her family.

Voices rose in the clinic entryway, and Nolan glared at the door. Why wasn't anyone stopping them from causing such a ruckus when it was clear Koukla needed to sleep?

It took a few moments for him to realize what they were saying.

"You don't understand, Marietta. She warned me. Koukla told me Darian meant her harm, and I ignored her. This is all my fault."

"Hush, child. It is Darian's fault and no one else's."

"But—"

"Hush!"

The bark of order surprised him. He knew the Alpha mates were attending to business in America, which meant they couldn't have arrived so quickly.

Who else would dare speak to Talia Trudale that way?

A whispered conversation followed, probably the doctors reporting to the women who'd just been arguing.

The door opened slowly, and Nolan forced his muscles not to tense. There was nothing wrong with what they were doing, whether they were enjoying each other's company or more.

Talia came around the door first, moving fast. She took one look at Nolan and went stock-still, her mouth agape.

Under other circumstances he might have laughed, but one considered his life carefully before laughing at the eldest child of the Alpha mates, female or not. Instead he smiled and motioned her in.

She looked nothing like Aurora, but he'd known that already. Talia had raven black hair that reached her backside and dark brown eyes. She was the perfect female complement to her twin brother.

Talia didn't question him. Instead, she came directly to Aurora's side of the bed and reached for her sister. She stopped short, working her lip between her teeth, seemingly in indecision.

"They gave her something to help her sleep," Nolan informed her in a whisper.

"I know, but I don't want to wake her."

"She's awake," Aurora grumbled.

Talia touched her uninjured cheek with a shaking hand. Tears dotted her lashes. "Oh, Koukla. I am so sorry. I should have listened."

"Please stop calling me baby." A wide yawn followed, and Aurora winced and hissed, probably at the pull of the stitches.

Before she could demand more pain relief for her younger sister, an older woman came into the room, trailed by two of the doctors. One of the doctors administered another shot, but Nolan focused on the servant who'd been with Koukla at Matriculation.

By the looks of her, she had seen more than a few generations of work with the royals. Her fur was silver, though he didn't doubt she could carry out her duties, even now.

She handed paperwork back to the doctors, then focused on the group on the bed. She tipped her head low in a practiced move, though it was unclear who she was bowing to.

Most likely Talia.

"Lord Nolan, I presume," she greeted him.

"I'm no Lord, grandmother wolf." Nolan wasn't certain he'd found the correct reverent address for her, but he'd tried. No one could fault him that.

She chuckled. "More like great-grandmother. And, I believe I have addressed you correctly, Lord Nolan. It was my understanding that you bested Darian in a challenge?"

"I...suppose, but I was only protecting Koukla from him." His cheeks heated at the truth of it.

I'm admitting what Aurora is to me.

Surprisingly, no one seemed upset by it.

The old wolf nodded. "Then you have proven yourself an alpha. It isn't unusual for a beta wolf to take his place as an alpha when the situation arises to spur him to motion. With your permission, I will have your belongings moved to Regina Hall." She said it as if there wasn't a question in the world that it would happen.

"I'm not sure I want to move. I like my friends at Paris Hall." It sounded lame, even to himself.

"You must," Talia decided. "You can spend more time with Koukla that way, and you'll be living right next to the gardens."

"*Stop* calling me baby." She was more vehement every time he heard her say it.

She did say she was sick of the name. But she doesn't complain when I use it.

"I'm not sure *some* of the alphas will welcome me with open arms." Nolan tried for a diplomatic response instead of an emotional one.

Talia let loose a very unladylike snort and rolled her eyes. "Just because my twin brother chose that adult-sized bratty toddler as his den brother — "

"Which has been remedied," a male voice spoke up from the doorway.

Tyler Trudale was impossible to mistake for anyone else. He wore his dark hair in a mane, not cropped short like most male wolves did. Moreover, he carried himself like the future leader he was.

He made his way to the bed, and proffered his hand. Nolan took it, stunned by the move.

"I've made a lot of mistakes, not the least of which was making Darian my den brother. They say hindsight is twenty-twenty, but I should have seen what he was sooner. I doubt my parents will allow him to stay here after the attack on the two of you, but I've already kicked him out of the suite." He shrugged. "It's yours, if you want it."

Nolan considered that. If Talia and her den sister were on the top floor and Tyler had the floor below... "No. It's not right."

Tyler cocked his head to one side. "Why?"

"Koukla isn't on Alpha level. I shouldn't be either."

Talia laughed shortly. "She will be. Something tells me you two are going to be spending a lot of time together."

Aurora smacked lightly at her sister's arm, her face going crimson at the insinuation.

"What? Do you think I can't smell it?"

Nolan shot a sideward glance at Tyler, but the young prince was smiling broadly.

The male in question started talking. "There is another advantage to you and Koukla—"

"Stop calling me Koukla!" she shouted at her brother.

Tyler motioned for her to calm down. When she did, he continued. "The advantage to you and...Aurora using the room is that our guards have established security already. There's no guesswork."

Nolan couldn't argue that. "It's up to Koukla," he deferred to her.

"I say we take the suite and make my brother and sister lose sleep."

Nolan considered that. "On one condition."

"I'm listening."

Was that disappointment in her voice? "Only *I* get to call you Koukla."

An smile pulled up the uninjured side of her face, and her eyes glittered. "I can live with that."

The End

Brenna Lyons

Alpha Son

WEREWOLF U III

Blurb

Tyler made a bad decision when he was a first year student. Now that his den brother has been dishonored, Tyler wants to make all the wrongs in his life right, not the least of which is claiming Julianna as his mate.

Alpha Son

WEREWOLF U III

Tyler stood at the corner of Kythera Hall, watching the group of girls laughing together.

Not quite, he admitted to himself. He wasn't watching the group. He was watching *her. Julianna.*

She dressed in a Bohemian style...ankle-length, flowing dresses made of linen, ramie, hemp, or double gauze. Her coppery-brown hair was long and loose, pulled back at the temples to a ponytail at the back to keep the strands out of her eyes. Still, waves escaped and framed her face.

She was tall for a female, nearly Tyler's height. Were they standing face-to-face, he would be able to look directly into her medium gray eyes.

I want to be that close to her. It's what he came here to do, and unless Julianna sent him away, he would have that wish.

* * * *

"Ladies," a male greeted them.

Julianna focused on the book in her lap. She had no interest in randy males sniffing for something appealing.

A gasp from one of her friends made her stiffen.

No. It can't be. Julianna raised her head slowly, panning her gaze up strong, male legs encased in tailored suit pants.

The shirt was undoubtedly a fine twill, and his arms were crossed over his broad chest.

His. No, Tyler's. She didn't question that she was correct. When their gazes met through the fall of his unruly hairstyle, Julianna wasn't surprised.

"Hello, Alpha Tyler." She tried to act unaffected, though his mere presence made her heart pound in excitement.

"Hello, Julianna." He smiled at her, though it wasn't reflected in his eyes.

Her friends shot uncomfortable looks at each other. When Tyler didn't continue speaking, they started mumbling excuses and taking their leave. Far too soon, they were alone together.

"You wanted to see me, Alpha Tyler?" she inquired, still trying to act unaffected.

"Call me Tyler. Please."

Not on your life. Julianna waited to see what he would say next. *Can't be worse than anything I've heard before.* At least she hoped not.

He sighed and rubbed a hand along his lower lip and jaw. "I was wrong."

She raised an eyebrow in surprise. "About?"

Tyler ground his teeth, but he nodded. "You're due a full apology. I know that. So...yes, what I said about you...about lowborn wolves in general... It was wrong. I was willful and arrogant and hurtful. I can't lead if I don't respect all wolves equally."

"I'm...stunned, to tell the truth." She was. "Thank you."

186

"Don't thank me. I'm trying to make right the things I've screwed up."

"Good start," she admitted. *Grudgingly.* She could almost grow to like this Alpha Tyler, though previous encounters with him still stung.

He stood there, seemingly waiting for something she couldn't name.

"Was there something else you wanted?"

"Yes. No. Sort of." He took a calming breath. "Not the right time. Do you mind if I talk to you later? Another time?"

Julianna tried to come to grips with this new, unsettling side of him. She'd never seen an Alpha so tongue tied. "Sure. You can talk to me another time." *But why?*

Tyler nodded and strolled away, more at ease than she'd ever seen him.

"So what was that all about?" Veronique asked, appearing from the distance as he disappeared the opposite direction.

"I have no idea." *But I may find out when he returns to talk to me again.*

"What did he say?" Vanessa asked. She was shadowing her twin, as usual.

"He apologized."

"Just like that?" they asked together.

"Just. Like. That."

* * * *

Four days later

Julianna slowed her steps, discomfited, though she couldn't put her finger on why she would be. Warmth at her back startled her. Before she could react, his scent reached her.

"Alpha Tyler."

His breath teased at her cheek. "I told you to call me Tyler, I believe."

She licked her lips, trying to calm her thundering heart. "Did you want something in particular?" *I will not call him Tyler.*

He inhaled deeply.

Taking in my scent. It aroused her. *This isn't smart. This is Alpha Tyler. He's not to be trusted.*

Julianna glanced around, relieved to see that no one else was in this section of garden. Then again, it was after nightfall.

"You." There was no hesitation in the reply.

Neither was there in hers. "So that's what the big apology scene was about." Her stomach ached at the truth of it.

I don't know the truth of it. Was he hoping his attraction to her was a fleeting thing, and he wanted to scratch the itch and toss her away? Or was he fully aware of what they were to each other, and he finally gave in and decided to accept his *fate*?

I'm not sure I'm willing to help him with either.

He turned her toward him, and Julianna braced herself

for his anger at being called out. It wasn't forthcoming. He shook his head, his color less than robust. His expression said she'd wounded him. It was almost enough to spur her to comforting him.

Almost.

"No. Not at all. You know I've apologized to more than you. I've... I won't say I've changed, so much as I've stopped letting the other alphas define my actions for me. Please believe me, I was never comfortable with acting that way."

"Then why did you?"

"I made a mistake."

She straightened her backpack and prepared to leave. "Yes. You did."

"More than one, but a few major ones. And I never knew how to fix them."

"You don't have to fix it. Consider yourself forgiven." Julianna nearly choked on the words, but she spit them out when she wanted to spit in his face. *No. I don't, and that's the worst of it.*

"I'm not, and we both know it."

She couldn't argue that. "A wolf never forgets." It was one of her father's favorite sayings.

He sighed. "I should never have chosen Darian as my den brother."

"Then why did you?"

"I don't know." For a moment, he looked lost and forlorn.

"I don't believe that." What caused this certainty was a

mystery, but Julianna didn't question it.

Tyler shifted his feet, looking not one milligram the Alpha he was. "I was awkward. I guess a lot of guys are at that age. He was...larger than life."

"That's one word for it," she muttered.

He winced, then nodded. "I know. He's unstable, but at the time, he seemed confident. He seemed like a leader. I wasn't those things, and I wanted to learn to be. I thought Darian could teach me."

"Those things come with time. There are no shortcuts." *Now I'm lecturing him? When did my life become so weird?*

"It took me a long time to learn that."

Something in his tone said there was more. "But—?"

"By then, I'd alienated everyone *but* Darian and a few others. Even my sisters considered me a lost cause."

"So why didn't you get rid of Darian then?"

He shrugged. "I don't know. I wanted to, but—"

"You couldn't figure out how to without looking foolish, so you waited until Darian did something unforgivable."

His throat bobbed. "Yeah. I guess that describes it well enough."

Again, he'd stunned her. It took a moment for Julianna to collect her wits.

"Why did you come here?" At the last moment, she reminded herself not to call him by name.

"For you." That time it was matter of fact and not a seduction.

"You think it's that simple?" The heat gathered in her

stomach, and Julianna felt the need to strike out at him. Her sight went red-tinged.

"No," he admitted. "I know it's not."

Julianna didn't know how to answer that, so she waited to see what he would say next.

"I want you. I've always wanted you. If you can't be with me after —" He rolled his hand in demonstration of a vague collection of reasons she might have. "— I understand. I won't hound you for it. I think I've squandered my right to pursue you."

He waited for a moment to see if she would form an answer. When she failed to, he nodded and turned away, making his way back to Regina Hall, his shoulders slumped.

Julianna watched him go, her mouth and throat dry. Tears stung at her eyes, and her emotions were in a flat spin.

Tyler was no end of surprises. She'd almost expected to see him cry. Or beg.

Would that I could trust him...

What? I would give him precisely what he wants? Not a chance.

* * * *

Three days later

Julianna reached for the doorknob, then pulled her hand back. *For the third time. Night Mother, when did I become so indecisive?*

The answer to that wasn't hard to come by. Anytime she considered the open-ended possibility Tyler had left her with, she became indecisive.

He hadn't said he wanted her as his mate.

Good thing. I am so not going there.

He'd just said he wanted her.

I want him too. She could admit that much without appearing weak. Tyler was a gorgeous male, and she'd weathered thirteen heats since she'd known what he was to her. *Thirteen heats, with him right across campus and unavailable to me.*

He's available now. And she was going into another heat. Julianna shied when she thought about that part.

I shouldn't. This is the answer. She considered that carefully, working her way through the possibilities.

If they weren't mates, any young she carried were her own, and—despite his status in the pack—Tyler would have no hold over them. If he later had heirs, her own son or sons could challenge for the position of heir, if they chose to. But the same would be true of any children he sired out of mating.

I could have children. After Tyler alienated her, Julianna had given up on the idea of children. She didn't want another male, and she certainly didn't want Tyler long-term.

But I can have him for this.

That decided, she grasped the doorknob and turned it. Each step she took was easier, and in no time at all, she was across campus and approaching Regina Hall.

Julianna rehearsed the lie that Tyler had invited her on the way. She'd never been an adept liar, and the idea of lying had her palms sweating.

She pasted on a smile and breezed into Regina Hall. The smile faded, and she looked around in disbelief. She'd expected to have to pass a guard or porter on her way to the stairway up to the Alpha levels, but the foyer was deserted.

As were the stairs. Halfway up, Julianna started getting nervous. There had to be guards somewhere. Why weren't they showing themselves? Why weren't they questioning her?

Am I going to crumble and cry...or wet myself when they finally show themselves?

Julianna smiled. Humor had always been her way of dealing with stress. She'd rather laugh than cry.

I did my share of both when Tyler broke my heart.

All too soon, she stood outside the door to his rooms. Julianna took several calming breaths, then knocked on his door.

With every heartbeat she stood there, more of her resolve evaporated. What if he wasn't here? That would explain why his guards didn't stop her. What if he was here with another woman?

Tears pooled in her eyes, and she blinked them away. Irritation that he could still make her cry pricked at her, and she turned to leave.

The door opened behind her, and Julianna turned to it, prepared to apologize to Tyler's servant for disturbing him.

Her breath caught in her throat at the sight of Tyler.

He stood in the doorway, dressed only in a loose-fitting pair of knit sleep pants. Tyler moved his mouth as if he meant to say something, but nothing emerged.

He's with someone else. Of course. He's a male. Why wouldn't he be? Julianna tried for a smile but failed. "I should go."

Her move to turn away short circuited when Tyler wrapped his arms around her and lifted her inside. He closed the door and pressed her to it, crowding her with his larger body.

"No. You really shouldn't. Not when you've come here to see me."

She managed a jerking nod, her body balking her simple commands to respond to him verbally.

"What did you come here for, Julianna?" There was something wistful in his tone. He wasn't taunting her.

The need to sate her rising heat drove her on. Julianna wrapped her hands around his head, sealing her lips to his.

Tyler didn't hesitate. In a matter of heartbeats, they were pressed to the door, his cock hard against her lower abdomen. He groaned into her mouth.

Julianna echoed him at the feeling of Tyler dragging her skirts up her body.

Yes. This is what I want. He's going to be everything I want. And no more.

Tyler grasped the meat of her ass in his hands, venting another groan. He pulled back abruptly. "No. I want better for you."

She raked her fingernails down his scalp to his back. "Here. Now." She demanded it, the need scorching at her nerves.

The sound of ripping clothing made her shiver. It wasn't her dress he was tearing, so it had to be his sleep pants.

He met her gaze, his expression fevered. "You want this?"

"Now." If he wasn't inside her soon, Julianna wouldn't guarantee her patient acceptance.

Tyler didn't test her resolve. He lifted her to spread her legs around him, then thrust deep inside her.

Julianna felt the shift coming over her, stronger than she'd thought it would be. Her senses sharpened, and her claws sprouted. She dug them into Tyler's back.

Far from fighting it, he moaned. He increased his pace, the door rattling from the onslaught.

She reveled in the mixed sensations. His scent tantalized her. The press of his skin against hers teased her with the solid reality of him. His cock worked its way through the rings of inner muscle, imprinting the memory of his length and girth on her senses.

Pleasure gave way to sparks of bliss. Julianna pitched her head back and howled, her senses whirling. Tyler joined her, jetting heat into her.

He parted her lips, enticing her into dizzying kisses. In a series of overlapping, seemingly random motions, Tyler carried her to what she assumed was his bed.

He broke off the kiss and stared down at her, his

expression a potent mix that paralyzed her.

The bird before the snake.

I may not be an alpha, but I'm hardly a helpless bird.

"Don't go."

He's pleading with me. I never thought Tyler would plead for anything.

"Julianna?"

Her heat forced an answer from her. "I'm not done with you yet."

* * * *

Tyler snapped awake, his senses muddled and his back aching. He turned toward the opposite side of the bed with a smile.

Empty.

He sat up, scanning the room.

There.

Julianna was across the room, dressing in the clothing they'd discarded the night before.

"Where are you going?"

"I have to get ready for class." It was rational.

I don't want rational. I want fire. I want the passion we indulged in half the night. She was in heat. Wouldn't she want that as well?

"I wish you wouldn't," he admitted.

She sighed. "I have tests to take, a lab—"

"Come back later?" Tyler tried not to show his nervousness, but he feared it slipped out.

Julianna stared at him, seemingly considering it. "Yes."

Before he could ask what time or suggest they have dinner together, she was gone, out the door and down the corridor at a run.

He dropped to his back on the bed, thanking the Night Mother for Julianna.

I have my mate. She's in heat. I will have children with her.

Tyler chuckled. Then he laughed...long and hard. Her scent settled in his lungs, causing his cock to rise in response. He groaned.

It's going to be a very long day. I should get a bath. He threw back the quilts and rose to accomplish the task.

As if taking that as his cue that he could begin his work day, Oalo bustled into the room and started stripping the bed.

Tyler bristled at the move. "Leave the pillows and pillowcases."

"Excuse me, sir?" He looked up from the bed in seeming confusion.

Tyler stared him down, unwilling to explain himself to his servant.

Oalo took a deep breath. He stood still, the linens in his hand. At last, he nodded. "As you wish."

Tyler turned toward the bath again.

"Perhaps I should send your regrets to the coach, since you will be missing practice today," Oalo suggested.

He stopped walking and turned back. "What are you talking about?" And why did Oalo annoy him so much today?

His servant sighed. He dropped the quilts on the bed and turned to face Tyler. "I presume you have seduced your mate."

Tyler didn't bother to correct him. Oalo didn't need to know Julianna came here and demanded what he'd offered. He crossed his arms over his chest and waited to see what was coming next.

"The female is fertile, and you wouldn't be that sloppy."

He nodded grimly.

"I also deduce that the two of you are not prepared to make this relationship public."

"Not yet," he admitted.

"The coach usually calls shirts and skins —"

"And I'm typically skin." *Damn, he's good.* "Thank you, Oalo." He started to turn away.

"If I may be so bold, Tyler?"

"Yes?"

"A servant has the ability to learn things."

Tyler peeked back at him, confused. "Things like what, Oalo?"

He smiled. "Things to help you in your quest, of course."

Tyler nodded, biting back a laugh. "Thank you, Oalo. That would be wonderful."

* * * *

Two days later

"And where have you been hiding?" Veronique asked.

Vanessa popped into the doorway beside her twin. "We stopped by last night, and you were nowhere to be found."

Julianna didn't look up from her work. "Just busy," she lied.

Veronique dropped into the chair beside her, looking completely unruffled in navy blue. Vanessa took the chair on the other side, wearing matching deep purple. Other than the colors they chose to wear, they were nearly identical girls, both dark-haired and with eyes that fluctuated between green and light brown.

"Ah...hem."

Julianna looked up at Veronique, then straightened with a sigh. "Yes?"

"Details?"

Vanessa leaned closer. "Spill."

"I...went on a date."

It wasn't entirely a lie. Tyler had made a show of providing her favorite foods, her favorite music, and a nightgown in her favorite color the night before. Whatever his means and whatever his reasons, he was treating her like a date.

As long as I get what I want, I don't care what his reasons are.

"Oh. My."

"Night Mother, you're serious?" Veronique overpowered her sister's voice.

Julianna nodded. Against her better judgment, she

smiled. Her nightly meetings with Tyler were quickly becoming an addiction.

Of course it is. I'm in heat.

"Is he your mate?" Veronique started the interrogation.

"Does he have to be?" Julianna countered.

Vanessa rolled her eyes. "It helps."

"Does it?" Since she'd never told them what Tyler was to her, she could tap dance around this subject all evening long, if she had to.

The twins stared at each other, seemingly — as it often did appear — trading information or conferring without words. Before they could question her further, Julianna started talking.

"There's more than one kind of mates in our world, you know."

They gaped at her.

"You aren't going to wait to find your actual mate?" Veronique asked, seemingly aghast that the notion.

"Why should I?" *I can have what I want without that complication.*

Vanessa shook her head violently. "What happens if you...you know, and then your actual mate shows up?"

"Unlikely." *Impossible. There is no future for us. Tyler made that more than clear long ago. He's always wanted me. I won't be an Alpha's possession.*

"Julianna?"

She looked up at Vanessa, her heart tripping at the concern in her friend's eyes.

"What will you do if you're wrong?"

Can my heart be broken any more than it already is? Julianna managed a brittle smile.

I should end this.

No. Just a few more days. A week at the most. I want young. I won't live my whole life without them.

* * * *

Two weeks later

Tyler moaned as Julianna shifted her hips, intensifying the sensation. She arched her back, her hair trailing over his thighs. When she levered her head forward, her fangs were extended.

Tyler shivered at the sight of them. *How many times have I seen them and hoped she intended to use them?*

Too many.

As if she heard him, Julianna came down over him, her breath warming his throat. But she didn't bite down.

He bit back a half dozen curses, trying to avoid showing his frustration with a shift.

Her teeth scraped lightly at his throat; she retreated abruptly.

"Do it," Tyler begged. "Please. Please do it."

Julianna went still, no longer riding them both toward release. She backed away from him, her eyes wide, shaking her head.

"What is it?" What would cause that look of disbelief?

She pushed off of him and rushed to her clothing. Her hands shaking, Julianna scooped them off the foot of the bed.

"Julianna?" Tyler came to his feet, his heart racing.

She dragged her dress on, then turned to face him, her hair still trapped beneath the back. "What is this, Tyler?"

He stroked his hands up and down her upper arms. "What is what?"

"Why am I here? Why do you want me here?"

Her confusion skewered him. "Don't you know?"

"You said you wanted me. You've had me."

There was something left unsaid, but he couldn't guess what it was. "I meant as my mate, Julianna."

She closed her eyes, weaving on her feet. Tyler moved to lift her into his arms, but she pushed him away. In the next moment, she was sprinting for the door, her shoes left behind on the floor.

"Julianna!"

The door opened, then slammed shut behind her.

She left me. She'd left him standing—naked and erect—next to the bed they'd just shared.

And I'm still not sure why.

The only thing he was sure about was that she needed time. Chasing her right now would be a very bad choice.

* * * *

Julianna thanked the Night Mother that no one observed her wild dash across campus. How she would explain her disheveled appearance and the tears rolling down her cheeks was anyone's guess.

I certainly don't know what I would say.

She wasn't sure she would come out with anything but a blubbering mess of half-formed phrases.

When the door to her room was closed behind her, Julianna sank to the floor, venting sobs into her hands.

I thought it couldn't hurt worse. Why did I let it go on this long? Why did I let myself continue to be sucked in?

Some traitor part of her heart rejoiced that he wanted her as his mate. Squelching it was difficult.

I have to.

Why? He wants me as his mate! I can have everything I want.

No. I can't. But Julianna could no longer remember the reasons why she couldn't just accept Tyler as her mate.

She dragged herself up, then lurched her way to the bed. Curled up on the mattress, Julianna tried to decide what to do next.

He'll either give up or chase me. If he gives up, I should let him go.

What if he chases me?

That wasn't as simple.

I guess I'll find out if it happens.

* * * *

Two days later

Tyler looked up at the knock on his door. He didn't answer. He'd told Oalo he didn't want visitors. How someone even made it to his door was beyond him.

It's probably one of my sisters.

All the more reason not to answer.

The knock repeated, a harder knock.

Definitely not one of my sisters. Not that it mattered. There was only one person whose presence he would welcome, and it seemed she wasn't coming back.

Why? What did I do to push her away?

"Damn it, Tyler. Are you going to keep sulking all day?"

Nolan. He considered inviting his brother-in-law in, then dismissed that idea.

The door opened, and Nolan strolled across the room. He stopped in the doorway to the bedroom, crossing his arms over his chest. At last, he cleared his throat, hinting at an explanation Tyler didn't want to give.

Tyler reached for the quilt; he didn't bother to cover himself. Instead, he let his hand drop to the mattress with a sigh.

Nolan didn't address him.

"Why are you here?" Tyler asked.

"Seems to me you made me your den brother. That comes with certain expectations."

He curled his lip to show one fang. "Expectations. Responsibilities. I'm starting to loathe the whole thing."

"Okay. As your brother-in-law and your friend, I'm here to kick some sense into you." He offered a fang-heavy smile.

"Don't push it."

Nolan ambled across the room. "So what went wrong

with her?"

"With who?"

His bark of laughter made Tyler want to attack.

Who am I kidding? I'm not going to move.

"Come on, Tyler. The walls aren't completely sound-proofed. For the last few weeks, you've been banging—"

Tyler launched off the bed with a growl, shifting mid-leap. He landed...where Nolan had been a moment before.

"Oh, that hurts," Nolan taunted him.

Tyler leapt for him again. The results were just as disastrous as the last time.

He's making a fool of me. Tyler growled, his hackles coming up in warning.

Nolan laughed at him. "If that's the way you feel, why did you let her leave?"

That took the fight out of Tyler. He collapsed to the rug, folding his ears.

Maybe that's the answer. Maybe I should stay in this form for the rest of my life. Sebastian can lead instead.

Nolan's smile disappeared. "Wasn't it you and your sisters who told me an Alpha always get what he wants?"

He snuffed and turned his head away.

"It's your choice. When I was angry and walked away, Koukla came after me. It just seems to me that females do what they expect you to do for them."

Before Tyler could consider that, Nolan left him alone to sink or swim.

* * * *

A feminine scream echoed down the corridor. Julianna ignored it. Chances were, it was some sort of prank. Some young wolves got off on pranks.

The last thing Julianna needed was to be exposed to anyone else's frivolity, so she curled onto her side and tried to ignore it. Any moment, she would either hear raucous laughter or sounds of annoyance.

"What do you think you're doing here?"

The challenge brought Julianna to sitting. Whatever was going on, it wasn't a prank.

The door to her room opened, and she tensed to attack whoever was coming through it. It was Tyler, and he looked entirely pissed off.

"Julianna?"

She didn't have to look at the person standing behind Tyler to know it was Vanessa. Julianna vaguely wondered where her twin was.

She's asking if I want her to call the guards. "It's okay."

"Close the door behind you," Tyler ordered.

Vanessa did so.

"And go away," he added.

The whisper of Vanessa's footsteps made Julianna's heart pound. She was alone with him.

His expression eased, but his stance didn't. "How are you?"

The words to answer stuck in her throat. She nodded, instead.

"I know the feeling."

When she didn't answer, he walked toward the bed with the same determination he'd used to come through the door.

And probably up the corridor. Across campus. Down from his suite of rooms...

To her surprise, he settled lightly on the edge of the mattress and stared at her.

"Why are you here, Tyler?"

He sighed. "A very smart wolf reminded me of a few things."

"And what would they be?"

"The first one is that females expect us to follow when they run."

Julianna wanted to deny it, but she couldn't. How many hours had she dreamed of him demanding what she'd run away from?

I never knew what I would answer. She swallowed hard at the fact that she would have to decide soon. *In moments.*

Tyler's hand cupping her cheek shocked her back to the present. He smiled slightly, and her stomach did flip-flops.

"Why did you run?"

Explaining it was harder than Julianna thought it would be. *Why? It seemed so clear to me when I ran.*

"Julianna?"

"I didn't think there was a future for us."

"Why?" he pressed.

"You said..."

Tyler turned her head to meet her gaze directly.

That freed up her tongue. "You said you couldn't

imagine spending your life with one of my kind."

He winced. "I told you I was wrong about that. I was...insecure, trying to learn to be a confident Alpha. I made the wrong choices and said the wrong things. I think I knew it then. My words weren't intended to hurt you. They were intended to hurt me."

Her heart skipped in joy. Julianna tried not to show it. "That doesn't make it right."

He eased his hand away from her. "Are you saying you can't forgive me?"

"No. I'm not sure what I'm saying." Admitting that galled her.

"I understand that too." Tyler paused for a moment. "What did you think was happening between us? All that time I was trying to make my sincerity clear to you, but I failed."

Julianna swallowed down a lump in her throat. "You couldn't imagine spending your life with me, but you wanted me."

He groaned. "After everything we've shared, you still believed that about me?"

"I didn't want to. The only reason I stayed so long was that... Well, I didn't want it to end, and I hoped you didn't."

"Then why did you run?" He seemed genuinely perplexed by it.

"It was so sudden." Julianna blinked back tears she couldn't account for. "I don't know," she admitted.

Haven't I spent the last two days trying to figure out why I ran? And why I didn't go back?

"I can be patient if you can."

"You mean... We go on as we have been and let it come naturally?" That sounded a lot less frightening.

His smile came naturally that time. "That's precisely what I mean."

The answer to that came readily to mind. "I think we should."

His eyes shifted, and his fangs came down. "That's good."

It wasn't a threat, but Julianna couldn't guess what it was. "I hope so."

He leaned toward her, his arousal rising, based on his scent. "Maybe I should tell you the other thing I was reminded of."

Her nipples peaked, and her body came to life for him. "Maybe you should."

Tyler came down over her, and Julianna sank to the pillows beneath him. His lips closed on hers. The kiss heated, and Tyler unfastened his trousers. He pushed them away.

Taking his lead, Julianna pulled up at her dress, urging him on. Tyler thrust inside her, and they parted long enough to voice their pleasure.

Then he parted her lips again. Tyler started moving, and Julianna wrapped her legs around him, drawing him closer.

The time apart made their joining all the more potent. In a matter of minutes, she was lost in climax, his seed coursing into her, waking her nerves with memories of how well they meshed sexually.

Julianna screamed in pleasure, and Tyler howled in triumph.

In the quiet moments afterward, Tyler chuckled darkly.

"What is it?" she asked.

"The other thing I was reminded of."

She stared at him, confused.

Tyler pushed deeper inside her. "An Alpha always gets what he wants."

"Only if I agree," she countered stubbornly.

One eyebrow went up in challenge. "Are you telling me to leave?"

"No." *If I decide to do that, it won't be today.*

* * * *

Julianna dragged the brush through her hair, glancing toward the clock. She was running late. Her maestros had excused her absence over the last two days, but she highly doubted they would excuse her being late on her first day back.

Tyler came out of the bathroom, tucking his shirt. "I'll have just enough time to run to my rooms and dress in fresh clothes before class."

She laughed. "You can't possibly make it to class on time."

"Oh, I'll miss the first few minutes." He shrugged. "Maestros don't begrudge Alphas being a little late on occasion."

"Lucky you." He was. She was somewhat envious of the leeway he had.

Tyler snuggled up behind her, his cock hard. "It could be lucky you, as well. Just say the word."

She was sorely tempted, but Julianna had already said she would be back at class today. Instead, she peeled his arm away from her waist and stepped forward. "We have places to be."

"You didn't say 'no'." There was a smug note in that.

Julianna laughed. "I didn't say 'no'. I *am* saying 'not now'."

He sighed. "Fair enough. Well then... Dinner at Regina Hall? Or would you rather go out somewhere?"

"Ohhhh... Dinner out? I will take you up on that." It would be yet another first step for them.

"Good. I'll pick you up at seven." He rounded her and laid a kiss on her lips. "Until then." His smile lit his eyes.

Julianna couldn't help herself. She wanted him. She sealed her lips to his.

Tyler didn't argue her choice. The kiss deepened, and he started to lift her onto the bureau.

I'm not an Alpha yet. Julianna extricated herself from his embrace slowly, feathering her lips across his.

He reached for her again.

"Not now. We have classes."

Tyler nodded. "You're right. Until tonight." He placed a kiss on her cheek and loped away.

Julianna watched him go, torn. She'd secretly hoped he might seduce her anyway.

No time now. I have to go to class.

That firmly in mind, though the kiss continued to niggle at the edges of her attention, Julianna scooped up her backpack and raced out of the dorm and toward the psychology department.

She made it with minutes to spare. Julianna dropped into her usual seat, to the right of Veronique and Vanessa. She pulled out her books and tried to appear unaffected by Tyler.

"Ah..hem," Veronique annunciated.

Julianna gritted her teeth, then looked up and managed a smile for them.

"And?" Vanessa prompted her.

She motioned for them to be more specific.

Veronique rolled her eyes. "I take it he's your mate?" she prompted in a whisper.

Julianna bit her lower lip for a moment. "Yes," she admitted. "He is."

"Hooooly Night Mother," Vanessa breathed. "What now?"

"What do you mean?" They couldn't have missed the sounds coming from her room last night.

"Well..." Veronique leaned closer to her. "Are you going to give the other guy the heave ho?"

Julianna's face flamed in embarrassment.

It only took the other two a few heartbeats to catch up.

"Oh. My. Are you serious?"

"Wow," Vanessa overpowered her.

"Yes and yes." Julianna smiled at the memories. If there

was one thing Tyler was, it was 'wow' in bed.

"Ah, Ms. Garson," Maestro Evanston spoke up from the front of the room. "So nice of you to join us."

Julianna winced at the snub.

"Perhaps you would be kind enough to start our discussion of Jungian archetypes?"

She straightened in her seat and called the previous class's readings to mind. "Certainly, sir."

* * * *

Tyler shot a warning glare at Oalo. His servant's hovering was really starting to get on his nerves.

The male in question backed off to a respectable distance. "My apologies. I just want everything to be perfect for you."

He smiled. "It will be." Whatever minor details Tyler might have forgotten, Oalo surely wouldn't.

"Should I call the car around?"

"No. Have the driver meet me at Kythera Hall in fifteen minutes."

"As you wish, sir."

Tyler buttoned his suit jacket and made his way out of Regina Hall. Halfway through the foyer, he realized people had stopped to stare at him.

All speculating on whether or not I've found my mate. He bit back a chuckle. There wouldn't be any question in the days to come.

He was at Kythera Hall five minutes early. Julianna

was already outside waiting for him.

With a crowd milling around behind her. Tyler recognized some of them from the study session he'd interrupted. Others, he'd seen around campus. Some were strangers to him.

Tyler ignored them and focused on Julianna. She was dressed in a floor-length black sheath dress with a slit to mid-thigh on one side, and her hair was loose around her face.

She smiled and held her hand out to him. Tyler took it and pressed a kiss to her lips.

"You smell divine," he complimented her.

Julianna moved closer. "Just smell?" she teased.

"Look. Feel."

"Good."

The car pulled up, and she gaped at it.

Tyler opened the door for her, and Julianna glided to his side. He helped her in, offered a wave to their audience, then joined her inside.

Alex—their driver—closed the door behind them.

She seemed preoccupied as they drove away.

"Julianna?" he prompted her. *Have I blown it already?*

"It will be all over campus by morning." Her voice was falsely cheerful.

"Is that a problem?" His stomach wriggled in fear. If it was, she might back out.

"Not really." Julianna trailed her fingertips up his cock, bringing it to readiness. "I suggest a light dinner."

"And after that?" He hoped he was reading her

intentions correctly.

"I've never had sex in a limo before."

"Alex!"

"Yes, sir. We will arrive in fifteen minutes. I will call ahead."

He smiled. *Whatever we're paying Alex, I'm going to give him a raise.*

* * * *

Two weeks later

Tyler seated himself inside her, taking her from behind in the traditional manner, stoking the flames in her blood.

Ever since the limo, she'd been insatiable for him. Every evening started with dinner: sometimes in his rooms, sometimes in the dining hall at one of their dorms, and sometimes at a restaurant. Every night ended with them in one of their beds.

Tonight is mine.

Tyler's servant—Oalo—had stocked clothing and toiletries for her in Tyler's suite, duplicates of what was in her rooms. She didn't ask how he learned her favorites. She supposed Alphas had their ways.

Or perhaps Tyler saw what she liked and told him.

He'd also delivered some of Tyler's belongings to her rooms, making sure neither of them would be late to class because of the need to return to their own rooms to dress.

The male in question stroked his finger over her clit, forcing a gasp from her. Julianna thrust her hips back into the cradle of his.

Her fangs sprouted, and her mouth watered. She was starving for him. Literally. The need to taste his blood was maddening.

Julianna reared back; Tyler tried to push her down, and she turned on him with a growl. Before he could react, she was astride him, easing down his length.

She bit into his shoulder, sucking greedily at the hot cinnamon essence coursing down her throat. The climax that washed over her sent hard tremors rattling through her body.

It's not enough. More. I need more of him.

Julianna pushed herself down on his length. Harder. Faster. Tyler screamed in pleasure. The sound urged her on.

He pushed at her head.

Not away. Just to the side. Julianna obliged him, releasing him long enough to move, then latching on again.

In the next instant, his fangs were sinking into her throat. Tyler did it gently, as if he was afraid to harm her while laying his mark.

His come flowed into her, and he pulled his head back, gasping in the force of his climax.

Julianna wasn't finished yet. She thrust and rocked against him, all the time drinking his blood.

"You're going to kill me," he breathed.

She was sure he was exaggerating, so she didn't ease off. His wound started to heal over, and she bit down again, reopening it.

"Night Mother, this is good."

He climaxed again, setting off a warm, more soothing release of tension in her.

Her mind cleared, and Julianna found herself horrified at what she was doing. *This is wrong. I'm taking too much from him.* Though she still craved his taste, she backed away, looking up at him guiltily.

"I'm sorry. I don't know what—"

"Are you pregnant, Julianna?"

His question caught her by surprise. She hadn't expected him to make such an assumption.

It's the hunger. Pregnant females often require blood, and I'm craving it.

But how to answer him. "I'm not sure yet. I believe I am."

"The doctors will be able to confirm it in the morning." He inhaled her scent, his eyes closing in apparent bliss. "I am certain you are."

Before she could answer, Tyler guided her face to the spot she'd marked. His blood inflamed her senses.

"Drink. I have enough for all of us."

The offer was touching. Moreover, it was what she needed to hear.

Julianna bit down, but she restrained herself to a gentler suckling. Tyler's sounds of pleasure drove her on. Time lost all meaning.

At last, sleep pulled her down. Julianna went from sucking to licking. The blood slowed and stopped, and she laid her head against his chest. The taste of him echoed in her mouth, and she slipped into the darkness.

* * * *

Tyler awoke from a night of sweet dreams. He looked down at Julianna, biting back a chuckle at the lightness in his heart. His shoulder ached, but he'd welcome night after night of the same if their young needed the sustenance.

Oalo would surely balk at that idea, though.

Careful not to wake her, Tyler reached down; he slipped his cell phone from the back pocket of his jeans. He silenced it, then texted his servant with orders for the day.

Oalo answered a moment later. No surprise, everything would be taken care of to Tyler's wishes. Within the hour, a breakfast of blood rich meats would be delivered to them. The clinic would be prepared to do an initial prenatal exam. Both their belongings would be moved to from her rooms to their suite.

The only thing left for them to accomplish personally would be an announcement to their families. If he knew his parents well — *I know I do.* — her servant would arrive within the day.

He reclined to the bed next to her. Julianna turned toward him, settling against him with a sigh of contentment.

"What time is it?" she mumbled.

"Early," he lied. "You've got plenty of time."

She nodded, then dropped off to sleep again.

Perfect. Everything is perfect.

* * * *

"I really should have gone to class." Maestro Evanston was sure to be in a bad mood over her unexcused absence, especially so close to midterms.

"A pregnant female has leeway, especially a pregnant Alpha."

"I know." At the same time, it was understandable that Julianna hadn't embraced those conditions. She'd been an Alpha less than a day, and it wasn't common knowledge that she was yet. Though she'd suspected she carried for several weeks, it had never occurred to her to request accommodations for it.

As if reinforcing her sense of dread, Maestro Evanston appeared in her peripheral vision, making a beeline for her with all due haste. Julianna tensed, and Tyler turned his head to follow her line of sight.

He remained calm, seemingly waiting to see what the maestro would do next.

True to form, he moved to block her way. " Ms. Garson, I am certain you know the rules for absences."

Tyler cleared his throat, and the maestro stiffened a notch.

He panned his gaze up Tyler's body, but he didn't react with any sign of respect. "If you wouldn't mind, Alpha Tyler?" he requested formally.

"I do mind." Tyler looped a lock of hair around Julianna's ear, uncovering her healing mating mark. "If *you* wouldn't mind, my mate and I have an appointment at the clinic to evaluate our young."

That time, the maestro paled considerably. "Of course, Alphas." He focused on Julianna. "I will email your work to you, if that is your wish."

"Thank you. It is." Trying to appear unaffected by the change in him was difficult, but Julianna thought she managed it.

He started to turn away.

"Maestro," Tyler called out to stop him.

Julianna expected a veiled threat. *Or an overt one.*

Neither was the case. "Your classroom will be outfitted with a mother's care area within the day. Julianna will be returning with a nurser's servant."

Maestro Evanston nodded. "Of course. Do you require a specific position, Alpha Julianna?"

"To the far left of the row I usually sit in," she replied. *That way, Veronique and Vanessa will still be next to me.*

"I will make myself available to direct the installation. Good day, Alphas." With that, he turned and hurried away.

Julianna watched him, stunned by the reversal.

Tyler wrapped an arm around her waist and drew her toward the clinic. "You see?" he asked.

"I'm starting to." She smiled. "Isn't it a little early for a nurser's servant?"

"Not for an Alpha, and you are now an Alpha daughter."

Julianna laughed at that, giddy in disbelief.

"What are you thinking?"

"About an Alpha son."

"Any one in particular?" he teased.

"The only one who matters to me...at least right now."

He growled deep in his throat. "I like the sound of that."

"In that case, I think we should take the rest of the day off."

"Anything my mate wishes."

Brenna Lyons

Never Alone

WEREWOLF U IV

Blurb

Veronique and Vanessa have never been apart. Wolf twins are often close, but none closer than these two sisters. When outgoing Veronique finds her mate and shy Vanessa's is nowhere in sight, the pair concoct a wild plan to stay together.

Berne and Barden have never seen eye-to-eye. Being in the same room for more than a few hours usually leads to a fight. But no fight they've had before can compare to the one that's coming when Barden finds his mate.

Prologue

Sounds intruded on Vanessa's sleep. She forced her eyes open, though she wanted to stay curled with her twin, sharing heat in the den they'd appropriated.

We have to start moving soon. Though they were hungry and exhausted, chapped, injured, and — in Veronique's case — fevering, every minute wasted was a minute closer to death.

She shook her sister's shoulder.

The uninjured one, of course.

Vanessa buried the guilt at seeing her sister's bandaged arm deep down inside and called out softly to her twin. "Veronique? You have to get up."

She moaned.

"I think we'll reach the bottom this evening." Vanessa didn't promise that they would find shelter there. For all she knew, it would be a valley with only mountains in every direction. If so, she had no idea where they would go next.

Follow the water. There are always people near water.

But will they be people we're safe with?

Only the Night Mother knew that for certain.

Loose stones and frozen dirt shifted at the entrance to their den. Vanessa covered Veronique's mouth, just as her sister started to answer. Veronique's eyes went wide and wild, and her trembling became more pronounced.

The next shift of earth was closer, sending the slide down to the floor across from them.

They've found us. Vanessa had heard sounds of pursuit on and off for the last four days. She'd hoped they'd finally lost the hunters, but it seemed luck was — as usual, of late — not in their corner.

Vanessa drew her hand away from Veronique's face and turned slowly toward the opening. Snuffling sounds got louder, and she spied a snout peeking past her camouflage of limbs and leaves.

They're using dogs. A wry smile twisted her lips up, and she shifted. *I may be new to this and a female, but I am a wolf, with all the intelligence and prowess of a wolf. No dog is going to get the better of me, even in the half-shifted form females take.*

The dog pushed through the cover and started down the steep incline. Veronique covered her mouth with a shaking hand.

Vanessa didn't waste any time. She vaulted at him from below, aiming for his unprotected throat.

Another body hit her solidly, knocking Vanessa to her side. She scrambled up, only to be knocked back again. A huge paw settled on her chest, pinning her.

Veronique screamed.

"Easy, pup."

Vanessa startled and looked toward the opening.

A nude human male crouched where the dog had been before.

Not a dog. A wolf! I attacked one of our own.

Vanessa forced herself to shift back, panting under the

pressure exerted by the wolf pinning her to the ground.

Veronique sobbed, then started coughing harshly.

"Let her up, Brand," the one in human form ordered.

The wolf backed away, grumbling warnings she only half understood in human form.

The other helped her to sitting and started checking her for injuries.

"Veronique needs help," she interrupted him, pointing at her sister to emphasize the point.

He nodded. "Brand, check the other pup. Then call in our men. We need to get them off this mountain before the next storm rolls in."

He didn't bother to shift. One moment, he was snuffling at Veronique, then he was climbing the incline, reporting back to his alpha in a myriad of vocalizations. Once he was outside, he let out a series of howls.

A call to gather and hunt.

Vanessa gasped. "No. The hunters."

Veronique shot them a panicked look.

The one still with them snorted. "We took care of them a week ago." His fangs peeked past his upper lip, a sign of his anger.

"But I heard—"

In the distance, she heard answering howls. *No, others spreading the call.*

"Probably us searching for you."

Her cheeks heated in embarrassment. All this time, help had been a shout away, and they never knew it.

"We found the bag you discarded. That's when we

knew you were close."

The dirty clothing. We couldn't see any reason to carry it. "We tried to hide it, but I suppose you could smell it."

"Yes. We did. That gave us hope we'd almost given up on."

He unbuckled a pack from his shoulders and started pulling things out of it. He handed each of them a small canteen of water. Then he went to work, putting together a travois.

Vanessa gorged herself on the comfort she'd come to respect highly. Every time they drank, it had been a hard decision to lose body heat gathering water from the stream for their use.

Veronique finished hers, then curled herself into a ball and settled down to sleep again.

"We need a second," he noted, seemingly frustrated. "I hope one of the close teams has one."

Vanessa did a visual assessment of the wide cot. "We won't need a second."

"You've done well, Vanessa, but we need to move quickly. Much more quickly than you can, in your present condition. Another storm is rolling in."

"No. I meant... It's wide enough for us to ride together. Unless that would be too heavy for you." *Please say it's not.* If they were on separate cots, they could be separated from each other, and that was intolerable.

He scanned his gaze up and down the travois, then nodded. "Let's get you both on board."

Before Vanessa could move toward her twin, he'd

crossed the den and cradled Veronique gently to his chest. He placed her twin carefully on the travois, then put out his hand to help Vanessa on as well. Once they were snuggled together, he wrapped blankets around them and then fastened the netting that would hold them in place.

The blankets were heated, probably by battery-operated systems. Vanessa fought to keep her eyes open, but the warmth was hypnotic.

"Brand! Clothing."

The wolf leapt into the den again and shifted to his human form. He pulled off his pack and started splitting the contents between himself and the other. In short order, they were dressed for winter travel.

The two wolves lifted the travois out of the den and set off downhill at a trot, each holding to a strap. The gentle bouncing put Vanessa back to sleep.

When she woke again, two more wolves had joined them. They passed information back and forth, without slowing.

Snow started falling, and the wind picked up and turned bitter and biting.

The storm they said was coming. She turned her face to the heat radiating from the blankets.

More wolves joined them. And more. By the time they reached the line of vehicles, they had well over a dozen wolves surrounding them, and the falling snow was thick and wet, heavy snow that would impede travel when it stuck.

A stream of wolves exited the largest vehicle, a touring

bus. A female raced toward them and threw herself into the arms of the one who'd brought the travois.

"I'm glad you're back safe."

He pressed a kiss to her lips. "I'm just fine. The pups will need a doctor and hot food before we deliver them to their grandmother, though."

"Benjamin," she roared.

A tall male came running. "Yes, Alpha Samara?"

Vanessa swallowed hard, her head spinning. *He kissed her. I attacked one of the Alpha males. Dear Goddess, what did I do?*

A hand cupped her cheek, and Vanessa looked up into the doctor's face.

"Inside. On the beds," he ordered.

Vanessa's breathing came in ragged gasps, and darkness embraced her before she could voice her opposition to being separated from her sister.

Chapter One

Eleven years later

Vanessa took a peek over her shoulder as the limo pulled up in front of Regina Hall. It wasn't the royal limo, and most of the other residents had cleared out for the holidays, so chances were it was the limo they'd been waiting for.

Please let him have a brother. Night Mother, I beg of you.

The back door opened, and an older male stepped out, a huge male who dwarfed most she'd met in her life. He hadn't waited for the driver, a sure sign of an alpha on the move. His back to her, he offered his hand to aid a petite, red-haired female out after him. One look at her cinched the determination.

Berne's parents. Though her hair color didn't match her son, it was impossible to miss the similarity in their features.

A gangly, young female emerged next. A pre-adolescent male followed close on her heels.

The driver shut the door behind them and withdrew with a tip of his head. The sound of the door slamming home seemed to resonate around her.

Sealing my fate.

"Well, shit." Veronique huffed, clearly irked.

It's not ideal for me either. Her sister knew that, so it was hardly worth the breath to say it.

Veronique fidgeted, a sure sign that she was very upset. "If you don't feel you can go through with this—"

"I can." *She's suffered twelve heats, waiting for me to find a mate. Or for me to be comfortable with the idea of being alone.* "It's not right to make you wait longer."

Her sister turned to face Vanessa, seemingly pained. "Maybe I could explain it. Insist on you coming with me. You could meet males through Berne's connections. In the meantime, we would be together."

Tears stung at Vanessa's eyes, and she blinked them away. "No family would go for that." *No mate would.* A lump formed in her throat. *Veronique needs Berne.*

But I need her.

Or someone. A mate. Where is he?

It was the truth and they both knew it. This plan—*this madness*—was the only solution available to them.

Veronique reached out and pulled Vanessa into her arms. "If this doesn't work—"

"It will." *For Veronique's sake, I have to* make it *work.* She pulled away and managed a stiff smile. "When he gets home from dinner with his family?"

Rumor had it that Berne had a few loose ends to tie up on campus before he left for the holiday. Vanessa only hoped he hadn't changed plans.

Her sister shot a wistful look toward Berne, and Vanessa followed her lead.

He and his family were sharing hugs and kisses. Laughter filled the air.

I remember that. Family get-togethers full of laughter and love. All of that was gone now. Veronique was all Vanessa had left. *Veronique and an empty house.*

"After dinner," Veronique confirmed.

Vanessa managed not to cringe, by the grace of the Night Mother alone.

That settled, they stood and — arm-in-arm — made their way back to their dorm.

* * * *

Berne raised his head, taking in Veronique's scent on the crisp winter wind.

She's in heat again.

He scanned his gaze upwind, picking her out in the distance.

Walking with her twin sister. Always with her twin. Never with me.

A growl built in his throat, and Berne swallowed it down.

Another fucking week of blue balls, while I know she's in heat, and she's not going to offer. Again.

The two times he'd tried to approach her, she'd played it off and disappeared with her damned twin. He wondered — not for the first time — why she wouldn't give him the time of day, even when she was fertile and should want to share his bed.

Maybe the problem is twins. Mine is a pain in the ass. Maybe hers is the fly in the ointment as well.

"Is there a problem, Berne?" his mother asked.

He smiled, and it felt natural, but his mother would probably see right through it. "No. I'm fine," he lied.

* * * *

Veronique smoothed her coat, her nerves on edge. *If this doesn't work, how can I convince Berne?*

Stop. She took a calming breath. *Assume it's going to work. Figure out what to do next, if – and only if – it fails.*

"If you don't want to..." Vanessa offered.

Veronique shot her a strained smile, then knocked on the door.

Berne answered it without delay. He stood there, dressed in a loose pair of trousers and a button-down shirt, half the fasteners undone. He gaped at them, seemingly at a loss for words.

Veronique swallowed to wet her throat. "May we come in?"

"Sure." He didn't take his eyes off of her.

She smiled at that. *He only has eyes for me.* That sobered her a bit. *He* has *to want Vanessa as well.*

Berne backed away, letting them round his body. He closed the door behind them.

Veronique glanced around at his room. It was a mess, despite the fact that he surely had a servant to clean it for him. *Maybe he prefers the mess.* A smile tugged at her lips. *I guess that's the one thing we'll have to change.*

In those few seconds, he recovered his wits. "You wanted to talk to me?"

Her heat driving her, Veronique sauntered to him on spike heels. "Oh, we want something, but talking is the least of it."

She untied the belt on her coat and let it slide open to reveal the royal blue, lace teddy and matching silk robe beneath. Beside her, Vanessa did the same, revealing her matching pink set.

He licked his lips, his cock rising, outlined in pants she was sure he was glad weren't snug to his body.

I wish they were. I'd love a better look at that beauty.

"Really?"

Veronique reached out and unbuttoned the top button still fastened on his shirt. "Yes. The question is... Are you game?"

His eyes narrowed, and he looked from Veronique to Vanessa and back again. "Both of you?"

Vanessa picked that moment to speak up. "We're a matched set, Berne."

Nearly in unison, they removed their coats and tossed them over the plush chair in the corner of the room behind him.

Berne scanned his gaze up and down their bodies. He deliberated so long and intensely, Veronique felt a bead of sweat work its way down her spine.

"Sure. Anything you want," he assured her.

What now? How do I proceed from here? Galling as it was, Veronique had to admit she hadn't thought they would get this far.

Berne had ideas of his own. He pulled Veronique flush

to his body and parted her lips in a searing kiss. Her knees shook, and her heart pounded in excitement.

Gods, but I should have done this years ago. She'd considered it. During more than one of her heats, Veronique had considered coming to Berne, pushing him down on the mattress, and impaling herself on—

He pulled away, leaving her reeling, leaning on him for support.

Berne wrapped a hand around the back of Vanessa's neck and pulled her into a kiss as well. Veronique swallowed down a shout of protest at the sight of it.

We offered this. It's our only chance of staying together. Vanessa was there for me when I needed her. It's my turn now.

Still, it hurt to see her sister in Berne's embrace. *My sister and my mate.*

Berne didn't kiss Vanessa as he had her. Their kiss was softer, almost tentative.

He broke off the kiss with a hum of appreciation. Again, Veronique felt a stab of jealousy.

"I think we should retire to the bedroom."

The liquid heat pooling inside her scorched her in her need. "Oh, yes."

Berne turned them, wrapped an arm around each, then led them into his bedroom. The queen-sized bed would be snug with three of them, but it would suffice.

More than suffice.

Veronique shot a smile at Vanessa. They'd discussed what they intended to do at this juncture long ago. They strutted ahead of Berne and draped themselves across his bed, side by side, offering themselves to him.

Vanessa slipped her robe off.

That wasn't part of the plan. The scars on Veronique's arm pulled tight. *I'm not removing mine. He'll want to know. I'm not ready to tell him. Not yet.*

Berne took a moment to strip off his shirt and drop it to the floor.

Veronique had seen him shirtless before, but the sight never ceased to enflame her senses.

She didn't have long to admire the view. In the next heartbeat, Berne was on the bed between them. He turned toward Veronique and kissed her. It was much more intense than their first kiss, and his hands made fiery trails up her body.

He pulled at the ties at her hips, uncovering her core. Veronique moaned in response, and her heartbeat thundered in her ears.

He's going to do it. He'll be inside me within a minute. Does he know I'm in heat? Surely he did. *Why else would he rush this way?*

As if Vanessa sensed it as well, she reached between them and started undoing Berne's belt, urging him into Veronique.

His cock sprang free, stroking her inner thigh. Veronique strained toward him, anticipating his slide into her. Savoring the thought.

Veronique squawked in fear, and the bed shifted. Veronique looked up, and Berne did the same.

Vanessa was draped over a man's shoulder...a very

angry man, who glared down at her.

Berne. But it couldn't be Berne. Veronique slanted a look at the man in bed with her, then back at the one holding her sister.

Brothers! Maybe twins.

"Veronique!"

The panic in Vanessa's tone cleared Veronique's mind and spurred her to motion. She slipped from Berne's side and reached for Vanessa.

Berne wrapped his arms around her and dragged Veronique to him, her back to his chest. She squirmed, trying to break his hold.

The male holding Vanessa backed off a step, baring his fangs in warning. A low rumble escaped his throat, and Veronique backed off slightly, terrified of the unknown but angry wolf.

"Veronique!"

He hesitated. "You're safe with me, little one." With that, he was gone—out of the bedroom, then out of the suite, the door slamming behind him.

"Vanessa," she breathed. He was taking her sister away from her.

Something in her snapped. *He can't. I can't let him.*

* * * *

Barden parked his car behind Regina Hall and turned off the engine. He looked up at the building and sighed.

Why am I bothering to do this?

It wasn't as if they had anything in common. Barden lived a neat and ordered life, while Berne was a slob. Barden was a composer, while Berne was an engineer. Only in their looks were they, in any way, similar.

Why am I doing this? Because he's my brother? My twin?

It wasn't as if Berne had ever gone out of his way to be brotherly with Barden. Though they were both alphas, Berne felt the need to prove himself the *more* alpha of the two, painfully more often than not. He'd snubbed Barden at every turn.

Does that mean I can't be the bigger man?

He sighed again. Succeed or fail, he would keep offering the olive branch.

Like the idiot I am.

Barden exited the car, closed it behind him, then made his way inside and up to Berne's rooms. He didn't bother knocking. Instead, he entered the unlocked room and made a beeline for the bedroom when he found the main room empty.

The sounds from inside stopped him cold with the door halfway open.

You've got to be kidding me. He's getting laid?

A feminine moan confirmed it.

Barden started to turn away, but an enticing scent caught his attention. He drew it in, filling his lungs and biting back a groan.

Realization made his heart skip.

My mate. He's not having sex with my mate.

Barden barged through the door, his eyes narrowing as

he took in the sight of Berne bracketed by two females in similar lingerie. His twin was fully engaged with one of them—the one in deep blue—while the one in pink was opening his pants.

It took a moment for Barden to separate the scents and identify the latter female as his mate.

Thank the Night Mother for that much.

Still, he's got my mate in bed with him! It was intolerable.

Barden stormed across the room and scooped her up, settling her over his shoulder. She grasped at his shirt, bunching it in her hand with a squawk of fear. He wanted to soothe her, but his fury was too high.

Berne and his playmate looked around slowly, seemingly only vaguely aware of the fact that the other female was gone.

Barden stared at the playmate, his eyes shifting in anger.

Twins. Berne was getting his rocks off with a set of twins. And after all the bitching he's done about being one.

"Veronique," his mate shrieked.

The female on the bed reached for her twin, and Berne dragged her into his embrace.

Barden backed off, showing his fangs. It was the only warning he would give his brother. Or her sister.

"Veronique!"

His mate's terror gave him pause. He wasn't being rational. *I'm abducting my own mate.*

I cannot allow her to stay with Berne. "You're safe with me, little one."

With that, he turned and made his way back to the main room. Almost as an afterthought, Barden grabbed up a long, feminine coat and tossed it over her. The last thing he wanted was other males seeing his mate half-dressed.

"No. You don't understand," the female with Berne argued.

The one in Barden's arms whimpered and tried to scramble off his shoulder. He clamped his hand down tight to hold her there and marched back toward his car, slamming the door behind him. He settled her in the passenger seat, his cock aching at the sight of her nearly nude.

She shoved her arms into the coat and tried to escape. Barden eased her into the seat, shushing her. He pulled the seatbelt around her body.

"You don't understand," she pleaded with him.

"Shhh. We need to talk. You're safe with me."

She didn't try to escape again. Barden buckled her in, closed the door, then circled the car and got in. He pulled out and headed for the house he'd borrowed from the Alphas, his emotions on a dangerous pendulum. As if his mate could sense that, she made herself as small a target on the furthest edge of the seat as she could.

I would never hurt you.

Berne? If I find he's been sleeping with my mate, I will gut him.

The need to know everything about her burned at him. "What is your name?"

"Vanessa." Her voice squeaked a little, and her throat

241

bobbed in what was probably swallowed tears.

"My name is Barden," he offered.

"You're... You're related to Berne, I guess."

"His twin."

She nodded, her eyes wide in seeming wonder.

It was so enticing, it was almost more than he could bear.

Outside, the snow started to fall.

"I have to go back, Barden. I have to see Veronique." Though her voice was calm, her hands trembled.

"I promise I'll take you back, but for now... We need to talk."

Vanessa nodded. "I would appreciate that. Thank you."

Chapter Two

The door slammed behind Barden, and Berne breathed a sigh of relief as Veronique went still in his arms.

For the first time in his life, Berne thanked the Night Mother for his twin's arrival. Whatever his reason, he'd taken Vanessa away, leaving Berne the luxury of spending time alone with Veronique.

He probably thinks it's unseemly to indulge in a ménage or something. Berne couldn't have cared less. He would have had the ménage if it meant having Veronique, but now he could focus all his attention on his mate.

My fertile mate. His cock ached to finish what they'd started, and he laid kisses along the line of her shoulder. *I could take her like this, from behind. She's fertile, and this is the traditional way to plant young.*

That thought in mind, he started to bend her at the waist, positioning her for it.

Veronique elbowed him in the ribs with a growl that sounded far too deep for her slight form. Confused, he released her, and she turned on him.

She'd shifted, and Berne admired her deep, brown coat and sharpened fangs.

It took a moment for him to realize the full import of her shifting. *That's a bad sign.* Veronique was angry with him. Furious. Or afraid.

No, she's not afraid. She wants to gut me. But why? What

have I done wrong?

"Bring her back."

His head spun. "What?"

"Make him bring her back." She annunciated each word, a clear warning.

"I can't."

She lunged for him, and Berne backpedaled, coming to his feet at the far side of the bed.

"Take me to her. Now."

He swallowed hard and motioned for a moment of peace. Berne pulled the mobile phone from his pants pocket and dialed his father's mobile. It went directly to voice mail.

Every muscle strung tight in frustration, Berne waited for the tone to leave a message. "I need to know where Barden is staying. Immediately. Kindly call me back as soon as you hear this message. Thank you." He hung up and placed the phone on the bedside table.

Veronique didn't relax. She stared at him, issuing a silent challenge.

"I don't know where Barden is staying. My parents will call back when they get the message."

She glared at him. "Call Barden's mobile."

"Even if he carried one, I wouldn't have the number. My brother and I don't see eye to eye."

Another growl escaped her lips.

"Vanessa is safe with him. Barden wouldn't hurt her. You have my word on that."

Veronique stepped off her side of the bed and made

her way to the main room, her ears and claws disappearing as she walked. Berne followed her, tucking his half-erect cock into his trousers as he went.

She picked up her coat, then swore fluently.

"What is it?"

"Your brother grabbed the wrong coat."

"So?" He tried not to sound peeved. *And failed,* he admitted to himself. Who cared which coat she wore? She and Vanessa were the same size, after all, and the coats, unlike most of their clothing, were identical in both color and style.

Veronique pulled it on with a roll of her eyes, fastening the belt a little too quickly and tightly. "*My* coat had the key to our room in it. Your brother has taken off with my sister *and* the key I need to get into my room."

"You don't have to leave," he suggested.

She gaped at him, as if he'd said something inconceivable.

Berne chanced a smile, his cock twitching at her proximity. "Vanessa is safe with my brother. I'll take you to her as soon as I find out where Barden is staying. There's no reason not to finish what we started." He let the invitation hang between them.

Veronique shifted again. In a single leap, she was face-to-face with him, her claws at his throat. "You. Let. Him. Take. My. Sister. From. Me."

Berne nodded solemnly. "Where will you go?"

"I'll find the residence head and have her unlock the door for me."

"Can I walk you? Just to make sure you arrive safely in your room?"

She deliberated on the offer. "No. Thank you, no."

He nodded, his heart sinking. "If you can't find the residence head, you know you're welcome here."

Veronique blinked. She turned away, seemingly rattled. "Take me with you to pick her up. Anytime. Day or night. I won't be sleeping anyway."

Not sleeping. Berne wished she would be 'not sleeping' with him. "Of course. As soon as I hear back from my parents."

She offered one look back at him, an enigmatic expression on her face. "Thank you, Berne."

"Anytime, Veronique. Anything." He meant it.

Veronique tipped her head and let herself out of his room, closing the door with a click.

Berne dropped to the desktop with a sigh, his body aching at the near miss with Veronique. "Will I ever have a chance with her?"

Hopefully. Maybe once she sees that Vanessa is in one piece.

* * * *

"Excuse me?" Vanessa dropped her fork to the plate with a clatter, her temper rising at the question he'd posed.

Barden raised an eyebrow, punctuating his demand for an answer without verbalizing it.

He's an alpha male. Of course he thinks he has the right to question it. "No. I did not have sex with your brother.

246

Okay?" Her appetite fled that quickly, and she cursed him for it silently.

"Why did you even agree to it?" Barden seemed frustrated by the idea that she had.

I didn't want to. He didn't need to know that. "It's...complicated." *And I don't know you. I'm not sure I want to explain my life to you.*

"Not too complicated to explain it to Berne." His anger was at the surface again. It seemed he was quick to anger.

Another reason I'm not sure I want to tell him. "We didn't explain it to Berne. Berne was getting what he wanted out of the deal, so he didn't ask any questions." She waved Barden off before he could protest. "My sister. I'm sure he couldn't have cared less when you took me away. Veronique is Berne's mate."

"Then why — ?"

"It's *complicated*."

He glared at her. Vanessa pretended not to notice. Mate or not, she wasn't sure she wanted Barden. Until she was, this was none of his business.

Barden visibly calmed himself. "I see."

He didn't, and that was fine with her. *For now.* Despite his mercurial temper, something told her he was worth offering herself to.

But his withdrawal made her stomach ache. Vanessa folded her napkin and set it on the table.

"Maybe you should take me back to my dorm room," she suggested.

Barden raised his head. He stared at her for a moment,

then looked toward the windows. "Not tonight. The storm is too wild."

Her heart stuttered at that. She and Veronique hadn't spent a night apart since they were five and Vanessa had to have her tonsils out. She tunneled her shaking hands into the coat pockets, gasping as her fingers closed on a room key.

No. No. No. "I have to go," she blurted out. Vanessa leapt from the chair and headed for the door. "I'll call a taxi...or call the school and have them send — "

His hand closed on her shoulder. "Dressed like that? You'll freeze. Your sister will survive a night without you."

But will I survive a night without her?

Vanessa tried to come up with a compelling reason to convince him that she had to leave. He couldn't lend her clothing; his would be much too large.

The key. "You grabbed Veronique's coat instead of mine. I have the key to our room. If I don't go back, she won't be able to get in." It was skirting the truth, and she knew it. Technically, Veronique could get the campus guards or the residence head to let her in.

Barden stared down at her. "Veronique is Berne's mate."

"So?" she inquired lamely.

"What makes you think she won't want to stay the night with him?"

There was no way to explain it without telling him the whole bloody story. *Literally.* "I know my sister." *Please let that be enough for him.*

It wasn't. "She'll get over it. I'm not going to risk you."

Vanessa tried again, but she couldn't come up with a compelling argument to change his mind. At a loss, she shifted from foot to foot and wrapped her arms around her chest.

Barden sighed. "Come finish dinner."

"I'm not hungry." That wasn't a lie. Vanessa was sure she was about to vomit on the floor.

"Then let me show you to the bedroom."

She drew away from him, shaking her head adamantly.

Barden sighed. "*You* will be using the bedroom. I will make due on the couch."

Her cheeks burned. After the way he found her, it was no wonder he didn't want to share a bed with her.

"There's no way you're going to let me leave tonight. Is there?"

"None," he confirmed.

"Then I guess I should."

He didn't touch her. Barden motioned with his hand, letting Vanessa lead the way down the corridor to a large bedroom. Once they were there, he didn't waste time.

"The bath is through here. There is a half bath I'll be using, so you needn't worry about me intruding on your privacy."

The bitter bite in his tone made her shiver in awareness of the strength of the wolf she'd yet to see.

Barden removed two items of clothing from a drawer. He set one the bed and headed for the still-open door with the other. "Just in case you want to sleep in something more comfortable."

He paused in the doorway, looking back at her as if waiting for something.

"Thank you, Barden." It came out a whisper.

One side of his lip curled in a smile. "Sleep well, Vanessa." With that, he closed the door behind him. His footsteps echoed back to her, growing fainter with each step.

"Sleep well?" She snorted. Vanessa wasn't certain she would be able to sleep at all.

The wild urge to call Julianna and have her arrange transport back to the dorms gripped her. The princess could surely find a way...

Her heart sank at the truth of the matter. Julianna was in transit to wherever Tyler's family was spending this holiday season. She could be on a plane or in a car. She could even have retired for the night early.

And she's bearing. There's no need to worry her needlessly. That wouldn't win her points with the Alphas, to be sure.

Vanessa sank to the edge of the mattress with a sigh. Like it or not, she was stuck here for the night.

At a loss for something better to do, she picked up the piece of clothing Barden had left for her. It was a thick, long-sleeved t-shirt. Vanessa didn't question that it would extend a fair length of her thighs, considering the difference in their heights.

Much more comfortable than this horrid teddy.

While their tastes in outer clothing matched well, their taste in lingerie did not. Veronique had wanted to play on the matched set novelty when approaching Berne, so Vanessa had agreed to wear the lace she found so uncomfortable.

I should just burn it. It was a tempting idea.

She took her time: stripping off the coat and the teddy, then pulling on the luxurious cotton shirt. There was something decadent in wearing nothing but Barden's shirt. Though one could see less of her body this way, the lack of fabric molded to her breasts and nether regions felt more daring.

Visions of Barden walking in sent her scampering onto the bed and burying herself beneath the blankets.

I suppose I'm not that *daring,* she conceded.

Vanessa examined the room in detail, calmed by the dark cherry furnishings and the deep blue and green accents. The house was large but cozy...and it was clean enough to run a white glove, she was sure.

Maybe I can sleep here, after all.

Chapter Three

Veronique laughed, and Vanessa joined her. In the rear view mirror, she could see their father's smile.

"We'll be there soon," he announced.

Gram's. Vanessa wriggled in her seat. They hadn't seen Gram for more than a year.

Not since mom's funeral. That cast a pall on her mood.

As if Veronique were thinking the same thing, she curled up on the seat next to Vanessa. The car fell into a brooding silence.

The dark mood took on a potent edge, and their father's scent changed.

Vanessa raised her head, breathing it deep into her lungs. Her heart pounded in response.

Fight. Father is prepared to fight.

He looked up at the rear view mirror over and over. The fur at the back of Vanessa's skull rose in warning. Veronique tensed, then started to shake.

A sharp crack of sound made all three of them duck. Vanessa looked up at the spider web cracks in the rear window in horror.

A rock would crack the windshield or a side window. That wasn't a rock. She wanted to ignore the obvious answer, but it stuck with her. *A bullet. Someone is shooting at us.*

A second struck, and the rear window shattered. Veronique screamed and dove for the floorboards.

Their father grunted. He pressed the accelerator down, and the car slipped to the right before it caught on the slick roads. Then it shot forward like a horse leaving the gate with the crack of a whip on its quarters.

Vanessa held to the door handle, turning to look out the window.

"Down!" Her father was growling more than he was talking.

It was a tone no young wolf ignored. Vanessa curled herself into a ball on the seat, holding to the edge as the car swung in tight curves.

From the floor, Veronique whimpered and cried out. Vanessa wanted to reach down and soothe her, but she couldn't risk letting go of the seat.

Then disaster struck. Vanessa squeezed her eyes shut as the skid gained steam. The seat bucked beneath her, then dropped away. She grasped for it and caught.

Veronique crashed into her, as the car rolled. Vanessa grabbed hold of her and held tight.

There was a bone-jarring thump from below, then one from above. Her shoulder slammed into something metal, and the picnic basket hit her shin before disappearing through the hole where the rear window once was. The sound of ripping fabric was eclipsed by the cacophony of crunching metal and breaking glass. Their duffel bags tumbled around them.

They landed in a heap on the seat, the car slamming to the incline on its wheels. The wild ride continued, the car heading down the snowy slope like a sled on the luge track.

They slowed and came to a stop, snow pouring through the windows. Vanessa tried to push herself to sitting, but she was stuck. She yanked at her hand, looking at it frantically.

Claws.

The life-threatening experience had forced her to a partial shift. She tried to disengage her claws from the shredded car seat, but they were trapped in the mangled material. She tried to reason her way out of it, to make her claws retract, but with her heart pounding and the icy wind whipping through the car, she couldn't do it.

Veronique moaned, bleeding from a cut on her forehead and another on her arm. Her eyes fluttered open, and she looked around, apparently dazed.

Voices came from far away, and Vanessa used her enhanced senses to gather information. They were human. With guns. Dogs. Chemicals that smelled dangerous.

The surge of adrenaline in her system gave her the strength to tear her hand from the seat. She reached for their father, hoping to rouse him.

His eyes were wide and focused on nothing. Vanessa didn't have to touch him to know he was dead. The scent of rot came quickly when a wolf was killed.

The sounds of the hunters approaching got louder. Vanessa grabbed their duffel bags and shoved Veronique through the downhill window.

Her sister yelped when she landed face-down in the snow. Vanessa vaulted after her and covered Veronique's mouth with her hand.

"Sh." She listened. "They're coming. Come on. We have to keep moving."

Veronique looked back toward the car. "Dad?"

"He's gone."

She nodded, swallowed hard, then took her duffel. They took off at a run, downhill and away from their pursuers.

Vanessa looked back, sighing in relief at the wind whipping away their footprints in the snow. If they were lucky, they might find somewhere to hide for the night. In the morning, they would have to continue the trek to Gram's house.

* * * *

Barden raised his head from the pillow, listening for the sound that had roused him from sleep to repeat. It took a moment for him to identify it.

Crying. Whining. Vanessa is in distress.

He didn't question what he should do. She was his mate, and she needed his help...or his comfort. Until he saw her, he couldn't know what she needed from him.

I will offer whatever it is.

He made his way down the corridor, paused at the door, then opened it with a sigh.

Vanessa was curled on the bed, whimpering in her sleep. She moved restlessly.

A bad dream?

Before he could decide what to do about it, she moved. In a heartbeat, Vanessa was in a crouch at the foot of the bed. Her claws were out, her mouth full of fangs, and her eyes and ears were shifted.

He stood still, ready to fight but not willing to harm her in a gut reaction. Barden marveled at her shifted form.

Has she had sex, or has she been endangered? He wasn't sure, but it wasn't the time to ask it.

Her growls tapered off. She shifted back slowly. At last, Vanessa crumpled to a heap on the mattress, her breathing labored.

Barden moved cautiously, trying not to startle her again. When he reached the bed, he eased down next to her and reached a hand out to stroke her back.

Vanessa didn't fight him. She didn't strike out. She lay there, shivering.

"We should get you under the blankets," he breathed. "You're cold."

She let him get her settled. Barden wrapped himself around her, and she turned toward him, burrowing her face in his chest.

"Tell me. Please." Barden didn't just *want* to know; he *needed* to.

At first, he was convinced she wasn't going to tell him. Then Vanessa started speaking.

"We were nine. Our father was taking us to our Gram's house." She paused for a long moment. "We didn't know, but there were hunters following us."

Barden pulled her closer, his heart thundering at the

mention of the curs.

"They started shooting into the car. My father tried to escape, but we rolled off the road and down the mountainside. He didn't survive the crash. We ran before the hunters could reach us. Into the storm." She shivered again, as if the cold was from her memories and not due to the current weather conditions.

Something sparked in the deep recesses of his mind. "I think I remember this. My father took part in the search."

She nodded.

"You were missing for a while. Many wolves thought you were dead."

"Eleven days," she confirmed.

The sensation of ice shards in his stomach made Barden's head spin. "At nine years old. In the wilderness." Her reaction when he entered the room resonated with him. "Was that when the two of you learned to shift?" *At nine? Dear Goddess!*

"Just me. Veronique hasn't had her first shift yet."

"So...you were your sister's protector." Was that why she was afraid to leave Veronique alone?

Vanessa shuddered hard in his arms. Then she sobbed. "A piss poor one." Misery fouled her scent.

"I don't understand. You were nine and untrained. Anything you did was heroic."

"Heroic?" Her voice went shrill. "I nearly crippled my sister the first time I shifted. I couldn't hunt, so we nearly starved." She swallowed hard. "And I nearly tore out Alpha James's throat."

The urge to laugh at what she considered her failures warred with the need to comfort her. "Even a wolf who *can* fully shift would be hard pressed to hunt in the dead of winter, and I will assume you attacked the Alpha because you thought he was a foe."

"But Veronique—"

"How was she injured?" He suspected it was an innocent error.

"I put my claws through the meat of her upper arm and to the bone, then ripped."

"Why?"

She looked up at him, seemingly lost. He could almost picture her as a pre-adolescent, half-starved and freezing.

"Why?" she echoed him.

"Why did you do it?"

"It's not like I *meant* to," she countered hotly.

Barden bit back a smile. He'd expected as much. "What did you mean to do?" He was goading her.

Vanessa's eyes shifted in anger. "I was trying to anchor us. The car was rolling."

He allowed the smile to creep out. "Heroic."

She shoved at his chest, grunting in frustration.

"It was," he assured her. "If you hadn't, your sister might not have survived the crash either."

Vanessa huffed at him, and her lips settled into an adorable pout.

"You've heard that before," he guessed.

She didn't answer him.

Barden sobered. "I'm so sorry."

"You weren't responsible for the hunters...or for us getting lost. We just kept going downhill. We didn't know what else to do."

He cupped her chin in his hand, marveling that so delicate a woman could have survived so much. "No. For making you leave Veronique. I didn't know. She must be a nervous wreck without you."

Her laugh was heartbreakingly brittle. "No. I'm sure Veronique is fine. It's me who can't be without her."

Barden wasn't sure what she meant by that. As if she understood his confusion, Vanessa offered an explanation.

"Being lost in the storm... Being afraid that Veronique might die and leave me alone... It broke me, I guess." Tears pooled in her eyes. "After huddling together to keep warm all those days and nights, it's difficult for me to sleep alone. At least...in a room alone."

His mouth went dry at that statement. "Do you want me to stay?"

Her indecision was palpable. Just when Barden was about to get up, her voice emerged.

"Yes. Please."

He settled Vanessa to his chest, then pressed a kiss to her forehead. "You're not alone."

Never again. Not if I have anything to say about it.

Chapter Four

Vanessa smiled, feeling warm and safe. Barden's scent enticed her, making her mouth water.

She'd slept soundly, probably better than she had since before her father had died. Vanessa was rejuvenated, nearly supercharged.

I could do this. I could make a life with Barden.

Vanessa stroked her fingertips along his chest, and Barden moaned in his sleep. He tipped his hips toward her, and his cock rose between them, setting off an ache at the apex of her thighs.

Barden opened his eyes, staring down at her, his arm muscles tightening. Vanessa didn't hesitate. She molded her body to his and sought out his lips.

The brief kiss she'd shared with Berne couldn't hold a candle to the heat of his brother's. Where she'd found Berne merely pleasant, her entire body came to life for Barden.

He worked his hand beneath the edge of the t-shirt, his fingers stroking upward along bare flesh. Though she was overheated, his touch raised goose bumps in its wake.

Vanessa broke off the kiss, and Barden startled. He stared down at her, questioning her silently. She peeled the shirt up and off, met his gaze, then tossed it aside.

A smile appeared on Barden's face, and he nodded. He rolled slightly off her, reached down, and untied his sleep pants.

Barden came to his knees on the mattress, pushing the sleep pants away. Vanessa levered herself up on her elbows, watching his body appear from behind the fabric, a breath catching in her throat.

His skin was a uniform creamy beige, the nest of golden hair around the base of his cock a near-glowing beacon, leading her gaze in and up. His cock was long and thick, standing at attention.

Vanessa swallowed the lump growing in her throat, then licked her lips. Barden groaned. His fingers encircled his cock, and he stroked it once...twice, bringing up beads of pre-cum. Her breathing went harsh.

In the next heartbeat, Barden was easing her to the pillow, his body covering hers, their mouths meshing. He retreated, leaving her gasping for breath. Vanessa arched up, moaning as Barden suckled hard at a nipple. His growl in response sent shivers down her spine.

Then Barden was in motion, licking and nipping at her skin, sending her heartbeat into a skittering non-rhythm. Her legs trembled as he approached the apex of her thighs. Barden paused, then parted them slowly.

His rough tongue bathed, then parted her, and his growls drove her toward what she suspected was climax. Unable to contain herself, Vanessa found herself shouting, crying, screaming as her body exploded in pleasure.

The shift slid over her, a comfort for the first time in her life.

* * * *

Berne raised his head, drunk on her arousal. She lay beneath him, shifted to her wolf form again, but this time she wasn't threatening him. Vanessa didn't attack him, as many females did their first time.

It's not her first time shifting. Maybe it has nothing to do with sex and everything to do with a first shift. The fact that it usually coincides with sex may be confusing the issue.

I don't know if this is her first time having sex either. Nothing she was doing seemed to indicate lack of knowledge.

Vanessa started to move against him, moaning. The need to stake a claim on her seared him, and Berne thrust deep inside her. She gasped, then wrapped herself around him. Her claws bit lightly at his hips.

Berne cycled his hips, alive to every sensation of her: the silk of her sheath, the enticing female scent of her, her taste on his tongue, the polite demand of her claws against his skin. His fangs sprouted, and his breathing streamed between them.

The urge to make her his own burned at him, and Berne doubled his speed. Vanessa's moans and squeals became screams of delight again, and her sheath massaged his length.

He thrust to the hilt, his seed rushing forth. Her claws dug deeper, and her screams echoed off the walls, encouraging him.

Berne forced Vanessa beneath him, pinning her to the mattress, his hips moving restlessly in the need for more of her. As if she agreed with the sentiment, Vanessa nibbled at his jaw line.

Mine. Her scent went to his head, pooled in his groin, confirming their bond.

The rest was a blur of motion and sensation. They kissed, rolled, touched. When the end came, Vanessa was astride him, cradled in his arms as he climaxed a second time.

Movement in the hallway put his senses on full alert. Who was in his house? Why were they here?

Barden wrapped the quilt around Vanessa's shoulders, intent on setting her aside while he investigated. She took advantage of his position to seal her lips to his. The heat rose between them, and Vanessa moved her hips back and forth, enticing him to readiness again. All other concerns faded away.

Until the bedroom door opened.

Barden left the kiss with a growl, focusing on— *Veronique.* Trailing behind her was Berne, but his twin was—ever so wisely—looking the other way.

Vanessa's twin moved her mouth as if to speak, but nothing came out.

"Would you give us a few moments?" Barden asked.

She nodded, took a step backward, then paused. "I brought... Sorry." Veronique rushed to the bed and dropped a small stack of clothing on it. She fled the room, red-faced and wide-eyed, Berne in her wake.

Berne shut the door behind them, and their footsteps echoed down the hall.

Vanessa sat astride Barden, her teeth making dimples in her lower lip.

"You don't have to go," he invited.

She looked at the doors, her expression tortured. "I should... I have to. I think Veronique needs to talk to me."

"Allow me to see you again."

Her cheeks went an enticing pink. "Yes."

"Tonight?"

She slid another look at the doors. "Call me? I'll give you my number."

"And you mine. Before you leave." He didn't want to think about her leaving. An ache set up deep in his heart at the thought of it.

Vanessa pressed a kiss to his lips, then levered herself off of him. She turned her back to him, then leaned over to grab the clothing her sister had left for her.

The sight of her in the ancient mating pose stirred his cock to readiness again. Barden didn't question what he had to do. He placed one hand on her lower back and slid his cock home inside her.

Vanessa sighed, then moaned.

"Like this. When you come back." Barden knew they didn't have time to—

"Now."

Then again. "Anything you want."

He rolled his hips, thrusting faster and deeper inside her. She stifled her sounds, and he did the same, swallowing down all manner of verbalizations.

"Vanessa?" her sister called out.

"Just a minute." She gasped. "Coming soon."

"Me too," Barden whispered.

She wasn't lying, and neither was he. Her inner muscles fluttered then massaged hard at his cock, and she buried her face — and a squeal — in the quilt. That was all it took to send him over after her.

Holding in the howl he wanted to vent took all he had and left Barden gasping for breath in the aftermath. Before he could recover, Vanessa eased off his cock, turned with a giggle, then placed a kiss on his lips.

She hurried into a pair of snug pants and an oversized sweater. Barden was face-down on the mattress and holding tenuously to consciousness when she had him scribble his phone number on a sheet of paper for her. Vanessa padded out of the bedroom and to her sister's care.

He glanced at the paper with her number on it and smiled at the effect she had on him. He'd never had so little control over himself.

And I love it.

Everything changes now. Maybe Berne will even relax his animosity towards me.

* * * *

Veronique dragged her feet on the way into their room, exhausted in body and soul. Vanessa closed the door behind them, then made her way to her bed. They dropped onto them nearly in unison.

"So..." Veronique managed. "Barden?"

Her sister smiled, then stretched luxuriously. "Barden. He's Berne's twin, you know."

"I didn't." It figured, though.

"How did it go with Berne?" Vanessa asked.

Veronique grimaced, but her twin wasn't looking at her and couldn't see it. "I learned how to shift."

Vanessa laughed, a light, relaxed sound.

"We didn't have sex, Vanessa. He just... I..." She couldn't find the words to explain it. In the end, she sighed and wrapped her arm over her eyes.

The mattress shifted, as Vanessa joined Veronique on her bed. Her sister wrapped her arms around Veronique, and she turned to face Vanessa.

All of the sudden, the last day was too much for her. Veronique sobbed, then cried, her heart aching at Berne's single-minded approach to mating.

Vanessa made soothing noises. "What did Berne do?" The gravel in her tone said Vanessa had loosed her fangs.

"He doesn't care about me at all, Vanessa." It hurt to admit it, but it was true.

"He seemed interested enough last night."

Veronique snorted in a most unladylike fashion. "That's *all* he's interested in."

Vanessa flinched. "Nothing else?"

"I hoped," she admitted. "After I...threatened him into trying to find out where Barden took you, he told me I didn't have to leave. I *hoped* it was out of concern for my feelings."

"It wasn't?" Vanessa stroked a hand down Veronique's

hair, soothing her as she had on those long nights in the cold.

"He thought it was a shame to waste the time we had alone," she imparted bitterly. "He wanted to finish what we'd started." Her stomach clenched painfully, as if she'd taken a blow to the chest.

Vanessa growled out a curse, and Veronique hurried on.

"Not to talk. Not to hold me. Just to sate himself. The swine!"

Before she could answer, the room phone rang. Vanessa turned away and scooped it up.

"Hello?

"I'm afraid not, Barden. I can't tonight.

"Yes, I know. I do too, but Veronique needs me.

"Well, no. Not exactly. She's upset..." Vanessa slanted a look her direction. "...for another reason."

She looked away. "Yes.

"What? What good would that do?" There was an edge of concern in her tone.

"Tomorrow night. You have my word.

"Seven is fine.

"Who said I want to go to dinner?"

She was teasing him. A spike of jealousy ate at Veronique.

"You too." Vanessa made a kiss sound and hung up the phone.

She turned to Veronique with a smile, her cheeks pink, her eyes focused far away in dreamy contemplation.

Guilt made Veronique speak. "You should call him back."

The smile faded, and Vanessa stared at her. "What?"

"Things seem to be going well with Barden. You don't have to deny yourself to stay here with me."

Vanessa pulled her into a hug. "Isn't that what you've been doing for me all this time? Isn't that what we've always done? It was your turn. Now it's mine again."

The words stuck in her throat. She forced them out. "Maybe it shouldn't be."

Her sister stiffened slightly. "What are you saying?"

Veronique took a calming breath. "Maybe it's not healthy...the way we've lived all these years. Not being able to be separated." She stopped short of suggesting they needed to learn to be alone. Veronique suspected it was long past time to learn a lesson like that.

Vanessa captured her chin between her fingers, forcing her head up. Her gaze bored into Veronique's. It was a look of order, the demand of the alpha, the firstborn twin.

Her voice brooked no argument. "We made a vow, you and I. Never alone. Never left behind."

"Yes." Veronique shuddered at the memory.

"You should go, Vanessa. I'll only get you caught."

"No!"

The shift came over her sister so suddenly, it made Veronique's heart stutter. She knew that look. Vanessa would never back down from whatever decision she'd just made.

"I will never *leave you behind. You are my sister." She shouldered Veronique up. "And you* will *never leave me alone.*

That means you walk, wolf!"

Veronique smiled weakly and managed a disjointed shuffle. "*Never left behind.*" Even if it kills us both, in the end. *Though she didn't want to admit it, Veronique was glad Vanessa wasn't going to abandon her.*

"*Never alone. Promise me.*" *Though she'd surely tried to hide it, the pain and panic made itself known in Vanessa's tone.*

"*I promise.*" *No matter how much hurt and how sick she felt, Veronique wouldn't abandon Vanessa either.*

"Never alone," Vanessa promised. "Nothing has changed.

But that was a lie. *Everything* had changed.

* * * *

Berne turned toward the door with a sigh. It was a solid bet the knocking at the door wasn't Veronique, so what was the point in answering it?

The knock repeated, a hard, demanding knock.

Masculine. Barden. I am definitely *not answering it.*

"Damn it, Berne. Answer the fucking door." A moment of silence followed. "I can hear you breathing."

That pissed him off enough to send Berne to the door. He yanked it open and glared at Barden, warning him off silently.

"About time," his twin grumbled. Barden pushed past him into the main room.

Berne closed the door with exaggerated patience. "Come to screw up another evening for me?" he challenged.

Barden scowled at him. "*I* didn't screw up last night for you. You managed that for yourself."

Before he could protest, his brother forged on.

"I admit I don't have all the details, but Vanessa made it clear that *you* upset Veronique."

"How is it *my* fault that *you* upset their plans for a ménage à trois? Oh, and how *did* you convince Vanessa to fuck you without her sis — "

Barden's punch sent him reeling. Berne caught himself against the desk, stunned by the ferocity of his brother's attack.

"I imagine your problem is that *you* view making love to your mate as fucking." Barden bared his fangs.

"She's your — "

"Yes. Vanessa is mine."

Barden winced, and his stomach gave a warning twist. He nodded sheepishly. No wonder Barden punched him. Though it galled him to do it, there was something that needed to be said. "I'm sorry. I didn't know."

Barden didn't seem mollified. He raised an eyebrow and screwed his face up in what appeared to be contempt. "Maybe you should say that to Veronique."

"For. What?" He still didn't know what he'd done to alienate her. Until Barden's pronouncement, Berne had believed his brother had been to blame for her upset.

Barden glared at him.

"Seriously. Give me a hint. I have no idea what I did wrong. Hell, I don't even know why they insisted on a threesome."

"And you agreed." It was nothing short of a condemnation.

"My mate is in heat...again. Trust me, a male will do almost anything a mate asks when she's in heat." Still, the accusation stung. He hadn't *wanted* Vanessa. He'd only agreed to fuck her to have Veronique. He'd actually been relieved when Vanessa had let him focus on Veronique.

I would have been fucking Vanessa, even if I had been making love with Veronique. Fucking. Barden's mate. He winced again.

Barden scrubbed a hand down his face, his muscles tensing and releasing. For the first time, Berne feared his twin might mean him real harm.

I deserve it. That didn't mean he wouldn't fight back. Berne had been pounding down his quiet twin since shortly after they were out of cradles.

"Didn't you talk to her at all?" Barden demanded.

Berne managed a sheepish shrug. "You know why. Don't you?"

"I *talked* to Vanessa."

"Then tell me, damn it!" *What is with Barden and these games?*

Barden shot him a warning look. "There are no convenient shortcuts this time, brother. You screwed up with your mate. You need to make it right."

He opened his mouth to protest, but Barden beat him to the punch.

"I will warn you once and only once. Your failures are

affecting my ability to claim *my* mate. If you ruin my chances, I will gut you. Do you understand me?"

Berne swallowed hard, more than a little unbalanced in the face of his brother's fury. Barden meant every word he'd spoken, he had no doubt.

Barden advanced a step on him, bringing Berne to within striking distance of his still-sheathed claws. "I said —"

"Yes. I understand you."

"Good." His point made clear, Barden headed for the door.

"Won't you tell me anything?" *I'm pleading.*

I don't care. I'll plead if it gets me answers.

Barden seemed to weigh that carefully. "Talk to her. Ask Veronique why they insisted on the ménage. Talk to her...about her sister." With that, he left Berne alone to consider his words.

"Talk to her," he muttered. From what he'd experienced so far, Berne knew Veronique wasn't easy to talk to.

Maybe she needs to talk to Vanessa first. He resolved to give her a day to cool off before he approached her.

Chapter Five

Vanessa laughed, taking a bite of the meat Barden was waving before her nose. He smiled and dipped in to press a kiss against her lips.

He was a playful male, and she found she liked that. It was all too easy to imagine spending a lifetime with him.

Only if Veronique isn't alone. That was enough to sober her.

Barden sighed; he placed his fingers below her chin and tipped her head up. "You're worried about her again. Aren't you?"

She managed a strained smile, then tangled her fingers with his. "I can't help it. I've always protected her."

He kissed the tip of her index finger. "It makes perfect sense. I know this can't be easy for you."

"But?" Something told her there was more he'd yet to say.

"We'll work it out. Whatever it takes to put you and your sister at ease, we'll make it happen."

Vanessa stiffened, color rising in her cheeks in a rush. He didn't think she wanted to share him, did he?

As if she'd spoken the thought aloud, Barden started shaking his head, seemingly horrified. "I'm not my brother. I didn't mean...that."

She laughed, but a tear spilled down her cheek. Barden wiped it away, a weak smile curving his lips.

"If the two of you need to be together... I make enough money that we can have a home with a room for her. If she finds a male she wants to mate with, I will welcome him and their young into our home. You have my word on it."

Her heart leapt at the solemn promise he was giving her. Barden was willing to upset his ordered existence and take on a mate with more than a little baggage in tow, without Vanessa asking him to do so.

I can't pass up a man like this.

Vanessa kissed him, smiling as his shock melted into a firestorm of male arousal. He growled, his wolf seemingly only millimeters from the surface.

In the next moment, she was in his arms. Vanessa didn't question that Barden was taking her to bed. She didn't protest it either.

Why should I? It's precisely where I want to be.

* * * *

Berne took a calming breath, then pasted on what he felt was his most charming smile. He knocked on Veronique's door and waited to greet her.

The door opened...then slammed in his face.

The shock of it left him silent for a moment. Anger rose up like flood waters in his gut, and he knocked again.

I shouldn't be demanding. Still, he knew he was.

The door didn't budge, and she didn't respond to him verbally.

"Come on, Veronique. The least you can do is talk to

me. You're my mate."

The door opened, but Veronique didn't move to let him pass. She blocked his way, glaring at him.

"Veron—"

"I'm your mate? And like all males, that means you think you have some right to me?"

The accusation stung. "No. I never said—"

"Didn't you? Didn't you just *assume* we would be finishing what we started? Didn't you ignore *my* distress and decide that was all I was good for?"

"Yes. I mean, no. Some of it, but no." *I can't even form a logical answer. What is wrong with me?*

He opened his mouth to try again.

Veronique poked a finger against his chest. "Aside from biological drives, I don't know what I ever saw in you, Berne." Tears misted her eyes.

Berne reached for her, the need to comfort her like a fire in his blood.

She slapped him. Hard.

He shook his head, trying to erase the sparkles of light dancing in his field of vision.

"I will *never* be your mate."

The door slammed between them, punctuating the sick twist of his stomach her words set off. Berne stood there, at a loss for words, hurting as he hadn't known a man could hurt.

The sound of someone clearing his throat had him whirling toward it.

The residence head stood there, a stately old matriarch

wolf, one hand folded over the other, her back straight, and one brow raised in challenge.

His face burned at the censure in that look.

"I believe the lady has spoken, sir. You should not return to this residence house."

She didn't need to say more. If he returned, she would tear into him with claws and teeth. *Then* she would turn him over to the guards, and not even his family or the Alphas would support him.

"Yes, Mother Wolf. As you say." He ducked his head respectfully, then made his way into the cold night.

Berne looked up at the sky, frustrated beyond words. *She will never be my mate.*

Of course, he didn't know that for certain. Veronique may have been speaking out of anger and hurt. She could change her mind.

But not if I push her. Not if I pursue.

What did that leave him?

Waiting, just as I've always waited for her.

What if waiting costs me her? What if she thinks I'm not interested?

There was no way to answer that.

Chapter Six

Vanessa woke, gasping for breath, her body on fire. She'd suffered heats before, but never like this.

I've never known who my mate was before.

I've never gone into heat already full of my mate's seed. That thought ramped up the flame in her belly another few degrees. Just the idea that she might already be conceiving Barden's young made her womb clench. Her fluids leaked down her thighs, a potent invitation Barden wasn't there to be enticed by.

Veronique arrived at her side. Her hand felt cool and soothing against Vanessa's forehead.

Not soothing enough. Vanessa forced the next scorching breath in and then out, trying to focus on anything but the unexpected pain.

Her sister raced to the phone, then scooped it up and started dialing.

"Don't leave me alone," Vanessa begged.

"Not happening."

There was a moment of nerve-wracking silence. Then Vanessa started speaking, an urgent note in her voice.

"Barden?

"No. It's Veronique.

"No...I—I mean...not really.

"No. There's not time to—

"Barden. Shut up and listen. I need you here.

Immediately. I mean...Vanessa needs you here.

"Look, I don't—

"No. You're—

"You're wasting time, Barden!" Veronique took a calming breath. "I have to hang up now."

She did, but Vanessa heard Barden's demand for more information as she settled the phone on the bedside table. Just hearing his voice made Vanessa moan in delight.

The phone started ringing before Veronique was halfway across the room. Her sister ignored it and kept going, all the way to the closet.

Vanessa started to rise.

"Don't you dare. Do you want Barden to come?"

Inside me. She nodded in response, trying to catch her breath to form speech a near-impossibility.

"The sooner he realizes no one is going to answer, the sooner he will be here."

Vanessa wanted to deny the sense that made, but in the end, she flopped back down on the mattress and curled into a ball.

The phone across the room went silent; Vanessa's started to ring. She stared at it miserably. One part of her wanted to answer it, just to hear Barden's voice. The other wanted to smash the phone against the wall, so she wouldn't have to hear it ring at all.

It's a torture. Why doesn't it just shut up?

Mercifully, it did.

Vanessa smiled, replaying her sister's comment in her mind. *He's coming. He'll be here soon.*

Veronique returned with the slit leg silk dress Vanessa used to wear for holidays. It was a deep Aubergine and molded to her body like a second skin.

Without a word, Veronique started helping her put the dress on.

Vanessa fought the process. She was already hot; why would her sister want to dress her?

Veronique growled low and in her throat. "You have to go with him, Vanessa. Where am I going to go if you don't?"

That stopped her fight. Hard as it was, Vanessa forced herself to think. Veronique needed the room. The only alternative was her sister going home.

Not an option.

Vanessa nodded her agreement and let Veronique dress her.

When she was done, Veronique slipped a set of black pumps on Vanessa's feet, then hoisted her up. "We'll meet him downstairs."

"Thank you." How she managed to say it was a mystery to her, but Vanessa suspected the Night Mother was responsible for it.

The night air was cool and crisp. Were she not in heat, Vanessa was certain she would be shivering, perhaps begging for a coat. As it was, she would compare the sensation to walking on an early Autumn night.

Her head cleared, and Vanessa glanced at her sister. "You knew you could calm it by using cold," she guessed.

Veronique managed a stiff smile. "I've never been as

affected as you are. I'm not sure it would work for more than a few moments."

"Then I forgive you for doing it this way."

A chuckle emerged, though it sounded of wry amusement at best. "After you have some time with Barden, I won't need forgiveness."

Panic lit in her chest. "What are you saying? I won't—"

"I won't be left behind. Promise me."

"Promise you what?" Why did this feel like goodbye?

"Just promise me I'll always have a room at your home, if it comes to that. Maybe I'll even find a family friend to have pups with. What I'm saying is... Mate if you feel the need to. Barden is a good wolf. He'll make you an excellent mate." Veronique seemed sincere.

Maybe even hopeful? At a loss for words, Vanessa nodded and hugged her sister close.

The roar of a car engine brought her head around. In a whirlwind of motion, Barden slid to a stop beside them, slammed the vehicle into park, then vaulted out.

Vanessa released Veronique and turned to him, her nerves sizzling in need. Her vision sharpened, a sure sign that she'd partially shifted in her scattered state.

"What is it?" Barden demanded, rushing to her side.

She threw herself on him, capturing his lips in a kiss. He was tentative for a moment. Then his hand closed in the back of her hair, and he took charge, deepening the kiss, his cock lengthening between them.

Heat licked down her thighs, drawn along by the wetness overflowing her heated core. The throbbing in

Vanessa's womb demanded attention.

Immediately. Now. Now. Now!

Barden broke away from her, his breathing ragged. "In the car."

Vanessa hastened to comply. *I don't care where he takes me, as long as it's soon.*

As if he agreed, Barden was next to her and driving in less than the time it took her head to stop spinning.

* * * *

Barden tried to pay attention to the road, but the scent swirling between them made that problematic. Just when he thought he had his wits about him again, her hand slid between his thighs, taking his measure.

Growls rose in his throat. Much as he would like to pull over and finish what she'd started, Barden knew it wasn't an option. Two wolves mating hard—and partially shifted—in public was too risky.

There has to be a way. He wracked his brains, trying to come up with a plan of action.

Inspiration struck, and Barden pulled to a stop. Taking it for agreement, Vanessa started pulling at his belt, in a frenzy to get him undressed. He let her, until she had the belt open. As she popped the catch on his trousers, Barden eased her hands away.

He shushed her complaints, smiling at her pleading expression. "Just until we reach the house." His voice came out rough, and his cock ached at the thought of the wait.

"Barden, please."

Her plea stirred something in him, and Barden kissed her solemnly. Then he pulled his belt from the loops and bound her hands behind her back with it.

He'd never considered bondage play before, but the sight of Vanessa tied up with his belt made him want all sorts of adventures. Without missing a beat, he untied his tie, pulled it off, then bound her ankles together with it.

Barden surveyed what he'd done, licking his lips in anticipation. He started driving again, calculating how fast he could travel without risking being pulled over by the local authorities.

That nearly wrenched a laugh from him. *It's just a sex game, officer. Really.*

This isn't sex. If she's willing at all, I'm going to bind Vanessa as my mate tonight.

Vanessa arched, no doubt trying to free herself. Barden's wolf reacted to the challenge, the drive to seek a claim on a fertile mate nearly undoing his typical ordered mind.

Not the right time. Not the right place. There were no wolf-owned hotels close by. If he dared risk an uncontrolled mating at a human hotel, he would change direction now.

I don't. Vanessa has already been terrorized by hunters in her life. The utmost care to avoid it again will be taken.

"Barden." She moaned, arching her back in a way that pressed her engorged breasts to the bodice of her gown. Her nipples tented the fabric out, begging for attention.

Barden chanced another five kilometers per hour.

"Barden, I'll do anything you ask."

The promise of it from such a strong female made him shiver in delight. "Is that a promise, Vanessa?"

Her eyes widened a bit, and her color rose. Just when he thought she would refuse, Vanessa gasped out 'yes'.

Barden took stock of their location, calculating the time he would need to reach the house. *Eight minutes. And I don't dare to travel any faster than I already am. Damn.*

"Barden, please." The sound of silk threads ripping made it clear she was intent on escape, most likely driven to it by her heat.

I have to keep her busy. Just eight minutes.

Inspiration struck. "Then you should start now, because when we get to the house, you're going to be full of me for hours."

Vanessa stared at him, seemingly shocked by the pronouncement.

Of course. I've never been so direct with her...so demanding.

That didn't mean he felt guilty about it. Far from it, Barden reached down with one hand and unfastened his trousers.

Vanessa watched the zipper slide down, licking her lips in anticipation.

Just what I want.

Barden reached across the car and loosened the belt, allowing Vanessa to free her hands. She moved on to the tie around her ankles.

While she was busy with that, Barden let her in on his

plan. "We have a few minutes before we reach the house."

She slowed her pace, glancing up at him.

"I want you to suck me, Vanessa. Get me ready for you." *Not that I need it.* He was already painfully hard.

Vanessa didn't question him. She didn't protest it. In a blur of motion, she was laying across the seat, pulling his trousers down to free his cock. Barden tipped his hips, aiding her, his breathing strangled, though nothing more than the heat of her breath had touched his cock.

That changed in moments. She engulfed him, taking him deep into her mouth. Barden fought to keep his mind clear and his eyes on the road.

The suction on her withdrawal was enough to make his mouth go dry. Barden swallowed hard, trying to wet his throat and to dislodge the lump rising from his chest.

He panted hard, as she sucked him in and out, driving him mad for more of her.

I will not come until we're home. I will not.

Vanessa tested his resolve, adding licks and nibbles to her avid attention. She sucked hard, then took him deep, scattering his mind.

Not yet. Not yet.

It wasn't that Barden was worried about recovery time. With Vanessa in heat, it was a solid bet virility wouldn't be a concern.

I just want to come inside her, to make the most of her heat. To have young with Vanessa.

The thought of planting his pups was nearly enough to send him over the edge. Barden tamped down the urge brutally.

The house came into view, and he pressed the button on the remote to open the garage door. "Enough," he grumbled.

Vanessa backed away and looked up at him, a feral expression on her face.

Barden's heart pounded in response. She was a strong mate, and every wolf wanted that. It was a dream come true.

He pulled into the garage, put the vehicle in park, and turned off the engine in a smooth series of motions. He hit the remote with one hand and pulled Vanessa into a kiss with the other.

They came together hard and fast, in a feast of tasting, their tongues dancing from mouth to mouth. Barden fumbled at the door release, toeing off his dress shoes in a frenzy to be rid of the clothing separating them.

As if in agreement, Vanessa pulled at the front of his shirt. It took a moment for Barden to realize her claws were out...just about the time they tore the linen and cotton blend to shreds, leaving shallow cuts in their wake.

That was his wolf's breaking point. Barden pushed the car door open and lifted Vanessa out with him. His trousers pooled at his ankles, and Barden kicked them away.

He made a beeline to the work bench, then tossed a packing blanket over it. With Vanessa deposited on the surface, Barden growled in frustration at the long, tight dress; he grasped the fabric at the split and tore it to high on her abdomen, baring her to just below her ample breasts.

Then he was inside her, shuddering hard at the molten invitation of her body. Reason deserted him, and Barden thrust hard and fast into Vanessa, her moans and pleas driving him on.

At last, she climaxed around him, and Barden followed her over. He gulped in lungfuls of air that brought her ready scent with it.

The bed. I need to get her to the bed.

That thought echoing in his consciousness, Barden dragged the ruined shirt off his sweat-soaked and blood-beaded torso. He set Vanessa on her feet. He didn't question when and where she'd lost her shoes; they would find them later.

Much later.

The trip to the bed was slowed by their petting and kissing. Just when he thought they would make it, Vanessa stroked his cock.

Whatever humanity he'd salvaged from the encounter in the garage fled. He was a wolf, and his wolf was demanding his mate.

A fertile and willing mate.

Before his mind cleared enough to follow where his instincts were taking him, Barden had her bent over the back of the couch, full of him and meeting his thrusts.

A sound at the front of the house had him in a partial shift.

If it's something I have to stop for, I'm going to gut

someone.

Barden didn't relax his muscles when his mother turned the corner and stopped cold in the doorway.

The facts he needed coursed through his mind. When Veronique had called, he'd been dressing for dinner with his parents. He'd abandoned the house without a suit coat or top coat.

It doesn't matter. They will understand and leave, or I will throw them out. After we finish.

Barden didn't even slow. On one level, he knew he was being rude. On another, he knew that—even if his wolf wasn't running the show—this moment demanded a challenge be issued.

His mother's shock was impossible to miss.

Of course she's surprised. This is unlike me. My life has always been neat, ordered, discrete...

I've never had a mate before, let alone one in heat.

She panned her gaze up and down their moving bodies, no doubt taking in every detail: the torn dress, the scratches on his chest, his claws wrapped around her shoulders, the socks that were the sole clothing he still wore... His mother's chest moved in a deep intake of breath.

Confirming that Vanessa is in heat.

Her face went a vivid red, and she placed a hand across what appeared to be a smile. She offered a wiggle of her fingers, then crept toward the door.

A sure sign that Vanessa's eyes are closed, and Mother doesn't want to embarrass her. No wonder she hasn't reacted to

Mother's presence.

A moan from his mate recaptured the whole of Barden's attention, and he lost himself in their coupling. One climax led to another, a patchwork of loving.

At last, Barden forced himself back a step. Vanessa turned to him, seeking his lips.

He held her at bay, trying to clear his head. "No. By the Goddess, the next time will be in bed."

"Your bed."

He growled, at the edges of control. Though it wasn't technically his bed, the thought of her in any space he called his own—even for the holiday season—was far too appealing.

* * * *

Vanessa woke slowly, smiling at the feeling of Barden's arm encircling her waist. Memories of the night before— the hours of touching and tasting—sent a flush of warmth up her chest to her hairline.

Barden stirred beside her, and Vanessa's mouth watered. She reached down and wrapped her hand around his cock, stroking his length up. He groaned, his hand tightening around her hip.

Before he had a chance to take the superior, Vanessa came up over him, pushing his shoulder with her free hand, pinning him to the mattress. His cock still cradled in her left hand, she levered it up and pushed herself down his length.

His moan shook the bed, and rumbled from her thighs up her center. There was something about making a wolf like Barden moan that made her feel powerful. Vanessa moved faster, pushing him toward climax. His set hers off, a flurry of sensation that made her head spin.

She sat astride Barden, sweat-soaked and trembling in the depth of their connection.

Barden smiled, running a fingertip down her lower abdomen. Vanessa didn't have to ask what he was thinking. He was thinking what any wolf would when his mate was in heat. Or when *she* was in heat and had a mate or lover, for that matter.

"Have you thought about us mating? Formally, I mean?" he mused.

The question made her mouth go dry. "Yes."

He raised his head, meeting her gaze, seemingly speculating on the lack of more.

Vanessa managed a smile. "We have three days until the holiday party with your family."

One brow went up, and he cocked his head to the right. "Uh huh."

"You said you have use of a bunch of houses."

"You want to mate somewhere else?"

"Wherever you want."

Interest lit in his eyes.

Vanessa pushed back on his shoulders. "I didn't say whenever."

Barden sighed. "Okay. What *are* you hinting at?"

She took a deep breath. *Bad idea. Smelling our sex while*

I'm in heat...

Enough! "Are any of the houses...remote?"

His confusion was palpable. "Yes."

Her smile spread. "Good."

Chapter Seven

"I'm so glad you came with us," Vanessa repeated. Her smile hadn't dimmed the entire way.

Veronique managed a return smile and reached over the seat between them to grasp her sister's hand. She wanted to be happy for Vanessa, but the sensation of being a fifth wheel was hard to shake.

Her smile smoothed into one of pleasure, as they came over the last rise and the house rose before them. It wasn't huge; she estimated one bedroom per family member and maybe a guest room or two. It had the look of an upscale cabin, but she didn't doubt that it was well-appointed inside.

As quickly as it bloomed, her smile wilted. It was a holiday party with Barden's family. That meant Berne's family. *Berne.*

As if she was reading Veronique's thoughts, Vanessa started patting her hand. "He'll behave himself," she promised.

"If he doesn't, he answers to me," Barden intoned.

Veronique sighed. "I don't want to cause you to fight with your brother."

"Oh, you won't." He slanted a feral smile her direction. "I owe Berne a whole lot of pain I've never taken out of his hide. I don't mind cashing in on a few payments due. He's had them coming a long, *long* time."

Veronique laughed at the typical alpha wolf mentality. He was protective, competitive, and more than a little irreverent.

If Berne was more like his twin, she could easily see herself mating with him. Her cheeks darkened in a blush. *Not an appropriate thought. Not at all.*

"Well, let's hope it doesn't come to that," she offered brightly. *Vanessa will know it's fake.*

Her sister didn't call her on it, and they pulled up in front of the house in silence.

Veronique let herself out of the car, while Barden aided Vanessa out.

"Why don't you show your sister the solar pool, while I take the bags inside?" he suggested.

"That's a *great* idea," Vanessa gushed. "I can't wait to try it."

Veronique nodded her agreement, though she wasn't a fan of swimming. Since they spent so much time together, Vanessa rarely indulged in the little pleasures Veronique found disturbing.

Guilt ate at her. *It has been grossly unfair of me to ask that of her. I should have met Vanessa halfway...somehow.*

Despite her dislike for swimming—or at least for wearing a swimming suit—the greenhouse-style building with the fifteen meter long, salt-water pool and deck beneath was a wonder. Vanessa pointed out the many benefits of it in excitement.

"And it's connected to the house over here." She pointed the way.

Veronique took advantage of the opening to head that direction. Vanessa fell into step beside her, and they emerged into a kitchen bigger than their rooms at school combined.

The sight took her breath away. Veronique spun in a circle, taking it all in. She wondered if Barden's mother would allow her free rein in the kitchen.

Barden joined them, wrapping an arm around Vanessa's waist. "Veronique, your room is second to the right at the head of the stairs. If you don't mind, I need to make sure I have Vanessa's full shopping list before I go."

She turned with a chuckle. "I'll see you upstairs." Veronique trotted toward the front of the house and made her way up the stairs, past the festive greenery strung on the walls; she started snickering halfway up.

Vanessa wasn't fully out of heat yet, and Barden was already treating her as if she was pregnant. It was sweet, but it was also funny as hell. *Watching an alpha male falling all over himself to make Vanessa's every whim a reality.*

At the turn in the stairs, she looked out the large picture window with the reading nook built into the U of glass. Barden was already heading back down the road, probably driven to get to a store and return to Vanessa as soon as possible.

She continued up the stairs, then into the room Barden had sent her to. It was breathtaking; a king-size four-poster bed in what appeared to be mahogany, covered in cream Battenberg lace linens, dominated the room. A matching bureau, chiffarobe, and dressing table with bench played accent. Off-white brocade drapes with gold thread covered two large windows, and deep, cream-colored, silken carpet reached wall-to-wall.

Veronique ambled across the room and threw herself into the literal lap of luxury with a heartfelt laugh.

A sound intruded, and she snapped to sitting. It wasn't someone on the stairs or Vanessa calling out for her. There was no sign of domesticated animals kept within the house. Ill at ease, Veronique waited for it to repeat.

The scrape of heavy furniture moving against bare floor was followed by what she suspected was a grunt.

Her heart pounded in warning. Veronique eased to the carpet, then shed her boots and socks onto it.

Muffled shouting made her cringe, and Veronique took stock of her situation.

No one except she and Vanessa were supposed to be here. Barden said they would be arriving hours before his family did, but even if he was wrong, the noises she was hearing raised red flags.

Barden is gone. Vanessa is here...and unaware. If I call to warn her, I will alert anyone else in the house with us. If there is an enemy, I have to try to protect her. Quietly.

Veronique forced herself through a shift, shaking in the effort, cursing herself silently for not practicing it after her first shift.

Who knew I would need it?

She crept across the room, then drew in a deep breath. There was no smell of human hunters, but she'd heard they'd discovered a way to mask it. The thought of it made her shiver in dread.

Another scrape gave Veronique a direction, and she padded that way, hoping the floorboards were in good repair. They were, and she made it to a closed door without announcing herself.

Every nerve on edge, she turned the knob, then eased the door open, ready for attack. None came, and the noises from inside the room stopped.

She peeked around the door, gaping at the sight of Berne, clothed only in a pair of sleep pants. Someone had tied him to an upright post on his bed. He'd been there long enough to attempt shifting, which had resulted in him tangling himself in the ropes and nothing more. He'd shifted back to human form, and the ropes were biting into the meat of his biceps and chest.

He looked up at her, anger morphing to misery. It was almost enough to make her feel sorry for him.

Almost.

Veronique lost concentration as she fought back gales of laughter. Her ears and fangs retreated, and her claws retracted into her human hands. She crossed her arms over her chest, certain now that there were no enemies.

If human hunters had invaded the house, they would have killed Berne and removed his body. He'd obviously been bound for hours, and this smacked of a practical joke.

"Barden said he had years of pain to pay you back for. Looks like he got a good start."

He glared at her, then started shouting gibberish against the gag that was uncomfortably tight against the corners of his lips.

"I should leave you there for Barden to release, I think."

The expression on his face was nothing short of panic.

Veronique's arms went leaden, and her blood ran cold. She started putting the clues together.

Barden tied Berne up.

No one was here when they arrived...save Berne.

The house had the minimum of decorations. *As if there wasn't a holiday celebration planned for this house.*

Vanessa still hasn't come up to talk to me. The house was completely still, save herself and Berne.

Vanessa could have left with Barden. Veronique hadn't seen him bring in the bags, and she hadn't seen him—or them get in the SUV.

"Oh, they wouldn't dare."

Berne grumbled something that sounded suspiciously like "Yes they would."

Her head swam in sickening circles. They'd trapped her here with Berne.

Questions fought for her attention.

How long did they intend to leave her here?

They didn't really think she was just going to jump into bed with Berne, did they?

If not, what did they think this would accomplish.

"Ve-on-eek?"

She glanced at Berne, aghast that she'd forgotten him so quickly and completely.

There was a boning knife on top of the bureau. Veronique collected it and cut through the ropes, marveling at how sharp it was.

Berne sank to the floor with a groan, then started wrenching at the gag in his mouth.

She turned and headed for the door, dropping the knife halfway across the room.

"Veronique?"

She hesitated, until the sound of him pushing to his feet made it through the numbness. Then Veronique sprinted to her room and slammed the door.

* * * *

"Do you think she'll be all right?"

Barden chucked as he ushered Vanessa into the plush honeymoon suite. The hotel was owned by wolves, and the floor had extra soundproofing to avoid unsuspecting humans overhearing a mating couple.

"Laughing isn't an answer," she reminded him sweetly.

"She will, and she will forgive us...after my brother proves he has a brain. One that isn't zippered in place, of course. She knows he has the other, I'm certain."

Vanessa laughed at the joke. Then she released his arm and glided across the thick carpet, shedding her shoes along the way. At the bed, she spun in place, then settled on the edge of the mattress, her gaze straying along the deep-hued opulence.

"I still don't understand why we had to come here. Couldn't we have stayed at the house you're renting?"

"Borrowing," he corrected her. "From friends, and that

would have been an unwise choice."

"Really? Why? Was the person you borrowed it from coming home?" There was no concern in her tone.

"No." In fact, he'd told Auntie Samara he would be using the house well into the new year.

He sighed. "My mother would have demanded to meet you within another day, and I want you all to myself."

She smiled at him, then the smile faded into a speculative look. "You're not joking."

"No. I'm not." He ambled across the room and sank into a comfortable club chair.

"But how would she—"

"She saw us together last night."

Her mouth moved as if she had something to say but couldn't force the words forth. Her look of horror twisted his heart.

"She realized...and she left."

"How do you know—"

"I know my mother. Not to mention the little wave goodbye she gave me on her way out said she wasn't upset. At all. The woman *lives* to be a grandmother, so a mate in heat... I'm sure she's overjoyed."

Vanessa chewed at her lower lip, her face crimson.

"They'll love you, but beyond wanting you to myself, if we didn't disappear, we wouldn't hear the end of them...given another twenty-four hours."

"I don't understand," she admitted.

Barden tipped his head to one side, trying to keep his tone light, though he knew his mother was going to have *something* to say about him leaving Berne tied up for his mate to find. "When she can't reach Berne, she's going to *assume* I know where he is."

"And you do." She stated the obvious.

"Yes. And I'm going to do my best to make sure no one finds them before they work out their differences."

"They only have two days," Vanessa protested. "We can hardly show up to the holiday celebration without them."

"So?" If Berne couldn't convince Veronique to talk to him in two days, his brother was hopeless.

She huffed. "You really don't know how stubborn my sister is."

He seemed to consider that. "I'll go in alone. If they still haven't worked it out, I'll leave them there and tell the family where to find them in another few days."

"Veronique and Berne will kill you."

Barden smiled widely at the thought. *Or maybe at the idea that she's worrying about me. I can't tell.* "Unlikely, but if they try..."

"Yes?" she asked nervously.

"It means they've found a common enemy and common ground. That might just help them learn to get along."

Vanessa gaped at him for a long moment, then started laughing. After a few moments of mirth, she laid back on the mattress and stretched.

His trousers abruptly felt too tight.

"Barden," she called in a sing-song voice.

The vixen. "Yes, my love?"

"I believe I was promised a mating."

His rush to the bed passed in a blur. Then they were pressed together, their mouths meshing.

If Berne tries to kill me... If my father does... It will be worth it.

Chapter Eight

Berne stared at Veronique, at a loss to fix what his brother had done. *As if I didn't already have problems with her?*

He'd been waiting for her to emerge for nearly twenty-four hours, but Veronique had stayed in her suite, skipping meals, pacing, sleeping, and—based on the slight sounds he could make out—crying.

Now that she'd emerged, things hadn't improved overmuch. Veronique sat in the reception lounge, staring at the snow falling on the mountains as if considering throwing herself off the closest cliff.

Before he could figure out how to start a conversation, she did.

"I don't suppose there's anywhere close enough to walk to." She didn't ask it; he suspected she knew she didn't have to.

"No. If we had a car, it would take three hours or more. It would take us well over a week in this weather, and I'm sure our siblings will be back before then."

She didn't reply.

"If I don't show up for the holiday, my parents *will* question Barden, and I guarantee—"

"I get the picture," she snapped.

Berne sighed. Why couldn't she see this wasn't the worst thing that could happen to her? Hadn't he proven he was trustworthy yet?

I have to find a way to calm her down. "Look... We're...here together. We should make use of the time, don't you think?" Berne ground his teeth in frustration. He'd barely avoided saying they were 'stuck' here. Night Mother only knew how Veronique would interpret *that* phrase.

She turned on him, coming to her feet, volatile as she'd been since the night she and her twin had come to his rooms. "I'm sure I know how *you* want to spend the time. Don't you think about anything else?"

"I'm not trying to get into your pants," he growled at her, his muscles strung tight.

"Aren't you? Isn't that what all—" She waved her arms in wide arcs. "—this is about? Isn't that what we're supposedly here to accomplish?"

"No and no." Considering Barden had all but bitch slapped Berne into the idea of *talking* to Veronique, it was unlikely his brother's aim.

He forced himself to continue. "I'm just tired of not understanding you. Aren't you sick of it too?" His patience had frayed nearly to its breaking point, and it doubtless showed in the tension of his body.

Veronique stared at him, no answer forthcoming.

She's not storming off, and I have to start somewhere. It might as well be with what Barden told me to ask. "Why did you want me to have sex with your sister?"

She snapped. Veronique slapped him hard across the face, her eyes shifting back and forth in fury. "You... Dolt! I *didn't* want—" She turned with a growl, seemingly intent

302

on stalking away.

Oh no you don't. Though he knew he was inviting trouble, Berne grabbed her by the upper arm and spun Veronique to face him. "You are the most infuriat—"

Ridges of uneven skin under his hand stopped Berne short. He ran his thumb back and forth, evaluating the scars.

Wolves rarely scar. What would it take to scar her this way?

Veronique pulled at his hold. Berne raised his head until he was focused on her face, noting her discomfort, the way she avoided meeting his gaze and moved her weight from foot to foot.

In a daze, he reached for the buttons on her shirt.

"No!" She twisted away from him, trembling wildly.

Her response irked him. "I. Am. Your. Mate."

Veronique stopped fighting him.

"I'm going to look. Now."

She didn't help him; neither did she make a move to stop him. Veronique stood, stiff and still, as he unbuttoned her shirt and eased it off her shoulders.

The scars reached from above her elbow to a few scant centimeters from her shoulder. There were four furrows, not quite evenly spaced, the edges ragged.

The skin ripped. It wasn't cut.

Berne started making connections. He'd never seen Veronique's upper arm. She always wore sleeves that covered her arms, even if it was a dress with a three-quarter sleeve over the scars and no shoulder on the opposite side or a half-length wet suit for swimming.

And she seldom swims.

Even when she'd come to his bed, Veronique had worn the robe. "Vanessa removed hers. You never did."

Veronique cringed. A scarlet flush rushed up her neck and face.

"Come with me." Berne led her to the sofa.

She dragged the shirt up the affected arm. "I should — "

"No. You shouldn't." Berne slipped the shirt off her arms and tossed it over the chair she'd been sitting in. "Never hide from me."

When Veronique didn't answer, Berne led her to the sofa and got her settled on one side. He took the opposite end, trying not to crowd her.

Veronique peeked up at him, then wrapped her hand over the worst of the scars.

Still trying to hide herself from me. He decided to let it slide. Whatever this was, it was deeply ingrained. "Tell me. How did you get the scars?"

"It was an accident."

"Accident?" What was she talking about? What *kind* of an accident could scar a wolf so deeply?

"The car was rolling."

"You were in a car accident." That made a certain amount of sense, though he couldn't remember reports of a wolf being in a car accident.

She managed a shaky nod. "The hunters shot into the car. I don't know if that killed our father or...or if the crash did. I didn't see him. Vanessa did."

His throat closed down, and he choked on words. He

didn't know anyone who'd been chased by hunters personally. *Until now.*

Veronique continued. "When the car was rolling, Vanessa tried to hold onto me, but her claws— She shifted. I would have been killed if she hadn't grabbed me. She didn't mean to scar me."

His stomach lurched at the mental image. "How old were you?" The scars were old. Moreover, if the accident was long ago, it would explain why he hadn't heard of it.

"Nine."

A memory stirred in him. "In the mountains," he guessed.

Veronique paled, swallowed hard, then nodded.

Of course. They wouldn't have told us about the hunters, only that the girls were missing and had to be found.

Berne remembered the search well. His mother had been pregnant with Allison, so they'd been left at home while their father joined the search. He'd thought, at the time, that their uncle had been there in case their mother had any problems while she carried. Now he knew. He'd been there to protect them from the hunters.

I have to know the rest. "Why did you bring Vanessa to my room with you?"

She winced and didn't offer an answer.

"Tell me," he invited.

"We made a promise back then."

It couldn't be a promise to sleep with the same male. Not at nine.

Veronique continued before he could decide what to

ask. "I was slowing Vanessa down. I begged her to leave me before the hunters found us. She refused to."

"What was the vow?"

"We would never leave each other behind. Never leave each other alone."

"Never alone. Vanessa hadn't met her mate yet."

Veronique sighed. "And I couldn't wait much longer. Each heat was worse than the one before. Our only chance of staying together—"

"Was convincing me to accept both of you?" He could hardly form the words. *I knew it was wrong from the beginning. Vanessa was willing to prostitute herself to avoid being left alone...and to spare Veronique pain.*

"We thought..." She shrugged, looking wholly miserable.

At a loss for a way to reassure her, Berne pulled Veronique into his embrace. She fit him perfectly.

As she should. "You don't have to worry about being alone."

"I... I don't know if—"

"Relax. We'll discuss it later. For now, let's get something to eat."

Veronique slanted a look toward the discarded shirt.

Berne removed his own and added it to the growing pile.

Her lips twitched, and a slight smile curved them. "I could use a meal."

* * * *

Veronique tried not to stare, but the sight of Berne's bare chest was hard to ignore. Every movement formed a ballet of visual delight.

He didn't notice.

Or he's pretending not to. That was more likely, though — to his credit — Berne was hiding it well. *That means I won't have to kill him.*

It was an empty threat, at best. The more time she spent with Berne, the less animosity Veronique felt toward him.

"Did you enjoy the omelet?"

His voice broke her out of her reverie. "Yes. It was wonderful. Thank you."

He smiled. "So was the glazed bread dish you made."

Veronique stacked his plate on top of hers and headed for the sink, secretly happy that he'd enjoyed it. "I like to cook. When I saw this kitchen..." That brought back sobering memories of being stranded here by Vanessa.

His heat against her back was a delight. "What? What about the kitchen?"

She turned on the water and started rinsing the dishes. "I was hoping your mother would allow me free rein to use it."

"You have it."

Her heart skipped in pleasure at the answer. *Still...* "Shouldn't the lady of the house have a say in something like that?"

One thick digit trailed up and down her spine, playing

at the catch at the back of her bra. "Since mother has always had a cook, she won't mind someone else using the kitchen."

"Oh." It was slightly breathless, and she cursed herself for showing how he affected her.

His breath bathed her shoulder, and heat pooled between her thighs.

"So, your mother didn't teach you to cook then?" Veronique suspected, if she didn't keep him talking, they would be all over each other on the kitchen floor.

"No. Our first cook was also our nanny. We used to watch her make our meals. When I was old enough, Suzanne humored me and started teaching me to cook." He plucked lightly at her bra again, seemingly asking permission to remove it. "Other cooks continued my education."

I want him to educate me, but not in cooking. Not in the kitchen, either. A wicked idea took hold, and Veronique decided to run with it.

She slipped away from him and sauntered toward the solar pool. Halfway down the glass corridor, she unfastened her bra, stripped it off, then let it fall.

Berne gasped, and she didn't doubt he was hard and intent on her.

When she reached the poolside, Veronique slipped out of her plush sleep pants and the underwear beneath. She let them fall, then stepped out of them. With one assessing look at Berne's rigid cock, outlined behind his jeans, she dove into the warm water and started to swim away.

The shockwave of water around her let her know he'd taken the bait. Veronique surfaced, planting her feet on the bottom of the 1.25m section, looking around for her pursuer.

He came from seemingly nowhere, lifting her at the waist and pulling her to his chest. Veronique opened her mouth to his, savoring the taste of him inside her, his tongue laying claim to her.

Berne broke away, his breathing heavy. "If you want me to stop, you need to say it."

Veronique licked her lips, and he moaned. She smiled at the response.

I have him exactly where I want him. She wrapped her legs around his waist, gasping as his cock moved against her needing core. "I'm not telling you anything of the sort." The last embers of her heat ignited at the reality of what they were about to do.

As if he sensed it, Berne came at her like a ravenous... Veronique almost laughed at the idea of comparing him to precisely what he was.

He started moving through the water, but Veronique couldn't identify what direction they were going with her head spinning as it was. Berne pushed her into the side of the pool, chest to chest, their mouths meshing and parting.

His lips traced the line of her throat, and Veronique dropped her head back, encouraging him.

"Goddess, but I need you."

His words raised goose bumps on her skin, despite the temperature of the water. "I need you too."

Berne straightened, capturing her lips in a brutal kiss. His lips left hers, and he thrust inside her with a growl.

Veronique gasped, raking her human fingernails along the lines of his shoulders. He retreated and thrust again...and again, driving her mind to distraction. Nothing existed but the solid length of him pressing to and into her in a sea of swirling warmth.

The drumbeat of anticipation coalesced into a knot pulling tight within her. Veronique gasped for breath, her fingers tightening, claws extending, needing something she couldn't name.

Berne had no problem interpreting what she needed. His thrusts quickened, deepened, touching more of her. The change sent her over; Veronique felt she was floating, surrounded by the brightest stars she'd ever seen, her body pulsing in waves of pleasure.

He followed her over with a howl, his essence filling her, wrenching mews of delight from her. They panted in tandem, her nipples aching at the brush of his chest against them.

Berne growled. "Tell me I can take you to bed." It wasn't a request. Inflamed as his wolf was, he was barely leashed, she was sure.

"You can take me anywhere."

He didn't laugh at the reply. "I intend to."

That simply, he set off aftershocks that wracked her system. *Anywhere. Anytime. Just take me.*

I can even forgive Barden and Vanessa for leaving me here, given more of Berne.

Chapter Nine

Barden startled awake at the sound of the bedside phone ringing. He grumbled a curse and reached for it, wincing at Vanessa's sigh.

Who the hell is calling? We didn't leave a wake-up call.

If this idiot wakes Vanessa, he's in a world of hurt.

He scooped the phone off the base and slid from the bed, whispering 'hello' into the receiver.

"Did you *really* think I couldn't find out where you were?" his father demanded.

Against his better judgment, Barden smiled. He shut the bathroom door behind him. "I knew you could find me. I was hoping Mother would let us conceive a grandchild or two in peace. Besides, my mate deserves every luxury."

The old wolf grumbled something he suspected was a series of curses. "And what about Berne?"

"What about him?" Barden thought he affected innocence well.

"*Where* is your brother, Barden?" There was a note of warning in the question.

"He's spending some time with a she-wolf."

"Doing?"

He chuckled. "I wouldn't know, Father, and I refuse to speculate. There's only so much brain bleach available in the world."

"So much...what?" he asked incredulously.

"A term I learned from my mate."

"And when—?"

"You'll meet my mate tonight, when we show up for the holiday party," he answered what was surely the question.

"If that wasn't the case, your Mother would be on her way there now. Still, I was *going* to ask when Berne will be back," his father replied patiently.

"As I said, I wouldn't know. I haven't spoken to him in a few days, but I would hope he's coming to the party tonight."

"Barden." That was a clear warning.

He wasn't biting. "I'm hardly my brother's keeper, Father. Besides, I have a mate that needs my...attention."

His father sighed. "The story of where your brother is had better be interesting, and I expect to hear it tonight."

"I'm sure it will." *One way or the other.*

"Take care of your mate, Barden. We look forward to meeting her."

He smiled. "I look forward to introducing her to you. You've never met a she-wolf like this one. I guarantee it."

His father hung up without a goodbye.

Barden opened the door...and came face to face with Vanessa.

She looked at the phone in his hand, and her gaze sharpened. "So, I did hear the phone."

"Just my father."

Vanessa rounded him, on her way to the toilet to take care of her morning needs. "He tracked us here?"

Barden laughed. "That's his specialty."

She didn't respond to that.

"They can't wait to meet you." His smile went strained. "But I hope Berne and Veronique have come to terms. If not, I may have a slight problem with my father tonight."

Vanessa winced. "For instance?"

"If I don't show up with my brother alive and in one piece, my parents aren't going to be happy with me." *If things went badly with Veronique, showing up with Berne in one piece may be a stretch.*

Her expression announced she was thinking the same thing.

* * * *

Berne smiled down at Veronique, savoring the mixed scents of sweat and sex. Now that he'd had her, it seemed he couldn't get enough of her.

Not that Veronique was complaining about it. Far from it, she was stroking at his ass, enflaming him for more though they'd spent more than half the night sating themselves, then—aside from having breakfast—the entire morning.

Veronique sighed. "How long do you think they'll keep us here?"

He stroked a fingertip down her nose. "Trying to get rid of me already?"

A light smack on his rear and the rumble of her laughter let him know she wasn't thinking that.

Good.

"No." She tipped her hips, making him shiver in delight. "I was just wondering how much time we have."

"By now, my parents have realized I'm missing. They will have assumed Barden knows something about it."

Veronique cocked her head to one side, regarding him seriously. "And?"

Barden considered it. "I would say, by now, our father has inquired as to my whereabouts. If Barden doesn't show up at the holiday party, my father will track him down and make him pay."

She let out a bark of laughter. "And if he shows up without you?"

"Oh, he would pay for that too, I imagine." Some childish corner of his mind reveled in the thought of their father making Barden pay for this. He squelched it. He owed his brother for forcing him to face Veronique. Without Barden, they might never have solved their differences and come together.

Veronique sighed. "Three hours to anywhere, you said."

"Four hours to where we have to be tonight," he corrected her.

"What does that mean?"

"It means we have time for a shower and lunch before they show up."

"You're on."

* * * *

Veronique pressed her hand to the shower wall, her breath coming in shallow gasps of air. Berne ran his hand in lazy trails down her stomach, tangling his fingers in her pubic curls as he washed away the slick of soap.

His breath buffeted her cheek, and he laid a kiss on the side of her neck.

Night Mother, he learned so quickly that I like it.

He massaged at her mound, moving lower and lower, settling over her clit. Berne drove her on, and Veronique closed her hand in a fist, needing something concrete to concentrate on in the throes of mounting bliss.

She wanted more...all of him. "Berne."

He chuckled, a dark promise delivered against the shell of her ear. His cock pressed to the small of her back. "Have to make sure all of you is clean," he teased.

Veronique wanted to protest, but some small kernel of her mind urged her to let him pleasure her. Instead, she leaned her head back to the curve of his shoulder, riding waves of delight.

"Berne?"

She startled, snapping upright so quickly she slipped and started to fall forward. Berne caught her against his body, shushing her while Veronique sputtered and wiped water from her eyes.

"Berne!" The voice was getting closer.

Berne turned the water off, then opened the shower door and stepped out. He gathered the closest towel and wrapped her in it, tucking it tightly around her chest.

"Goddess take it, Berne! Where the hell are you?"

He motioned for Veronique to stay where she was, turned, then crossed the room and yanked the door open.

Stark naked. Veronique licked her lips. Oh, yes, that was sexy.

"You're early," Berne noted.

"My... You decided to use *my* rooms?" Barden complained from somewhere out of her line of sight.

Veronique snickered. Berne hadn't told her he'd done that; the rooms had been cleaned and only retained a faint family scent, so she hadn't known. *I wonder if his room is a mess?*

"I figured I owed you that much after you tied me up and left me here."

Barden didn't respond to that.

"Well?" Berne challenged him.

"Well, what?"

"Are you going to go downstairs, so Veronique and I can dress?"

Barden hesitated.

"So we can have lunch before we leave," he pressed.

"We could pick something—"

Berne glared at him, and his brother fell silent. For a moment.

"Do you mind if Vanessa and I join you?"

Fur sprouted on Berne's neck and face, and his snout elongated, making room for his wolven teeth. "As long as you *leave* so we can dress." There was a threat couched in that. "Unless you want me to take a few ounces of flesh for tying me up?"

"Not necessary. I'm going."

His footsteps faded away, but Berne took his time, waiting until his twin had nearly reached the stairs before he shifted back to human form. Then he returned to her with a second towel and started drying her hair.

"Shouldn't we get dressed?" Veronique knew she was teasing him. After that show, it was a solid bet Berne intended for them to take their time.

One side of his mouth quirked up in a smile. "We'll get to it."

"I'm hungry." She was, but Veronique acted as if she was starving for effect.

"So am I." Berne swung her up into his arms and headed for the bedroom.

Barden's bedroom.

"We're not going anywhere, until I eat." Before Veronique could reason that they were both going to eat, he continued. "You're going to come for me again."

She bit back a laugh. It was a challenge to Barden and to Vanessa, and Veronique supposed it was better than the two males tearing each other apart.

One brow went up when she didn't answer. "Well?" he prompted her.

"Carry on," she invited him.

"I fully intend to."

* * * *

Vanessa stared at the huge manor, stunned by both the size and the variety of holiday decorations. She'd heard about wolves who made such an outward show of celebration, but she'd never seen it.

"This is your family's home?" she blurted out.

Barden chuckled. "No. My family tends to spend holidays with the Alphas."

She furrowed her brow. "Really? Why?"

"That means Julianna is here." Veronique's answer overlapped with hers.

Berne answered her question. "Our mother is Alpha Samara's den sister. They've been nearly inseparable since they went to school together."

"Oh." It shouldn't have surprised her, she supposed. She'd known they were alphas, after all. "Well, it will be nice to spend the holidays with Julianna."

Barden and Berne exited the vehicle. Each rounded the SUV, then aided their respective mates out. They went in together, Vanessa and Veronique in the center, Barden and Berne a protective shield to their sides.

All talking stopped short when they entered the house. Vanessa looked around at the gathered Alpha family and their friends, offering a tip of her head for Alpha Samara and her mates.

Her panning gaze short circuited, and her smile went brittle. At the far side of the room was another familiar face.

And he doesn't look happy. At all.

Vanessa swallowed a painful lump in her throat. When

318

they'd spied on Berne's family, she hadn't looked closely at his father.

I was looking for a younger male. I didn't care about anyone else in their family.

He took a step toward them, and Veronique took a step back, no doubt reading Vanessa's tension and reacting to it.

Berne looked back at her sister in confusion, and Vanessa realized he'd let down his guard. Her wolf took over, as it always did when Veronique was in danger.

The old wolf straightened, and his eyes shifted. Nearly in unison, Berne and Barden closed ranks between their father and their mates.

"What is this?" the old male demanded.

Barden tensed. "Our mates. You have a problem with it?"

"Just making sure the elder sister isn't going to try to rip out anyone's throat."

The irreverent tone made Vanessa laugh, and she shifted back, tears filling her eyes. "Maybe my mate should make sure you don't crush my ribs again."

He winced, hurt clouding his expression. "It was one bruised rib, and it was an accident."

She raised an eyebrow in challenge.

"I was only protecting my Alpha." He huffed, then managed a grim smile. "You couldn't know we were friends and not foes, but you *did* attack an Alpha."

Both brothers relaxed.

Berne snickered. "Just what you need to shake up your ordered little world, brother."

Barden smiled widely, but he didn't answer.

"Well, that much is true," Vanessa conceded.

"To which comment?" Berne teased.

"Oh, stop," Veronique ordered.

He nodded his agreement.

It was Barden's turn to laugh. "And yours will keep you in line."

"When I want to," Veronique intoned.

Alpha Samara waved them toward open chairs and love seats in the huge room. "Julianna will be glad to see you, but she's napping right now. Why don't you tell us how this all came about so quickly."

"That's a long story," Vanessa admitted.

"The best kind," the Alpha female invited her to continue.

Yes. Yes it is.

The End

Her Christmas Wolves

Wolves

Brenna Lyons

WEREWOLF U V

Blurb

Evan and Eric have been patient, wolves waiting for the moment to act. Now that Talia is in heat...and in the same place they are, it's time to pounce.

Talia has known her mates for the last three and a half years, but she's avoided finalizing their mating. By the grace of the Night Mother, Talia hasn't had to face her mates while she's been in heat...until now. It's Christmas Eve, and everyone is celebrating their new matings at the Alphas' holiday gathering. The time has come for Talia's mates to claim what is theirs. But, can they convince Talia her reservations about mating are unfounded?

Chapter One

Talia stopped to take a calming breath, cursing her state silently. It was the day before Christmas and her traitor body chose now to go into heat.

It's not bad enough that I'm halfway through my final year of uni and am dreading the duties of my job to come instead of looking forward to them like everyone else. It's not bad enough that it seems everyone is settled with their mates, while I'm still unsettled. It's not bad enough that I don't know what I am. Now this?

A questioning yelp brought her head up, and she scowled at Lawrence, one of her two Husky companions. As if she agreed with Talia's annoyance, Gracie nipped at her mate, then huffed. Lawrence licked at Gracie's face, and she begrudgingly returned the gesture.

Mate. Gracie had it lucky. One female. One male. Not multiple mates to deal with. No animal-human instinct confusion. No loathsome duties to perform for the majority of her life.

Talia, on the other hand, had all three. *In abundance.* She was a cross-bred human-wolf, but she further had been born to a life of duty and had two horny males waiting for her inside the house. *Two horny males, who won't hesitate once they scent I'm in heat.*

If only I was so sure. About anything.

She silenced the errant voice that proclaimed she didn't *want* them to hesitate. She wanted Evan and Eric to pounce, lick, suck, and fuck her into a pup or two.

If only it were that easy. If only there were no feelings involved.

Stop it! Wishing doesn't change things.

So far, she'd been lucky. Talia had known from the first time she laid eyes on the brothers that she wanted to sink her teeth deep. She'd managed to avoid being in the same place with them when she was in heat for three and a half years.

Time has run out.

That fact didn't speed her toward the house. Talia ambled along, considering how best to approach her mates. She wasted time, taking out the long, dangling diamond earrings that matched the pins in her hair.

She considered throwing them toward the woods, then tucked them into her coat pocket instead. *I hate these things, but there's no cause to waste them that way.*

If I hate them, why do I wear them?

It was a nonsensical question. *Josephine sets my jewelry out with my clothing, and I wear them.* Like everything else in her life, it was expected. She dressed the part, accessorized to her role, and played the 'pampered princess' to the hilt. Her teeth sprouted at her irritation with that fact, and Talia forced them back.

You're a princess. Always keep your composure.

Her thoughts returned to her mates. *They don't have to be a duty. I want them.*

But I'm a duty to them.

Am I?

As if in answer, they exited the house together and made a beeline for her, intent as she hadn't seen them since the first night they spent together, loving in her suite at school. The sight left her weak in the knees.

Talia stiffened her spine and planted her feet. *I am the primary Alpha daughter. I run from no man and no wolf.*

In the moment she spent reassuring herself, her mates bracketed her, Eric at her back and Evan in front. Eric buried his face in the side of her neck and inhaled deeply. Dual cocks rose against her, stealing her breath.

"I told you I smelled her heat musk." Evan's voice was rough in arousal, an alpha pushed to the edge by his instincts.

I want them over the edge. Talia grasped Evan around the neck and pulled his lips to hers, savoring his taste as his tongue swept into her mouth. She spread her legs, went up on her tiptoes, and rubbed the heat between her legs up and down his length.

He didn't hesitate, not that she'd expected him to. Evan took the lead, as he always had. The kiss was primal, passionate, and full of promise.

Thankfully. It would be a shame to scar him for teasing me.

Far from it, the brothers guided her behind the cover of the barn, toward the door on the side opposite the house. Visions of the three of them coupling in the hay loft left her light-headed.

She'd never considered such a crude escapade before. It was what she would have expected from her younger sister. *Maybe Aurora isn't so far off. When we mate, even royals are animals; our wolves take charge.*

Gracie yipped her farewell, and both of her companions trotted away.

Probably in search of food in the kitchen.

There was no wasted time, no useless words. By the time they were halfway across the barn floor, they'd divested her of her coat and tunic. Talia tore at Evan's t-shirt, and she felt Eric remove his own in response. The younger twin went to work on her skirt, unbuttoning it and pushing it away, just as Eric dragged her panties down her thighs, leaving her thigh-high stockings in place, the knee-high boots over them.

"I'm not going to make it upstairs," Evan warned, pulling at the buttons on his jeans.

Talia couldn't find the words to respond to that. She tipped her head back, arching her body in invitation.

Eric cupped his hands over her breasts, stroking her into a frenzy. "I don't think she minds." There was a note of amusement in that.

She didn't complain about it. Talia wriggled against Evan, trying to hurry him along while he removed his shirt and dropped it to the floor. Eric lifted her, positioning her for his brother's first thrust.

There was something primal and exciting about two strong men handling her as if she weighed ounces, positioning her for mutual enjoyment.

In the next heartbeat, Evan was inside her, thrusting hard and fast, driving her to climax after climax. The need to have him join her was too much, and Talia dragged his mouth down to hers, urging him on in heated kisses. When he still didn't climax, the need to demand his participation beat at her, and Talia dug her claws into his back.

Evan bowed forward, his eyes shifting, fur sprouting on his abdomen, teasing her senses with the animal within him. He let loose with a strangled groan, pouring his hopefully-potent seed within her, his chest heaving in deep breaths of the crisp air.

It took a moment for him to regain his senses, but she wasn't doing much better. The need for more swept her into its dark embrace, a state where nothing mattered but what sexual delights her two mates could provide.

"My turn," Eric announced, the rough tone confirming that his teeth were extended.

Visions of him sinking them into her made her inner muscles flutter in delight, and Evan sucked in a breath, shivering.

"Now, Evan," his brother demanded.

Evan placed a kiss on her lips. "Don't get too complacent. I'll be back inside you soon."

The vow set off aftershocks, and she moaned as Evan left her body and turned her toward his waiting twin.

Eric was inside before she could complain at the emptiness, as fevered Evan had been, most likely driven to near madness by her heat.

She touched his abdomen, and fur sprouted in the wake of her fingertips. Talia moaned, enjoying the call of their instincts to mate with her.

"You like that, don't you?" Eric asked.

"Yes. More."

Evan nibbled at her ear, taunting her with his ready teeth.

Not now. Not yet. Just this.

Eric shifted more of his body, letting fur sprout on his chest. Then he pulled her flush to him, the fur tickling and pricking at her skin, pulling lightly at her nipples.

Her moans turned to excited little cries she made no effort to stifle. Eric doubled his efforts, nearly matching his brother in fiery display.

A sound niggled at the edges of awareness. Talia knew she should pay attention to it, but the loving was so sublime, she resisted leaving it to attend to anything else.

Certainly something less appealing. Besides, Eric and Evan will protect me. The truth of that sent a little thrill through her, heightening her arousal. There was something about a strong, able male that she'd always found appealing. *One of the few signs of my Alpha nature,* she supposed.

"Oh, my."

Talia looked lazily toward the sound of the voice, biting back a groan at the sight of Josephine turning her back on their play, her face crimson, though Talia dared not ask what emotion drove it.

Jealousy at the idea that it might be arousal fired her anger as she'd never felt it before. *Jealousy. Such a human emotion.*

Eric pushed deep, his climax demanding her full attention. Hers followed, and she screamed in pleasure.

Her teeth itched, as they often did, to stake a claim on them. *Especially with that bitch here.* Her anger resurfaced that quickly.

"What do you want, Josephine?" It wasn't as cool and detached as a princess should be, she knew. *I don't care.*

"My apologies, Talia. I came to tell you dinner will be served in a matter of minutes." She didn't peek back at them.

Good thing. I'd have to gut her. Talia worked at regaining her composure. "Very well. Go."

Josephine fled the barn, the door banging shut behind her. Her footsteps crunched along in the snow.

Is she stomping? Talia pushed that thought away. She didn't care if her servant was angry or embarrassed. She didn't care what Josephine thought.

But my parents will. She sighed.

"Talia?" Eric called out. "What is wrong?"

"I suppose we should go in."

"Should we?"

The invitation in Evan's tone sent flutters of movement through her core, stoking the flames of her heat.

Reality dragged her back to Earth, cooling the need, killing her fair mood. "We should."

"As you wish," he conceded.

They dressed slowly, the brothers alternating between putting on their own clothing and hers, as if reminding her she was theirs. Talia didn't balk at it, enjoying their ministrations too much to complain about it.

When they were all dressed, Evan pressed a kiss to her lips. "After dinner," he vowed.

Eric pulled a bit of straw from her hair, and Talia realized her fancy style was a mess.

"I think we should just take this down," he suggested.

Years of lessons on personal bearing and image made her rankle at the idea. His fingers working through the tight style sent shivers of delight through her.

"Yes." Agreeing seemed to lift a weight from her heart, and Talia took a deep breath.

Evan helped him undo the braids and remove the pins from her hair. He scrunched a handful of curls, moaning. "I'm not sure I'll make it until after dinner."

The idea of skipping dinner and going straight to bed was appealing. *It's a duty to join the family. Another expectation. After dinner will come soon enough.* "Well, you will have to. Won't you?" she offered crisply. *As will I.*

Talia wasn't certain if she was angry with herself, with Evan for teasing her with what she couldn't have, or with her family. *Definitely the last, though I'm not sure about the other two.*

"Whatever makes you happy, Talia," Eric stated calmly.

But it doesn't. None of this does.

Her tender core called her a liar. There was *something* that made her happy.

But that's only one part of a very large and unpalatable life.

Chapter Two

Talia stretched leisurely. She knew without opening her eyes that it was still dark outside.

It's Christmas morning. The moment the deep, velvety blue of night lightened the slightest degree, one or more of her younger cousins would be awake and howling to start the day.

Eric and Evan shifted closer to her, and she focused on their breathing sounds.

"You're awake." She didn't question it.

Eric buried his nose in the side of her neck, dark laughter sensitizing her skin. "Our mate moved."

Talia wanted to act unaffected, though it touched her that they were so attentive to her. "You won't get much sleep, if that's all it takes to wake you. I move a lot in my sleep."

Evan shook his head. "You don't when we share your bed."

They fuck me into a stupor.

It's not fucking. "I'll take your word for it."

Eric nipped at her throat. Talia shivered, though she knew he wouldn't dare mark her first.

"When are you going to follow your drives? You torture us by making us wait for your mark."

So Eric. Her heart fluttered in excitement at the plea. "Eventually."

Evan brought her nipples to hard points with a series of masterful licks of his rough tongue. Talia bit back a moan, fighting her wolf for control of her drives.

As usual.

"When?" Evan didn't demand an answer. His voice was full of sinful invitation.

Do not fall for it. It's nothing more than instinct talking. "And have you two following my every move at uni? I have one more semester as a free she-wolf, and I intend to enjoy myself."

The line of licks heading south on her abdomen — *Evan* — reminded Talia how much she "enjoyed" her mates. Her stoic exterior cracked, and she arched her back, begging silently for his talented tongue.

In the blink of an eye, Evan had her thighs wrenched wide and both brothers were busy sampling her fast-heating musk. Moans became pleas for more, then screams of climax.

That probably woke a few wolves.

The adults will go back to sleep, and the young ones don't dare howl the Christmas morning wake-up until daybreak.

Their dual growls set off aftershocks that wiped those concerns from her mind. She trembled in need of the two of them filling her conspicuously-empty channel.

It's those damned human emotions. Stop it. Much as she wanted more, Talia had long-ago decided the brothers couldn't provide it. No wolf could. *I'm too human for my own good.* Her heart ached at the truth of her situation.

"What is wrong, Talia?"

Eric's spoken breath puffed against the shell of her ear, and Talia startled at the fact that she'd been unaware of her movements.

"Talia? You're upset again," Evan chimed in.

She searched for any excuse she could logically use. *This isn't logical...or even instinctual.* "It's bad enough I'm probably going to be hugely pregnant by graduation without two doting males."

Evan snapped. "If you carry, at least one of us will be with you at all times."

My heart won't survive it. As it was, Talia was running out of reasons not to do her duty.

It's not just a duty to me. Not just Alpha instincts pushing me to strong mates. Why does it have to be for them? Why can't anything in my life be more?

Her heart aching, Talia let her frustration show. "Because it's instinct to protect your young."

"And you," Evan corrected her hotly.

Instinct. Duty. I always knew it. Tears misted her view of the darkened room, and she blinked them away.

"Talia..." Eric sighed, sounding weary.

Not as weary as I am. She pushed them away, her teeth sprouting in anger. "Animals. Instincts. Duty. You protect me because you believe you *own* me."

Evan pinned her to the mattress, heavy breaths flowing through clenched teeth. "If I thought that, you would already be ours."

His show of masculine force aroused her. *It's not enough.* "As if I'm not already," she countered hotly. "I—"

"Promised. Yes. We know. You've been promising to be ours for the better part of three years."

The answer confused her. As if she'd questioned him aloud, Eric explained the statement.

"Promises are human mating rituals, Talia. We never asked for promises."

Her heart ached at the rebuke. Her eyes burned, and the first tear spilled down her cheek. "If I'm too *human* for you, you can find your way out." She blurted it out without decorum, abandoning her regal bearing completely. *Ansella and Josephine would be appalled. They trained me so well to hold to it.*

I'm losing them. Talia bit back a howl of loss at the idea.

Stop it. Better to lose them now than be tied to males who feel that way about me. She'd secretly hoped—all this time—that they didn't see her humanness as a weakness.

That's what I get for hoping.

There was a potent moment of silence, and her heart stuttered as if she found herself prey instead of predator.

At last, Evan spoke, a cool edge to his voice. "You're throwing us out?"

Were they looking for an excuse or was he simply questioning her challenge?

Part of her wanted to answer in the affirmative, lie though it was. *End it now. Live alone for all your days rather than living in longing for what they can't offer.*

I'll long for it, with or without them in my bed.

That was immaterial. Longing would be easier without their constant presence.

She couldn't force the words out. Talia couldn't even force her jaw to unclench. *I'm weak. Human.*

Eric found his voice before she did. "Is that really what you believe we think of you?" There was a note of hurt in his tone.

I don't want to hurt them. Talia hadn't wanted that, almost as much as she hadn't wanted to *be* hurt.

Wait. His words resonated with her. "That hurts you?" *Why would it?*

Evan snorted in seeming disgust. "So now we're heartless as well." He flopped to the mattress beside her.

"I didn't say that," she snapped. *How dare they make me out to be the villain here!*

Evan tensed beside her.

Eric cut off whatever was about to come out of his twin's mouth. "Let me handle this, Evan." He wrapped an arm around her and eased Talia to his chest.

She didn't want to feel comforted by the move. *I do. Damn it all. Can't anything in my life be easy?*

"Now... Slowly and clearly, answer my questions."

She bristled at the order.

"None of that. Answers."

"You haven't asked me anything."

"I'm about to."

Talia didn't respond to the gentle reprimand.

"Good. Now... Are you telling us to leave?"

Again, words failed her. Her mouth went dry, and she swallowed a lump of tears. *Just tell the truth. Worst case scenario, they decide to leave of their own accord.* "No. I don't want you to leave." She reached back, threading her fingers through Evan's. "Either of you."

Evan's hand tightened minutely. "Then, why—"

"Evan, quiet."

Eric's command was uncharacteristic, but he obeyed, though Evan fairly vibrated in anger.

"Have we ever done or said anything that that made you think we were dissatisfied with you?"

Talia re-ran memories of her years with them, though she didn't need to. "No. I suppose... I must have misunderstood your comment." On some level, she didn't question that she had, that she'd overreacted, tried to push them away to end her own uncertainty.

"Where did the idea that you're too human come from?"

Taunts of the other young she-wolves ran on a loop

through her mind, making her dizzy. Talia had never shown them they struck home, of course. Her servants had trained her well enough to avoid that embarrassment. Shame stopped the words before she could spit them out.

"Talia," he prompted her.

"Well, I am, aren't I? Everyone knows my grandmother was a—"

"What does it matter if *she* was human?" Evan demanded. "You're nothing like her."

"Aren't I?" Her stomach squirmed uncomfortably at the thought. Talia was nothing like the rest of her family; her...oddness had to come from somewhere. Maybe she was like her grandmother.

Even if I am, how would they know it? They've never met my grandmother. Only my mother, Grandfather Travalian, or Grandfather Tyler would know for sure, and I'm not about to ask them!

"No," Eric replied before Evan could. His answer was crisp and sure. He shifted on the bed, looking down at her in the near-dark they could all see well enough in. "Not enjoying playing in the dirt has nothing to do with being human and everything to do with being raised a princess."

Aurora got over that. Saying it would make her sound peevish.

"How many servants did you have in your formative years?"

"The family?" He was joking, wasn't he? They were the Alpha den, after all.

"You."

She winced. "Two grandmother wolves and six or so guards."

He smiled. "Thought so. And I bet they were *so* happy to

336

let you run wild and get dirty."

Heat rose in her cheeks. Talia didn't offer an answer.

Eric laid a kiss on her forehead. "The question remains... Who made you think you were too human?"

"It doesn't matter."

Their silence said they disagreed.

"I think I know," he replied confidently. "You know, when your mother went to uni, the she-wolves were merciless. One was so convinced your mother didn't belong with us, she attacked Samara with a blade in hand."

"The Hunter's Fang," Talia recalled. Her mother still had the scar from that attack. "Having one is punishable by death now."

"With good reason," Evan grumbled.

"True." Eric paused for a moment. "They taught you nearly everything you needed to know."

"Nearly?" Talia wasn't sure what he was hinting at.

"It's up to you to put your foot down and assert yourself as an Alpha."

"Meaning?"

He didn't rush to an answer. "I suppose when you decide it's time to put your foot down about something, you'll know."

Talia was at a loss for words.

That left her ill-prepared for Eric to abandon that line of questioning and adopt another. "Did you enjoy what we did in the barn?"

Her breathing hitched; her body reacted fiercely to the riot of memories.

Evan pressed to her back, his cock recovered from his anger that quickly.

Eric chuckled. "Just as I thought."

How could he question it?

Behind her, Evan's breathing went rough in arousal. Talia's fangs sprouted in response.

Eric continued. "If I demanded we go there now?" His cocked bobbed against her, leaving a wet trail that fired her senses.

Anything. Anywhere. "Now."

"Your instincts say now. If we go to the barn, it won't *be* now."

Talia's need bubbled hotly in her belly. What was he saying?

"Follow your instincts. Do you want here and now or there and later?" It wasn't a taunt. He seemed to be posing serious question to her.

In her state, answering that was easy enough. "Both."

Evan chuckled darkly, and Eric's smile spread, showing a peek at his fangs. Her own lengthened in answer, and her mouth watered. The pheromones surrounding them went thick and drugging, and still they waited.

Why aren't they doing something? Talia wondered if they might be *trying* to drive her mad.

Eric whispered to her, a sound of invitation. It took a moment for her to make sense of the words.

"Follow your instincts, Talia. Wherever they lead."

She knew what her instincts were screaming for. Talia pulled Eric's face down to hers, opening to a ravenous kiss.

Evan groaned, probably at the wait until he could do the same.

When Eric made no move to mount her, Talia pushed him to his back with a curse, taking him in with a downward thrust of her hips. A scrape of her claws down his chest drew droplets of blood and forced a shiver of delight from Eric.

The reaction was too much to ignore. Talia rode him, a brutal race toward climax, the fire in her blood driving her on, their sounds rising together.

They are mine. Mine. She'd thought that before about them, but never with such a fierceness.

Her fangs lengthened fully, and her eyesight went red-tinged. Talia stared at the blood droplets on Eric's chest, the hunger to taste him almost more than she could bear.

Mine! She came down over him, sinking her teeth into his shoulder, suckling hard on rich blood with hints of musk that went to her head. Her body exploded in climax, wracking pulses of pleasure that washed away her thinking mind. Talia released him, drunk on Eric's blood, riding wave after wave of aftershocks.

She vaguely noted Evan easing her hair from the side of her neck, baring it to his brother. Neither of them moved.

"Now," she breathed. "I need you now."

Eric tipped her head further to the right and sank his teeth deep. The slight edge of pain quickened her crest, shooting her over the edge again, while his cum swirled against her inner tissues.

There were no words to describe the feeling of trading blood and sex fluids. Talia didn't question why so many wolves did this more than once.

At last, Eric released her neck. He pulled her into a slow, deep kiss, and the blood in their mouths mixed and mingled, making her crazy for more of them.

Of Evan. He's going to be marked as my own as well.

She turned off of Eric and came face-to-face with Evan. Taking his cue from his younger twin, he let her approach him.

Talia didn't hesitate. She pushed Evan to his back and mounted him, prompting a series of curses from him.

"Problem?" she taunted.

"No. I like this side of you."

"Good. I would hate to have to scar you." Before he recovered enough to speak, she started moving.

Evan was less restrained than his brother, raising his hips to meet her thrusts when Eric had lain still and allowed her to set the pace. Her arousal rocketed, but she wanted to tease him.

Talia raked her claws down his chest, smiling as his cock tightened. He was on the edges of release, his expression feral.

Just as I like him. She raised her half-paw and licked his blood off her claws, her inner muscles clenching at the allure of his heavier musk.

That was Evan's breaking point. "I am going to make you mine, Talia. Ours. Our marks will burn on your skin."

She hummed a note of satisfaction. "Then you better get to it."

The challenge was too much for him, she was sure. Evan flipped her beneath him, his thrusts bordering on the violence of ancient wolves. He bit down hard, his mark resting halfway over Eric's.

His heat filled her, and he groaned, most likely at her flavor washing over his tongue. It wasn't enough. She needed to drink her fill. A taste of him wasn't sufficient.

Talia bit down on the opposite side of his neck, taking the mind-altering nectar in. Evan released her with a growl, panting hard as his cock erupted and jerked inside her. When she finally released him, he howled in triumph.

She drew his mouth to hers, sharing the blood as she'd done with Eric. There was something inherently sensual in the move, something that made her want more of them.

Now. Now. Now.

But there was something else her instincts were telling her to do. *Follow them. Wherever they lead.* Was it really that simple?

"I love you both," she blurted out, her face going hot in a mixture of embarrassment and outright fear. *Why did I wait to say this until after we mated formally?*

There was a moment of tense silence, and Talia cursed herself again for cementing a union with them before she was sure they could return her very human emotions.

Eric appeared at his brother's side and drew her into a gentle kiss. "We love you, too. You do know that, don't you?"

Answering that was a minefield. Besides that, Talia wasn't sure she could form words.

"You were afraid we didn't," Evan guessed. "You thought it was all duty and instincts?" There was no bite of accusation in the question. If anything, she would term it as concern.

"I...wasn't sure," she admitted.

"Well, we do."

Talia managed a smile. It grew as they returned it.

A crisp knock on the door brought her head around. "Yes?" Talia called out.

"The pups are awake, Talia," Josephine reported. "It's time to open presents."

As if punctuating her report, a youthful howl to gather rose up from the far corner of the house.

Blinding anger that her servant was interrupting so precious a moment seared in her chest. "We're still opening our own presents," she snapped back. *My Christmas wolves. My mates.* "Tell my parents we will emerge when we're finished."

341

Josephine didn't answer for a moment. "Yes, Talia. As you wish." But her indecision and upset were impossible to miss. She padded away, and Talia turned her attention back to her mates.

Mates. What a lovely word.

They both stared at her, wearing twin expressions of amusement.

"What?" she asked, ready to defend her curt manner with her servant. *Not a servant I chose.* All her servants had been assigned to her by her parents, and—for reasons she still didn't fully understand—Marietta had passed to Aurora instead of herself.

"You're following your instincts," Evan stated the obvious.

"I told you that was what she needed to do," Eric added.

"Yes. Yes. Very smart of you."

"I don't understand," she admitted. They wanted her to snap at a servant?

Evan cupped his hands around her hips, making her more than aware of his cock lengthening inside her again. "You are Alpha daughter, but you have never been encouraged to claim your own power and voice." He tipped his hips, teasing her with his ready length. "I don't mind telling you it's incredibly sexy to see you do it."

Eric brushed a kiss against her lips. "You have been unhappy for some time. At first, we thought it was with us, but then we realized it was a general unhappiness." He kissed her again, a little deeper that time. When he broke away, he met her gaze. "We are your mates, Talia."

"I know," she offered breathlessly. They were well on their way to proving it again.

As if in agreement, Evan tweaked a nipple, wringing a moan from her. Before she could beg for his mouth, he was speaking again.

"We've talked about this at length. Whatever makes you unhappy makes us unhappy as well."

Eric demanded her attention by rubbing his thumb in maddening circles over her sensitized clit. "And whatever makes you happy makes us happy."

She tipped her hips back and forth, working Evan in and out slightly, while she encouraged Eric's massage. *I'm going to come. This simply. This quickly. Night Mother! We'll never get out of bed.*

Eric continued. "You are going to start doing what makes you happy, no matter how monumental those changes are."

"We insist," Evan added. "Whatever it is, we will support you fully. You have our vow on that."

She nodded, on the edges of climax.

"Oh, that's right," Evan breathed. "You want to climax again."

Not without both of them. "Eric. I want you too. Now."

He didn't question her. "Whatever makes you happy."

In the next heartbeat, Eric was at her back, using their mixed fluids to work her back channel looser. She moaned, leaning forward to help him.

Evan took a nipple into his mouth, teasing then suckling hard at it. Talia moved more frantically, driving Evan's cock and Eric's fingers in and out.

"Now. Please, Eric."

He complied, thrusting deep into her. The feeling of the two of them, nestled close inside her and moving in tandem, had always excited her. This morning, it was a sign of more.

343

No matter what, we are in this together.

But did she have the fortitude to stand up to her family, her duty, her obligations?

Her rocketing climax washed away that concern, and the brothers followed her over into bliss.

The rising sounds from the corridor announced the family moving, en masse, to the large family room for presents, while the servants made breakfast.

Eric sighed. "We will get no peace until we join them," he voiced her concerns perfectly.

A rebellious streak raised its head, and Talia marveled at it. "For now. After breakfast, I intend to feast on the two of you again."

Both their cocks jerked. "Whatever makes you happy," they vowed in unison.

* * * *

Talia smiled at the rush of young wolves, trying out new toys while they waited for the next of their own presents to be unearthed in the piles. Hard as she tried to recall it, there were no memories of her doing the same, in her youth.

My servants probably hadn't allowed it. A pang of regret drew a wince from her. All Talia could remember was holidays of sitting primly and offering prompt thanks for the lavish gifts bestowed upon her.

She vaguely remembered Tyler giving her a floppy doll one Christmas. As she recalled, Talia had stared at it, confused by such a useless bit of fluff, while her twin wiggled in anticipation of her response. She'd thanked him and had tucked the doll next to her, all the while trying to understand his confusion and upset.

I don't even know what happened to the doll. But she wanted to. Talia didn't question the urge. Hadn't Evan and Eric told her to let he instincts guide her?

I should ask Josephine. Though she was only Ansella's assistant at the time period in question, Josephine would know what—

"Talia?"

She snapped her head up and stared at Daddy James. Though both of her mother's mates were technically her fathers, James had taken on her care immediately upon birth, she being first born and he being the elder of the two brothers.

I suppose that explains some of my rigid behaviors. Daddy Jason has always been the more relaxed of the two.

"Talia?" he repeated.

It took a heartbeat for her to focus on the package in his hand. Talia managed a weak smile and took it with a nod of thanks. He watched her, his eyes narrowing, but he didn't comment on her inattention.

The tag said it was a gift from her mother, which probably meant it was something beautiful. It was no surprise to find a stunning embroidered shawl inside the box.

Her mother didn't hesitate. "I saw it when I was out with your grandmother, and I thought you might like it for when you move to your office in Barcelona in May."

Talia's smile went brittle at the reminder. Eric wrapped an arm around her waist, and Evan shifted closer to her on the sofa they'd claimed for the day.

Showing their support. They said they would support any choice I make. Still, the words stuck in her throat. She tried to clear them with limited success.

345

"Talia?" Daddy Jason prompted her.

Always the more empathetic of the two. I am so James's daughter.

Talia looked from Eric to Evan, then took a calming breath. "Thank you for the lovely gift, mother, but I'm afraid I won't be taking the position in Barcelona this May."

Silence fell for a moment. Even the children stopped playing. Around the room, newly-mated couples straightened from their cuddling and surreptitious snogging to gape at her.

Her mother's smile widened. "Are you—?"

"I won't be taking it, at any time." Her heart pounding made her head ache in the rush of blood.

Evan squeezed her hand. Neither brother offered comment or expression that might give away the fact that this was the first they'd heard of her choice not to follow her duties where they led.

"I don't understand," James offered in a carefully-neutral voice.

Talia opened her mouth to reply.

Grandfather Tyler beat her to speech. "Of course you do. Talia doesn't want to be a politician. She never has."

"Ambassador," James corrected him.

"She doesn't want to be that either." He winked her way.

Talia laughed in response, covered her mouth with her fingertips, then composed herself. "You are correct, of course. I have never really wanted to be an ambassador."

Grandfather Travalian sighed. "I owe you ten thousand dollars."

"Yes, you do," Grandfather Tyler replied smugly.

They were taking bets on me? Well, that's just galling.

"Why didn't you *tell* us?"

The exasperation in her mother's question made Talia wince. "I didn't know what else to do," she admitted bluntly, then hurried on before anyone could protest. "It was my duty...I thought." *Thought, hell! Ansella and Josephine drilled it into me from the time I was a toddler. Or earlier.*

No one seemed to know how to respond to that.

They'll figure it out soon enough. Of that, there was little doubt.

"If you're not going to be the ambassador to Barcelona, what *are* you going to do?" Tyler inquired.

"I don't know," she admitted. "I'm still working on that problem."

"Whatever Talia wants to do," Eric vowed.

"Whatever makes her happy." Evan's answer overlapped with his twin's.

"Perhaps this will help," Marietta announced.

Talia looked around, noting two of the male servants carrying a large wooden chest into the room. At Marietta's direction, they brought it to Talia and set it before her. Then they withdrew with a respectful tip of their heads.

"What is it?" Talia asked.

"Yours," her sister's servant answered simply. "Your mother told me to do whatever I felt the need to in order to calm your upset. This needed done."

Talia considered that. Though Grandmother Trudale had provided Ansella as her servant at birth, and Josephine had taken the post when Ansella was aging, Marietta would have been the lead female servant of the household.

"Thank you, Marietta."

She smiled and waved Talia on. Talia took her time, undoing the latch. When it clicked open, Evan leaned forward to lift the lid.

The contents took her breath away. "Toys." There were so many toys, of all types and made of all sorts of materials. *Stuffed animals and tops. Trains and musical toys.*

She plucked a stuffed wolf from the top, smiling at it, then pulled out the two baby wolves that matched it. Talia had never understood why someone would give her stuffed wolves, when her fathers and other male relatives could change into real ones at will.

Marietta started talking again, while Talia touched one toy after another.

"Anytime you seemed confused by a toy or looked at one in longing, I made sure to buy it...or to keep it for you, if was already in your possession." Her weathered face lightened in fondness. "I knew the day would come when the shackles of expectations would be too much for you to bear. I simply hadn't expected it to take you this long to voice your concerns. And, I admit, I didn't know which *portions* of the expectations on you were so stifling."

"All of them," she breathed. Talia stared at the wealth of her childhood, stunned to silence. Her mind locked on one thing Marietta had said.

Confusion. "The doll." The mad urge to start tearing toys out of the trunk to find it assaulted her.

Marietta didn't question her. "It's here." She moved a few toys from the top, pulling the precise doll Talia had wanted from beneath.

Talia took it with shaking hands, hugging it to her chest. After a moment, she found her voice. "How did you know?"

"When I took the doll from your room, you noticed. You'd never noticed before. A toy would be forgotten, and it would disappear. You never reacted to it. Every time you entered your rooms...or when you woke, you glanced toward the shelves where the doll had rested. I'm not even sure you realized what you were looking for, but—"

"I didn't." Tears welled in her eyes. Talia made no move to wipe them away.

No one spoke. For that, Talia was grateful. She let the tears fall, relieved at so simple an indulgence.

At last, she managed a tremulous smile. "Thank you, Marietta." She sought out her brother in the crowd. "And thank you, Tyler."

"Anytime," he replied, but his throat bobbed.

Talia wished she knew if it was in laughter or in the same nameless emotion that gripped her.

Marietta bowed and took her leave.

Talia marveled at her composure. *All these years, she's known what I needed.* She took a calming breath, then sank into a comfortable position between her mates, watching the present opening resume in earnest.

What do I do now? The trunk full of toys indicated that Marietta had no more clue about it than she did herself. *No help there.*

From across the room, she could see the concern on Josephine's face.

She's concerned for herself, for how her little world has been upset. In a flash, Talia made another decision. "I won't be taking Josephine with me to school this year. Diane has offered me one of their servants. I would like to take her on, as a sign of our alliance with Eric and Evan's family." *And because Carol doesn't try to order my life for me.*

Her mother nodded. "I hate to put Josephine out of

349

service, but—"

"There's no need to," Talia interrupted her. "Julianna will need several servants in the coming months, especially once her pups are born." *Tyler won't allow her to run roughshod over his mate and children, and Josephine will be in service to royals in line for the throne. Overall, everyone will be happier that way.*

Her mother's smile widened. "Excellent idea."

James sighed. "You are a born ambassador. The post will be there...if you ever decide that *is* what you want to do."

His acceptance warmed her, and Talia considered hugging him close. *Not now. Later, when I'm not so raw.* "Thank you, but I doubt that will be the case."

Epilogue

"No decision yet?" Eric asked.

Talia moaned as he massaged the arch of one foot, lifting it from his crossed legs to apply more pressure. She savored the scents of flowers and grass at the intake breath. Basking in the summer sun with one or both of her mates was becoming her favorite pastime.

"I don't know." She sighed. "I'm not good at anything."

He chuckled darkly. A nudge with her other foot ended that.

"Any *marketable* skills," she qualified.

"Since you don't want to be a diplomat for your parents, you could be a spokesperson for a cause or product. You're certainly qualified for that."

Her curled lip revealed a flash of fang, she was sure.

"I know," he soothed her. "Don't worry. You'll find your calling. We just need time."

Now that her mates had freed her from perceived constraints, Talia had no intentions of going back to it. *I am more than a voice and face for someone else.* That meant she wasn't going to use her primary skill set, the one she'd been trained to use since toddlerhood.

I suppose I could do something in translation. Part of being a raised a wolf meant exposure to multiple languages. As a royal, Talia had been required to acquire a working knowledge of the language of every country they traveled to.

As the firstborn Alpha child, I will never be allowed to work for humans. That would make it too easy to kill off the secondary heir to the throne.

Moreover, the only translation jobs she could get from wolves would include her being a representative, would depend on her using her position to raise their status. *I'm done with that.*

She wasn't the type to sit around and do nothing, though her mates and their family wouldn't balk at it.

"You have time," Eric reminded her. "No need to obsess over it."

Of course. Her pregnancy meant she wouldn't be starting any sort of job for at least six months, even a wolf-run endeavor.

Talia smiled at the tickling sensation at the arch of one foot. She pulled both feet back with a squeal of delight, startling Gracie.

The Husky mother started barking at Eric, and Lawrence came running. He nosed his napping pups, then added a growl to his mate's warning.

"I'm sorry," Talia apologized to her companions. "Eric promises not to do that again."

"I promise no such thing."

Talia swallowed a laugh. "Then I make no guarantees to call her off when she bites you."

Eric bared his teeth.

She scowled at him, though she knew her mates wouldn't dare harm her canine companions. *If something displeases me, it displeases them.*

Lawrence's snuff of distaste broke the stand-off. Eric drew his fangs in, then tipped his head to the protective parents.

Gracie turned away, circled her sleeping pups twice, then settled down to nap with them. Lawrence planted himself beside them, protecting their sleeping backs.

Eric levered himself up to lay next to Talia on the blanket.

He traced one hand up and down the pronounced swell of her womb, humming a note of contentment as one of the babies shifted under his touch.

Talia sighed and combed her fingers through his hair. *Content.* No word was more appropriate, she decided.

His tender touching stirred more than a smattering of interest. Eric didn't question what she wanted. His mouth came down on hers, parting her lips in a heated kiss.

His stroking became more purposeful, down her body then upward, beneath her summer frock, his fingertips teasing the sensitive flesh of her inner thigh. Talia parted her legs further, immersing herself in the kiss.

Eric snagged the edge of her panties and tugged them down to the top of her thighs. Just when she was convinced he would finish removing them or rip them away — *oh, yes* — he thrust two fingers inside her.

Talia moaned, tipping her hips to speed him on. Eric didn't take the hint. He pleasured her in slow, even strokes, forcing her arousal higher.

It wasn't enough. She knew what she wanted from him. *What I need from him. Now!*

Talia pushed Eric to his back, working at the fasteners on his shorts frantically. A lazy smile curved his lips, and Eric pulled his shirt off, gifting her the delightful sight of ripped, male chest.

She wanted to taste every millimeter of him.

Later. Right now, I want to feel *every millimeter.* Talia shot a look at Eric, a silent order to be still; a slight tip of his head marked his concession. She stripped away her panties and straddled his waist. In the next heartbeat, she'd come down over him, taking him deep inside.

Eric didn't attempt to take charge.

He knows I need to this time.

She rose and lowered over him, taking what she wanted so desperately from him. Eric moaned; his cock tightened, massaging her inner walls. Stroke after stroke stoked the fire within her.

"What a delightful sight," Evan called out.

He's home. Her inner muscles clenched tight, and Eric moaned. He panted beneath her, seemingly at the edges of control.

Evan started peeling his clothing off, dropping them at the edge of the blanket. "Room for me? Or do you want me to take care of myself while I watch?"

The offer further emboldened her. Talia's vision sharpened, as her eyes shifted. "I have a craving." She focused on him fully. "And you're next. Be ready for me."

His cock jerked in response to the order, and he swallowed hard. "At your service." He stretched out on the grass, watching their sexual exploits breathlessly.

That pushed her over the edge, and she shattered, pinpoints of light dancing before her eyes. Eric's climax set off aftershocks that stole her breath.

Need clawed at her, and Talia moved from Eric to Evan. Their mouths meshed, and they came together hard and fast.

Eric had come into the loving from a quiet moment, and he'd been content to let her set a leisurely pace. Evan had walked in at the height of their arousal. As a result, he was less restrained.

I don't want him to be. It was the truth. She wanted to experience the polar opposites of her mates—Eric's sweetness and Evan's fire.

He gave it without pause, his hips moving in a smooth rhythm beneath her. Evan held her mouth to his, plundering her.

Eric pressed his cock to the cleft of her ass, laying it against her in the offer of more. He didn't presume to join in.

Not when I've made it clear I want something specific. She rarely asserted herself sexually, but her mates didn't fight it when she did.

An odd sensation niggled at the last of her thinking mind. Talia dismissed it and sought her pleasure as she hadn't done since the height of her heat at Christmas.

It didn't take long to achieve it.

In the afterglow, she panted hard, impaled on Evan, Eric nestled to her back and supporting her lightly. Two pairs of masculine hands cradled and stroked at her womb.

Talia closed her eyes, relaxed, sleep calling to her.

The change came so abruptly, only a whimper escaped her throat in response. Both of her mates tensed.

"What was that?" Evan choked out.

The pain in her gut made her eyes water. She tried to force an answer out, but her lungs and throat refused to comply.

"Talia?" Eric prompted her. "Tell us what you need."

"The...blanket." The pain dissipated, and she gulped in lungfuls of heated air.

Eric lifted Talia and deposited her gently on the empty side without disturbing Gracie in the process. Instinct driving her, Talia moved to her hands and knees.

Just as the next pain hit. Talia grunted, weathering the pain as she had countless Braxton-Hicks contractions in the last few weeks.

This isn't Braxton-Hicks. Now that she'd felt the real thing, Talia didn't question it.

Gracie appeared at her side and swiped her rough tongue over the sweat on Talia's brow.

"She's bleeding," Eric reported to his twin.

Evan swore vehemently. "Something is wrong. The sex was too rough, maybe?"

The pain subsided, and Talia stretched her back. "No." If there was something wrong, her instincts would be to panic, to grasp for aid, to run for help...or at least to demand someone else do so. "This is right. It might be bloody show." The blood wasn't coursing down her thighs, which meant it was a miniscule amount.

"We should call for Benjamin." Evan wasn't as calm as she was.

"He's seeing to Vanessa's girls," she reminded him. The identical triplets had been born well over a month premature, and with a wolf's stunted gestational period, that was significant. Her mother had lent the services of the Alphas' personal doctor to the worried new parents.

"Fuck! He's six hours away."

"Steven is—"

"We don't need him," Talia interrupted Eric's sentence. The pain returned, and she let her instincts guide her. At last, it passed.

The brothers were still discussing the best course of action, it seemed.

"We should move her to the house," Evan insisted.

"After the next contraction," Eric agreed.

"No." She looked up to find both of her mates gaping at her. Talia licked her lips. "Here. Our pups will be born *here*."

It took a moment for them to recover from their shock.

Eric managed it first. "Here?"

"You two taught me to follow my instincts. My instincts say here," she informed them. *Great. Now I sound like a princess.*

"Get the servants," Evan ordered.

Eric glared at him. "Are you insane? I'm not leaving her."

"And you think I *am*?"

Talia chuckled, and they both whipped around to face her. She ordered her thoughts, not the easiest thing to do, given the circumstances.

"Your instincts tell you to stay. Stay with me."

"But..." Evan faltered, an uncharacteristic move for an alpha male. "We can't do this alone."

The pain ramped up, and Talia gasped. "We're not alone." *We have each other, and we have our instincts. This is how wolves used to have pups.*

"We need—"

Talia shifted her mouth and throat, then vocalized a query to Gracie. The Husky licked Talia's cheek, then passed the command to Lawrence in their shared language. He darted away, and Talia shifted back to human form, trembling in the outlay of energy it required to make a controlled shift.

Twice.

"Don't do that while you labor," Evan stormed.

"You can converse with your canine companions?" Eric asked. He'd learned quickly that Gracie and Lawrence didn't like to be referred to as 'dogs'.

Talia bit back the urge to smack each of them back to focus. *Or maybe to share the pain.*

No. I'm not that vindictive.

"Only...Gracie. Her mother taught me when I was a toddler." The pain subsided again, and Talia breathed a sigh of relief. "I could have trained with Lawrence, when he joined the pack, but it never seemed necessary, since Gracie translates for me."

Far off in the distance, a howl gained steam.

"That's the howl a wolf in danger makes," Evan stated the obvious.

"You taught them *our* language?" Eric asked in disbelief.

Why are they asking stupid questions now? "Only a few important communications. Huskies have a wide range of vocalizations, and teaching them new language is fairly simple."

"Talia, don't you—?"

"This isn't getting our children born any faster," she snapped, at the edges of patience and slipping fast. Whatever Eric was about to say, it could wait.

The warning succeeded in focusing them on the task at hand. They gathered close around her, massaging her back and thighs.

"What do you need?" Eric asked.

Ever the pragmatic one. The pain headed to a crest...and the urge to push came with it. "He's coming." Talia bore down hard, shouting at the burning pain streaking down her channel.

The pains overlapped, the downturn of one melding with the rise of the next. Talia cycled between pushing and resting, the latter getting shorter with each crest she endured. Finally, the first of their pups slid free, and she collapsed into Eric's embrace, gasping for air.

"Wrap him and trade places," Eric ordered.

"Wrap him? In what?"

"Use a shirt."

There was a moment of furtive motion. Eric eased Talia to her knees, then pressed a kiss to her forehead.

"You're doing fantastic," he breathed.

The pains racing down her thighs had her whimpering, begging the Night Mother silently for a reprieve.

"I know," Eric breathed next to her ear. "Hurry, Evan."

"Coming."

Eric made room for his twin, then eased her into Evan's one-handed embrace. His other arm was full of a disgruntled-looking newborn.

Talia took a moment to admire him.

"What should we name him?" Evan asked, already seemingly besotted with the pup.

"Bastian," she panted out, preparing herself to start pushing again.

"Sebastian," he crooned.

"No. Bastia—" The 'n' was lost in a grunt as she started pushing their second pup forth. *No overly complex names for my children.* She'd decided long ago that Tyler had gotten it easiest in their parents' naming scheme.

"That's good, Talia," Eric urged her.

Had Evan done the same? Sadly, she couldn't remember those fevered moments, even now.

And it doesn't matter. Talia doubled her efforts, slightly panicked at her waning stamina.

"Almost here," Eric assured her.

I know. She nodded.

At the next push, the pup slipped into Eric's hands, and what could only be the afterbirth followed directly after.

"What do you need?" Evan asked, taking up Eric's usual question.

"Down." It was the most direction she could force out of her battered throat and from her muddled mind.

He eased her to the blanket, and Eric wrapped the far

corner over her, leaving Gracie and her pups undisturbed next to Talia's shoulder.

A few long minutes passed in a patchwork of sensation. Her trembling eased as warmth soaked into her fatigued body. The scent of grass and flowers overpowered the tang of blood and sweat, calming her jangled nerves.

Her mates moved in and out of her field of vision. One moment Evan and Eric were nude; the next they were dressed in pants and shorts respectively, two wriggling infants wrapped in their shirts and held to their chests.

They settled on either side of her, bringing their sons to her for a mother's inspection. Talia looked from one to the other, momentarily overwhelmed.

Relax. You knew this was likely. With both herself and her mates as twin births, it was nearly a given they would have twins. Mother forbid it had been triplets like Vanessa had given birth to!

"You have to name our younger son," Eric reminded her.

Talia fought to remember the names they'd discussed in the last few months. She'd already decided to forego the alliterative names so common in wolf multiple births. *No B names.*

C? Connor. Corwyn.

D? Damon. Douglas.

No E names. Not with Evan and Eric.

I know. "Finn."

He smiled and tickled their younger son's chin. "Happy birthday, Finn."

The first sign of approaching wolves was the sounds of urgency from Lawrence. He bounded over the hill, sniffed each of the new babies, licked Talia's cheek, then hurried over to check on his own mate and pups.

In the next heartbeat, wolves in human form poured over the same hilltop, half-dressed and prepared to shift. They carried a variety of weapons, everything from kitchen knives to farm tools.

Whatever they had close at hand when the call came to rally.

They stopped short and stared in disbelief for a moment. Patrick, Evan and Eric's father, dropped the machete at his feet and rushed toward them, dropping to his knees near her head. He checked her pulse, then started giving orders.

"Gideon, get to the house. I want a van here, the back seats removed and the storage area padded so Talia can travel in comfort. Tell Diana to collect as many women as she needs...and supplies she might need. Talia is stable at the moment. We keep her that way."

"Yes, sir." Gideon was on his feet and running before Gideon turned to another.

"Michael, call in Steven. I want him here by nightfall, even if we have to fly him in."

He was gone an instant later.

"Andrew, call the Alphas. Tell them..." He looked at Evan, seemingly confused.

"Bastian," his older son informed him.

Eric chuckled. "And Finn."

Patrick smiled wider. "Tell them our grandsons have arrived."

"Immediately." He loped away.

Her mates' father hovered over her, seemingly at a loss. "Is there anything you need, Talia? I can send another. I should have asked earlier," he berated himself.

Her vision blurred. "Sleep."

"Then you should."

Darkness closed on her.

* * * *

Talia woke to the smell of roasting meat...and the sound of a squalling baby.

Eric hummed a tune and rocked their son back and forth, trying his best to win her a few more moments of sleep, she was sure.

"Finn," she guessed, her voice rough in her own ears. Chances were the brothers had kept hold of the same babies they'd started with. It normally worked that way.

Evan rushed into the room, their other son in a sling.

"He needs to eat." She tried to push herself to sitting to do so.

Evan helped her, then stacked pillows behind her. Once she was settled, Eric placed the fussing baby in her arms. Finn latched on and went to work procuring his first meal.

The peace resonated with her, calming Talia's normally riotous mind.

Bastian started to fuss.

Probably reacting to the scent of mother's milk.

Evan helped him settle at the other breast, and both brothers stacked pillows under her arms to support their sons. Her mates murmured to her, and Talia rested, on the edges of sleep, her eyes drifting shut.

The boys were still eating when someone entered the room quietly and left a plate of food for her.

Probably Diane, peeking in on the pups. Or Carol.

Talia didn't remember the women arriving in the van or the ride back to the main house. She didn't remember someone bathing her and changing her clothing, though it was clear someone had. She only vaguely recalled Diane urging her to drink some cold water before she pitched back into sleep again.

"Talia," Evan whispered.

The smell of red meat won out over sleep, and Talia opened her eyes. Her mouth watered, and her stomach rumbled. The tray on Evan's lap held more than enough meat for the three of them.

The five of us, she reminded herself.

Eric raised a slice of the rare meat to her lips, smiling as she sucked it in and started chewing. Warm, succulent blood ran down her throat, and she detected healing herbs cooked into it.

Probably whatever Steven told them to use.

Ravenous, Talia ate slice after slice. Once in a while, Evan bathed her face with water that smelled of lavender. At last, she shook her head at the offer of more and sank back into the pillows, uncomfortably full.

I haven't been able to eat that much in more than a month.

Finn finished first, and Eric took him to the table for a nappy change. Shortly after that, Evan did the same for Bastian. With both babies snug in the crib on the opposite side of the room, her mates returned to bed with her and helped her lay down again.

Eric kissed her on one cheek and Evan on the other. Though she wanted to go back to sleep with them, Talia found her mind occupied with the question of what came next.

"You're thinking too much," Evan opined.

She nodded, her face heating at how well they knew her.

Eric sighed, then pushed up on one elbow. "What is wrong?"

"The clock is ticking, I suppose."

"Clock?" Evan questioned. He mirrored his brother's pose.

Before she could answer, Eric did. "We told you we would give you as much time as you need. You don't need to rush into a job, if you don't want to."

Though it was true, she felt guilty for considering it, for her relief at the vow.

Eric sighed again. "I had wanted to save this."

She stared at him, lost at the change of topic. "Save what?"

He left the bed...then the bedroom. It was several minutes before he returned, and Evan's expression announced he had no more clue than she had about what his twin was talking about.

Eric came in with one of his presentation boards in hand. "I know what marketable skill you possess, and I think you know it too. If you think about it, that is."

She shook her head, lost. He stared at her, and she started rethinking the last week...then the last day.

His surprise resonated with her. "I can talk to Gracie?" But what use was that?

"And you can learn to talk to other Huskies. You can teach other Huskies to talk to you."

She nodded, still lost.

Eric smiled and turned the board toward her. The sketches were rough and without his usual finesse.

He probably did them while he had Finn in one arm.

The message took longer to sink in. "You want me to train Huskies to be bodyguards to young wolves?"

"Is it possible?" Evan asked.

Talia considered that. "If I started with the pups and the

children young enough, I could teach them to talk to their companions. I don't know if they would be able to talk to the next generation without me to aid them. I've had two canine generations to learn."

Now that she thought about it seriously, it was a great idea. It was certainly something she could be happy doing. "And I can start with our sons and Gracie's pups," she mused.

"What do you need to get started?" Evan asked, clearly excited that she was making plans already.

The many possibilities made her head spin.

"Take your time," Eric soothed her. "Make lists. Don't rush. And for now..."

She yawned, her body picking up his cue. "Sleep," she mumbled.

"Sleep," Evan echoed her.

Talia looked toward the toys she'd taken from the chest the first day: the wolves and the baby doll. They had a spot together on the window seat. She smiled and closed her eyes.

I knew. Somehow, I knew and chose the right toys. Marietta was correct. As were my mates.

The End

About the Author

Brenna Lyons wears many hats, sometimes all on the same day: former president of EPIC, author of more than 100 published works, owner of Fireborn Publishing, columnist, special needs teacher, wife, mother...and member in good standing of more than 60 writing advocacy groups.

Since she started publishing novel-length works in 2003, she's won 3 EPIC e-Book Awards (out of 16 finalists) and finaled for 3 PEARLS (including one Honorable Mention, second to NY Times Bestseller Angela Knight), 2 CAPAS, and a Dream Realm Award. She's also taken Spinetingler's Book of the Year for 2007.

Brenna writes in 26 established worlds plus stand-alones, poetry, articles and essays. She's a bestseller in indie/e fantasy and horror, straight genre and cross-genres thereof. Brenna has been termed "one of the most deviant erotic minds in the publishing world...not for the weak." (Rachelle for Fallen Angels Reviews) Milieu-heavy dark work is practically Brenna's calling card, with or without the erotic content.

She teaches classes in everything from POV studies to advanced editing, networking to marketing. Brenna enjoys hearing from people who read her work and can be reached by e-mail.

Website: http://www.brennalyons.com/

Facebook: http://www.facebook.com/brenna.lyons

Email: brennalyons@FBP.comcastbiz.net

Also by this Author

Available from **Fireborn Publishing**

KEIF'S DEN AND PACK
Keif's Pack
Mother of the Keif
Keif's Den (Coming Soon)

PROPHECY
Prophecy: Revelations
Prophecy: Rapture
The Prophet's Mate
Prophecy: Rampage - Meet Gavin
Prophecy: Rampage (Coming Soon)

THE FANTASY CLUB
The Consort

WEREWOLF U
Werewolf U
Second Daughter
Alpha Son
Never Alone
Her Christmas Wolves
Werewolf U Stories (print)

RENEGADES SERIES (Coming Soon)
TYGERS
Renegade's Run
Max Sec

URBAN GRIMM (Coming Soon)
Catch Me, If You Can
Three Wishes

Temptation of Eve

Beyond the Veil
Fairy Wishes (Coming Soon)
Mine for the Night
Once in a Blue Moon
Overtime Pay
Stay With Me
The Fire God's Woman
The Punishment of Phoebus Apollo
With Great Power (Coming Soon)
Undead in Blue (Coming Soon)

Available from **Fireborn Publishing** in PRINT ONLY

NIGHT WARRIORS
Night Warriors
Will of the Stone
Bearing Armen
Hunter's Moon
Veriel's Tales I: Crossbearer Turned
Veriel's Tales II: Losing Regana
The Blutjagdfrau Chronicles

Bride Ball
Fire and Ice
Lovers' Kiss anthology
Monsters and Mayhem anthology
Paranormal Paramours anthology

Available from **Phaze Books**

ANGEL-WING SAGA
Sons of Heaven: Beldon
Daughters of Man: Prize Match
Sons of Heaven: Unexpected Mates

Daughters of Man: Claiming a Princess

BRIDE BALL
Bride Ball
Poison, Lies, and No-Win Choices

COLOR OF LOVE
The Color of Love

FIRE AND ICE
Magmon's Hunger
Magmon's Lover

INSTINCT SERIES
Animal Instincts

KEGIN SERIES
Conquest
The Last of Fion's Daughters
Last Chance for Love
Rites of Mating
In Her Ladyship's Service
Matchmaker's Misery

KIELAN SERIES
The Lady's Lowborn Lover
Time Currents
Cubed

NIGHT WARRIORS
Night Warriors
Will of the Stone
Bearing Armen
Hunter's Moon
Maher Men
Choosing a Mate/Starting a War
Raised to Be His Own

Veriel's Tales I: Crossbearer Turned
Veriel's Tales II: Losing Regana
Blutjagdfrau Lost
The Warrior's Man
Damsel in Distress

STAR MAGES
The Master's Lover

XXAN WAR
Daahan Rising
Crossbred Son
Raashh Decisions

Enslaved
All I Want for Christmas is You
Fates Magic
All's Fair...
Black Sail
Mama's Tales
Dream Walk
Unexpected Daddy
Phaze in Verse
We Shall Live Again
May the Best Man Win
Nevermore
Marked
And It Was Good

Available from **Mundania Press**

STAR MAGES
Written in the Stars

Fairy Dreams
Monsters of Myth Anthology

Available from *Under the Moon*

Evil Overlords Union Issue #1 Anthology
Undead Embrace
"*Playing Games*" in *Forbidden Love: Bad Boys*
"*Marked*" in *Forbidden Love: Wicked Women*
"*The Master's Lover*" in *Forbidden Love: Sacred Bands*

Available from *Logical Lust*

"*Mine for the Night*" in *The Cougar Book* Anthology

Available from *Coming Together Charity Anthologies*

INSTINCT SERIES
"*Foundling*" in *Coming Together: Into the Light* Anthology

"*Claim Mate*" (available separately and as part of the
Coming Together: Against the Odds Anthology)
"*The Fire God's Woman*" in *Coming Together: Under Fire*
Anthology

Available *self-published*

KEGIN SERIES
Earth-Born Lord
Graham: Training the Earth-Born Lord

NIGHT WARRIORS
Claiming a Lady
Stone Lord
Mother's Son

COLOR OF LOVE
A Safe Heart

Snapshots from a Poet's Life

Award-Winning Books

EPPIE/EPIC eBOOK AWARDS WINNERS
Coming Together: Against the Odds- 2010
Time Currents- 2010
Coming Together: Into the Light- 2011

EPPIE/EPIC eBOOK AWARDS FINALISTS
Fion's Daughter- 2004
Collected Poems: Book One- 2005 (now titled *Snapshots of a Poet's Life*)
Renegade's Run- 2005
Rites of Mating- 2006
All I Want for Christmas- 2006
Phaze in Verse- 2008
"The Fire God's Woman" in Coming Together: Under Fire- 2009
Three Wishes- 2010
Matchmaker's Misery- 2010
The Cougar Book- 2011
The Master's Lover- 2011
Bride Ball- 2011
Keif's Pack- 2016

DREAM REALM AWARDS FINALIST
Last Chance for Love- 2003

PEARL HONORABLE MENTION
Night Warriors- 2004

PEARL FINALISTS
Schente Night- 2003 (now included in *The Last of Fion's Daughters*)
König Cursebreakers- 2004 (now titled *Will of the Stone*)

JOYFULLY REVIEWED BEST BOOKS OF 2010

Written in the Stars- 2010

SPINETINGLER'S BOOK OF THE YEAR 2007
NOBODY: An Anthology of Dark Fiction- 2007 (Brenna's
pieces of the anthology can be found in *Beyond the Veil*)

TRS's CAPA FINALISTS
Ultimate Warriors- 2004 (Brenna's portion is now available
as *With Great Power*)
Written in the Stars

LOVE ROMANCE AND MORE CAFÉ BOOK OF THE
YEAR RUNNER UP
Last Chance for Love- 2008

ROAD TO ROMANCE REVIEWERS' CHOICE AWARD
Prophecy: Revelations- 2004

LOVE ROMANCES REVIEWERS' CHOICE AWARD
Black Sail- 2003

ROMANCE JUNKIES BOOK CLUB STAFF PICK
TYGERS- 2003

FALLEN ANGELS ROMANCE RECOMMENDED READ
Devon's Price-2005 (now available in *Bearing Armen*)

JOYFULLY RECOMMENDED READ
Fairy Dreams- 2008
The Last of Fion's Daughters- 2009

TREBLE HEART FINALIST
Prophecy: Revelations- 2003